THE DOUBLE VICE

THE 1ST HIDDEN GOTHAM NOVEL

CHRIS HOLCOMBE

*To Parisa,
Stay Fabulous!!!*

**BOOKS
LIKE US**

Published by Books Like Us, LLC

90 State Street, Suite 700, Office 40, Albany, NY 12207

"Alice Blue Gown" by Harry Tierney and Joseph McCarthy © 1919 by Leo. Feist, Inc. Public Domain.

"Gambler's Blues" by Carl Moore and Phil Baxter © 1925 by Phil Baxter. Public Domain.

"Five Foot Two, Eyes of Blue" by Ray Henderson, Lewis and Young © 1925 by Leo. Feist, Inc. Public Domain.

Printed in the United States of America

ISBN: 978-1-7364458-9-1

For David, whose love changed my life.

ACKNOWLEDGMENTS

The author wishes to acknowledge the invaluable assistance of the following people:

David Bishop, for being the personification of *hope* and *joy*; Erica Obey and Leanna Renee Hieber, for encouragement and guidance; Wendy Alexander, Kristen Cothron, Alberta Hardison, Tony Holcombe, Sonoko Jacobson, Rob Karwic, Leigh Pettus, and Justin Rudy for being early readers and becoming the very first supporters of these characters; Trista Emmer, for killer (pun intended) editorial edits; Mary Louise Mooney, for her razor sharp eye in helping me finalize the manuscript, and Robin Vuchnich, for the evocative cover.

A NOTE FROM THE AUTHOR

LGBTQ+ terminology has certainly evolved over the years. In doing the research needed for this novel, I discovered that evolution and wish to clarify a few items to avoid confusion.

The terms "heterosexual," "homosexual," and "bisexual" as we define them today—which are based in the main on the sex/gender of one's sexual partners—were adopted in the middle of the 20th century, specifically by the 1940s and 1950s.

But in the 1920s, much of LGBTQ+ terminology was based on an individual's gendered appearance and mannerisms. Therefore, those men who were more feminine, or dressed in women's clothing, called themselves "fairies" and "pansies"; and those women who were more masculine, or dressed in men's clothing, called themselves "bulls" or "bulldaggers." The terms "drag king" and "drag queen" were not used until later in the century, though "drag" was used (as in, men's gowns would *drag* across the floor). Instead drag kings and queens were often referred to as "male/female impersonators."

Those men who did not adopt a more feminine appearance but still desired other men referred to themselves as "queer." These men would identify as "gay" later in the century. Women who desired other women were called, as they are today, "lesbians."

Straight people were referred to as "normal" (please note, this does *not* reflect the views of the author) and those masculine men, such as sailors, construction workers, etc., who welcomed the advances of "queers" and "pansies" were called "trade."

Outsiders referred to the LGBTQ+ community in a variety of terms: invert (as in, her internal nature is masculine because she pursues other women, but she is anatomically a woman, thus she is "inverted"), pervert (always used derogatorily), and degenerate (a legal term referring to "degenerate disorderly conduct," which was often punishable by a prison sentence in the work yards).

I have tried to use the derogatory terms as sparingly as possible, unless it is to demonstrate a character's prejudice for the purposes of narrative tension. And although drag queens were more casually called "fairies" over the more formal "impersonators" during the early-to-mid-20s, I switched the term with the less jarring "pansy," which would become more adopted by the late 20s/early 30s (i.e., the "Pansy Craze").

And now, I hope you enjoy this fictional crime story set in the real queer world of the Roaring Twenties.

—Chris Holcombe

THE DOUBLE VICE

He is not one of us.

Dash Parker tried to shut out all the noise around him and pinpoint exactly what it was the man had said—on his birthday, of all days—to cause this hurried thought. Not an easy feat given both the house band and the tiny dance floor of his club, Pinstripes, were hitting on all sixes.

Still facing the dancing men, Dash tilted his head towards the outsider. "I'm sorry?"

The outsider stood just at the edge of his peripheral vision. A darkened shoulder. A faintly outlined jaw. And, of course, the voice.

"A pansy is here. And you will take me to *him*."

Ah, it was the "him."

Every female impersonator Dash knew referred to themselves and others as "she" and "her," and required everyone else to do likewise. They were "Duchess," "Doll," and "Flossie," not "James," "Robert," or "Allen."

Then there was the belligerent tone, the brusque manner, the clipped accent, the demands—especially the demands. Wanting Dash to take him to a "pansy," then bristling when Dash had replied he was in the wrong place and ought to try Mother Childs near 59th Street where, at this hour, they'd be showing off their latest drag.

And now, the "him" drenched in contempt.

This was a man who disapproved of the recent changes in the world. A bluenose. Dash pitied those who couldn't keep up, though he had to admit the world was flying through this decade. Just as fast as the drummer's sticks across his snare and the dancers' feet across the floor. Why, here it was, the middle of August 1926, and already so much was different. Women were voting. Telephones were ringing. Radio waves and motor cars crisscrossed the country. The farms shrank, the cities grew. Jazz was quickly becoming America's music, and secret clubs popped up to celebrate the nature of Dash and many others.

And yet, so much had not changed. Hate, for one. Fear, for another.

This outsider represented both.

How did he get in here?

It was Sunday, August 15, approaching midnight, and they were standing in a room hidden behind a men's tailor shop called Hartford & Sons on West Fourth Street between Sixth and Seventh Avenues. A secret knock was needed to enter the shop itself. Then once inside, one had to find the secret door in the back wall of the curtained-off changing area. An elaborate system. Pinstripes, like many clubs of its kind, was designed to be the very height of discretion. It had to be to avoid the raids. Now how did this outsider figure it all out?

More importantly, *who* was this outsider? A cop? A federal agent? A newshawk for a low-rent tabloid writing an expose of the "invert underworld"?

Unnerved, Dash turned to face the man. "My good sir,

you are free to walk around to see if *she* is here. Many fine gentlemen such as yourself do the same when they come to a club."

A scowl rippled across the outsider's face as he straightened the lapels of his blue-gray suit. He did not want to venture any farther into this narrow, darkened room.

He is not one of us.

Dash brushed his misbehaving brown hair behind his ears while his hazel eyes measured this threat. They mirrored each other in some ways, he and the outsider. Their slim figures totaled up to the same height, roughly six feet, and they were about the same age; newly twenty-six on Dash's part and the other appearing to be just past there. But whereas Dash's features were warm and inviting, this outsider was all hard angles and warning signs. Clenched jaw and razor-blade cheekbones. Blazing blue eyes unwavering in their stare. Blond brow creased in anger.

Such incongruity, what with the joyous dancing on one side of them and the lively bar on the other.

"Very well," Dash said to the lack of response, speaking in what his younger sister Sarah used to call his "Father Voice," which was amusingly (at least to her) formal and old-fashioned. It often came out when a situation was going wrong . . . or about to. "May I ask who you are?"

"That is none of your concern."

"Why are you here?"

"Also, not your concern."

"Listen, my good man, if you're here to start trouble, then I'm afraid I'll have to ask you to leave."

"You don't have the authority."

"Oh, but I do," Dash said. "I'm the owner, and I'd very much like it if you left the premises."

The moment the words were out of Dash's mouth, he realized his mistake.

You dope. He's not going to leave now until you tell him everything.

The outsider gave him a curious look. "You own this place? I should've realized sooner. You don't look like the other men here."

Dash gestured to his own black tuxedo and white silk shirt. "Because of this?"

"Yes. You have money." A curt raise of his chin. "These men do not."

The outsider wasn't wrong. Most of the patrons here tonight couldn't afford the finery Dash wore, not having been born into the privileged upper class like he was. Instead, they gathered what mismatched glad rags they could find to celebrate his birthday. In the case of the bell bottom standing next to them, he still wore his navy whites, albeit freshly laundered. Dash's former uptown friends would've taken offense, but Dash was charmed by their efforts.

And now, now he must protect them.

"Be that as it may, my loyalty is to my patrons, something I should think a gentleman such as yourself would appreciate. And it is *you,* good sir, who clearly doesn't belong." Dash grabbed the man's elbow. "Off you go."

In response, the outsider quickly grasped Dash's hand, the grip hot steel. "I am not leaving until I find this . . . this *thing.*"

The clipped accent became clearer and harsher, the consonants landing like bombs.

German.

Dash stifled a grimace. He didn't dare show the pain he

felt in his crushed hand. "I'm afraid you don't have a choice."

The outsider's eyes blazed blue like hot flames. His lips twisted into a cold smile. "You do not want to make an enemy of me."

Dash's jaw tightened, his pulse pounding. "You are outnumbered in here."

"I will find this pansy."

"No, you won't."

"Why is that?"

"Because there isn't one. Look around you!"

The outsider kept his eyes on Dash's face for a few more seconds before relaxing his stare as well as his grip on Dash's hand. The release in pressure sent a dizzying rush to Dash's head. He took a few deep breaths, hoping he wouldn't faint. He also hoped that what he said was true. He watched as the outsider took in the sights surrounding them.

At one end of the club was the band, a trio of drums, bass, and cornet played by two black men and one white. Scandalous and highly illegal. In the center was the busy dance floor, filled to the brim like a martini, men and their male partners threatening to slosh over the sides. Those men who weren't dancing with one another leaned against the surrounding blue-painted walls or sat at wobbly wooden tables, smoking, drinking, laughing.

On the other end of the club was the bar, jammed so full you couldn't even see the bartender. Dash watched as the outsider's eyes took in the hunched shoulders, bent heads, and shirt backs with damp circles just above the trousers. No matter where the outsider looked, it was a sea of suit jackets, waistcoats, and suspenders. Not a dress in sight.

The two eventually faced each other again.

"There," Dash said, his dry throat causing him to clear it. "She appears not to be here."

The bell bottom standing next to them put his arm around a young man on a barstool, who was dressed in a sharp green suit. Loudly bragged tales of sexual conquests followed, as his dimpled cheeks spread into a grin. His young quarry looked up at him with lips parted in breathless anticipation. Their colognes, citrus and sawdust, intertwined with one another like their bodies would soon be.

The outsider flashed them a look of disgust, then said, "*He* is here."

"What makes you certain?"

"I followed a companion of his."

Cold sweat licked Dash's palms. Only law enforcement and private detectives followed people, didn't they? "Tailing," the pulps called it. Now who was this female impersonator? And why the urgency over her? If the cops or the Feds wanted to raid Dash's club, this outsider had all the evidence they needed to shut Pinstripes down: men drinking liquor, men dancing with men. Who would care about just one girl gallivanting around the Village in her latest drag?

Unless . . . unless she was rich, and her wealthy family was trying to stop a scandal.

Just like mine did.

Dash cleared his dry throat again. "Perhaps she gave you the slip. This city at night can trick many a man's eye. I'd look elsewhere, if I were you."

The outsider sighed, as if Dash were a misbehaving child. "You are being difficult."

Dash projected a cockiness he didn't feel. "'Stubborn' is the word most men use to describe me."

"Give me your name."

Dash was about to reply *none of your concern* when his name was called by a familiar voice to his left.

The man arched his brow. "Dash?"

Hell.

First, he said he was the club's owner, now someone else said his name. The only information left to volunteer was his home address!

He forced a smile. "Short for Dashiell. Excuse me."

He turned and pushed his way to an open space at the crowded bar. Once he laid his hands on the polished wood surface, he called out, "Evening, Joe!"

His bartender, business partner, and roommate Joe O'Shaughnessy stood behind the wooden bar, grinning one of his mischievous smiles. "Happy birthday, me lad!"

Joe placed his hands on hips tightly clad in brown trousers. Broad, wide shoulders strained against the matching suspenders, and the wrinkled white shirt worn with no tie (no matter how much Dash begged him) featured rolled-up shirtsleeves exposing thick forearms covered in fiery hair.

He bent forward at the waist. "Or is it me lass?" he added with a wink.

Dash wanted to reply to Joe's usual flirtation in his usual way, *you've seen my bed from time to time, you tell me.* Instead, he lit a cigarette and flicked a wary look to the outsider behind him.

"We have a problem."

"Ya tellin' me." Joe reached down underneath the bar and brought up a bottle of clear liquid. He poured the elixir into a snifter glass and passed it to Dash. "Taste this."

"Joe, I—"

"Taste it, lassie."

Dash acquiesced. He didn't want to alert his patrons about a wolf in their midst—not yet, at least. Better to avoid a brawl and go along with Joe's banter. Which was disarmingly easy. Not only was Joe forceful, he was right irresistible. A big six of a man with eyes the most vivid green, made even more luminous by the flaming red of his hair and the paleness of his freckled skin. A woman on the street once described those eyes as emeralds on the neck of the Queen. Joe replied they were the only things royal about him. Everything else was purely second class.

Well, thought Dash, *not* quite *everything.*

He picked up the snifter. "Gin?"

Joe nodded.

Dash flipped the liquid back. It burned his throat like coal smoke.

"Dammit, Joe." He dropped the snifter onto the bar and brought up the cigarette to wash the taste out of his mouth. "The past two weeks, it's gotten worse and worse."

Joe nodded. "I know, I know. It's just that by the time the truck gets here—"

"—the good bottles are all taken."

"I've been mixing 'em with fruit juices and seltzer like usual. Only now I'm startin' to hear complaints."

Dash exhaled a thick cloud of blue-gray smoke. Not all of the changes in this decade had been good. Ever since the ridiculous Volstead Act, beer and wine had been replaced with "cocktails," concoctions to hide the vile taste of the bootlegged alcohol. Glasses were now loaded with lemon juice, honey, sugar, and mint leaves. Like drinking candy. Appropriate since the federal government and its nannies continued to treat its citizens like children. But if the childish disguises weren't working anymore, then how could they compete with the thousands of other speaks in town?

Joe put away the snifter and said, "All right, lassie. What about this problem?"

"Dash, is it?" the Problem said. "We have not finished our conversation."

Dash placed his cigarette on the lip of an ashtray, murmuring to Joe, "A bluenose snuck in."

Joe was confused. "What was that?" he said at the same time the outsider called out Dash's name.

Hell, Dash thought for the second time tonight and turned around.

The outsider had stepped closer to him. At that moment, the band ended their song with a squealing high note and a mighty cymbal crash. The crowd of men exploded into cheers and whistles, drowning out the outsider's words.

"I'm sorry?" Dash said once again, cupping his hand behind his ear while he thought to himself, *how do we get him out of here without causing a fight?*

The outsider's mouth moved, but still Dash heard no words over the din. A few of the men surrounding the dance floor started to mill about. In between the patterns of glad rags, Dash thought he saw the flash and sparkle of a blue and gold dress. Was he imagining it? He narrowed his eyes. There. At the back-right table nearest the band. A blue and gold dress. Now where did she come from? She was probably in the water closet when Dash and the outsider scanned the room the first time. Lucky for her. She sat with two darkened figures in tuxedos, the only other tuxes in the place besides Dash's.

The outsider's eyes sparked. He started to turn to see what was behind him.

Dash touched the man's shoulder to stop him. "I can't hear you!" he shouted.

The man's frowning lips moved in a frustrating pantomime.

The cheering and whistling eventually stopped and the band began a slow waltz. The men on the dance floor, breathing hard, wiped their faces with their handkerchiefs and grabbed their partners again to sway to the soft music. Heads rested on shoulders and hands pressed against backs, eyes half-closed in bliss. This gentle moment was considered "degeneracy" by those nanny lawmakers, and Dash marveled, not for the first time, at the cruelty of the language used to describe the tenderness on display.

"I said," the outsider continued, "I will pay you handsomely if you can find this . . . person. If that's what it'll take for a man like you."

Before Dash could reply, another voice cut through the noise. "Pardon me, boys, a lady is coming through!"

Like a miniature Moses, Finn Francis—Dash's other roommate and partner as well as the club's only waiter— parted the sea of men to get to the bar. He inadvertently separated the bell bottom from his green-suited prize, and their dimpled smiles were replaced with momentary frowns. They rejoined each other's limbs immediately after Finn passed.

Once in front of Joe, Finn said, "I need three gin martinis, extra dirty, no olives, and one beer from the secret stash. And I cannot emphasize the no olives part enough, Mr. O'Shaughnessy. I got a Your Highness who is just *in*sufferable, and if this Queen Mary sees any trace of olives, she will raise all-holy hell."

He turned his mascara-lined blue eyes to Dash.

"I swear to Athena, she thinks this place is the Ritz-Carlton and the service should be the same. No offense, dearie."

Caught off guard, Dash replied, "None taken."

"But this *is* a bar in the Village, and you get what you get. Why people act like they're the Astors when their bank accounts look like the O'Shaughnessys—"

"Finney," growled Joe.

"—I'll never know." He caught Dash's expression. "What's that look for?"

Dash stared into his friend's wide blue eyes which sparkled with intelligence, the painted lashes magnetic in their effect. For the life of him, Dash couldn't get the words out fast enough to warn this "wisp of a lad" with short black hair, a smooth oval face, an impish upturned nose, and a pointed dimpled chin that an outsider had broken into Pinstripes.

The outsider quickly set his sights on the small man. "You said 'she.' A queen, I believe?"

Dash tried to catch Finn's attention with a quick and forceful shake of his head. Alas, the little man didn't see it, or more likely, ignored it.

"I did," Finn replied, turning towards the outsider, "and not that I'm a flat tire, but *she* can sometimes be *too* much. And dearies, I am quite at home with being too much."

He gestured to his own outfit, a crisp white vest with no shirt underneath, showing off his sinewy arms and narrow, hairless chest. Despite the fact he wore no proper shirt, he still placed a matching white bow tie around his neck. A sparkling comb in bright red flashed from the corner of his dark-haired head. The cherry on top of a soufflé of a man.

The outsider was persistent. "And one of the men at this table, he ordered a beer?"

"That's what I said. Little kraut." Finn caught himself. "I don't mean to offend. A German boy. Nice enough. A bit shy."

"Where is this table?"

"Why, back there next to the—"

"FINN!"

All three men—his waiter, his bartender, and the outsider—were surprised at the sudden rise in Dash's voice. Even the bell bottom and his green-suited companion paused their conversation.

Dash forced a polite smile and spoke softer. "I believe this man was just leaving. He was looking for someone, but she is not here."

He glanced meaningfully at Joe and mouthed the word "bluenose."

Joe finally got the hint. "Aye," he said, aiming his green emeralds at the outsider's blazing blues. "She's probably elsewhere. Best be on yer way."

The outsider replied, "I can see the men here lack the proper breeding."

"What was that, bub?" the bell bottom said, tearing his gaze away from the boy in the green suit, his hackles rising.

The man ignored the sailor. "And the proper respect of those who have good breeding."

The accent got thicker, the consonants harsher. Bigger bombs landed.

He looked at Finn. "Take me to the table. Now."

Finn's eyes flashed. He tried to redirect in his own way. "Why choose a Queen Mary when you can have almost every man in this room? A tall, strapping thing like yourself, you could have your pick of the litter."

Finn quickly saw his error.

Dash did as well.

The outsider stepped towards the small man, his body tight with promised violence. "What did you say to me?"

"I-I just thought—"

"Do you honestly think I want to engage in this, this *filth*?!"

Dash grabbed the man's shoulder to pull him away from Finn. "Sir, I will *not* ask you again—"

The outsider gave no warning. He quickly whirled around to Dash with his right hand closed into a fist. By the time Dash registered the motion, it was too late.

2

The blow struck the side of Dash's face, and his head snapped back into the shoulder of a patron behind him. A teacup tumbled to the floor and broke. The band halted abruptly.

The outsider grabbed the front of Dash's vest, crumpling it, and brought him forward. Instead of waiting for the next punch, Dash tried to knee the man. He was a little off —his kneecap connected with the man's hard ribcage instead of his soft groin—but the outsider let out a surprised yelp, regardless. Dash kneed him again, hitting the other side of his ribs. He felt the crowd surge around them.

"Get 'im, sister!"

"Ya meat-packing piece o' shit!"

"Hit the Hun!"

"Dash, duck!"

That last one was yelled by Finn. Dash crouched down as the outsider's fist sailed over his head and connected with the jaw of the young man next to him, the one in the green suit who had been talking with the bell bottom. The one some men would call "a fairy."

Big mistake.

The boy shook off the blow and left his barstool, pushing Dash out of the way. He grabbed the outsider's crotch and practically lifted him up by his delicates. The outsider's face twisted in pain. The boy released him, seized the back of the outsider's head by his hair, and raised it high before slamming it down onto the bar, hard, three times. *Bam! Bam! Bam!*

The outsider dropped to the floor.

The boy looked down at him and said in a low, gravelly voice, "Hit me again and I'll feed you your own gospel pipe."

Then, as if he hadn't been engaged in an altercation, the boy returned to his place next to the bell bottom, who stared at him with a mix of awe and fear. The boy said to the sailor, in a much higher, softer voice, that his enjoyment had been interrupted by a "rude kraut."

Finn rushed over to Dash. His delicate hands reached up and cupped both sides of Dash's head, turning him this way and that. The red comb sparkled in Finn's black hair, the pinpricks of light temporarily blinding Dash.

"Hmm," he said, "you're going to have the most *brutish* bruise in the morning."

"Oh hell."

"Don't be upset. Why, there isn't a man in here who wouldn't want to be your nursemaid and check your temperature." A grin danced across his elfish face.

Dash rolled his eyes. "There's nothing wrong with my temperature, Finn."

"Just that it's not being taken by anyone lately. Unless you've been using Joe's thermometer while I'm away."

The outsider groaned at their feet, interrupting them. They turned their attention to the man on the floor. He spit out blood. Two teeth lay beside him, a pair of dice from a losing throw.

Finn called down to him, "Do you *mind*? I have to clean that floor later."

He then went to calm down the customers, telling them "it's all right, Mr. Parker has it all under control." Other than a figure in a tuxedo excusing himself towards the door —one of the two Dash had seen at that back table—the rest of the crowd stayed put.

At least the fight hasn't cleared the room.

Joe came around the bar and stood beside him. "Let's get this blowhard outta here."

They lifted the outsider, each throwing one arm over their shoulders, and aimed him towards the hidden door.

"I'll get you," the outsider said, his words muffled by the fast swelling of his cheeks and lips. "I swear to God, I'll get you."

Joe looked over at Dash. "What is he, lassie? Rough trade?"

"I tell you I don't know this man."

"Huh. Seems awfully angry at ya for someone you don't know."

The three of them shuffled to the club's hidden door, which was actually the mirror embedded into the back wall of the tailor shop's curtained-off changing area. As Joe pulled it open, the glass caught the reflection of the three men, plus another shadowy figure rushing towards them.

"Excuse me! Excuse me!" she said. "I need to catch up with my friends!"

They stepped aside for a tall, dark-headed girl pushing her way through. Her dress shimmered blue and gold. The other person at that back table.

Is she the one this bluenose was looking for?

"Easy, lass!" Joe called out.

She didn't seem to hear, just crossed the threshold and disappeared.

Joe growled, "Impatient, these young ones."

"Careful," Dash replied. "You're sounding like a Father Time."

Joe's response was lost under his breath, but Dash got the idea. They walked into the tailor shop's changing area, pulling the mirror closed behind them. Only a single wooden chair occupied this space, which was surrounded by a dark green curtain, still swaying from the girl's hasty exit.

As soon as they set the stranger down into the chair, the curtain was pulled open with a high-pitched *ring*! Dash turned to see their doorman—and their lookout—Atticus Delucci, backlit by the shop's sewing table lamp.

"Boss," Atty said, "I saw a couple of people running out of here. Is everything . . . ?"

He paused when he saw the bloody face of the outsider. Then questions came out fast and furious, followed by righteous anger on his employer's behalf. Atty yelled at the German man that *they lost the war,* that *it's no reason to ruin a man's birthday,* and *they better act right or go back to where they came from.*

"All right, Atty, all right, enough," Dash said. "We've got it under control."

"You sure, boss? We can teach this fella more of a lesson."

Dash looked down at his doorman. At first glance, Atty was an admittedly odd choice to stand guard, as he barely stood five foot and barely saw over the bars he regularly attended. He would've been taken advantage of by men of ill will and ill repute had he not the muscles blessed by a boxer, a baseball bat blessed by the Yankees, and a pistol blessed by Smith & Wesson—which didn't often hit its target but was dangerous, nonetheless. Despite Atty's eagerness, Dash wanted to avoid more violence tonight, if he could help it.

He patted Atty on the shoulder. "That won't be necessary."

Joe said, "Close the curtain, lad. We don't want the entire street seeing this mess." He nodded towards Hartford & Sons' front windows, which overlooked West Fourth. Anyone looking in right now would see a stage-lit view of the changing area.

Atty reached back and did as he was asked, the curtain slinging around them again. The changing area darkened by half. Shrunk too, what with four men in a space made for one.

Dash turned his attention to the outsider. "May I have your name, sir?"

For a moment, the man just sat there, stunned. He reached for his handkerchief in his front breast pocket and spit out more blood into it before responding with "Walter Müller."

The name meant nothing to Dash.

"A pleasure to meet you," he said, demonstrating good manners. "And why is this female impersonator worth getting your head beat in, Mr. Müller?"

Walter wiped his mouth and looked up, his eyes unfocused and dazed. Three men stared back at him. He furrowed his bloody brow and considered his options. He wisely chose to be forthcoming.

"He corrupted my brother. He has brought him here to this . . . this *place* . . . and others like it, which has made my brother believe he is also . . . unnatural."

"Your brother is the man you followed here? The one who met up with her?"

"Yes."

Dash sighed. Another family member who found out about their sibling's secret life. The desires that were left unspoken yet found a way to get satisfied, nonetheless. Some families simply turned a blind eye to the midnight activities of their sons. Others wanted to put a stop to "such foolishness." That's what Dash's own father had tried to do. *Leave this schoolboy nonsense and accept your responsibility!* He meant marriage to an upstanding society girl. For Dash, who was madly in love with someone else at the time, that would never do.

Dash crossed his arms over his chest. "And what were you planning to do with her once you found her?"

Walter's eyes cleared, the spark reigniting those blue flames. "Talk to her."

Atty leaned forward. "Tell it to Sweeney, you lying son of a bitch. Youse was gonna—"

"Atty." Dash shook his head at his doorman, who backed away from Walter.

"Sorry, Boss. These bluenoses just get me so sore."

"They get me sore as well." Dash returned his attention to Walter. "You never heard of this club before?"

"I don't even know its godforsaken name, and I don't care to know it. I only want to stop my brother from further corruption by degenerates like you and perverts like that, that pansy."

"I'm afraid you're all wet. A pansy can't force a man to do things he doesn't want to do. Face it, mister, your brother wants to be in the life."

"He would *never*. He is confused and confounded by your wickedness."

Joe leapt to his defense. "There's no wickedness here, ya bloody fool. Only people having a good time."

"And we will not," Dash said, "let you harm anyone in this club."

Walter paused for a moment. More wipes of his bloody mouth with the handkerchief. "Very well. I wish to collect my brother and go home."

Atty was incredulous. "Your brother's a grown man, sir! He can do whatever he wants."

"He lives with me and Mother. We follow her rules."

"Great," muttered Joe, "someone who's still on Mother's teat."

Walter's look hardened. "If I cannot confront this pansy for *his* involvement in my brother's degeneracy, then I'm not leaving here without my brother. Even if I have to fight you all to do it."

Atty responded by pulling out his Smith & Wesson from his pocket and aiming it at Walter.

Dash cut in. "Wait a moment." He looked at Walter. "It wouldn't be just us, I'm afraid. As I said before, you're outnumbered in there. That damage to your face is the result of just *one* fairy. Can you imagine what an entire roomful would do to you?"

Dash let the thought simmer with Walter's anger.

"I'll tell you what I'll do," he continued. "I'll go back in there and see if your brother is really here."

"He *is* here."

"*If* he's here and *if* he wants to leave with you, then I will not stop it. But if he doesn't, then he stays, and *you* can be on your merry way. Is that understood?"

"I want to talk to him."

"It's either me or no one at all."

Walter tried to stand up to muscle his way back in, but

the young boy in the green suit at the bar had clocked him good. His balance was off, and all Joe had to do was push him back into the wooden chair with a gentle palm. The pistol cocking in Atty's hand helped to end the argument.

Walter glared at Dash. His pride would not allow him to admit defeat, but he knew good and well who had won this round. He folded his bloody handkerchief and placed it in his trouser pocket, then held open his hands, indicating acquiescence.

"Excellent," said Dash. "What's your brother's name?"

"Karl."

"What's he look like?"

Walter reached for his inside jacket pocket.

Joe stiffened. "Easy, there. I wouldn't try nothing."

Walter gave him an annoyed look and slowly pulled out a small square of paper with bent edges. He handed it to Dash.

A photograph.

Dash supposed the image to be of Karl Müller. He was slight, the very opposite of his intimidating brother. A soft face with delicate features. His hair appeared ghostly white, as did the color of his skin. Gentle hands clasped in front of him in the stiff pose, the fingers looking like they trembled a bit before the flash bulb went off. He couldn't have been more than sixteen years old.

"Alright," Dash said, "I'll go see if he's here."

Atty gestured towards Walter with his pistol. "We'll make sure he behaves."

Dash leaned towards Joe and whispered, "Make sure Atty doesn't accidentally shoot him."

"Hmph. Wouldn't be the worst thing."

"Then *you* can get down on your hands and knees to scrub the German's brains off the floor."

Joe begrudgingly nodded.

Dash prayed all three men would keep their tempers in check. Last thing his birthday needed was a shoot-out on top of a fight. He walked towards the mirror in the back wall and pushed the left-hand side. The mirror silently swung open on its hidden hinges.

He no sooner entered the main room of Pinstripes than Finn glided up to him and shoved a cloth filled with ice into his hands.

"For your poor, battered face."

Dash gingerly placed the makeshift ice pack against his cheek. The cold sent a searing, sharp pain to the back of his eye. He sucked in air between his teeth.

"It's not that bad, is it?"

"Not yet, but soon it'll be a *spectacular* black and purple. Did you find out why that man hates you so?"

Dash told him the situation.

"Oh dear," Finn replied. "And he wants to drag his brother out by his hair? How caveman! Why would you turn this boy over to a brute like that?"

Dash shook his head. "I'm not. I'm simply giving the boy the choice. If he doesn't want to leave, he won't. Simple as that."

Finn peered over Dash's shoulder. "Where is this Walter, by the way? He's not coming in here again?"

"Atty has our angry German under guard."

"I hope the gun doesn't go off."

"Has anyone ever told you what a comfort you are? His brother may not even be here. He's adamant about that but he could be mistaken." Dash handed Finn the photograph Walter gave him. "Look like anyone you've waited on tonight?"

Finn studied the photograph, purring, "He is a choice

bit of calico, isn't he?" He returned it to Dash. "Have you ever had one, a German? They are *quite* the specimen. Tall, muscled. And what's hanging between their legs is simply—"

"Have you seen him, Finn?"

Finn pouted but then answered the question. "I seem to recall one blondie tonight. It could be that fellow's brother." He pointed to the photograph in Dash's hand. "This looks an awful lot like him, now that I think about it."

"What can you tell me about him?"

"Young. Blushing. Nervous. I'd say it's his first time in a club like this, or very nearly his first time. When I asked him what he'd like to drink, I thought he'd faint. I wanted to hold him to my breast and say, *there, there, it will be alright.*"

"Anything else?"

"He seemed to be waiting for someone. Always checking his wristwatch, which I'm just *dying* to have if *some*one will give me a raise."

"You're trying my patience, Finn."

"I didn't realize you were one for virtues. Anyhow, he was always looking at his wrist and checking the door. Like he was watching Helen Wills on the court. Back and forth, back and forth."

"Did anyone arrive for him?"

"I don't believe so. His table was already full. Not sure how they could've fit one more person, unless he sat on someone's lap."

Dash nodded, making a guess. "Right, the woman in the blue and gold dress and the man in the tuxedo."

Finn's eyes widened. "How on *earth* did you know that?"

Dash tapped the side of his forehead. "I've got spiritualist powers."

"Hmm, they're only working at half-speed, I'm afraid. You got one wrong."

"Oh?"

"It wasn't a man in the tuxedo. It was a woman."

"Ah."

Dash peered over Finn's shoulder to see the table in the back-right corner. It was empty.

Finn turned around. "My, my. Everyone must've run off. Where do you suppose the pretty boy went?"

Either Karl was the tuxedo-ed figure Dash saw running out of here, or . . .

"If he's still here, he's hiding. And I know where." Dash patted Finn's shoulder and returned to him the ice pack. "Thank you, Finn. Back to work you go."

Finn faked offense. "All I am to you is a hot number to parade around for tips."

"And no one does it better."

"I see. Well, dearie, while I'm out here degrading myself, something else you should consider."

"What is that?"

"How did this Walter fellow even know about this club?"

"Simple. He followed Karl here."

"Yes, but how did he know the secret knock?"

And with that, Finn glided off.

Dash nodded to himself, recognizing the question was a damned good one. The secret knock to get into Pinstripes was a series of syncopated hits not unlike the jazz that was roaring across Manhattan like a thunderclap. Patrons had to give it on the tailor shop's front door. If the knock didn't match the code, Atty, who was sitting at the sewing machine in the right-side window, would press a button on the side of his table. The button was wired to a red bulb inside Pinstripes. The red light would glare, causing everyone to stop the music and quiet themselves. Joe would lock the club's secret door while Atty dealt with whomever out front. Only Dash gave out the secret knock, and he certainly wouldn't have given it to a bluenose by accident. Perhaps one of his patrons parted with it by mistake? He'd have to sit down with Atty to figure out what went wrong. In the meantime, he had to contend with the Müller brothers.

Damn. This was not how his birthday was supposed to go.

He placed the photograph of Karl in his inside jacket pocket and made his way toward the back of the club, maneuvering around clusters of couples and trios. A few reached out and shook his hand, some wishing him a happy birthday, others saying what a glorious club this was. Crossing the dance floor, Dash walked through a cloud of nicotine mingling with the juniper of gin, the yeast of beer, and the sweet musk of sweat. Joy, freedom, and desire all in one fragrance.

At the back of the room and to the right of the band was the water closet. Dash knocked on the door. "Karl? Are you in here?"

A pause.

A nervous voice stammered, "Who is it?"

"My name is Dash Parker. I am the owner of the place. May I please come in?"

A longer pause this time.

"I promise I won't make you leave with your brother."

Silence still.

Then the lock clicked, and Dash went inside.

3

A young man stood nervously in front of the toilet. Unlike most of the patrons tonight, he wore the appropriate formal wear for a night out: tuxedo jacket, white shirt and waistcoat, white tie.

Money, Dash thought. *I see I was right about the family being rich.*

Like in the photograph in Dash's pocket, Karl's hands were clasped in front of him. Unlike in the photograph, in which his smile was forced, here the smile was gone, replaced by a panicked thin line.

"Is he gone?" Karl asked.

Dash shut the door behind him. "Not yet."

Karl looked to the side wall, as if he could peer through it and see his brother. "I can't go back there. Not after tonight."

"Go back where?"

"Home."

"Is home that unwelcome for you?"

Karl swallowed a cry, trying to keep the tears down. He looked even younger in the flesh than in the photograph in Dash's pocket. A nymph's nose, a child's eyelashes, an aristocrat's slicked-down hair. His smooth palms didn't speak to long days of hard work, and his unblemished knuckles didn't tell a story of fight and flight. Either he lived high above the streets or he was extremely careful walking them. He had to be with that wristwatch of his. Not many Village men owned one, and some would think it was theirs by virtue of seeing it on someone else.

Karl's head was still shaking from side to side. "I can't go back there. He knows."

"I can tell him you're not here."

"He won't believe you."

"My men will keep him from searching the place, I promise you."

The kid stopped shaking his head. "Why are you helping me?"

"Because I'm like you. Because . . . I had a very unwelcome home too."

Especially towards the end.

Karl scrunched up his face, but this time, he couldn't stop the tears from rolling down his pink-suffused cheeks. "Not like this."

Dash reached out and laid a gentle hand on the boy's shoulder. Karl recoiled from the touch, almost falling against the toilet.

Dash held up his hands in apology. "I don't want to hurt you. I can help, if you'd let me."

"No one can help me. They tried to help, they all tried to, but it didn't work and now, now I have nowhere else to go—"

"Who tried? Your friends?"

Karl's response was made unintelligible by his sobs.

Dash tried another tact. "Were you going to move out? Was someone going to take you in?"

A low moan like a barge horn hummed from Karl's chest. "You don't understand."

"But I do."

"No! You don't!"

Dash wasn't getting anywhere. He needed Karl to calm down so he could get Walter out of his club.

"I will go back out there and tell your brother you are not here. You can stay in the club for as long as you like. My doorman, Atty? He can go outside and make sure your brother isn't waiting for you on the street. And then you can leave and safely rejoin your friends. For now, just stay here. Can you do that?"

It took effort, but the tears managed to subside enough for Karl to nod.

Dash nodded in return. "I will return shortly."

He left the water closet, closing the door behind him. A strange emotion filled his chest, a mix of sadness and regret. *I can't go back there!* Dash had uttered those same words as well when he was near that age.

The band members weren't at their instruments. Probably using the fight as an excuse to grab a drink. Dash didn't blame them. He wanted one as well. Instead of accepting various drink offers from granite men or returning the fanciful gazes of porcelain boys, he entered the tailor shop's changing area again, preparing himself for the lies he had to tell a man who most likely wouldn't believe them.

Joe gave him a harsh look. "Took ya long enough."

Atty had returned the pistol to his front trouser pocket. Now he stood with his arms folded across his chest. "Yeah, this fellow here is no good for conversation."

"Apologies, gentlemen," Dash replied. "I wanted my

search to be thorough." He looked at Walter. "Your brother isn't here."

"Liar!"

Dash held up a hand. "I asked my waiter, who saw him leave. He must've seen you enter the place and while you were getting your face pounded by the boy you shouldn't have hit, even if it was by accident, young Karl walked behind everyone and snuck out."

Joe said, "The bloke in the tuxedo. I saw him leave as well."

God bless you, Joe, Dash thought.

Walter pointed at Atty. "How come he hasn't said anything about a young boy leaving?"

"Because people come and go all the time in a place like this. Right, Atty?"

Atty gave him a curious look, then cleared his throat as well as his expression. "Right, right. It's a never-ending parade."

Walter wasn't buying it. "You're all lying to me. You're *lying!*"

Dash had an idea. "If you're done accusing us of deceit, I can show Atty here the photograph you gave me. He hasn't seen what the boy looks like."

He took the picture out of his pocket and handed it to Atty.

"Does this look like the fellow in the tuxedo?" Dash kept his face benign, but he hoped Atty caught the hint in his eyes.

Atty turned his head to the side in a display of thought. He handed the photograph to Dash, who returned it to his inside coat pocket.

"Yessir, that's him in the tux, alright. He was pretty nervous too. I didn't put it together, his leaving, your fight, but uh . . . this boy definitely came out here and left through that door. Went to the right, I think, towards Seventh."

God bless you too, Atty, Dash thought with relief.

Walter kept his burning eyes on the doorman. "I want to search the club for myself."

Joe scoffed. "And start trouble again? I don't think so, lad. If Mr. Parker says the boy is gone, then the boy is gone."

Dash added, "I'd go home and see if he's there. If not, I'd search the cafeterias. At this late hour, they tend to cater to boys like him."

Walter grimaced at that last statement and turned his glare towards Dash. A tense silence followed.

Don't let the fear show on your face, Dash's older brother Maximilian always said. *That's how you get away with lies.*

Walter stood up. Joe's fist clenched, and Atty reached for his pistol. Walter held up his hands and forced a grotesque smile, his lips and tongue bloody from the two missing teeth in the upper right corner of his mouth.

"Alright, gentlemen. If you say my brother is not here, then I shall look for him elsewhere." He pointed a threatening finger at Dash. "But he is not to come back. Understood? You see him, you turn him away. I do not want to return to this despicable place."

Atty started, "You can't tell us—"

Dash placed a calming hand on Atty's shoulder. "We will advise young Karl to go elsewhere. Though I doubt he'll come back after seeing you here."

Walter said, "He better not."

Atty opened the changing area curtain and grabbed the German by the arm, leading him to the tailor shop's front door.

Dash remembered what Finn had said earlier and stopped Atty. "Mr. Müller, one question before you go. How did you know the knock to get into this club?"

Walter kept his back to Dash. "What was that?"

"The knock. On the front door of the tailor shop. How did you know it?"

Walter turned towards Dash, his expression bemused, his tone condescending. "I heard him practicing it last night. Many of these secret clubs use such knocks. When I saw him go into your shop, I knew why he was practicing something so *childish*."

Joe demanded, "What kind of brother spies on his own?"

Walter gave him a fiery look. "One who protects his family. He is *my* responsibility. I taught him everything from when he was a boy. To read, to write, to know right from wrong. He has been corrupted by the likes of you—"

Dash interrupted the tirade. "And the mirror. How did you know about that?"

Walter's lips curved into another jack-o-lantern's smile. "This is not the first club I've seen my brother enter. Many of you degenerates use the same tricks."

Damn it all.

Atty, still holding on to Walter's arm, said, "We done with him, boss?"

Dash reluctantly nodded.

Atty opened the front door and pushed Walter across the threshold, saying "Go chase yourself!"

Walter kept his blazing blue eyes on Dash as he stepped into the street, bloody grin still in place. "Good night, Mr. Parker. You should hope we never meet again."

Dash swallowed the lump in his throat.

Atty slammed the front door shut and locked it. "Good

riddance!" he said, returning to his post at the sewing table in the right-side window.

Joe shared the sentiment. "What a bloody fool. Coming in here trying to place blame for his brother's actions. Not yer responsibility."

"Yeah, not your responsibility."

Except the scared kid hiding in my club is *my responsibility.*

Dash stood in front of the left-side window, watching as Walter sauntered down the street heading west towards Seventh Avenue, looking entirely too pleased with himself. "Did he say anything of interest while I was gone?"

"A bunch of ramblings," replied Joe.

Atty nodded. "He supports the Temperance Committee and the Anti-Saloon League. And he is a member of the Committee of Fourteen. Proud of the fact he works for the nannies."

Dash cursed under his breath. The Committee of Fourteen was an independent organization designed to "discipline" the broader culture. Nannies, indeed. They hired undercover investigators to spy on New York's dance halls, saloons, theaters, and other, what they called, "commercialized amusements." A man working for a place like that was the *last* person they needed to know about Pinstripes.

Atty kept on. "Bet his Mother does all his thinking for him. Did you hear him, Joe? 'Mother' this and 'Mother' that."

Joe's eyes were afire. "Ha! I bet he don't take a piss without dear old Mum telling him so."

Atty raised his voice to mimic an elderly woman's. "Remember to shake proper, Walter boy!"

Dash said, "Did he say he'd report us to anyone? Make any threats like that?"

Walter hadn't. It didn't mean he wouldn't though.

Dash turned away from watching the street and glanced around the tailor shop, trying to get a handle on their situation. The parlor-green walls felt like they were closing in on a space already too small. The modest furnishings he'd found left on the city streets were crammed together: the sewing table by Atty and Joe, a small writing desk at Dash's hip, and, next to the curtained-off changing area, a wardrobe standing against the back wall, which functioned as a display case for jackets and ties and was topped with various hats. In this mix of light and shadow, those hats looked like vultures staring down at the doomed.

Dash started walking towards his two friends. "Atty, what happened tonight?"

The question caught Atty by surprise, which didn't bode well for the conversation to come.

"What do you mean, Boss?"

Joe saw where Dash was going and joined him. "He means, lad, how in the name of Mary did *that* bluenose get inside Pinstripes?"

Atty's face creased with panic. His eyes flicked from Joe to Dash and back again. "He—he knew the knock. He did it perfectly."

Dash now stood next to Joe, his brow wrinkling with questions. "He didn't seem threatening to you?"

"Not a bit! He was excited. He spoke with a high voice, you know, like Finn. Said how he couldn't wait to get inside. It had been a monstrous day and he was ready to forget it."

Joe muttered, "He put on an act."

Dash nodded. "And when he walked inside the tailor shop, did he know exactly where to go?"

Atty swallowed. "No, not at first."

Joe said, "Ya didn't think that was suspicious?"

Atty got more defensive. "Some of our regulars some-times forget where it is. A lot of people think it's behind the wardrobe. Hell, I'd think so myself. It's not easy to guess."

"It's not supposed to be, lad."

Atty crossed his arms over his chest, which he started to puff out. "It's easy to criticize, but it's not so easy sitting here trying to figure out who's legit and who's dangerous. If youse think you can do it better, than why don't either one of youse sit in this chair and do it for a change. I did my best and—"

Dash held up a hand. "Atty, Atty, it's alright. Every-thing is jake. Or it will be. We just need to figure out how and why Walter Müller snuck inside so it doesn't happen again. That's all." He put on a friendly smile. "The knock is one security measure. The mirror is the other. If someone doesn't go straight to the changing area, press the button."

Joe sent Dash a worried look. "Lassie, are you sure about that? He's gonna be pressing that button every other person."

Atty was offended. "No, I won't! I know exactly what Mr. Parker wants. They knock, they come in, if they walk around the shop or go in the wrong direction, that's a warning sign." He looked to Dash. "Right, Boss?"

Dash smiled. "Exactly right." He returned his gaze to Joe. "See? He's got it."

Joe just shook his head slightly. "I sincerely hope so."

I as well.

"Speaking of security, gents," Dash said, "we have to change the knock."

Joe and Atty nodded in agreement.

Then Joe clapped a hand on Dash's shoulder. "Where is young Karl? I think we should buy the poor boy a drink."

"You may need to buy me one as well. He's hiding in

the water closet. Atty? Can you take a look outside and make sure Walter has left our block?"

Atty nodded. "Aye aye, sir."

"And Atty? Be sure you don't accidentally shoot him."

Atty grumbled but left the shop with a sharp click of the front door.

Dash turned to Joe. "We got a terrified little lamb in there. Doesn't want to go home."

"He can't stay here!"

"I know, I know. At the moment, he's not budging. Hopefully in a drink or two, he'll be on his way."

"Hope so. We don't need any more trouble tonight."

Only I can't send him back to a dangerous place. But where else can he go?

Dash nodded towards the club. "You better get back to your post, Joe. Our boys might start picking the bar clean."

Joe swore under his breath, turned, and pushed open the secret door, disappearing into the shadows.

Dash sighed and followed after him, saying aloud, "Happy birthday to me."

4

Back inside Pinstripes, Joe was urgently taking orders from the impatient and thirsty. Dash pushed his way through the noisy throng and crossed over the idle dance floor. The band had returned to their instruments, readying themselves to start again. He gave them a nod as he passed.

When he opened the WC door, he found Finn standing in front of Karl.

Oh no.

"Finn." Dash shut the WC door behind him. "Shouldn't you be attending to your tables?"

The three of them barely fit in this space, what with Finn and Karl pressed against the walls near the toilet and Dash practically overflowing into the sink.

Finn smiled. "Only if you let me have next Sunday night off." He held up a blue card. "This lovely boy told me of the most *excellent* party."

"I see." Dash flicked a look towards Karl, who averted his gaze.

Finn continued. "Yes! It's in Harlem." He said to Karl,

"Don't worry, Dash isn't a whites-only kind of fellow. Why, one of his good friends is a famous bulldagger up there—"

Dash held out his hand. "May I see the card, please?"

Finn slipped the blue card in between his fingers. Dash squinted to read the black type in the jaundiced light:

Come on Boys, don't be Ruff, go from Heaven to Hell and Strut Your Stuff—AT—a Social Whist Party.
Given by Zora Mae at corner of 150th Street & St. Nicholas, Sunday Evening, August 22, 1926.
GOOD Music. Refreshments Served.

The party was one week from tonight in Sugar Hill, Harlem's rich neighborhood full of castle-like mansions.

Dash said, "Impressive." He tilted his head towards Karl, "Do you know this Zora Mae?"

The kid shrugged. "Perhaps."

Dash looked at Finn. "And this came up in conversation how?"

Finn rolled his eyes. "Look at you, being all suspicious. I find this beautiful boy in here, so naturally I strike up a conversation."

"And Harlem rent parties was what you were conversing?"

"Not *initially,* dearie. The boy was nervous—and you're making him more so, shame on you—and so I just asked if he knew where there was a good party. It *is* 1926, and the champagne is *flowing,* praise goddess."

Dash looked at Karl. "Kid, is that what happened?"

Karl nodded meekly.

Finn put his hands on his hips. "Now that you're done interrogating him, can I have next Sunday off?"

"Most Harlem rent parties aren't for whites, Finn."

Dash then said to Karl, "Your brother has left. My doorman is making sure he's gone from the block."

"Thank you." Karl hesitated. "Although, I don't know where to go. I don't . . . I don't think I have a home anymore."

The kid had the face of someone too anxious to stay but too fearful to leave. The last time Dash saw such an expression, it was in his bedroom mirror at his family's sprawling townhouse.

"What about your friends?" Dash asked. "Surely you can stay with them?"

Karl began fidgeting with his hands. "I wouldn't call them close friends."

"I see. And there's no one else you can go to?" Dash looked down at the blue card in his hand. "This Zora Mae perhaps?"

"She doesn't take in strays. Or so she said the one time I asked her."

"A . . . lover then?"

Karl's tone was low and flat. "Not anymore."

Finn stepped towards Dash and whispered in his ear, "He can stay in my room."

"And invite more trouble to our apartment?"

Finn flicked a look at the kid. "We can't just throw him out. That's heartless."

"I am aware, Finn." Dash looked from Finn to Karl, thinking, *what am I going to do with you?* He glanced down at the blue card again. If not Zora, then maybe . . .

He held up the card. "You're comfortable being in the black part of Harlem?"

Karl nodded.

"And your brother? Is he comfortable being there as well?"

"No, sir. He said he'd rather be shot dead."

Finn narrowed his eyes at Dash. "What are you doing?" he murmured.

Dash just smiled. "Helping." He pocketed the blue card and looked at Karl. "I know just where to hide you. There's a friend of mine in Harlem who can assist you. *If* she agrees, that is."

Finn's eyebrows shot up. "You don't mean—"

"Yes, I do."

"Do you think she'll do it? Hide him, that is."

Dash blew out a breath. "I can convince her."

"She won't be happy about it."

"No. No, she will not. Will that suffice, kid? It's not permanent, mind you, but it will allow some time for you to find another place to live."

Karl hesitated, then nodded. "Thank you. Thank you very much, sir."

"You are most welcome. Once the coast is clear, we shall journey uptown. Now, gentlemen, if you continue to hide out in the WC, everyone will think the good time is in here instead of out *there*." He gestured towards the door. "Away we go."

In an aside to Karl, Finn said, "He thinks he's the boss of us. It's adorable." He grabbed the kid's hand. "Come with me! I'll show you how to do the Black Bottom!"

The two men brushed past Dash and exited the room. Dash shook his head and followed them. What a night this was turning out to be. And what a lesson to be reminded of. For every person striving for freedom, there was always another trying to take it away.

The band had started up again and was in the throes of another song, this one loud and fast. Dash could see Finn teaching Karl dance steps, Finn moving with ease but Karl struggling to keep up with the beat.

When the cymbal-crashing crescendo finally came, Dash strolled up behind the drummer and whispered into his ear. The drummer, a black man shimmering with sweat, nodded. Dash went to the front of the band and held up his hands, waiting for the applause to die down.

"Ladies and gentlemen! Boys and girls! (And those somewhere in between.) May I have your attention, please!"

Finn yelled, "Yessir, missus sir, yessir!"

The crowd quieted.

Dash grinned, his teeth flashing like headlights. "Thank you for coming to Pinstripes. We are *so* glad you chose to celebrate with us."

"I'll celebrate with you anytime!" called out a flute-like voice from the shadows.

The crowd responded with laughter and whistles.

Dash gave a wink. "You wouldn't be able to last five seconds, my dear."

"Five seconds is all I'll need!" a different, deeper voice replied amidst more laughter.

Dash pretended to fan himself. "Such men! Such offers! How can I refuse? But business first. As many of you know, there's a little knock you need to enter our humble club. From time to time, we may change it for security reasons. And tonight, tragically, we need to do just that."

The crowd booed.

Dash waited for them to finish cursing the nannies, then said, "I know, but some things can't be helped. Now Calvin here will demonstrate for you just what our new knock will be. Mister Calvin!"

Calvin did a rat-a-tat-tat on the snare, a short but complicated series of hits. The crowd applauded.

Dash waited for them to quiet down. "All right? Let's see if you can do it with Calvin. Get ready to knock on your tables or on the bar. And please, be careful not to spill any precious drops from your drinks. Everyone ready?"

Finn, with more voices joining him this time, responded with an excited "Yessir, missus sir, yessir!"

For the next few moments, the drummer and the crowd did a call and response until the knocks and the snare were in solid unison.

"Beautiful!" Dash said. "I believe you've got it. Carry on!"

The band began another fast number, which caused everyone to rush to the dance floor. Out of the corner of Dash's eye, he saw Karl smiling as he danced. So innocent. So free. The way they were all supposed to be.

Dash returned to the bar. Joe came up and handed him a much-needed Gin Rickey.

"What are ya going to do with the brother?" he asked. When Dash told him his plan, Joe scoffed. "Good luck, lassie."

Dash raised his glass to his lips. "Thank you, Joe. I have a feeling I'm going to need all the luck in the world."

———

An hour later—when they were sure Walter was really gone —Dash and Karl grabbed a cab at the corner of Sixth Avenue and West Fourth and rode uptown in conspiratorial silence until the driver dumped them at their destination, 133rd and Lexington.

Dash led the way towards a club called the Oyster House, their pale skin earning them a few wary looks. Whites were often called "downtowners" up here, but the

Oyster House allowed a mixed audience. Which apparently was a large audience. Already a line formed down the street to get into the infamous speak. Luckily, they didn't have to wait, as Dash knew the doorman.

Horace was a giant black man with a square-shaped face that always wore a mean expression. His broad shoulders and bulging arms, crossed over a massive chest, threatened to tear the fabric of his shiny, black coat. Despite this intimidating presence, he smiled when he saw Dash and Karl walk up.

"Evening, Mr. Parker," he said, his voice surprisingly fey.

"Evening, Horace."

"Big crowd tonight. El should be happy."

"And if El is happy—"

"—then everybody else is miserable." A good-natured laugh followed.

"You are absolutely right about that, sir." Dash introduced Horace to Karl, then said, "Hot as Hades out here."

"Now *that's* the truth. I'm melting like a candle in this jacket. Wool don't breathe."

"Bet you're jealous of your lady's sleeveless dress right about now." Dash winked.

Horace laughed again. "I'm not man enough to try it on just yet."

"She over her cold?"

"That she is, thank you for asking."

"Summer colds are beastly. Tell her I'm happy she's feeling better." Dash nodded towards the speak. "Want me to get you a drink?"

Horace shook his head. "I go on break in half a chime. You two get on in there and grab something cold."

Dash slipped a bill into Horace's hand, saying "thank

you, Horace, stay jake out here." Then he and Karl ducked underneath the doorway.

They were greeted by the smell of spilled gin, pungent but sweet, reminding Dash of early-morning kisses from last night's passions. Walls painted deep red surrounded the mostly black patrons, a mix of male and female dressed in either fashion, with a few downtowners sticking out like white hairs. Conversations crashed around them like cymbals and snares, punctuated by sudden laughs echoing off the silver tin ceiling. One would never know it was a Sunday night.

Dash and Karl found a spot at the end of the bar nearest the stage. A beat-up brown upright piano stood at the center.

Dash ordered their libations and turned to see Karl glancing around the room in childlike wonder, his eyes wide opened, a half-grin tickling his lips.

Hang onto that joy, my boy, Dash thought. *And don't let this world take it from you.*

Rickeys in hand, they touched rims and took some much-needed sips.

"Alright, kid," Dash said, setting his glass onto the bar. "What's your story?"

5

Karl hesitated, clearly not comfortable being asked about himself.

"I was born in Germany. Berlin. I do not remember it. My brother does. He often talks of the countryside villages, the lush green hillsides covered with blue cornflowers and bright yellow chamomile. And the city rising upwards with tall buildings brushing against the giant blue sky. A lot like here."

Dash smiled, then nodded for Karl to continue.

"He said the country was filled with passionate, artistic, engineering geniuses. The most superior people in the world making the very best of things." Karl paused. "Sometimes I wonder if it's more fantasy. Other people speak of the poverty, the desperation, the violence. He never does. It seems the longer he's away from it, the more romantic he becomes."

"A keen observation. Would you ever go back?"

"Why should I return to a place I do not know?"

"Fair point. Is your family in America as well?"

"Only my mother."

"Your father stayed behind?"

"In a manner of speaking. He died."

Dash frowned. "I'm so sorry."

Karl replied, "It's alright, I didn't really know him. I was still young when it happened."

"What happened to him?"

"He was attending a cabaret and was mugged on his way home. They beat him and took his money and some other belongings. He had hit his head on the curb. The doctors told my mother his brain had swelled and that it caused his death."

"That's terrible! How can people be so needlessly cruel?"

Karl gave a bitter smile. "Cruelty is in our nature more than kindness, I'm afraid. Ever since my father's death, my mother has been very much against cabarets, saloons, clubs. She says it took her husband and she would not allow it to take her sons as well."

"I see," Dash said. "An overreaction, but an understandable one, given her circumstances. And you, your brother, and your mother came here after that?"

Karl nodded. "In 1924, a few years ago."

"And what do you do for a living?"

Karl's reply was slow in the making. "I work with my brother."

"Walter? I can see why you don't want to go home again. Living *and* working with him must be a nightmare."

"If you only knew. If only anyone knew." Karl didn't elaborate further.

Dash tried to reel him back in. "Where do you and Walter work?"

"The Committee of Fourteen. Walter helps manage the money. He's always been good with numbers. Meticulous.

Keeps perfect records and diaries. Says it's important to know what came from whom, for you never know when that information will be useful again. He bragged that the Committee never saw a more thorough, detailed report than his."

"I see." Moral views aside, Dash thought Walter sounded insufferable. "And what do *you* do?"

"What do I do? I . . . offer him support. Help him with the books."

Dash took another sip of his cocktail. The kid was a terrible liar. "And your friends? The people you came with to my club. How do you know them?"

A cautious look. "What do you mean? How do you know about my friends?"

Dash shrugged. "I saw them at your table. A female impersonator and a woman in men's clothing, now that's some interesting company. Especially given your mother's and your brother's personal views on cabaret nightlife."

Karl rubbed nervous fingertips up and down the sides of his glass, the surface already beaded with condensation. "One cannot change one's nature. On either side. As for my friends, I met them in other places—places like this." He shook his head. "But we are not very good friends."

"Casual acquaintances?"

"I suppose." Karl's face darkened again.

Dash gave what he hoped was a friendly smile. "Not every person in this city needs to be a confidante. Sometimes you just need superficial company. Do you go out with them often?"

Karl shook his head. "Tonight was special."

"Wonderful! I feel honored you chose my club for a celebration."

"It wasn't a celebration." He left it at that.

"Well, whatever it was," Dash said, "I'm still honored." He paused, thinking of how to ask his next question without scaring off the kid. "Did you choose my club? Or was it someone else?"

Karl stopped rubbing the slick sides of his cocktail glass. "Why do you ask that?"

So suspicious, so nervous. What are you afraid of, Karl?

Dash kept his manner and his voice nonchalant. "I'm a business owner. I like to know how my patrons learn about my place. That's all."

He sipped his Gin Rickey and let Karl work out his response.

The kid thought for a moment. "It was Miss Avery. She lives nearby and heard of it from a friend of hers."

"Glad to see the Village Grapevine is just as strong as ever. Miss Avery, was she the one in the blue and gold dress? Or the suit?"

Karl's eyes widened. "Why are you interested in them?"

Careful here, Dash.

He shrugged. "I'm not, really. Just making conversation. I ask you questions, then you ask me questions." He took another sip of his gin, then nudged Karl's elbow. "Ask me something."

The kid quietly debated with himself, then said, "Alright. Who is your friend we're about to see?"

"Ah, yes." Dash set his glass down. "I met her in a Harlem speak once upon a time. Not this one, some place I don't think I could find again. This incredible woman at the bar was just so lively, so fiery, so *funny*. A true bearcat in the best sense of the word. One couldn't help but be drawn to her. Naturally, I introduced myself, and we spent half the night and half the morning talking. Well, arguing mostly."

"Arguing?"

Dash grinned. "Why, yes. I had mentioned I loved jazz music and just adored the band who had invented it, the Dixieland Jass Band. It was the first record I ever heard and of course, in my naiveté, I thought it was the first one ever made."

He laughed at the memory.

"Oh my, she about levitated off her barstool. 'Those white boys did *not* invent jazz!' she said. 'They *stole* it from us, and anyone who says differently is a goddamn liar!' She set me straight and gave me new music to listen to. That's when I discovered Louis Armstrong and his band, who will change your life if you ever hear them in person. She and I have been friends ever since."

Karl's brows lifted with disbelief. "Friends with another race? Is that even possible?"

Dash gestured to the room around them. "Anything is possible in these modern times! And if it isn't, then it ought to be, and we're the people who can make it so. Besides, those of color are human beings. Just like the Irish, the Italians, the Polish." He touched Karl's arm. "And the Germans."

The kid smiled, which made Dash grin in return.

"What is her name?" Karl asked.

"El Train."

Karl titled his head with puzzlement. "Why is that her name?"

"She's as powerful as a locomotive, that's why! Of course, it's not her real name. Her real name is Eloise Ankins, though nobody calls her that—not if they want to stay alive, that is."

"Why would she change her name?"

"She's a take-charge kind of woman, not a refined, passive Eloise. Certainly not an Ankins. Horrid-sounding name and she'd tell you so. Sometimes the names we're given don't reflect who we truly are."

"Like the pansies." Karl quickly glanced around, worrying someone would overhear him.

Dash placated his fears. "This is a safe place. Yes, exactly, like them. Now other times, people change their names to protect themselves."

"How so?"

"Take the tailor shop for example."

"Ah, you changed *your* name," Karl said. "I was wondering why the shop was called *Hartford & Sons* and not *Parker & Sons*."

The kid hadn't missed the sign out front.

Dash chuckled. "Well, almost. My family name is indeed Parker, though I don't have any sons of my own." He leaned in. "Accuracy isn't the point; anonymity is." He sat back on his barstool. "I actually inherited the shop from a, uh . . . friend."

The friend had been the Parker family tailor. Just the thought of Victor with his dark hair flecked with gray, dark eyes, and dark pinstripe suits—always pinstripes—lit a fire buried deep within Dash. He hoped Karl didn't see the tell-tale blush on his cheeks.

"He was a Hartford?" Karl looked at Dash expectedly.

Dash shook his head, trying to recover. "This is where it can get confusing, especially after a few of these." He gestured to their drinks. "Yes, publicly the original owner went by Victor Hartford, but his real family name was Agramonte."

Karl wrinkled his brow. "What name is that?"

"Spanish. Apologies, Catalan. Victor would gasp if he heard me call him Spanish. We Americans aren't into the fine nuances of other countries and other cultures."

Though he certainly taught me the nuances of a glance or a handshake held too long.

"Why did he change his name to Hartford?"

"Because no one would buy from a Spanish tailor, let alone a Catalan one. And when the Spanish Influenza hit, can you imagine the scorn they endured? They were deemed responsible for bringing the 'plague upon our house,' as it were."

Dash's father certainly thought so when by Christmas of 1918, Dash's younger sister Sarah—the one who coined "Father Voice"—was added to the list of the fallen. If Thomas Parker had ever found out the true nationality of his tailor, God knew what he would've done.

Karl nodded, his voice solemn. "I understand. Just like they blame all us Germans for the War."

Dash's smile curved towards sadness. "When tragedy hits, people will need someone, or something, to blame." He took a long drink to cleanse his palate. "Anyhow, Victor simply picked his new name from a map. He said, 'if Hartford's good enough for a state capitol, it is good enough for me.'"

"He must've been a good friend to have left you his entire business."

Dash's body warmed with the memory of those secret nights in the back of the tailor shop—where music swelled from the Victrola and he and Victor discussed everything from worldly politics to the pulp stories Dash read with abandon. The air thick with cologne, laughter, and spilled wine. And then later, humid breaths on skin, lips salty with sweat. The room seeming to spin like the record on the turntable, the needle scratching as no one seemed to care the song had long ago finished.

"He most certainly was a good friend," Dash replied.

"Was?" Karl approached his next question with care. "Did he die?"

Dash quickly shook his head. "No." Thank God that wasn't the case. "No, no, he—" Dash didn't want to explain, not just yet, so he settled for: "—he had to leave. Circumstances beyond his control. You know how life can be."

That was 1925. A bad year all around.

Karl said, "And this new name, it gave him a new life when he moved here?"

"It does for most who come to this country."

"I wonder . . ."

Dash looked at Karl with interest. "Wonder what?"

Karl was speaking barely above a whisper, not talking to Dash at all, but to himself. "I wonder if I should do something like that. Go to a different place. Give myself a new name. A new life."

"Why would you need to?"

Karl didn't answer.

Dash leaned in closer. "What are you running from, kid?"

Before Karl could answer, El Train appeared onstage.

6

The roar from the crowd was deafening. Half the room stood up—a few even stood on their chairs—to applaud and whistle the tall, broad-shouldered, busty woman. She was dressed in a man's black tuxedo with tails. A top hat cocked to the side on her head, a face round like the moon, a snaggletooth dead-center in her grin. She placed her hands on her hips and scanned the crowd, seeing if they met to her liking.

After a full minute of cheering, she raised her hands and yelled her usual greeting. "Well *shee-it!*"

The crowd replied back, "Well *shee-it!*"

"You act like you've never seen a woman before! Some of you probably never even been with one. I *know* some of you never been with a woman like me. That's alright, baby, that's alright. Better late than never. Now tonight, I'm gonna educate you on the subject of *l-o-v-e*."

Dash watched as El pulled out the piano bench, flipped her tails back, and sat down.

"Tonight's first lesson is Alice Blue Gown. You know Alice Blue Gown? She one *baaad* little girl. Most don't want to admit she's around and those that do, well, you get told to keep your mouth shut. It's not appropriate conversation for polite society. Uh huh. As I look down from this stage, I can plainly see you're not society. And I'm not polite, so we're gonna tell *all* tonight!"

The crowd applauded with anticipation, then quieted down as El began to play. The music belonged to "Alice Blue Gown," a well-known song often performed in cabarets, rumored to be inspired by Alice Roosevelt's signature dress. To the Roosevelts' chagrin—or horror, more likely—El had rewritten the lyrics to be about something entirely different.

The intro was slow and teasing, full of dramatic pauses. She sang in her full, husky voice:

> *I once had a gown, it was almost new*
> *Oh, the daintiest thing, it was sweet Alice blue*
> *With little forget-me-nots placed here . . . and here . . .*

To the crowd's giggles, El paused to point to either side of her substantial bosom.

> *When I had it on, my love I just had to share . . .*
> *Then I whored and whored and whored*
> *'Til it ripped and it wasn't no more!*

The music then changed to a more stomping blues number, El's voice guttural and full of power, her fingers flying over the piano keys.

> *In my sweet little Alice blue gown*
> *When I first let my panties down*
> *He was so proud inside*

As I ground his gospel pipe
He shouted "Mama, mama!" as he shuddered and closed
his eyes

Then he said, "Dearie, please turn around"
And he shoved that thing right up my brown!
He tore it, I bored it, Lord, how I adored it
My sweet little Alice Blue Gown!

The room gasped, whooped, and hollered in response to the new lyrics. Several women in the crowd laughed so hard, tears streamed down their faces. The men doubled over as well, some even stamping the floor in a fit. Dash looked over at Karl, whose face was bright red.

The song concluded with a trilling flourish on the piano keys, and the audience applauded enthusiastically. El beamed, taking it all in.

She played songs in that profane vein for the next hour. When she finished, she took a bow, saying, "Well *shee-it,* I guess y'all weren't a bad crowd after all!"

As she strolled off the stage, she said over her shoulder to Dash, "You're just going to stand there and gawk? Or are you going to get some stones and come on back?"

Dash smiled. He patted Karl on the shoulder, and they followed El's imposing frame into the back office.

The room was a cramped affair with a desk right next to the door. The three of them squeezed past it and the man sitting in the chair as they entered. The man was talking on the telephone. Karl's eyes flashed when he saw the contraption. Dash regarded the kid with a quizzical look.

I wonder what that's about?

The three of them gathered in an open space on the other side of the desk by a half-opened window. The man on the phone—Leslie Charles, the club's owner—finished his conversation with a "I told you I would, now leave well enough alone!" and then slammed the receiver down. He shook his head to himself, muttering, "Goddamn, nobody has patience anymore," then swerved around in the swivel chair with an ear-piercing squeak and looked up.

Every time Dash saw Leslie, he was always shocked by the man's appearance. Dash had never seen such bright blue eyes on a dark man. They were like the fake sapphire jewelry dancers and actresses wear on stage.

"Mr. Parker," Leslie said, his voice flat, his expression bored. "What brings you back here?" He looked Karl up and down. "And why'd you bring a friend?"

El rolled her eyes. "They're not here for you, fromby, they're here to talk to me. And judging by that bruise on Dash's face, it's a fraughty issue, isn't it?"

Dash nodded. "We are in a bit of a situation."

El shook her head. "You downtowners sure know how to get into trouble. Les."

The man flicked his sapphires to her. "What, girl?"

She put her hands on her hips. "Don't you 'what girl' me. Do I have to teach you manners? We have to talk about something private."

Leslie pointed at his chest. "You want me to leave my own office?"

"Considering all those ladies and gents out there came to see me, and all their sugar is going into your cash drawer, honey, this might as well be *my* office."

He stood up, though there wasn't much height differ-ence from when he was sitting down. Leslie Charles was a short man who desperately wanted to be tall. Dash had heard he added inches to his shoes' heels. He also coiffed his hair high, a thick black valance over a window display of a face. El once said, "God spent extra time on him, and he knows it." An accurate assessment in Dash's view. But even with the tall hair and the tall shoes, he was still dwarfed by the formidable frame of El Train.

"El," Leslie said, "you gotta learn to respect a man. This is *my* club, that is *my* money, and this is *my* office. And I am not going to be run out of it by a she-he like you and two pale, pasty white boys like them. We clear?"

When Leslie paused to take a breath, El said, "You done?"

Her lack of reaction flustered the angry man. "El, I swear to God—"

"Be a dear and bring us some refreshments. I'm parched and this boy—what's your name?"

The kid stammered at first, then managed to get out "Karl."

"Right. Karl here looks like he could use some liquid nerve."

She and Leslie stared at each other for a moment, Leslie's face scrunched with anger, El's face uncreased with angelic patience. Leslie lost the standoff—as if he could ever have won it in the first place—and left the office, slamming the door.

El chuckled. "I guess he had to have the last word."

She took his seat at the desk and gestured towards the half-opened window overlooking the small alleyway. Dash sat on the sill, grateful for the breeze coming through the opening. He swore August got worse with every passing year, the air thick and heavy with the smells of sweating bodies, urine-filled alleyways, and overflowing trash cans. At least tonight the wind was cool.

Karl stood near Dash, keeping close.

Dash said, "El—"

She held up a pointer finger. "Three, two, one—"

The office door opened, and Leslie roughly handed her three glasses. One was dark whiskey for El, the other two were Gin Rickeys for Dash and Karl. Leslie slammed the door again as he left, causing El to laugh.

"Whoo, he mad tonight. I think I've outdone myself."

She handed Dash and Karl their glasses and they clinked in a silent toast.

Once the first sips were completed, El said, "All right, boys. Talk."

It took a good half hour of verbal tap dancing on Dash's part to get El to agree to hide Karl.

"Are you crazy?" she initially said. "You want me arrested? Good Lord, Dash, I am *not* taking on that risk."

"He needs help, El."

"Then *you* help him."

"His brother won't come up here. He's scared to death of Harlem. Besides, my place would be too easy to find."

"You don't have any other white folks to take him to?" she asked over the rim of her whiskey glass. "Huh. I suppose you don't. Your family won't help you, that's for sure."

Dash held open his hands. "We need to help those persecuted by the normals."

"Says you. And don't you be using *persecuted* as if you're a preacher at a pulpit. I didn't fall for that when I was younger, I won't fall for that now."

"Come now, El. You've taken in many a white bull whose family, or husband, threatened to beat her normal. Why not take in him?"

"I take in those gals because they give me something in

return. And I don't want his white pipe." She nodded towards Karl. "No offense."

Karl blushed but remained silent.

Dash softened his voice. "El. We've all been in his situation. It doesn't matter what neighborhood. It doesn't matter how much money we got in the bank. When it comes to who we love and how we love, we all get reduced to the same curse and the same violence, sent to the crazy houses, to the jails . . . the work yards . . ."

She stared at him some, then rolled her eyes again. "Goddammit." She set her almost empty whiskey glass on Leslie's desk with a hard *tap*. She breathed in deep, then looked at Karl. "Are you afraid of hard work?"

"No, madam."

"It's *ma'am*. I am no madam. I'd be making more money if I was."

Dash asked, "Where are you going to hide him? Your place?"

She scoffed. "Hell, no! My building is full of busy bodies. They'd rat him out the first chance they get. No, we need a place where downtowners can visit and not raise too many eyebrows." Her snaggletooth grin beamed at Dash. "And I know exactly where we can put him." She leaned her head back towards the office door and yelled, "Les!"

"You're joking," Dash said. "Will he be willing?"

Her grin got bigger. "No, sir. He'll hate it, which is gravy for me. But I'll convince him. 'Cause remember this, boys: I always, *always* get what I want."

And get what she wanted, she did. Karl would work in the Oyster House's cellar, counting inventory, and then clean the bar once the patrons left for the night. He'd be allowed to sleep on a cot in the main room.

"Two days," Leslie said to Karl. "You got two. You hearing me? One. Two."

El sighed. "Les, we can count."

He turned his sapphire eyes to her. "I'm just making sure we all understand that I'm not, I repeat, *not* putting up this ofay indefinitely."

El ignored him and said to Karl, "That's the time you have. You better make it work."

Leslie held out a warning finger to Karl. "And under no circumstances, I mean none, are you to use my telephone. You hear me?"

"Y-y-yes, sir."

Satisfied with the kid's intimidated response, Leslie nodded. "Good."

As Dash got ready to leave, he said to Karl, "I'll ask around some of the hotels in midtown and see if they got a space open. Then we'll figure out how to get your stuff there without your mother or brother noticing. Don't worry. You'll be free in no time."

He reached into his inside pocket and handed the kid his card, the one that said PINSTRIPES and had the West Fourth address on it. "In case you need to find me. I'm there almost all day and night."

Karl nodded, taking the card and placing it in his own jacket pocket. When both El and Leslie weren't looking, the kid leaned in and gave Dash a fast peck on the cheek. "Thank you, Mr. Parker."

"Please. Call me Dash."

Karl's smile was radiant. "Alright. Dash."

"Atta boy. I'll be back in two days." He nodded towards El. "Mind your new aunt and uncle."

El's eyebrows shot straight up. "Uh-uh, I am *nobody's* aunt."

Dash just smiled and walked towards the exit of the Oyster House.

As he said goodbye to Horace out front, he glanced back into the club. He could see Karl standing in the doorway of Leslie's office, his trim body backlit by the desk lamp. The kid raised a hand in farewell. Dash did the same. He turned on his heel and hailed a cab, not knowing he would never see Karl Müller again.

7

Dash was rudely awakened when Finn Francis burst open the door to his bedroom.

"I am just *distraught!*"

Finn slammed the door shut behind him and swept across the room, where he collapsed into a wooden chair leaning against the wall.

Dash sat straight up in bed, his head pounding from the suddenness of it all. His jaw cracked with a mighty yawn as his eyes tried to adjust to the bright light of the late morning. He felt like a jalopy with rusted sides and slightly flat wheels, the engine wheezing and whining before finally starting up.

Twenty-six and already a Father Time, he thought ruefully.

The inside of the apartment wasn't helping matters. The ceiling had more water stains than plaster, the floorboards more splinters than polish, and the thin walls more arguments than peace and quiet. That last bit referred to their unique living situation: the apartment was above the Cherry Lane Playhouse on Commerce Street, a few blocks south of Pinstripes. According to Finn, who found the living space through a performer he was seeing at the time, in no existing world would playwrights, directors, and actors get along. Indeed, at this very moment, someone was yelling about his character's motivation and how he'd never say *that* line, to which another voice responded with: "Fuck your motivation, your job is to say the lines, not write them!"

Finn, momentarily distracted, raised his eyebrows. "Must be a new production."

"Previews start tomorrow." Dash stifled another yawn. "What time is it?"

Finn ignored the question and rolled his hand dramatically. "This is when you ask what I am distraught over . . ."

Dash ran a hand through his hair, trying to rouse himself. "Apologies. What's the matter?"

Downstairs, a door slammed, followed by a shouted "Get back here this instant!" and another door slam. That's when Dash noticed in Finn's hand a rolled-up newspaper, which Finn brought up and slapped on his thigh.

"My favorite screen star, the Latin lover Rudolph Valentino, was struck *ill*!"

"Who?"

"Rudolph Valentino. Don't tell me you don't know who that is." Dash's ignorance earned him an eye roll. "He's just the *god* of cinema. He's here in New York at the Hotel Ambassador. I was going to camp out there last night after my shift, see if I could run into him at the bar they have in the basement. An *oh hello there, how are you?* sort of thing. Now the man had to go get himself an ulcer and a ruptured appendix."

"I don't think those are the kinds of things you go and get."

Finn ignored him. "He was with his valet when it

happened. They were in his apartment when Rudolph suddenly gasped, put his hand to his side, and then collapsed. They rushed him to the hospital where the doctors performed a double surgery. A double surgery! Oh my poor, sweet Valentino."

"Did the doctors say how he'd fare?"

Finn's eyes were heavy with sadness. "We won't know for three or four days. I don't know how I'll be able to stand it while his life hangs in the balance."

"Must be some actor."

"He's more than that! Those eyebrows. Those cheekbones. Those *lips.* He practically screams masculine bravery, no matter what that anonymous writer wrote in the Chicago Tribune . . ."

This time, Dash hit his cue. "What did the Chicago fellow write?"

"Malicious lies, that's what! It was an inflammatory editorial called 'Pink Powder Puffs.' Said beautiful men like Valentino are lightweights and aren't real men. Ha! I never. Valentino was so insulted he challenged the writer to a duel."

"How courageous, challenging an anonymous man in a faraway city."

"Of course, the yellow-bellied boar didn't show. Do you know what Valentino's first words were when he came out of the anesthetic from his surgeries?"

"Haven't a clue."

"'Doctor, am I a Pink Puff?' And you know what the doctor said? He said Valentino had been very brave. Very. Brave."

Finn beamed a satisfied smile, though the smug victory over the Powder Puff article didn't last long. Within seconds, Finn's face crumpled again, and he clasped a hand over his heart.

"Whatever shall I do if he doesn't recover? Why I'll die, I'll just die."

"Don't be goofy, Finn. Doctors can do wonders these days."

Dash stretched his arms upwards, trying to wake his body up. That's when he noticed Finn's face had been scrubbed clean of last night's rouge, though faint black liner still traced his luminous blue eyes. He had also changed clothes, the white vest with no shirt inviting the kind of trouble from which one doesn't recover. He was now wearing blue-gray wool pants, wide with a two-button waistband and wide belt loops. On top of Finn's trousers were a simple white shirt and suspenders. Instead of wearing a proper hat—a fedora, even a bowler—he opted for the flat cap of a newsboy. His vain attempt to stay young.

Finn said, his words tumbling over each other, "A bunch of us will be attending a vigil later today. I might even sneak into a church and light a candle. Valentino's Catholic, I believe, so I have to pray to the right God. Though I'll be praying to the goddesses as well. Every little bit helps!"

What happened next was a miracle, for Finn seemed to acknowledge someone else's plight over his own.

"Ohhh, I see we're looking like a painted lady today."

Dash reached up and gently touched his face. He winced. Still tender. "How bad?"

"Like a giant thumb pressed itself into your eye."

Finn stood up and peered over the side of the bed. The neighboring cot—the landlord's suggestion for turning a two-room apartment into something more—was empty of Joe's usual presence. Not that Joe spent every night on it. He and Dash flipped a coin to see who got the bed. Sometimes, when neither side was willing to lose, they'd share it. Those were some of Dash's favorite nights.

Alas, Joe was not here to flip the coin last night. Finn noticed the man's absence.

"Did Mommy and Daddy have a fight?"

Not quite, thought Dash.

Joe had to bring medicine to his sister's apartment in Sunnyside, Queens, to help his nephew who, the poor lad, was suffering from the croup. While Dash admired Joe's dedication to his family, he often wondered if Joe's sense of family duty was born out of guilt of his own nature.

Dash shook his head. "We are not a couple, Finn. We are . . . sometime companions."

The little man rolled his eyes and returned to the chair. "Yes, of course. Lord knows I never hear *anything* from my bed in the salon."

"You mean the hall." New York landlords were certainly crafty in cramming as many tenants into a two-room apartment as they could.

Finn talked over Dash. "Casual acquaintances. Weekend friends. Separate candles, who only on cold lonely nights light each other's wicks. You can't fool me, Dashiell Parker."

"I'm not trying to fool anyone!"

"Only yourself. You share a room with the man! You can at least share his heart."

Difficult to do when half of mine is missing.

That other half belonged to Victor Agramonte, the man for whom Dash had abandoned his family. The man who sailed out of New York for good one cold bitter day last autumn, to be with the family who couldn't cross the ocean. A part of Dash never truly healed, and after that, he vowed he'd never allow himself to be that vulnerable again. One heartbreak in a lifetime was more than enough.

Dash didn't feel like going into it—especially not before coffee—so he asked, "How was the rest of last night after I left?"

Finn pointed to his own face. "This is me noticing you changing the subject. Let's see. I cracked my knuckles scrubbing Walter's blood off the floor in both Pinstripes and your silly tailor shop. I may need tonight off to recover."

"Finn."

"Oh! And there was some man, a huge baby grand, asking for you."

"For me?"

"Not you specifically. Just the owner."

"Did he give a name?"

"Yes, dear. Lowell Henley. I never heard the name before."

"Neither have I. Did he say what he wanted?"

"Only that it was about our inventory."

"Inventory?"

Finn tapped his chin. "I suppose he meant our booze. I think he's trying to sell us something. He said he'll try to catch you again."

"I see," Dash said.

Open only a few months and already someone was peeking into their business. He didn't know who this Lowell Henley was, but Dash suspected he knew his kind. And what he wanted.

I thought we'd have more time before we had to do something like that.

Finn stood up from the chair. "I need to go wash my face. I'm a tad puffy from being so upset over my Valentino.

I may be in mourning, but that's no reason to look like a Bloated Betty. Tah-tah!"

He didn't wait for Dash's response before sailing out of the room, which coincided with the third door slam that morning from downstairs. A voice trembling with fury shouted, "And I'll tell you another thing: without me, you *have* no play!"

Dash rolled his eyes as he got out of bed. Actors.

In desperate need of coffee and food, Dash returned to West Fourth dressed in his Banff blue pinstripe suit with an eye-catching red tie and topped with a new gray homburg he'd been dying to show off. He walked to the Greenwich Village Inn, his usual lunch and dinner spot situated on the triangle-shaped plot of land on Barrow and West Fourth. The Village was full of such odd geometric shapes, its isosceles triangles, trapezoids, rhombuses, and parallelograms at odds with the perfect squares and rectangles of the rest of Manhattan.

There's a metaphor in there somewhere, thought Dash.

The Inn sat across the street from Sheridan Square, just a few shops down from Hartford & Sons. The shutters of the pine-outlined windows of the downstairs tavern were folded open in a vain attempt to catch a cooling breeze.

Inside the Inn he saw the usual mix of bohemians—artists, suffragists, writers, and political anarchists—at the scarred round wooden tables, whose surfaces had equal parts stains and etched epitaphs. This morning, the bohemians were arguing over the state of the country and from the sounds of it, America was on the verge of collapse. No one in the place was a fan of the do-nothing Coolidge who, like his name, kept a cool, nondescript presence while robber barons and tycoons ran amuck. "Coolidge Prosperity" only benefited the rich and the bankers, one woman argued, while the working class still had the same wages as last year and the year before that.

"Mark my words," she said, her voice rising in volume, "this administration only cares for the wealthy few. Why else put one of the world's richest men as the Secretary of the Treasury? This Andrew Mellon cuts taxes for millionaires as often as flappers cut their hair! Newspapers every day talk of soaring profits. But do we see any of that? Have your wages gone up? Have yours? The only thing that's gone up is the rents! Hear me, folks. The wealthy only take care of each other and when this so-called prosperity ends, they'll retreat to their mansions while the rest of us scrounge for food in the streets!"

Her audience heartily agreed with her.

The only patrons who sat silent during these political arguments were the three ex–Wall Street traders sitting in the back against the exposed brick wall. "The Ex-Pats," they were called. Years of ulcers, trembling fingers, and night terrors meant the only items they traded these days were coins for booze. They kept their eyes on their drinks and nowhere else.

Behind the rough wood bar, which needed two more sessions of sanding, was the owner of the tavern, a tall, thin older gentleman Dash knew only as Emmett. He wore an apron over blue slacks and a simple white shirt with the sleeves rolled up to his elbows.

The warped wooden floorboards groaned and protested as Dash made his way to the bar.

Emmett glanced up, regarding him with cobalt-blue

eyes and an arched snowy white eyebrow. "Well, if it isn't our well-dressed friend. What has you slumming it today?"

Dash sat at the bar and smiled. "Had a slum-filled birthday last night. I figured I couldn't go any lower."

Emmett barked out a laugh. "I can see that. What happened to your face?"

There was no way to hide the damage Walter Müller had inflicted. This morning in the Cherry Lane Playhouse WC, the mirror had reflected a face with a swath of sickly purple around his left eye complemented by red spidery veins. Not a very Mode look.

"A gentleman's disagreement," Dash replied.

"I see how 'gentlemanly' it was. Whattaya have?"

"Eggs on rye and coffee."

Emmett's palm tapped the bar. "Done." As he set about pouring Dash's coffee, a creak of the floorboards turned his head towards the door. "Shit," he muttered.

Dash swiveled around and repeated the same curse.

Cullen McElroy of the NYPD was standing in the doorway. With the whirlwind events of last night, Dash had completely forgotten today was "Donation Day."

McElroy's beady eyes searched and found where Dash was sitting. He lumbered over. The bohemians went uncharacteristically silent, with a few of the patrons giving him wide berth, as if he were diseased. Round as a globe, his belt was a black equator dividing the copper's hemispheres. His face was a constant sunburnt red, made even more apparent by the yellow hair peeking out from underneath his police cap, as lifeless and as bland as straw.

Dash felt all eyes upon the two of them.

"Well, well, well," McElroy said, as he stood next to Dash. "Mr. Parker." McElroy reached into his pocket with a meaty hand and pulled out his timepiece. He flicked the clasp open. "What time is our usual meeting?"

"Ten o'clock."

"And what time is it now?"

"I presume a few minutes after ten."

McElroy regarded the face of his timepiece. "Ten-oh-seven." He shut the clasp with a loud snap. "And where are we supposed to meet?"

Dash swallowed the pride which wanted to tell this odious officer where he could go. "At my shop."

"So *why*, Mr. Parker, do I find you past our meeting time in a place we are not supposed to meet?"

Emmett spoke up. "Quit being a condescending ass and just take his money."

McElroy flashed him look. "These young ones don't respect authority. I've had to teach one or two how to be respectful and believe me"—he turned back to Dash—"you don't want to be a student of mine." He scanned the rest of the room. "None of you do."

Dash nodded. "Yes, sir."

McElroy's grin exposed gray and yellow teeth. "*That's* more like it. Yes, sir indeed." He returned the timepiece to his trouser pockets and gave Dash his full attention. "How goes business at Hartford & Sons?"

"Terrible. I'm barely making a dime."

"That's not what I hear. I hear if you want to have a good time, you visit good old Dashiell Parker on West Fourth. He'll set you up fine."

"Nasty rumors."

McElroy went on as if Dash hadn't responded. "Yes, you hear all kinds of things when you're on this beat. It would be a shame if I had to report half of what I hear. Do you have your weekly donation to the New York Police Department? Remember, it's selfless contributions from citizens such as yourself that help the NYPD keep this city safe."

There was a grumble from the bohemians behind them. Emmett shot them a warning look.

"Do not worry, I've got your payment," Dash said, thankful he actually did.

"*Donation*," Cullen corrected.

Dash forced a smile. "Coming right up."

He reached into his pocket and pulled out his billfold. He counted out the bribe—five dollars, almost as much as his rent!—and returned the billfold to his pocket. He reached out to McElroy to shake his hand, the money in his palm. He tried not to squirm as the officer's slimy fingers gripped his own.

"We're grateful for your generosity," McElroy said.

"We're grateful for your blind eye."

McElroy finally released his hand, the dollar bills now in his palm, which was being transferred to his trouser pocket. Dash wondered how many bills he had in there at one time. A fair amount of sugar, given how many businesses were on this block alone.

McElroy touched the brim of his cap. "Until next week, Mr. Parker." He looked at Emmett. "I'll see you next in a few days. And I better receive more respect from you, grandpa."

He exited the Inn and strolled down West Fourth towards Seventh Avenue—and, no doubt, towards his other victims—whistling along the way. As soon as he left, the tension level in the Inn dropped by half. A collective sigh of relief murmured throughout the room.

Dash turned to see the bohemians still watching him.

"Look at that," he said, gesturing to the front door. "There goes one of New York's finest."

Someone scoffed, "Finest, my ass. He's the worst thing about this city!"

Another voice said, "Yeah, get rid of the police!"

More voices joined in. "No more police! No more police!"

Dash looked at Emmett with a wry smile and raised his coffee cup. "I'll drink to that."

It was time to open Hartford & Sons for the day. Granted, Dash wasn't a tailor, not by any means, despite Victor trying desperately to teach him. (And heaven help him, Victor tried his best.) But a storefront couldn't stay closed all day without inviting the attention of some cop or federal agent—someone who wasn't accepting his bribes, that is.

Dash had the wherewithal to at least do measurements, which he would take during business hours, and have Atty, who surprisingly was quite adept with a needle and thread, do the alterations at night. Atty sat at the sewing machine in the right-side window of the tailor shop, the shine of his sewing table lamp the signal to those in the know that Pinstripes was open. Together, he and Dash gave the illusion of Hartford & Sons being a legitimate business. And the nocturnal alterations kept Atty from being bored senseless while standing guard.

Very clever, if Dash could be so bold to admit.

And yet, it wasn't too clever for Walter Müller.

Dash sincerely hoped the bluenose's presence wasn't a harbinger of things to come.

He spent an uneventful day taking measurements from

those who didn't know about the club and answering questions about "pinstripe suits" from those who did. No one named Lowell Henley stopped by, which eased some of Dash's anxiety. Maybe this Mr. Henley would forget all about him and bypass his club entirely.

Long shot odds for that one.

At 5:00, he closed up shop and went to a public bath, letting the steam and the water wash away the grit and dirt of the day. He returned to the Cherry Lane Playhouse apartment, where he napped, despite an incessant stage manager from below yelling "Theodore! Places! Anyone seen Theo? He's missed his entrance three times! God help me . . ."

At 9:00, he changed into his tuxedo jacket, white silk shirt, vest, and tie, and returned to West Fourth for dinner.

Walking the careless zigzag of the Village streets, Dash felt himself come alive. True, he worked during the daylight hours, but he was a night animal by nature, always had been. When he was sixteen, he would sneak out of the family home and explore all the neighborhoods his parents told him to avoid—especially the ones Thomas and Mary Parker disdained. Just the act of being where he wasn't supposed to filled him with euphoria. And with it came sharpened senses and a quickness and deftness he didn't have during "normal" hours.

Even now, years later, he thrived off the shadowy sounds of the darkened city. The purr of unseen motor cars. The squeal of the elevated trains navigating the curves from West Third to Sixth Avenue. The rapid click of shoes on pavement and the loose laughter of friends. In between the bursts of sound was the sensual swivel of a cap being removed from a bottle. Dash tingled with excitement and anticipation. Who knew what wonders the night would bring?

When Dash turned onto his portion of West Fourth between Barrow and Jones, he stopped. This section of street looked different tonight. He scanned the narrow area, looking for something out of place. What was it?

The windows in the apartments above him were lit, the sounds of clattering dishes from their occupants spilling out into the night. Nothing unusual there.

The gentle rush of the wind interrupted by the harsh metallic echo of trash being thrown carelessly into bins. A mouthwatering aroma of sautéing onions and garlic from nearby restaurants was interrupted by a toe-curling whiff of urine and vomit from rotting places unseen.

So far, a typical summer night in New York.

Dash scanned the street again.

Ah. It was his tailor shop.

The light in the front right window was out. Strange. Pinstripes wasn't closed this evening, so why did Atty have the light off? Were they late opening?

Trouble, he thought.

And his eyes found it. A darkened figure was weaving back and forth in front of Hartford & Sons. The figure looked familiar, but the distance and the shadows hid his face. He stumbled, caught himself, then stumbled again. The plate-glass window of Dash's shop was a backdrop curtain for this sloppy performance, the name of the shop the marquee. Intuition whispered a warning.

Run. He hasn't seen you yet.

But if the man was here now, then he would return again. And if Dash could point in the opposite direction, he might be able to keep the kid safe for longer.

Dash took a breath, then slowly walked east on West

Fourth towards his shop. The dark figure was now cursing to himself. Dash was ten feet away when stray pieces of gravel crunched beneath his feet.

The figure turned around and looked straight at him.

"You!" the German voice shouted.

"Oh hell," Dash muttered.

He had guessed right. The figure was Walter Müller.

8

Unlike last night, tonight Walter's state of dress was a state of anarchy. Jacket crooked, tie askew, elbows and knees smudged with dirt and grime, no doubt picked up from crawling across whatever surface he had fallen upon. And he had definitely fallen. The man couldn't maintain his balance. Was he drunk? Dash couldn't believe it. A bluenose? Dash would've doubted his observation, but enough time spent in speakeasies had made him an expert in determining who was half-seas over. And Walter had gone overboard.

"Mr. Müller," Dash said, keeping his voice steady and neutral.

"You bastard. You fairy bastard!"

Dash flicked a look around. Several passersby gave them wide berth, staring at the drunkard with equal parts humor and disdain. At the announcement of "fairy," some eyed Dash.

"Too much giggle water," he replied to the questioning stares.

One of the men said, "Get him out of here before he hurts somebody, will ya?"

"It's more likely he'll hurt himself," Dash replied. He closed the distance between him and the German. "Walter, let's get you some joe."

Walter swatted at the air. "I don't need coffee."

Dash tried to grab Walter's arm, but the man yelled "No!" before he stumbled backward, hitting the sidewalk with an awkward thump. Some of the spectators laughed.

Dash reached down and said, "Take my hand, Walter. Before you further embarrass yourself."

The German gave him a look of utter contempt. He tried to stand on his own, but he couldn't manage it. Reluctant, he let Dash help him up.

"This way."

Dash steered him to his storefront. He then placed Walter against the doorframe while he caught Atty's eye. The man must've watched the whole scene from his perch in the shop window. At first, Atty seemed confused. He rightly didn't want Walter coming in, but Dash needed to get Walter off the street before he said something even more inflammatory.

"You bastard," the German kept saying, his alcohol-stained breath offending Dash's nose.

The bruise on Walter's face was double that of Dash's. Red and purple circles surrounded both eyes; broken capillaries fanned out over his brow and down his cheeks. And, of course, the missing upper two teeth. He looked like a man with nothing left to lose. A dangerous man.

Dash nodded to Atty, who finally got up and walked towards the front door.

As Atty undid the locks, Dash said, "Mr. Müller, you are disrupting my place of business."

"What are you going to do? Call the cops? Ha!" Spittle landed on Dash's face. "Let's call them. Let's call them right now!"

He was leaning on the tailor shop door when Atty jerked it open. Walter almost fell onto the floor but Atty caught him, saying "Whoa, there!" Atty's eyes flicked over to Dash. "I need some help here, Boss."

Dash grabbed Walter's torso and helped Atty stand the German more upright. "Let's get him into the changing area."

"Youse sure?"

Dash said as he pushed Walter inside, "It's better than on the street when he can say all kinds of things. He's so bleary-eyed, God knows what will come flying out."

"And he a teetotaler? I knew it! Those bluenoses are nothing but a bunch of hypocrites."

Dash thought of his older brother Max sneaking out of their parent's house to visit one of four women who each thought she was his only girl. That was if he wasn't visiting one of the whorehouses down in Times Square. Yet *Dash* was the degenerate.

He replied, "You're not wrong, Atty."

He closed the door behind them and the three of them stumbled towards the curtained-off changing area. Atty pulled back the green curtain and Dash set Walter into the wooden chair, the legs scraping the floor with a groan from the backward motion of his weight. Satisfied Walter wouldn't slump off and hit the floor, Dash and Atty stepped back, their voices low so Walter couldn't overhear them.

"What happened tonight?" murmured Dash.

"He tried to force his way in here, but he didn't know the new code. Smart thinking changing it last night. I wouldn't let him in, even though he was hollering. I was hoping he'd eventually ankle, but no such luck."

Dash shook his head and stared at the angry drunk, who kept muttering profanities and slurs over and over.

I got rid of you one time. How the hell will I manage a second?

"Atty, can you go across the street to the Inn and grab some coffee from Emmett? We need to sober him up."

"Yeah, sure. Need anything else?"

"A sandwich for me. Whatever Emmett's got. And Atty? Let's keep the lamp light off. We don't want anyone else coming in right now."

"Youse got it."

Dash heard the clicks of the front door closing and locking. Now only the yellow from streetlights provided any kind of illumination in the darkened shop, their beams creating stripes on the wood floor. Prison bars. Where Dash would soon be if he couldn't figure out what this bluenose from the Committee of Fourteen wanted.

Dash went and grabbed a chair from the writing desk and dragged it over towards Walter. He pulled the curtain around them, cutting out the lights from the street, and sat across from the belligerent drunk. He let his eyes adjust to the darkness. Even in shadow, he saw Walter couldn't hold his head upright.

"Walter," Dash said, his voice sharp and clear.

The man jerked as if electrocuted. He slurred something incomprehensible.

"Walter," Dash repeated. "What did you drink?"

"I don't know," Walter mumbled.

"Clear or brown?"

"What?"

"What you drank. Was it clear or brown?"

"Clear."

Thank the Lord for small favors. Most of the poisonous liquors were yellow or brown in color. A clear liquid didn't necessarily mean Walter hadn't consumed something lethal, but it made his odds a lot better.

"Good," Dash said. "Where did you get it? The drink? Was it a speak?"

Walter's reply was incomprehensible.

"Walter. Talk to me. Where did you get the booze?"

Walter seemed to cry at the mention of the word. Dash felt a small pang of sympathy for the man. Walter had fallen from grace, from that pious podium on which he preached abstinence, sobriety, and purity of spirit.

Welcome to terra firma with the rest of us.

"Walter—"

The tailor shop door opening interrupted them. Atty with the coffee.

The curtain swung open. Dash reached over and took the hot mug from the short man. He thanked him and gingerly placed Walter's hands around the steaming mug. Dash hoped the heat from the porcelain would stimulate a few of his senses that had been dulled by the alcohol. With both hands overlaid on top of Walter's, together they lifted the mug to the cracked, dried lips. Walter took a few sips. After a moment, Walter could hold onto the cup of coffee on his own.

Dash released the mug and stood, beckoning Atty to step back a few feet from Walter.

Atty said, his voice quiet, "Your sandwich is on the desk."

"Thank you, Atty." Dash nodded towards Walter. "He wasn't with anyone tonight?"

"No, sir."

"Did he get here by walking or by cab?"

"By hack. Don't think he lives close by."

Dash ran a hand over his mouth. "What are we going to do with him?"

Atty shrugged. "We can just put him six feet under. That way, he don't bother us no more."

Dash shook his head. "Offing a man doesn't solve all problems."

"Yes, it does! This guy on my family's old street, some Sicilian fuck—'cuse my language, Mr. Parker—kept coming around and trying to mess with my sister. She's not more than fifteen and no one's gonna take her honor, least of all this scraggly do-nothing with no job, no shave, and no clean shirt. Finally, Papa confronted him one day and said, 'youse try that one more time, I'm gonna turn you from a devil to an angel with one shot.'"

"Let me guess," Dash said, "the 'Sicilian fuck' came back."

Atty grinned. "And now he has his wings."

"I doubt he's in heaven given what he tried to pull."

"The point is, Papa solved the problem. Might want to think about that with this fella."

Dash ran his tongue over his teeth and shook his head again. "We're not killers, Atty."

Walter must've overheard them, for he scoffed, "The hell you're not."

Dash walked towards the slumping, slurring man. "What was that?"

"I said, the hell you're not. You kill. You may not know it, but you deal in death."

Dash put his hands on his hips. "Oh yeah? Then whose untimely demise did we cause?"

The reply came out wet and mean, like a sudden ocean

wave catching a bather by surprise and slapping him across the face.

"My brother's."

Dash couldn't breathe. Karl? Dead? When? How?

Walter's eyes blazed with anger. "You fairy bastards. You corrupted him. And now he's dead."

Atty stepped forward. "You Dumb Dora, Mr. Parker didn't kill your brother! Why, he tried to help—"

"That's enough, Atty," Dash said. He looked at Walter. "We didn't cause anybody to get hurt, and we have no idea what you're talking about."

"Goddamn perverts!"

"And *you* are entirely too blotto to be reasoned with."

Walter must be wrong. Or playing a cruel joke. Karl was safe and sound up in Harlem, counting inventory in the Oyster House basement. He could not be dead. He just couldn't.

Walter was getting wound up. "You fucking hand-hippers. You caused him to die!"

"Why should we believe you?" Dash said.

Atty jumped in. "Yeah, how do we know youse telling the truth?"

A look of disdain flashed across Walter's face. "Why would I lie?"

"I don't know," Dash replied. "To trick us into doing something we don't want to do."

"Why would you think that?"

Dash leaned forward, his face inches away from Walter's. "Why else are you here? You could've called the cops to shut us down. You could've alerted the Feds. You didn't. Why? Because you want something, that's why."

Walter smiled that jack-o-lantern grin. "You are a very clever man, for a degenerate. This will come in handy."

"I do not believe your brother is dead."

"You want details?" Walter licked his dry, cracked lips. "I shall give you details. The cops when they came to visit Mother and I this morning said he was strangled in Central Park. Someone choked the life out of him and left him there like garbage. I had to go to Bellevue and identify his body. Do you want to know what he looked like?"

"No," Dash said, meaning it.

Walter, however, wanted to maximize Dash's horror. "The blood vessels in his eyes had burst. His cheeks were swollen. There was frothy blood in his mouth where he bit his tongue while he struggled. His nails were broken, and there were scratches at his neck where he clawed at the ligature around his neck—"

"That's ENOUGH!"

Dash stepped away.

Walter's bloody grin widened. "Have I convinced you I'm telling the truth?"

Now it was Dash's turn to say, "You bastard."

Karl could not be dead. No matter what Walter told him, Dash could not believe the words coming out of this foul man's mouth. How the hell did Karl get to the Park? And why? Dash began pacing the floor on the other side of the shop.

Atty cleared his throat. "He was found in Central Park, you say?"

Walter nodded.

A trick gone bad.

A man entering the Park out of curiosity, then

panicking when he realizes how much he enjoyed the illicit touch of another man. But if Karl was planning to run away, terrified of an unnamed threat, then why leave the safety of the Oyster House to go cruising in the Park? Libido makes many a man stupid, yet this seemed entirely out of character for the blushing, nervous kid.

Atty continued asking questions. "Was he robbed?"

"That's what they said."

"Money? Didn't he have a wristwatch?"

"All gone. Nothing in his pockets."

Odd. Robbers in this city didn't choke their victims. Their weapons of choice were more efficient, guns and knives being their favorites.

"How did they know he was your brother?" Dash asked.

Walter's eyes were full of disdain. "The robbers left his identification card. Apparently, no one in New York wants to be a German."

Dash stopped pacing and returned to the changing area. "If what you say is true," he said, "then your brother was a victim of rampant crime, not us."

Atty crossed his arms over his chest. "Rampant crime thanks to you bluenoses. If youse just have left well enough alone, we wouldn't have these mob bosses shooting up the city."

Walter's eyes burned bright. He stared down Atty. "I don't believe you're in a position to speak to me in this manner. As I see it, the police will be very interested in the speak behind Hartford & Sons. And if they don't care, if you've managed to buy them as most speak owners have done, then the Committee of Fourteen and the Anti-Saloon League would be abhorred to learn of an inverted club promoting degeneracy and *dancing* without a license, which I'm sure you're aware is against the Cabaret Act."

He returned his gaze to Dash.

"Either way, your club will be shut down and you all will be arrested. And then, of course, there's the matter of my brother who is in the morgue. My brother, who was last seen walking into this place."

Oh, hell.

Dash flicked a look to Atty. "Watch him."

"Yes, sir!"

Dash pushed against the mirror in the back wall and entered the club. The jubilant music felt otherworldly, bright and disconnected from the harsh darkness which had come over the tailor shop. He closed the hidden door behind him and walked towards the end of the bar.

When Joe looked up from his drink orders, he came over.

"Lassie! Not bad for a Monday night," he said, nodding towards the modest but lively crowd.

"Joe, there's—"

"Someone's looking for ya."

Dash was momentarily distracted from the Müller situation. "What was that?"

"Aye, a big man's here to see ya. Sitting over there by the band."

This must be the baby grand Finn mentioned this morning. Dash shook his head. "I don't have time to see him."

"He said it was very important."

"Be that as it may—"

"Said it had to be tonight or—"

"Joe!"

Joe finally registered the look on Dash's face. "What's the matter, lassie? You look like your mother just died."

The band finished their song to loud applause.

When there was a gap in noise, Dash forced a smile and

said, "Not quite. Remember the little German kid we snuck out of here last night?"

Joe's brow furrowed. "Ya?"

"His brother Walter is out front. According to him, Karl's been murdered."

Joe's face went white. "Bloody hell!"

Dash put a finger to his own lips, indicating they keep quiet about it. He didn't want any of the club patrons to overhear them.

Joe lowered his voice. "He's supposed to be up in Harlem with that Leslie bloke."

"He is. Or was." Dash drummed the wood bar with his fingers, agitated. "I don't know what's going on. I don't know if Walter is lying to me or—or if he's telling the truth. Oh God, I hope he's not telling the truth."

I tried to help Karl. I tried to save him.

"What does he bloody want?" Joe asked.

"He's about to tell me."

Joe gave Dash a long look. "We can't afford to pay him. Not him *and* McElroy."

"I know, I know."

Dash ran a frustrated hand through his hair and glanced back towards the hidden door, as if he could see Walter through it.

Just like Karl did when he was hiding in my water closet.

Dash muttered, "What are we going to do?"

"First thing's first. We get Walter out of here."

"And take him where?"

"Throw him in the street."

"He'll just boomerang back here."

"Pour him into a hack and send him home. Do we know where he lives?"

Dash sighed. "No."

He felt a light touch on his shoulder. He turned away from trying to stare through the wall and saw a glass of gin in Joe's hand. He took it and held it up in a mock toast.

"To our future. Whatever and wherever it may be."

He downed the contents in one swallow.

"Do you want me out there with you?" asked Joe.

Dash shook his head while he coughed. Goodness, their gin was vile. "You need to mind the club. Finn will just give our drinks away in the hopes of getting someone to take him home."

"You're sure you can handle him?"

"I'm not sure of anything at the moment."

Joe took another look at Dash, then tended to the next customer. The band began another song, the cornet moaning lustily.

Dash took a deep breath and returned to the tailor shop's changing area. He nodded to Atty that he needed to be alone with Walter.

"Keep a watch out for anything suspicious," he said. "God knows who this man called while he was drunk."

"Youse got it, Boss."

Atty left, closing the curtain around them.

Dash sat across from the German again, who was shakily taking short sips of the bitter black coffee. "What is it you want?"

"What makes you think I want something."

This response sparked Dash's anger. He said darkly, "Don't toy with me, it's unbecoming."

Walter smirked. "Very well then. I want you to find the pansy he was with last night."

Dash furrowed his brow, not comprehending. "You think a female impersonator robbed Karl?"

"Do not concern yourself with that. You remember him, yes?"

Just a darkened shadow in a blue and gold dress.

"What if I don't?"

"Then I'd say you're lying to me again. And you will regret it."

Dash lightly bit the inside of his lip. "I remember what *she* wore, but I didn't speak with her in any way."

"Then you will have to be clever because I want his name and address. I want to know where I can find him."

Vengeance. He wants to spill her blood.

"I understand why you'd want to know those things," Dash slowly said, "but it won't change—"

"*I* want to know. He let Karl lead a wicked life. Encouraged it even. And he caused my brother's death. I know this to be true. I want his name and where I can find him."

"Revenge won't solve anything, Mr. Müller. It certainly won't bring your brother back."

"It is not revenge."

"What is it then?"

The sick jack-o'-lantern smile was back again. "It's business."

Dash suppressed a shiver. "She wasn't with Karl last night. She left him behind after you so rudely started a fight."

"He wouldn't leave Karl. Not for long, at least."

"Why do you say that?"

"Karl had something this degenerate pansy needed."

"And that is . . . ?"

Walter didn't respond.

"Listen, mister, I'm not tracking this person down just because you asked me to."

"I didn't realize I was asking. As I said before, you're in

no position to argue. If you do not cooperate, I will have you and your friends arrested, your business shut down, and your lives forever ruined. Do you understand?"

Adrenaline pumped through Dash's veins. A surge of nausea hit his churning stomach as he wondered *How do we get out of this?*

The reply was swift and terrible: *We can't.*

"Where should I start?" he asked, his voice tight. "I don't know the first thing about your brother."

"Perhaps my brother's friend can help. His name is Tyler Smith. He would take in my brother when Mother told him to leave his wicked ways or leave our home."

"Is he the girl you were looking for last night?"

"No, Mr. Parker, though I'd often see that pansy with him."

"Was he with her last night?"

A shake of Walter's head. "He was not with the pansy when I followed him here."

"And where can I find this friend, this Tyler Smith?"

"I have the address. He's at the Shelton Hotel."

"Not to be difficult, but why not ask him yourself?"

"I believe he might be more forthcoming speaking to other men of . . . his kind."

"And if he's not?"

Walter wasn't interested in barriers. "It's in your best interest to make sure that he is."

"What happens after?"

"You come to me." Walter reached into his pocket and pulled out a folded piece of paper. "You will give me a report at this address immediately after your visit to the Shelton." He handed the piece of paper to Dash.

Dash unfolded it and saw an angular script very much like the man who wrote it: harsh and exact. The address was an apartment on 86th Street and Avenue A. In the heart of the new Germantown.

"No, sir," Dash said. "I meant what happens after we tell you whatever this Tyler Smith tells us? After we find the female impersonator?"

Walter took his time, his sinister tongue caressing the words. "That, you do not want to know."

"I will not allow you to harm innocent people, Mr. Müller."

Walter was clearly enjoying Dash's moral crisis. "You will not do as I have asked?"

"Not if it means murder!"

Walter's face then took on a mocking sadness. "Then I'm afraid it's prison for all of you . . ."

9

The cab could not get to the Oyster House fast enough. Karl was not dead. He couldn't be. Dash's hands rubbed together while he stared out the window at the city rushing by in flashes of light. The hack bounced over intersections and trolley lines, causing Dash to intermittently grab the door handle to keep from flying upwards into the ceiling. His foot tapped an urgent beat on the floorboards, all staccato notes, no rests.

This is just a devious trick by an evil man. That's all.

His pulse pounded in his throat, making it hard to swallow. Once the cab pulled up to 133rd and Lexington, Dash threw the fare at the driver and leapt out of the backseat. He barreled towards the speak, his heels clipping against the sidewalk. Nervous energy radiated from him, and people stepped out of his way, giving him anxious glances as he blew past.

Horace, tending to the long line, even on a Monday night, saw him approach and held up both hands in front, as if trying to stop a charging bull. "Mr. Parker, Mr. Parker. Wait a minute now."

"Where is he?"

"Leslie? He's in the basement doing inventory—"

"Not Mr. Charles. Mr. Müller. Karl. The kid I dropped off last night."

Horace's eyes opened wider. "The nervous looking one? Mr. Parker, he's not here anymore."

A pit opened up in Dash's stomach. "What do you mean?"

A black man a few feet down the line said, "You ain't cuttin' me, ofay, *that* I know!"

Dash ignored the remark. "He's really gone?"

"Yes, sir," Horace said. "And Leslie isn't too happy about it. That's why he's doing inventory now. The kid didn't stay to do it. He didn't stay long, period."

"Did someone come and get him?" Dash could not picture this boy who was scared to death of his brother leaving the safest place he could be.

"I don't know, Mr. Parker. I didn't see him leave."

This didn't make any sense. "I don't understand, Horace."

The irate man in line said, "What's to understand? There's a line and you get in it!"

Horace looked at the man. "Hey now! We're having a conversation, so mind your manners or you're gonna be standing there *all* night."

The irate man grumbled under his breath, but he seemed to be somewhat mollified.

Dash said, "What happened after I left?"

"He sat at the bar and watched the rest of El's show. Leslie made sure he paid."

"I'll bet so."

"Then we closed. I got myself a well-deserved drink and talked with some of the bartenders. They tell me the craziest stories about some of the people who come in here."

"I don't doubt it. Where was Karl during this time?"

"Cleaning up the main room. Thought it was a little odd seeing a downtowner cleaning up after us, but these days, I see lots of odd things." Horace's face creased with concern. "You all right, Mr. Parker?"

The irate man in line said, "What's happening? Y'all need a room?"

Horace jerked his head towards the line. "I *said* we're having a conversation. You better mind your manners, sir, or I'll never let your raggedy ass in. You understand me?"

A woman with the irate man jostled his arm and hissed something to him.

"I'm alright," Dash replied belatedly to Horace's question, lying through his teeth. "I'm just surprised he isn't here, that's all." He made believe his sniffing was due to the hot air, not the tears threatening to break loose. "Did he say anything before he left?"

Horace crossed his arms over his chest, shifting his weight from foot to foot. "He did but . . . you gotta promise you won't tell Leslie. I could get in serious trouble."

Dash held up a hand as if taking an oath in court. "My lips are sealed."

Horace looked him in the eye, making sure he saw Dash's sincerity. He nodded to himself once. "I was outside in the alley, having a cigarette, trying to have a quiet moment. Wanted some peace, you know? I'm halfway through my ciggy when I heard him—the little German boy, I mean— talking. At first, I thought he was talking to someone, but I didn't hear another voice speak back. Now you know Les's office window is right there so that's where I figured his voice was coming from. I snuck a peek to see who he was talking to. He was on Les's telephone. That's a big no-no around here. Only Les can use the contraption because he, and he alone, pays for it. If he finds out the little German boy used his phone and nobody told him about it? That poor sucker can find themselves another job. And I like this job, Mr. Parker, so please don't say anything to Les about this."

"Your secret is safe with me," Dash replied. "You didn't by any chance hear what the kid was saying, did you?"

"Bits and pieces. I heard him say: 'please try again, it's of the upmost importance. I said, try again! No, I will not lower my voice. It is an emergency, please try again.'" Horace shrugged. "That's all I could make out before I went back to my spot and minded my own business."

It sounded as if Karl was arguing with the operator. "And he didn't say out loud who he was trying to reach?"

"No, sir, but that's probably why he left. He couldn't reach the person he needed to."

Dash wondered who it could've been and why the urgency. "Did he mention any names either on the phone or around the club? A Tyler Smith?" Dash tried to remember the person who suggested his club to Karl and his friends. He got it. "A Miss Avery?"

Horace shook his head.

Dash thought of the blue card Karl handed to Finn. "What about a Zora Mae?"

More shakes of the head.

"And Karl left how long after his telephone call?"

"That I don't know. I left shortly after my ciggy break. When I come in today, Mr. Charles is ranting and raving about how the German kid didn't even work the night."

"Was he missing last night or this morning?"

"Last night. Mr. Charles said he ran an errand after I

left and when he came back, the club was left wide open, and the kid was nowhere to be found."

Another round of tears threatened to leave Dash's eyes. He sniffed again. "And, uh, no one has heard from him since?"

Horace's face was sad. "No, sir. Did something bad happen?"

Dash sniffed a third time. *Not here.* "Yeah, Horace. Something very bad happened." He cleared his throat, hoping that would keep the emotion in check. "I need to talk to El. It's important."

"She's onstage now."

"Is she making them cry?"

Horace nodded.

"Then she's almost done."

El liked to start the night with vulgarity and end it with sincerity. A successful combination that made her more than just a novelty act and kept people coming back for more.

Horace cast an anxious look at the long line.

Dash said, "I know, it'll cause a little trouble for you, but it's urgent. I wouldn't ask otherwise."

Horace sighed. "She's about to do her last number. You get on in there. But hurry out, you hear?"

Dash thanked him, slipped a bill into his hand, and started towards the speak's entrance.

The irate man in line said, "Oh *hell* no. Did you see that? Did you just see that? This is *our* neighborhood and we still get put second. Now tell me, y'all, why can't ofay wait? Huh? Why can't ofay wait? Why can't ofay wait?"

The man got other people in line to chant along with him.

Horace said, "He's not seeing the show, he's dropping off a message."

"Bullshit!"

"Hey! You know what? He paid me money, too. Y'all want in early? Pay the doorman. Otherwise, hush your mouths!"

To the chant of "Why can't ofay wait?" Dash entered the club just as El was introducing her last song.

El said to the crowd, "This next one comes straight out of N'awlins. Nobody knows who wrote it and nobody cares, 'cause it's like the truth of the heart, folks. And in a world of lies and disguises"—she paused to thump the brim of her top hat—"when someone tells you the truth, it doesn't matter who said it first. Just as long as it keeps getting said."

Dash found an open space about halfway down the bar. He ordered a Gin Rickey as she began playing the minor chords of a mournful ballad and sang in that deep, expansive voice of hers:

> *I went down to the infirmary*
> *Saw my sweetheart there*
> *And they had her stretched out on the table*
> *Poor child, so white, so pale, so bare*

> *Soon they'll be sixteen coal-black horses*
> *All hitched to a rubber-tired hearse*
> *There'll be seven gals goin' to the graveyard*
> *But I'm 'fraid only six of 'em is coming back*

As she mourned the death of her lover, Dash sat transfixed, filled with emotion. It wasn't sadness, per se. It was loss, a feeling he had more and more of these days. Was this what getting older meant? Dealing with increasing amounts of loss? He'd already lost his family, as they'd disowned him when they discovered why he spent so much time down in Greenwich Village.

Filthy, his mother had called him.

His father had called him something worse.

His older brother Max refused to call him anything at all.

Only his younger sister Sarah knew the truth before the rest of them. "I see you looking at Victor," she wrote in a letter as she lay in quarantine, dying from the influenza. "I see the way he looks at you. Promise me, Dash, you'll live your life your way. It's too damned short to live otherwise."

But how? Dash had asked himself at her funeral, fingering the letter's pages in his pocket. *It's not possible. It's not even legal.*

He tried though. Escaped to the Village, to Victor, who left him in the end. Now all Dash had was Victor's tailor shop and too many memories he tried to cover up with jazz and clinking glasses.

El sang on.

> *Now, when I die, I just want you to bury me*
> *With a box-back coat and a high roller hat*
> *And put a twenty-dollar gold piece on my watch chain*
> *So that the boys'll know that I am standing pat*

Then there was the loss of Karl, the loss of a friendship that might've been. Death—for Dash could no longer deny that Walter was telling the truth about his brother—had ended the possibility with cold, cruel finality. And the guilt of not having protected the kid made Dash's head feel as heavy as the weariness in El's song.

And I want six crapshooters for my pallbearers
And of course girlies sing me a red-hot song
And put a jazz band on ahead of my hearse
And let 'em raise hell as they roll along

Beyond that, Dash felt the loss of friends. Many died in the War, that bloody pointless conflict in Europe, the supposed War-To-End-All-Wars he had managed to escape because of his father's social and financial position. Young lives were ripped apart by shells or burned from the inside out by mustard gas, destroying families in the aftermath.

Now, in a different kind of war, friends were lost over arguments about the state of the country. Disputes over immigrants (let them in? keep them out?), workers' rights (an American value? Bolshevik anarchy?), the role of women (in the workforce and independent? married and at home?), and race (equal? separate?).

Life is filled with loss, El's voice seemed to say on the stage tonight, the blue notes bending and curling over and under themselves. And Dash—as well as the rest of the room—breathed in the melody and the words in a reverent silence.

And, now, my good friends, since you've heard my story
Mister Bartender, I'll take another shot of that booze
Oh, I guess I'll be on my way
I've got those gambler's blues

One could've heard a pin drop during the final note. When the concluding chord finally faded away, the room exploded into applause. A few shouted "Yes, girl!" "Sing it!" "Tell the truth, now!"

Something warm landed on Dash's face. He thought it

was an errant drop of liquor from a bartender's shaker, maybe even a squirt of fruit from the makings of a cocktail. When he reached up with his hand to wipe it away, he was surprised to discover it was his own tears. Guess he couldn't stop them after all. He joined in the applause, crying as he clapped and cheered.

El walked off the stage, not appearing to see him. He finished his drink, went to Leslie Charles's office door, and knocked. He expected the black man with the sapphire eyes to open the door, but instead, it was El.

When she saw him, she said, "Les is going to hit the roof when he sees you. You're lucky he's in the basement right now. That little friend of yours left after all we did for him. Hell, after all *I* did for him."

"El—"

"I tried to do him a favor, and he repays me by making me look like a fool to Leslie! I have a system of debits and credits with that man, and I always make it a point that he owes me far more than I owe him. Karl futzed that up. Next time I see him, I'm gonna raise some hell on his ass."

"You can't, El."

"Why the hell not?"

"Because he's dead."

El paused. She seemed to register, for the first time, Dash's tear stains, then the pain in his eyes. Her expression softened.

"Well, shit." She opened the office door wider. "Come on in."

10

Dash sat on the windowsill in Leslie Charles's office just like he did the night before and explained the whole story, including Horace seeing Karl on Leslie's telephone. El was sitting in Leslie's desk chair during this tale of woe.

When he finished, she sighed. "Les will not be happy when he sees that bill. You know that boy didn't call anybody in the next few blocks, so it's long-distance."

"He was trying to warn somebody, but I don't know who." Dash looked at Leslie's phone sitting on his desk. He nodded towards it. "Think we can ask the operator where that call was placed last night?"

El hooted a laugh. "I doubt it. How many people are in this city? You know those poor operator girls transfer at least a hundred calls a day."

"You're right," Dash said. "He didn't mention any names to you, by any chance. A Tyler Smith? A Miss Avery?"

"Nope, just someone named Pru."

"Pru?"

"Short for Prudence, I imagine. Sounds like a white bull, the way he was describing her."

"How so?"

"She wore suits. He said she wore them better than he did."

Dash nodded to himself. "There was a woman in a tuxedo last night in my club. She was with the female impersonator Walter was looking for."

"Might've been her."

"So if Miss Tuxedo is Pru, that makes the female impersonator Miss Avery," Dash said. "Why was Karl mentioning her suits?"

El adjusted herself in Leslie's desk chair and crossed her legs. "Because she was in a trouser-wearing profession. According to him, Pru's an attorney."

Dash blinked. "An attorney? A woman lawyer?"

El nodded. "They got those now. Not sure who would hire them, 'cause men only want to do business with other men." She tapped Leslie's desk. "This one is a prime example of that. Do you know how long it took for him to get used to dealing with just me? Damn near a year and even then, he still has his bad habits. The amount of training I have to do with menfolk, I swear. Slow and ungrateful learners. No wonder I don't want them in my bed."

Dash wasn't listening all that closely. When she paused to take a breath, he asked, "Why was Karl gallivanting around town with an attorney?"

El shrugged. "He didn't say."

Dash leaned forward. "Did he say anything else about her? What law firm she works for? Where she lives?"

"Nope. Only that Pru's plan failed. Kept muttering it under his breath. 'It didn't work, it didn't work.'" She flicked a look at Dash's confused face. "I take it you don't know what that means neither."

"He said a lot of things last night that were odd. First, he said they chose my club because it was a special occasion. Then he said he was thinking about changing his name and starting a new life."

"Running from something."

"Or somebody."

"His brother's a good guess."

"He knows!" Karl had said. "He knows!"

Dash asked, "And he never said anything about this plan?"

El paused a moment to think. "I got the feeling there was something he wanted to tell but for whatever reason, he couldn't get the words out."

"His brother said Karl had something this Miss Avery wanted."

"Walter didn't say what it was?"

"Not a word."

"Huh. If I were a gambling woman, I'd say it was money."

"Why do you say that?"

"Because it's the only thing we all spend over half our lives chasing!"

"True enough. Still. Seems a bit excessive given the lengths Walter is going to get it back."

"Unless it was substantial." El blew out a breath. "Lord, Dash. You are in some kind of mess. And I don't know a cop who could help you out of it by locking up Walter for black-mail without locking you up in the same breath for degener-acy." She hesitated. "Walter doesn't know Karl came up here, does he?"

Dash shook his head.

"Neither do the cops?"

He shook his head again.

"Thank God for that."

He looked down at his shoes. They were in desperate need of a shine. "And Pru was the only name Karl mentioned? I know I'm asking again, but I want to make sure. Not a Miss Avery? A Tyler Smith?"

"Nope on both counts."

"What about a Zora Mae?"

A slight pause. "He didn't mention her but . . ."

Dash looked up. "You know who she is?"

El replied, "I think the better question is how do *you* know who she is?"

He explained about the cards Karl had.

"I see," El said. "Why would a small white boy be working for her?"

"Who is she, El?"

"She the premier party girl of Harlem. Hosts rent parties, theme parties, and from what I hear, certain specialty parties."

Dash caught her hint. Naked petting parties. "So is she a . . . ?"

"She calls herself the 'Baroness of Business.' Not sure what this boy was doing with the likes of her."

"Handing out her rent party cards, at the very least. Could he have gone to her? He said she didn't take in strays, but maybe he had to work for her last night."

"Like I said, he only mentioned Pru. And then he disappeared."

"I see." Dash gathered his courage, knowing El wasn't going to like his request. "El, how do I find this Zora Mae?"

El closed her eyes. "Dash, listen to me. You do not want to mess with that one. She's dangerous."

"She can't be any more dangerous than Walter Müller."

"Oh yes, she can!" El opened her eyes and looked hard at Dash. "Listen now. You didn't grow up in the streets and in the alleys of this city. You were in palaces with doormen and the police at your beck and call. *This* world, the world she lives in? You don't know anything about it. And you can get yourself killed without realizing you caused offense to the one killing you."

Dash stood up and started pacing around the small, cramped office. "I don't have any options, El. I'm trying not to get innocent people hurt by Walter, but he is insistent on finding this female impersonator. And he is damn serious about putting me, Joe, Finn, and Atty in prison. If this Zora Mae can point me in the right direction or, hell, give me a clue as to who could've killed his brother, then I *have* to speak with her."

"I understand you're feeling panicked, Dash. Even desperate. I certainly would feel the same in your shoes." El leaned forward in the chair, her elbows resting on her thighs, her eyes pleading. "But you have to understand, you will be messing with some dangerous people. People with hardened hearts. People without a soul. You will not be safe with a woman like Zora Mae."

"If Walter puts me in prison, how safe will I be?"

El narrowed her eyes. "This isn't the only reason you're doing this, is it?"

Dash was startled by the question. He stopped pacing. "What do you mean?"

El sat up, leaning back in Leslie's office chair. "I *mean,* you're up to something. Why else would you intentionally go to a place you have no business going?"

"I . . ." Dash's voice faltered. He kept seeing the shy smile on Karl's face, the gentle way he clasped his hands together, the slight hesitation before giving Dash the quick peck on his cheek.

I tried to help him.

El saw the look on his face. "Oh hell."

Just then, the office door swung open and there stood Leslie Charles. It took a moment for the sapphire-eyed man to register Dash's appearance. When he did, he said, "Oh no. No, no, *hell,* no. What is this ofay doing in my office?"

"Les!" El replied. "Watch your mouth."

"I don't have to watch anything. This is my office in my club. And *that* ofay is causing me nothing but trouble. Your friend? The one who's supposed to help me out?"

"Les—"

"He done skipped out on me."

"Les—"

"And *nobody* skips out on a deal with Leslie Charles. Uh uh. He owes me two days of labor. When you see that little sauerkraut, you tell him—"

"Les!"

"What!"

The little man turned to El.

El said, "The little sauerkraut is dead."

Leslie stared at El. "Say again?"

"Somebody killed him."

Leslie turned and looked straight on at Dash. "Get out." His voice was low and guttural. "Get out now."

El tried to intervene "Les—"

Leslie held up a hand and, for once, silenced El. He pointed at Dash. "You're not bringing cops to my club over some dumb white kid. You got me? Now get out."

Dash slowly stood up. "I'm leaving. And don't worry, the cops don't know he was up here."

"They better not. You hear? They better. Not."

Dash made his way towards the door. El dropped her head, her eyes not meeting Dash's. He didn't blame either of them for their reactions. He hadn't meant to cause them trouble, but good intentions didn't change the outcome.

When Dash got to the doorway, he said, "Thank you both for trying to help. And I—"

"*Don't* apologize. Just get out."

Dash looked from Leslie to El and back again. He took a deep breath and left the office.

Out on the street, he said goodbye to Horace. The irate man in line, the one who started the chant "Why can't ofay wait?" said, "Hope you had a good time!"

Dash ignored him and stood on the curb, waiting for a cab, wondering what in the world he was going to do. He had just successfully hailed a taxi when he heard a rustling sound behind him. He turned and saw El. A few people in the line noticed her and started cheering and calling out her name.

She pushed a piece of paper into his hand. He took it out and read the hastily scribbled note: *Hot Cha, near Seventh and 134th, ask for Clarence, then say you're here to walk his dog and you're the dog walker.*

Dash looked up at El.

She replied to his questioning gaze, "That's where you'll find Zora Mae. She's there almost every night."

Dash tried to stammer a thank you when she waved him off.

"Knock it off with that. I'm doing this favor for you because I like you. I hate it and I'll deny it to my dying day, but I like you. But you can't futz this up, understand?"

"Yes, ma'am."

"Don't fucking ma'am me." The words were harsh, but the corners of her mouth twitched.

Dash nodded. "Thank you, El." He looked down at the note again. "I sincerely appreciate this."

"Don't thank me yet. First off, you can't just go there by yourself. They don't like solo downtowners. They look like cops."

"Will you go with me?"

"Hell, no! I am way too conspicuous. And this place ain't for B.D. women like myself. You need someone more refined, like fine china. See, I'm the bull in the china shop, but—"

"—I need a china cup?"

El put her hands on her hips and gave him a baleful look. "You know I hate it when you do that."

"Do what?"

"Finish my sentences like we some kind of boring married couple."

Dash forced a smile. "I'd make a good wife."

"Uh huh, and I'd make a lousy husband."

Dash chuckled a little. "So who's my china cup?"

"Flo Russell. She's a dancer at Connie's Inn. I've known her for years. She'll do right by you. Of course, I've got to convince her first."

"Didn't you say you always get what you want?"

"From men! They're too easy to convince." She blew out a breath. "But women? That's a whole other story."

"I never did figure them out myself."

El gave a sardonic smile. "Yeah, well. Tomorrow night. Half a chime past midnight. Meet me here. We'll go to her apartment. Flo and I usually have a cocktail and a ciggy there between our sets. If I can't convince her, maybe you can."

"What makes you think so?"

"You convinced me, didn't you?"

The cab driver leaned towards his opened passenger window. "Hey, are you goin' somewhere's or not?"

El said, "Hold your damn horses, son!" She then crossed her arms and looked at Dash. "What are you going to do in the meantime?"

"Find this Tyler Smith," Dash said, "and hope like hell he gives me all the answers."

11

The following morning, Tuesday, August 17, the rising sun behind the Shelton Hotel flared like an explosion against the top right corner of the thirty-one-story skyscraper. Glittering golden sunspots rained down against the walls, with a few careless ambers floating towards the neighboring buildings. The sight took Dash's breath away, and he marveled at how other worldly this city was—like nowhere else on earth.

When his vision cleared, the wonder didn't cease. The Shelton Hotel was a four-million-dollar spectacle practically taking up the entire block of 49th Street and Lexington Avenue. He and Joe stood across the street from its westward entrance, staring up as each bricked story climbed higher and higher until it reached a barely visible central tower at the top. Dash knew from reading the *Times* during its proposal and construction how the architects designed three setbacks which not only got around the zoning laws, but also created this stunning vertical effect.

The crick in their necks finally caused Dash and Joe to look down and at each other.

"You don't see that every day in the Village," Dash remarked.

Joe's response was more pertinent to their situation. "This Tyler lad most have a lot of sugar to afford this. Ya think Walter wants some of it?"

"El certainly thinks so. Finn says there's a year-long waiting list for an apartment."

"What's so special about it?"

"Right now, it's the site of Houdini's latest demonstration. Didn't you read about it? He was placed in a coffin and submerged in the hotel's swimming pool for an ungodly amount of time. Trying to disprove the spiritual trance the Hindi Rahman Bey claimed he went into to accomplish the same thing."

Joe arched a fiery eyebrow. "One of these days, Houdini is gonna do himself in trying to prove half the world wrong." His forehead wrinkled. "Lassie, why didn't Karl just come here? Why did he say he had nowhere to go?"

Dash sighed. "I don't know. I asked about a lover, and he said he no longer had one. Perhaps that's what Tyler Smith is. Or was."

"Still, desperate times and all."

"Depends on how badly they ended things." Dash gestured towards the limestone entrance. "Let's see what we can find out."

They may have been doing what Walter demanded of them, but it wasn't the only thing they were up to. Dash wasn't about to sit by and let some hypocritical bluenose take away everything he'd worked for. He certainly wasn't going to let his friends suffer neither.

Last night, when Dash returned to Pinstripes, he learned the mysterious man, the "baby grand" who tried to meet with him twice now, had disappeared. Joe had said the man would find another time.

"But he wasn't the least bit happy about it, lassie," Joe warned.

Given the news of Karl's death, Dash didn't care one way or the other if this baby grand was irritated with him. He had far bigger concerns.

For the rest of the evening, he sat at Pinstripe's bar, sipping gin, wondering how he was going to tell his friends they were being blackmailed to become accessories to murder. Perhaps multiple murders.

When Pinstripes closed for the night and Dash finally told them what Walter wanted, they reacted in their usual ways. Joe cursed all bluenoses. Finn lamented how first, he was going to lose his precious Valentino, and now he was going to lose his precious freedom. And Atty said Dash should've let him blow the German's brains out when he had the chance.

Once tempers finally crested, they set about creating a plan. Atty would be extra vigilant, making sure there weren't federal uncover agents watching them. Finn would put his flair for the theatrical to good use by disguising himself and, with the address Walter gave Dash, would watch and follow the German during the day. He could borrow some of the makeup and props from the Playhouse. It turned out there was a benefit to living above a theatre after all.

"We need to get something on him," Dash said to his friends. "I don't believe for a moment he's earning enough money from the Committee to afford his expensive suits. Or Karl's, for that matter."

"That divine wristwatch," Finn purred.

"Exactly."

"Maybe he's collecting bribes like the rest of them," Joe replied. "Just 'cause they say they're moral don't mean they are."

"He *was* drunk as a skunk tonight," Atty added.

Dash sipped more gin. "And he may have killed Karl himself and is looking to pin it on someone else."

Finn shuddered. "Killing your own brother. That would make me want to get zozzled. Keep in mind, I don't even *like* my brother, but still, why be a Cain and risk being cursed for all eternity?"

Joe crossed his arms over his chest. "I bet his defense is *the pansy made me do it.* Ya know how these moralists like to blame their own actions on others."

Atty scowled. "These bluenoses get me so sore, so sore, I tell ya!"

"Either way," Dash said, "extortion or murder, if we can prove criminal actions, then we can get Walter put away."

Joe's face was serious as stone. "We need to be careful, lads. Those in charge of morality need to keep up appearances, and they may do anything to protect themselves."

"Good point." Dash looked at his friends. "We don't trust anyone involved with the Müllers. Understood? Not until we know what the devil is going on."

All three men nodded.

"Alright, gents. Let's get some answers."

It felt good to have a plan, to take action.

Now he and Joe walked towards the Shelton's limestone entrance, which was two stories tall, with five archways upheld by five columns. Intimidating stone griffins perched overhead, their talons gripping the busts, their beaks sharp, their sightless eyes staring at all who entered. From the front, they looked like militant eagles, reminiscent of the war propaganda posters from a few years back—when the newshawks wrote of earth-shattering shells and the massacred fields of "no man's land." An involuntary shiver danced up Dash's spine to his shoulders.

Past the columns and their griffins were intricate brass sconces hanging above the three main doorways. Joe said, "After you, lassie," and Dash, with his friend behind him, entered the Shelton.

The lobby murmured with usual hotel energy. The excitement of new guests seeing the metropolis of New York for the first time. The nervousness of exiting guests worried they'd miss their trains. The hustle and bustle of bell hops as they wheeled brass-pole carts stacked with luggage to and from elevators. Rolling, clicking, and shuffling sounds echoed off the shiny tiled floor, itself a pattern of gold and sienna blue. The corners of the ceiling as well as the room itself were curved, making the entire room an oblong oval. In the center of the room stood a brass clock on a square-shaped granite base. The clock's face indicated it was 11:15.

Dash and Joe looked around and saw the front desk was tucked off to the side in an adjacent hallway. They waited in line as two other men, one short and thin, the other tall and stocky, checked in. Once they concluded their business, the concierge gestured for them to step forward.

"Good morning, gentlemen." The concierge had a slight flash in the eyes. "Do you have a reservation?" his voice taking on notes of suspicion.

At first, Dash didn't understand the man's haughtiness. Both he and Joe wore freshly spot-cleaned and pressed suits, a light tan with a blue-striped tie for Dash and a checked brown with a green-striped tie for Joe. They had even paused for a shoeshine, despite Joe saying it was a waste of time and money.

It's the bruise on my face.

Dash looked back at the concierge and replied in an even tone, "We don't have one, I'm afraid."

The concierge frowned, delighted to deliver his bad news to a pair of men he didn't believe belonged in his lobby. "I'm terribly sorry, sirs, but we are completely full—"

"That's all right, my good man, we are actually meeting a friend of ours. Mr. Tyler Smith."

Suspicion was replaced by skepticism. "I'll have to check my records."

Joe replied, "Ya do that."

The concierge gave him a withering look, then went through the logbook. He must've found the listing, for he frowned and said, "And what names shall I give?"

Dash gave the one name he thought would most convince Mr. Smith to let them up to his room. "Karl Müller."

The concierge looked to Joe. "And you?"

"Mr. Johnson," Dash answered for him. Instinct told him not to give their real names.

More skepticism from the concierge. "I'll just go in the back and—"

"Oh for bloody sakes," cursed Joe. "Ya got a telephone right there. Call him up now and let's get on with it."

For once, Dash didn't mind Joe's bluntness. The concierge was making a show out of something so simple, and all because they didn't have the appearance of the right class.

Did I do that when I was younger?

Most assuredly. It was how he was raised. Those with dirt under their nails and bags under their eyes were just spokes in the wheel that turned the rich's fortunes. A flash of shame blushed Dash's cheeks.

May I never think that way again.

"Alright," slowly replied the concierge.

He picked up the receiver of the telephone and flipped a switch on the switchboard. He kept his eyes on Dash and Joe while he waited for Tyler Smith to answer.

"Mr. Smith? There are two gentlemen here to see you. Yes, two. Their names? One is a Mr. Karl Müller and the other one is—" A look of surprise painted his face. "I understand. I will . . . send them up right away."

The concierge's earlier haughtiness had been replaced by a puzzled defeat. "Gentlemen, his room is 2119. The elevators are through the lobby and across the corridor."

Joe leaned forward. "We thank you, ya condescending ass."

Dash tugged at his arm. "Let's go, Joe."

They followed the concierge's instructions and soon they were in a small box climbing high above Manhattan. Stepping off into the quiet corridor of the 21st floor, they walked until they found Tyler Smith's room number. It was a corner suite.

Joe said, "What do we do now?"

"Simple," replied Dash. "We knock."

Once he did, a masculine voice said from the other side of the door, "Come in. It's unlocked."

Joe's brow creased. "That's odd."

Dash shrugged and turned the knob. The two men entered a short hallway before coming upon as ornate a room as they'd ever seen, all done up in the modern style taking over the city. Glass coffee table with a plumage of white feathers stuck in a cream-colored vase. A beckoning velvety blue sofa with gold and champagne-colored pillows. Two rounded chairs done up with ivory-colored fabric. Three-piece nesting accent tables, their gold legs able to fit inside one other like a Russian doll. And a silver bar cart glittering with bottles and glasses.

Two sets of corner windows overlooked the city, one set facing northward towards Central Park and the other westward towards New Jersey. The sky was clear, blue, and vast, making an already stunning room even more so.

Except it was missing Tyler Smith. The two men exchanged another look.

Joe said, "We did just hear him say to come in, didn't we?"

Dash nodded. This was *very* odd.

They ventured further into the room. A closed door was to their left, which Dash supposed led to the bedroom. Was the mysterious Mr. Smith dressing for his guests? It was late morning, but perhaps he was a night owl.

As Dash walked forward, he heard a slight crunch. He looked down. Beneath him on the intricate ruby red, gold, and sienna blue rug were shards from a broken glass, scattered ashes from past cigarettes—or perhaps from a dropped ashtray, given the multitude of them—and a large red wine stain. Dash doubted Mr. Smith would be getting his cleaning deposit back.

"Lassie," Joe said softly. "Where is Mr. Smith?"

He is *taking a rather long time to show himself,* Dash thought.

He turned around and nodded towards the closed bedroom door. "Dressing," he mouthed before calling out "Mr. Smith?"

A muffled voice behind the bedroom door replied, "One moment!"

"Something's wrong," murmured Joe.

A sudden tingling sensation tickled Dash's throat and chest. "I think you're—"

Dash didn't get to finish the sentence for just then the bedroom door opened, and a tall man dressed in a light gray suit stepped into the front room, brandishing a shiny black pistol.

"Alright, gents," he said. "Just who the hell are you?"

12

Standing across the room from each other, both Dash and Joe raised their hands upwards.

The man was closest to Joe, who dwarfed him in size. He jerked his head towards Dash, saying, "Get over there with him."

Joe nodded and sidestepped his way across the room, never once taking his eyes off the pistol.

Dash tried to keep his voice steady. "I think there's been some kind of mistake."

The man pointed his pistol at Dash. "You bet there has. I'm not gonna ask you a second time. *Who* are you? 'Cause neither one of you is Karl Müller."

Joe tried to intervene as he stood beside Dash. "Look, lad, we just want to—"

The man quickly aimed the pistol back at Joe. "I said *who*, you goddamned Mick!"

"All right, all right," said Dash, trying to make his voice steady. "Keep it jake, fellas." He pointed to his chest. "Mr. Smith, my name is Dash Parker, I'm a tailor down in Greenwich. This is my business partner Joe O'Shaughnessy."

Tyler Smith was confused. He frowned. "Bohemia? What are you doing in midtown?"

Joe replied, "We just want to talk to ya about Karl, Mr. Smith."

"What about him?"

Dash didn't see a way to soften the blow. "He's dead."

"Dead!"

"Murdered, in fact."

Tyler looked to Joe, who nodded in affirmation. "Oh. I see." The pistol sagged, the weight of the metal too heavy for his depleting resolve. His voice quieted. "That's why he hasn't been around."

"You were waiting for him?" Dash asked.

Tyler hesitated. "No, but he usually swings by." He cleared his throat, his voice strengthening. "He's like an alley cat that way. Seems to disappear and then one night, you hear a little pawing at the door and a pathetic little mew, practically *begging* to be let in."

Joe said, "Mr. Smith, we are in a bit of a situation. We need your help finding someone."

The gun came back up. "You coppers?"

Joe scoffed, "Christ bleedin' on the cross, do we look like coppers?"

Tyler waved the gun in an irritated fashion, causing Dash and Joe to tense at the metal nozzle aiming this way, then that. "How the hell should I know? They got coppers now dressed in everyday clothes instead of the usual blues. And, uh, not to point out the obvious"—he nodded to Dash's face—"but it looks like you got yourself into a fight with someone. Someone you were arresting, maybe?"

"I did get into a fight," Dash replied, "but not while arresting someone. A misunderstanding in a speak. A speak I own." He decided to take a chance. "A special speak for certain types of men who fancy, shall we say, different types of company . . ."

Wariness followed by understanding flickered across Tyler's face. He lowered the gun to his side. "You better not be chewing gum, mister."

"You have my word as a gentleman."

Tyler smirked. "Not much worth in that, these days."

Despite the confrontational words, the gun stayed at his side.

With the weapon not taking all of Dash's attention, other features of Tyler Smith came into view. He was thin, with short brown hair and delicate eyes and lashes. The smooth skin of his cheeks had not yet been touched by stress or age. The suit he wore was nondescript, a light summer gray, the bright blue tie the only splash of color on him.

Dash said, "I'm sorry to be the bearer of bad news. I understand you and Karl used to be close."

"I wouldn't say that."

"Oh?" Dash followed his instincts. "I thought you two were . . ."

"No. Well yes, but it wasn't what you think." Tyler was agitated, his eyes darting around like he was looking for an escape. He found one in the bar cart. "Would you two like a drink? My nerves are a bit overcome by the news."

"Aye," Joe replied. "Whiskey if ya got it."

Dash shrugged. Oh, why not? He just had a gun pointed at him. "Gin for me."

Tyler pointed to the weapon. "I apologize for this." He then laid the gun on the top surface of the stacked three accent tables. "I actually don't know how to use the blasted thing."

Joe asked, "Then why do ya have it, lad?"

A jaded look. "Have you *seen* this city lately? I'm

surprised you two *don't* have one, given the roughness of *your* neighborhood. Bohemia isn't exactly where the cream lives, though I mean no offense."

Tyler went over to the drink cart holding various bottles of liquor. He set out three empty glasses. He spoke over his shoulder as he selected the bottles: one whiskey, one gin.

"How did you learn about Karl?"

Dash noticed his voice was less rough and less forced, his cadence relaxing into the vamp-ish style of inverted men when they're in the company of each other. He replied, "His brother told us."

"You met the infamous Walter. What did you think?"

"A bloody no-good bluenose," Joe growled.

Tyler turned. "That about sums it up." He nodded towards Joe. "On the rocks?"

Joe replied that was fine.

Tyler turned back around and added a few ice cubes to the whiskey glasses. "Not to be morbid, but how did Mr. Müller meet his demise?"

Joe replied, "A bloke strangled him in the Park."

"Central Park?" Tyler gave a theatrical shudder as he corked the bottle of whiskey. "Terrible way to go. A trick gone bad then. I'll bet his brother is furious about the scandal."

"Aye, that he is."

"And what made you come up all this way to talk to me?"

Dash answered that one. "In all truthfulness, Walter made us."

"He *made* you? Pray tell, how does one do that?"

"He says to find someone, or he'll turn us into the police."

Tyler uncorked the bottle of gin. "Sounds like our

Walter." He poured the gin into the third glass, looking at Dash. "How do you take yours?"

"With soda."

"I don't have any limes, sadly. So, what does Walter want with *me*? I haven't seen his brother for a time now."

"Walter thinks you can point us to another friend of Karl's, a female impersonator."

A slight pause. "Did Walter mention any specifics about her?"

"Only that you might know who she is."

Tyler finished mixing Dash's drink and turned from the bar cart, three glasses in hand. "Unfortunately for you both, I haven't the foggiest idea who he's talking about."

Joe said, "Walter was adamant he saw you and her together quite often, lad."

Dash watched Tyler carefully as the man served them their drinks. "We're not the enemy, Mr. Smith. We won't put her or you in any danger."

Tyler arched his brow. "I don't know if that's something you can promise with Walter around."

Joe asked, "Why do you say that?"

"I direct you to Mr. Parker's face." Once all their drinks were in hand, Tyler said, "I would offer a toast, but it feels obscene given the present circumstances."

Joe raised his whiskey. "To calmin' nerves."

Tyler's laugh was a little too shrill for comfort. "To calming nerves."

They all drank their medicine and retired to the seating area. Dash and Joe shared the velvety blue couch while Tyler sat in the rounded ivory-colored chair next to the three accent tables . . . and the pistol.

Dash tried once more to appeal to Mr. Smith. "You can't help us at all in finding her?"

Tyler gave a beleaguered sigh. "I just *know* I'm going to regret this," he said. "Alright, I admit, I do enjoy the company of pansies. They're so irreverent and bubbly, full of life and wit. I know many, many girls, so unless you have a description—"

"Tall with dark hair. When I saw her, she was wearing a blue and gold dress."

Tyler blinked. "You *saw* her?"

"She was in my club. With Karl," Dash said. "I only saw her in shadow and only from behind. I noticed her dress when Walter came in, demanding I take him to her. I refused, hence, well, this." Dash pointed to his face.

"I see," Tyler said. "Tall with dark hair doesn't narrow down the list, I'm afraid."

"I have a name as well. Miss Avery."

Tyler considered the name, then shook his head. "Not one of my girls. You can finish your drink and then be on your way."

"Wait a minute, lad," Joe said. "We've got other names."

Tyler's brow furrowed. "I thought Walter only wanted this female impersonator."

Dash replied, "We've discovered a few other friends of Karl. Perhaps they can help us if you can't." *Or won't.* "Do you know a woman named Pru."

"Pru? As in, Prudence?"

"I suppose. She wears men's suits and is a lawyer."

"How interesting. A female lawyer. What will they think up next?" Tyler uncrossed, then recrossed his legs. "How did you come about that name?"

Joe leaned forward. "Why do you ask?"

Tyler shrugged. "I'm curious. I didn't know Karl had any friends. One of the reasons I broke it off. I had to be *all* of his life—lover, friend, acquaintance, family. It got to be so tedious after a while."

Dash replied, "Karl let the name Pru slip to a friend of mine."

Tyler rolled his eyes. "Discretion was never that boy's strong suit. Obviously, otherwise how would you know to come here."

"Walter did mention Karl would come to you often after his mother threw him out."

Tyler scoffed. "His mother. Have you met the woman?"

Both Dash and Joe shook their heads.

"Consider yourselves lucky. Karl told nightmarish stories of how she'd discipline them if they did wrong. Wooden spoons on the back of the hands, a switch to the back of the legs, hand slaps to the face. And yelling, he said. Always yelling. An absolute terror. She's the reason Karl's so clingy and Walter so rigid."

"Karl told me about their father, how he was robbed and killed coming home from a cabaret in Berlin. He said it was why she's such a fundamentalist teetotaler."

"I didn't realize you had spoken much with Karl."

"We had a brief conversation."

Tyler's eyes glinted with a shrewd look. "I see little Karl wasn't completely forthcoming then."

Dash furrowed his brow. "What do you mean?"

"It wasn't just any cabaret. It was a cabaret *in Berlin.* And, my dear boys, Berlin makes the Village look positively tame."

Joe said, "Ya mean—"

"Mr. Werner Müller liked to wear ladies' clothing and dance the night away with former army soldiers. The Nazi thugs—excuse me, the representatives of the National

Socialist German Workers' Party—decided ol' pansy Werner needed to be taught a lesson."

"Sounds like they taught him too much of one," Joe remarked.

Dash said, "That explains why Walter is so vehemently against female impersonators."

"He's vehemently against all members of the queer sex," replied Tyler, "but yes, pansies in particular. Mother Müller made sure of that."

"Did Karl know what really happened to his father?"

"That's how *I* knew about it to begin with. The boy didn't find out until years after, when he was older and got caught experimenting sexually. Walter told him to try to ward off such behavior. 'Death comes for degenerates' or some such thing." Tyler waved the thought away. "Thank God I cut that cord. Too much baggage for one man."

"How long ago had you ended things?"

"Fairly recently. I'd say five days ago, maybe a week?" Tyler paused. "Perhaps that's why he was in the Park when he died. Trying to cure his loneliness."

"That's not so," Dash said. "I hid him with a friend in Harlem. He was overheard arguing with a telephone operator. The person he was trying to reach wasn't available and it greatly upset him. He said it was urgent."

Tyler's eyes flashed with intensity. "My, my, you have eyes and ears all around this city, don't you?"

"I think he left the hiding place to warn somebody."

"Warn them of what?"

Dash held out his hands. "I don't know. Perhaps of Walter? You said yourself he's a dangerous man."

"Well, he didn't call here. I was out the entire evening, and when I returned, I had no messages waiting for me at the front desk."

Joe asked, "Where were you that night?"

"Not that it's any of your business, but I was at Mother Child's kicking it up for the jam. They do love to come and gawk at the pansies, bulldaggers, and the rest of us." He saw their empty glasses. "Now that you've finished your drinks, will there be anything else?"

Dash looked to Joe and back again to Tyler. "I don't believe so."

He stood up. Joe followed suit.

"Thank you for the drink, Mr. Smith," Dash said. "Apologies again for bringing you such horrible news."

Tyler stood up as well and walked them to the door. "I apologize I couldn't be more helpful."

"Oh, but you have been," Dash said, noting with satisfaction the slight blanching of Tyler's cheeks. "I'd be cautious answering the door. Once we tell Walter we didn't learn much from you, he might come up here himself and ask his own questions."

Joe said, his voice grave, "And he won't be as polite as us, I can promise you that."

Tyler's face hardened. "Is that a threat?"

"No," Dash replied quickly. "No, I just . . ." The guilt he felt over Karl was rising up again, like bile, hot and bitter. "I just don't want anyone else to get hurt."

Tyler watched him for a moment, then gave a short nod. He looked over his shoulder at the gun still sitting on the side accent table. "Perhaps I should learn how to properly use that, then."

Walking through the hotel's lobby with Joe on his heels, Dash saw the time on the brass clock and abruptly stopped, causing Joe to almost run into him.

"What's the matter, lassie?"

The clock announced it was five minutes past twelve. "One quick thing before we go."

Dash veered off to the front desk again. Joe stayed put, watching after Dash with an expression of irritation mixed with concern. Dash ignored him. If he was right, then there should've been a shift change at the front desk. In the adjacent room, he was relieved to see their haughty concierge had been replaced by a much friendlier-looking fellow. Much younger too. When it was his turn to step up to the counter, Dash put on his best smile, hoping to override the garish purple of his bruise.

"Hello there," he said, "my name is Tyler Smith in room 2119. I was wondering if you had any messages for me."

The young man's face flashed dimples as he smiled. "I'll check for you. One moment, please."

He turned and went to the back wall behind the desk, which was a honeycomb of small cubicles holding tenant's messages and mail. His fingers counted until they reached 2119 and he pulled out several pieces of small paper. He faced Dash again and placed them on the counter.

"Looks like you have several, Mr. Smith."

Dash slid the papers into his palm. "Thank you so much. Good day!"

He turned to the lobby where Joe hissed, "What are you doing, lassie?"

"Detecting." Dash held up the pieces of paper. "Looks like several people were trying to reach our Mr. Smith."

"So the lad lied."

"I suspect he was lying about a lot of things." Dash

flipped through the messages. "How interesting." He pointed to the stack of papers. "These first five are from Sunday night. Three are from Karl and two are from Pru."

"Lying little minx. Any of these messages have telephone numbers or addresses?"

Dash looked through the papers again. "Sadly not. Let's see here, two more from Pru dated yesterday. And this morning, a message from Atlas Travel Agency confirming two tickets aboard the Red Star Line for Boulogne-sur-Mer on August 27." Dash looked up at Joe. "Looks like Mr. Smith is leaving the country."

"Aye, makes ya wonder why."

"And makes you wonder who was going with him."

Joe tapped the messages in Dash's hand. "Lassie, why didn't Tyler pick up his messages? He's got three days' worth here."

Dash shook his head. "I honestly don't know."

13

Trying not to blow the week's remaining cash on cabs, Dash and Joe took the rattling, squealing elevated train uptown to Walter Müller's neighborhood. The address he gave Dash last night was on the corner of 86th and Avenue A in the Upper East Side neighborhood of Yorkville. Not surprising, since many of the city's Germans took up residency there after they left the Lower East Side at the turn of the century, so much so that New Yorkers started calling 86th Street "Sauerkraut Boulevard."

Walter's building wasn't the Wagner-glory of the Yorkville Casino and others surrounding the main drag near the station. Closer to the river, the neighborhood was a bit more modest and plain: three stories of square and brick with rectangular windows, elevated stoops, and flat roofs. The first floor of Walter's building, like all the others, was occupied by a business. This building hosted a spiritualist, someone who claimed to speak with the dead. Dash chuckled to himself. All-Holy Mother and Holier-Than-Thou Walter Müller lived above a charlatan. There was an anecdote in there somewhere, he was sure.

He and Joe walked up the stoop stairs, found the Müllers' apartment (Apartment 3B), and rang the buzzer.

Joe murmured in Dash's ear, "What are we gonna tell him?"

"I don't know."

"That Tyler Smith was lying through his teeth. He knew where to find the pansy and he definitely knew this Pru woman."

"I agree. I just don't know how to make him talk."

Through the door, they heard the creaking of stairs. Someone was coming down. A series of locks were undone, and then the building door squealed open. Walter had washed the drunkenness off his face, though the bruise was still a brash violet and crimson. Dash wondered how he explained it to Mother. He now wore a crisp white shirt underneath a gray vest and over gray slacks, the crease sharp, the fabric smooth with nary a wrinkle.

Walter made a show of checking his wristwatch, much like the one Karl had worn. The time annoyed him. "What did this Tyler Smith have to say?"

Dash kept his face neutral. "He hasn't seen your brother in days, and he doesn't know the female impersonator you followed."

Walter stared at Dash. "You are lying to me." He shifted his eyes to Joe. "You're both *lying* to me. Do I need to remind you of what is at stake for you? For *all* of you?"

Knowing what he knew about Walter's father, Dash saw the hatred for what it was: suffering. What had Dash said to Karl? *When tragedy hits, people will need someone, or something, to blame.*

Joe replied, "We're not lying, Mr. Müller. He says he doesn't know them."

"Did you question him thoroughly?"

"We didn't beat him to a pulp, if that's what ya mean."

Walter's blazing blues were pitiless. "That's exactly what I mean."

Dash said, "Mr. Müller, given how your father died, I would think you'd abhor such violent measures."

That threw him off his stride. "What do you know about my father?"

Dash decided to play it cagey. "We know enough," he said. "I think the better question is, does the Committee of Fourteen know about your father?"

"Lassie!" hissed Joe.

The three men stared at one another for almost a solid minute. Dash let the statement lie there, waiting to see what Walter would do with it.

The man licked his lips. "Are you threatening me? Because if you are, I will make you and anyone you love so very sorry."

Dash kept his face blank. "That's a no then for the Committee?"

Walter worked to get his anger under control. "Did you talk with the front deskman?" he asked, changing subjects completely.

Dash paused, considering how much to push him. No need. He knew where Walter was vulnerable. "We did," he said.

"And the front deskmen never saw this pansy walking through their lobby?"

Joe shook his head. "You think they'd know what one looks like?"

"And the day shift?" Dash added. "I'm not sure how familiar you are with them, Mr. Müller, but most female impersonators don't come out during the day."

"Then you must return at night then."

Joe was incensed. "We can't just wait around the hotel lobby for her to show. We have a business to run!"

"A business that breaks the laws of this country."

Dash stepped in. "Mr. Müller, what do you know about the woman who dresses in men's clothes?"

That stumped Walter. "A what?"

Dash repeated himself.

"Unnatural," Walter replied. "A woman who does that is flaunting herself against nature's, nay *God's*, laws." He ran his tongue over his teeth, pausing to probe where the "fairy" had knocked out two of them. "I presume she is yet another one of my brother's degenerate friends."

"You've never seen her before?"

Walter shook his head.

"Would it shock you to know the woman is a lawyer?"

Walter stared at Dash. "A lawyer?"

"Yes. Do you know why your brother was socializing with an attorney?"

Before Walter could respond, an older female voice interrupted them. "Walter! Why do you keep the door open to let in the heat?"

The accent was even thicker than Walter's. An older woman—Dash supposed her to be in her fifties, maybe sixties—stood ramrod-straight in the hall of the building, her posture perfect, her face determined. This was Mother with a capital M. The lines of age and experience creased her skin. She had on a dark blue dress with lavender daises printed everywhere. A long string of pearls decorated her neck with two strands hanging down to her waist, the white orbs small but gleaming fiercely in the dim interior light. A wide-brimmed straw garden hat was held in her hands, its lavender bow matching the daisies on her dress. The hat was a surprisingly modern choice given that Dash assumed her to be a Mrs. Grundy.

Walter turned and stood up even straighter when he saw her standing behind him. "Sorry, Mother."

Mother stepped forward. "Who are these men, Walter?"

Her appearance unnerved Walter, and he couldn't think of a lie fast enough.

Dash obliged him. "We work with your son, madam."

"At the Committee?"

"Yes, madam, at the Committee of Fourteen. We work in the same department."

Suspicion narrowed Mother's eyes. "You don't look like a Committee man. They don't get into fights."

This damnable bruise.

Dash gave what he hoped was a shy, embarrassed smile. "The truth is a bit more foolish, I'm afraid. My shoes came untied and I tripped on the subway stairs."

Mother's suspicion stayed put. "Why are you here? Can my son not be ill?"

Walter's lie for not being at work today. A nice cover for his hangover.

Dash watched Walter's face as he responded. "Normally we would, madam. Good health is very important. However, there was an emergency, and we needed your son's immediate opinion on the matter."

Mother was somewhat placated. "And is this 'emergency' resolved?"

Walter finally found his words. "Yes, Mother. Everything is all right."

The old woman looked from Walter to Dash to Joe, who nodded in affirmation. "Good. Then you can be on your way, and my son can get back to resting." She laid a hand on his shoulder. "Come, Walter. The heat will do you no good." She cast a glance to Dash and Joe. "He will return to the office tomorrow."

Walter let his mother turn him around. He added over his shoulder, "The other matter we were discussing? Perhaps this woman can lead you to the . . . other person. You will give me another report Thursday."

That was two days from now.

Dash said, "I'm afraid that isn't much time, Mr. Müller, for a . . . full report."

Walter's smile was cruel. "An update then."

There wasn't much to say, except "Yes, sir. Will the early evening suffice?"

"The evening?" Mother remarked. "Why don't you conduct your business during regular business hours?"

"It is all right, Mother," Walter said. "Sometimes these things happen."

Dash asked, "We will leave the information at the office then?"

"No, home is fine." Before his mother could object, he said, "The information is of vital importance."

Dash nodded. "As you wish. And madam? Our condolences for your son Karl."

She regarded him dispassionately. "Thank you. I assume Walter told you, though it is none of your concern."

She turned and disappeared into the shadows of the hall.

Walter looked at Dash and Joe once more before saying, "Thursday evening. Do not disappoint me."

They returned to the Village, opting for a cab when it was announced at the IRT station that there were significantly delays because of a stalled train.

"I am not waiting in this heat," Dash replied. "I'm already a sopping mess."

Joe replied, "As long as you're paying."

With the few grains of sugar I have left.

The cab dropped Dash off in front of Hartford & Sons before taking Joe home to the Cherry Lane Playhouse.

As Dash stepped out onto the street, Joe said, "Don't worry, lassie, we'll get outta this mess in no time. That story about Walter's father may be enough to do it."

Possibly, but then whoever killed Karl would get away with it.

Dash forced a smile. "From your mouth to God's ears."

He closed the cab door and watched it drive off. He tried to shake off the tension building in his shoulders from witnessing Walter with his mother. Joe and Atty weren't wrong when they joked Walter couldn't visit a toilet without his mother's say-so. She ruled him with an iron fist. At least she verified what Walter had claimed: Karl was dead. It was possible this was all an elaborate ruse, but Dash didn't think so.

He went across the street to the Greenwich Village Inn for a bite to eat, suddenly famished.

The tavern was surprisingly empty, with only The Ex-Pats scattered across the round tables. Emmett was sitting at the bar reading the latest issue of *The New Yorker,* his snow-white brow furrowed. This was a surprise given that Emmett only read those newspapers which were strictly news, "none of that fancy headline shit," he'd often said.

"Emmett," Dash purred, "I didn't figure you for a *New Yorker* reader."

"I'm not. I just see you reading it all the time and thought, what the hell, let me give it a go."

Dash pulled up a barstool next to him. "Verdict?"

Emmett pursed his lips. "Hoity-toity poppycock. Trivial nonsense. Rolls Royces, letters from Paris, stories about the Ritz-Carltons."

"I think the Carlton series is meant to be satirical."

Emmett went on as if he hadn't heard. "They had a whole column devoted to yachts and how the Sound is being overtaken by them."

"It *is* true, though. All of those white sails block the view."

"And for what? So rich men can get to work without getting on the train or on the bus like the rest of us? Next thing you know, they'll write about how the rich have *two* yachts."

Dash feigned reverence. "Of course they will, Emmett. You can't expect the idle rich to remain mono-nautical."

Emmett grumbled as he went around to the other side of the bar, grabbing a cup and saucer and pouring steaming hot coffee. "The only thing these writers got right is the pay-as-you-enter nonsense about the bus. Highly inconvenient. And those citywide franchises they're proposing? They'll be bad as the subways, and once again, the *real* New Yorkers will be cast aside." He gave a baleful glare to Dash as he set the coffee down in front of him. "To those of us who can't afford taxis, anyway. Your face still looks like hell."

"Thank you, Emmett." Dash then touched the cover of the magazine left on the bar. "But see? You're as mad as they are about the same thing. It can't be *all* poppycock."

"Huh. I'll give them credit for the bus thing. And for calling the Volstead Act the 'Volstead Cancer.' That's most appropriate. The usual?"

Dash nodded.

The front door opening interrupted their transaction, and they both turned to see who it was. A large figure momentarily blocked the light of the early afternoon. After a brief pause, the round shape walked towards him. Dash felt a spark of dread.

Not two days in a row of Cullen McElroy.

When the door closed and Dash's eyes adjusted, he saw it wasn't McElroy at all, just a bald, rotund man in a gray-green suit. Both he and Emmett sighed with relief.

"I'll get your sandwich," Emmett said.

"Thanks, Emmett."

The bald man walked up to the bar and said in a raspy voice, "Is anyone sitting here?"

Dash gestured to the empty seat to his left. "Have a seat."

The big man struggled to gracefully sit down. He could barely fit in the space between bar and stool. His poor vest looked like it had been condemned to rack torture, the buttons straining against the bulging fabric. The man eventually settled in with a sigh from his mouth and a groan from the stool.

Intuition fluttered in Dash's chest. He said, "I haven't seen you before. Are you new around here?"

"Been here a few times."

Dash offered his hand, despite his misgivings. "I'm Dash Parker."

The man's massive hand engulfed Dash's. The iron grip was hot and feverish. "Lowell Henley."

Dash slowly pulled his hand away, repeating the man's name. The name Finn mentioned yesterday morning. And if Dash had to bet, the same man Joe said was waiting for him in Pinstripes last night.

He cleared his throat. "I understand you've been looking for me."

"I was."

"And you found me here."

"I always find who I'm looking for."

Dash's pulse steadily climbed. Details of the mysterious man revealed themselves one at a time. The bald head buffed to a shine. The multiple jowls of his jaw. The impassive eyes that didn't blink.

Dash said, "Can I get you drink?"

"I don't need any. This is a quick job."

"I see. And what job is that, my good man?"

Lowell reached inside his jacket, causing Dash to involuntarily flinch. Lowell enjoyed this nervous reaction. He pulled out a single piece of paper, placed it on the bar, and slid it towards Dash. Dash picked it up, giving it first a cursory glance. A typed contract. How formal.

Dash skipped the half-attempted legal language and went straight to the man who was proposing a "distribution of quality spirits" and "protection from unjust and corrupt harassment from law enforcement" for his club Pinstripes: Nicholas Fife. The notorious gangster often referred to as "Slick Nick" by Manhattan's newshawks.

Dash tried to keep his voice steady. "I didn't realize he was interested in such places."

Lowell's impassive eyes didn't betray a flicker of emotion, neither humor nor offense. "He sees great potential in your club."

"Really? I wasn't aware he'd been a guest."

"He keeps his ear to the ground."

"A vigilant man," Dash said. "And what percentage does Mr. Fife want in return?"

"It's there on the paper."

"I like to hear men speak about money."

"Why?"

"It enhances their good looks."

Lowell glared at Dash, refusing to play along. "Fifty," came the reply.

Dash stared at him. "Fifty," he repeated. "He wants *half?*"

The number stunned him into a brief silence. How was he going to remain in business with half of his earnings going to someone else? On top of the bribes he already paid to McElroy.

Dash picked up the paper and shook it. "And what exactly do I get in return?"

"The chance to make some heavy sugar. Good booze is a rarity in this town."

"For half, I need more than just drinkable liquor." Dash set the piece of paper down on the bar and tapped it with his forefinger. "This so-called protection. I currently pay for it now, at a much cheaper price, I might add, and direct to the people I need protecting from."

"His offer extends beyond the cops and beyond your club."

"What do you mean?"

A long-suffering sigh. "If you and your fellow perverts run into any kind of trouble, Mr. Fife makes sure the troublemakers would be sorry for their actions."

"I'm touched."

"Don't get any ideas. He wants to protect his investments. By any means necessary, if you catch my drift."

"I'm buried beneath it."

Dash ran his tongue over his teeth while he thought. If just half the stories in the newspapers were true, then Slick Nick was a pitiless brute. A man who organized people to disappear with alarming regularity. Yet he was so far removed from his crimes no one even had a picture of him, much less an accurate description. (Hence his moniker of Slick.) Could Dash really do business with such a man?

Emmett stood at the other end of the bar. He saw Dash's distress and arched a snowy white eyebrow. Dash subtly shook his head, wanting to keep Emmett out of this. He returned his attention to Lowell. "And the high quality of booze?"

"Best in the city."

"Easy to accomplish when the standards are so low. Any reports of blindness? Vomiting? Dizziness? The Jake Walk?"

"Better than the truck you're buying from now. Why pay for scraps when you can have the Real McCoy?"

Dash felt his cheeks burn. Lowell knew about his agreement with another speak, in which they split the last delivery of the weekly booze truck. What *didn't* this man know?

Lowell went on. "I'm afraid if we were to do business, your present supplier would have to cease and desist. And we have ways, Mr. Parker, of making sure the desist is enforced . . . for both parties."

Dash slid the contract back in front of Lowell, his hand slightly shaking. "Would it be possible, Mr. Henley, to try the merchandise before I sign this?"

An annoyed grimaced. "That's not how it's done."

"Look around you. Rules don't matter here in the Village. If Mr. Fife wants my club, he needs to prove his value."

Lowell's sausage-like fingers drummed the surface of the bar while he processed this counterproposal. Those dead, shark-like eyes bored into Dash's. The ominous drum-beat continued for a moment before suddenly stopping.

"You're a bold fag, you know that?"

Dash forced a smile, flashing teeth. "I've always enjoyed being insubordinate."

"You talk like an uptowner."

"A man has to have goals."

Lowell stuck out a pugnacious chin. "I don't like uppity perverts. And I don't like high hats like you."

"Don't get yourself into a lather. A man doesn't buy a suit before trying it on. I should know; I've sold many of them that way. Tell Mr. Fife the offer is under serious consideration, pending an inspection of the merchandise. If he has good gin, I'll sign right then and there."

Emmett came by with Dash's sandwich on a round plate. "Here you go, Mr. Parker." He flicked a look at Lowell. "This man bothering you."

"I was just leaving," Lowell replied. He picked up the contract, folded it neatly, and returned it to his inside pocket. He said to Dash, "I'll convey your message. For your sake, I hope he accepts."

Fear pricked the back of Dash's neck. He hoped so as well.

Lowell left his barstool with a groan and sauntered towards the door.

When he was out of sight, Emmett asked, "What was that all about?"

Dash took a healthy sip of coffee, wishing it was gin. "Believe me, Emmett, you don't want to know."

14

Somehow, Dash made it through the rest of the day, despite his brain buzzing with questions. Nicholas Fife? Wanted his club? Dash didn't think gangsters wanted anything to do with "degenerates." And how was he going to tell his friends about the proposition? This Walter business was already a lot to handle. Now they had to navigate a working relationship with one of New York's most notorious mobsters!

When it rains, it pours.

He tossed and turned during his early evening nap. The nervous energy of the first night's previews from the Playhouse cast downstairs didn't help matters. The constant running to the water closet. The pipes groaning with every toilet flush. Voices rising and falling in pitch during vocal warm-up and diction exercises. "One hen, two ducks, three squawking geese . . . four limerick oysters, five corpulent porpoises . . ."

"Oh, to hell with it," Dash grumbled, getting up from the bed and dressing.

Joe, who was seated in the wooden chair by the window, smoking, said, "I don't know why ya think ya can sleep when they open a show. They'll be like this all week until the reviews come out."

"Why can't we live somewhere sane so a man can get some rest?"

Joe flicked his emeralds at Dash. "What's gotten into ya, lassie?"

Dash shook his head. "Nothing. Just a case of the grumps."

In the end, he didn't mention Fife to Joe or Finn. There wasn't much to tell anyway—at least, not yet. Besides, he had to focus on his next task: convincing El's friend to take him to meet Harlem's Baroness of Business.

At half-past midnight and dressed in his finest tuxedo, Dash walked up to the entrance of the Oyster House. The giant doorman, Horace, grinned when he saw him. "Good evening, Mr. Parker. Three nights in one week."

"Hello, Horace. Have I missed El?"

"No, you didn't," said the woman herself, as she moved through the entrance towards Horace and Dash. "I got one hour before my next set. Hurry up before Les sees you. He's likely to kill you on sight."

Horace gave Dash a worried look, but Dash just smiled. "Don't worry, Horace, I'll get back into his good graces."

While Dash reassured Horace he kept his secret about Karl and Leslie's telephone, El went to the street and tried to hail a cab.

Horace cleared his throat. "That's nice and all, Mr. Parker, I do appreciate that. Now I heard where you're going tonight. To see someone who will introduce you to Miss Zora Mae?"

"Yes, that's right."

Horace looked around to see if anyone was eavesdropping. No one in the line seemed to be paying attention. A purple and white cab pulled to the curb in front of El. He lowered his voice even more.

"I overheard something I think you should know."

"What is it?"

El whistled to Dash through her teeth, causing him to jump. "Don't just stand there. Someone will steal our hack."

"Mr. Parker," Horace pleaded.

"C'mon, downtowner, let's go!"

Dash smiled at the big man. "I'll be back, I promise."

Dash followed El into the cab. When the door closed, she gave an address on 140th Street. The driver, recognizing El from her publicity posters, said none of his friends was going to believe this and what an honor it was to drive her this evening. Then he pressed on the gas and they surged forward.

She looked over at Dash. "You cause any trouble since last night?"

"Only threatened Walter with exposing the truth about his father to the Committee of Fourteen."

El looked at him warily. "Which is what?"

"He was a female impersonator with a penchant for army soldiers in the underground cabarets of Berlin."

El smacked his shoulder. "What is *wrong* with you, downtowner? You have a death wish? You must. Going after a bluenose *and* the Baroness. Shit. We should swing by the undertaker and pick out your headstone while we're at it."

"Don't worry, El. I just let Walter know we're not going to be some easy mark for his schemes."

El took a deep breath. "Well. You better not try that with the Baroness." She paused. "Maybe we shouldn't be doing this. Maybe you shouldn't meet her."

"Come on, El. We've come this far."

"Don't mean we have to take it further."

Dash held up a hand. "I solemnly swear not to purposefully antagonize the Baroness."

El looked at Dash for almost two blocks before relenting. "Let's see what Flo has to say. You ready to work your magic?"

Dash gestured to his tuxedo. "Who could say no to such a finely wrapped package as this?"

Flo Russell crossed her arms over her bony chest and said, "Absolutely not."

El replied, "Flo! Don't be salty."

"I'll be plenty salty if I want to." She pointed her finger at Dash. "I'm not helping him get himself nixed. Or me, for that matter."

They were all standing in Flo's one-room apartment on 140th Street between Sixth and Seventh Avenues. Two large windowpanes were open, the copper-colored curtains fluttering in the whispering breeze. Two wooden chairs perched by the sill, where Dash and El sat to blow their cigarette smoke into the night air, the scent still present, tarry and sweet. Flo, who didn't smoke, stood on the gold and black rug which laid between the chairs and the bed.

El said, "You're not going to get nixed."

"Says the woman who won't be in the Baroness's line of sight."

"You won't be the star. It'll be him."

"But I will be the fool who introduced them!"

"Once he starts beating his gums, she's not going to care one bit about you."

Watching the two of them argue was almost like

watching a married couple. Here was El, tall, big, imposing in a man's suit. And there was Flo, short, thin, fiery in a red sequined stage dress. The cut was designed to expose as much as decency would allow. The cleverly draped fabric showed off her muscular legs and calves as well as her arms and shoulders.

Flo kept shaking her head, her bobbed black hair gently bouncing from side to side. "No, no. Just 'cause you got a soft spot for this downtowner don't mean I have to risk my life."

"Flo, I swear to God—"

"Ladies."

Both turned to look at Dash.

"I understand the position I've put you in," he said.

Flo muttered, "The hell you do."

"I am in a desperate situation. I need to give this Walter Müller something."

"It sure as hell can't be *her*. Otherwise, we're all dead."

"If she's as dangerous as you said, then she may very well have killed Karl."

"Uh huh. And what happens when you tell his brother that?" Flo asked. "Will he go on a rampage, enacting revenge on her like he did with your face? See, that's what *I* am worried about. We have no idea what this man is capable of. And if the War taught us anything, his kind are capable of a lot."

El nodded her head at Flo. "She's got a point, Dash."

Flo didn't stop. "And what if she turns out to be innocent? I know you downtowners like to place the blame on us, but if you ask me, strangling a little fairy boy and dumping his body in the Park sounds like a white man's game to me."

Dash looked away, his eyes taking in the room. Cracks

like spider legs fanned out in the corners of the plaster walls. The baseboards chipped from abuse were also dusty from neglect. A water stain that seemed to plague every ceiling in New York hung dead center over the room, a giant yellow cloud at sunset. Dash would've bet his last dollar the sink in the washroom dripped and the doors wouldn't stay closed unless they were locked. Whether it was the Village or Harlem, white tenants or tenants of color, landlords were still landlords, and, in the wise words of El, "They don't do shit but collect the rent."

Dash took a deep breath and returned to the conversation. "All the more reason to talk with Miss Mae. She might direct me to the real culprit, and I won't ever have to bother her—or you—again." He looked at Flo. "Miss Russell, will you please help me?"

Flo stared at Dash for a moment, then dropped her eyes. "I don't know."

"C'mon, Flo," El said. "We've got to help those like us when we can, right?"

"He's not *like* us. He's white and rich."

White, yes. Rich? *Not anymore,* Dash thought.

El replied, "He's a degenerate according to the law, just like we are, which means he'll go to the work yards, just like we would."

Flo gave El a look that said *I'm going to regret this* and then said to Dash, "The thing about the Hot Cha is it's where those with sugar go to show off how many grains they got in the bowl. It's all about one-upping the person next to you. And if they decide you're not high-class enough, they don't let you in, so you've got to be in your finest suit or in your most elegant dress. I hear the Baroness wears her furs there, even in August, like a regular Duchess. I don't think dressing is going to be a problem for you."

El chuckled. "He practically a Duchess himself."

Dash piped up, "I object."

Flo cut him off. "One thing you need to know when you meet Miss Zora 'I Wear Dead Foxes' Mae. I hear she got a girl now—can't remember her name for the life of me—but she's straight up crazy. Like someone permanently blew her wig off and she can't get it screwed back on."

El asked, "She's icky?"

"No, she's jealous. Thinks everyone is trying to take away her precious Zora 'I Wear Furs and Pearls' Mae. Anyone who tries to get close to Zora ends up having that girl go full-on Zulu on them. I heard from my friend Ruthie that she broke a beer bottle and aimed the jagged edge at someone's throat."

"Jesus!"

Flo nodded. "And even Christ might take his own name in vain meeting the likes of her. That's why I'm not all that thrilled about meeting Miss Zora 'I Got Minks in Pink' Mae."

Dash nodded towards Flo. "Would this girl have killed Karl?"

Flo furrowed her brow. "You better hope not. 'Cause if she did and you get her locked up or worse, Zora will come after us all." She looked from Dash to El, then back again. "So downtowner? This better not bring trouble back to my house. Or El's house. Bring it to your house, I don't give a damn. Have it burn down the whole Village for all I care. But bring trouble up here, we got problems. Understand?"

Dash replied, "I understand."

"I've got a show tonight, but I can take you tomorrow at midnight. Don't be late."

Dash said, "Thank you, Miss Russell. I am truly in your debt."

Flo crossed her arms over her chest again, shaking her head, whether at herself or at Dash, he couldn't tell. After a moment's silence, she took a deep breath and said, "Well, shit."

El barked out a laugh. "Hey now! That's my line!"

It was the following afternoon, Wednesday, August 18, when Dash finally found the mysterious Pru.

After a few appointments at Hartford & Sons, Dash closed the tailor shop early with the hopes he could charm his way to a name and address from the Bar Association of New York. He figured there couldn't be that many female attorneys registered. And even if there were half a dozen Prudences listed, he could narrow down the list in short order.

The Bar was on Club Row, a block of West 44th between Fifth and Sixth Avenues that was, sadly, not full of speaks, lounges, and dance halls. Rather, it was the epicenter of the city's power. The Harvard Club. The New York Yacht Club. The City Club. The St. Nicholas Society and the Penn Club. Nearby stood clubs for Yale, Princeton, Columbia, Cornell, and Brown. Judges, Congressmen, and Presidents sprouted from these gilded gated gardens almost as regularly as perennials. And amongst all this power stood the New York Bar Association, otherwise known as The House.

The House, Dash came to learn, did not approve of women attorneys. The male secretary, to whom Dash initially addressed his query, said, "They're a radical trend, if I may be so bold to say. A few bored women deciding to cause trouble. It won't last. Not only is the female mind incapable of maintaining the mental rigor needed to practice law, no one will hire them."

"I see," Dash said. "Are they not allowed to be registered with the bar?"

"They are."

"But they can't be members of the Bar Association?"

"No." A satisfied smirk. "They have their own, though. If you really want to degrade yourself, you can pay them a visit."

Dash's smile got even bigger. "I would be happy to wallow in the so-called degradation of the law. I do it on a regular basis. Address, please?"

The difference between the New York Bar Association and the National Association of Women Lawyers was striking. Whereas the House flaunted its marbled wealth, the Women Lawyers showcased their unadorned, plainclothes commitment to social justice. Divorce and marriage laws, a new concept called "minimum wage," even the right for women to serve on juries. Here lived the noisy, kinetic sparks of ideas and change.

An hour and three cigarettes after his request, the secretary—a woman this time—returned, motioning him to her desk. "You're in luck," she said. "We have only one Prudence registered with us. A Prudence Meyers of the firm Meyers, Powers, & Napier on East 14th Street between Third Avenue and Irving Place. Near Tammany Hall." She handed him a piece of paper with the exact address. "A perfect location for attorneys, I must say. I wonder how she managed that."

Dash placed the address in his inside jacket pocket. "Sounds like a formidable woman. Then again, aren't they all?"

The receptionist beamed. "I wish more men thought like yourself."

Dash returned her smile. "I as well."

Less than ten minutes later, Dash exited a cab in front of the imposing building of Tammany Hall, its three stories climbing high into the sky, decorated with large windows topped by rounded arches. In the shadow of ruthless political power, Dash pulled out the piece of paper he received from the Women Lawyer's receptionist, double checked the address, and began counting the building numbers.

He passed by the flashing neon signs of the Olympic Theatre, the Central Hotel, a cigar shop, and the Borough Lunch counter before eventually finding the front of Meyers, Powers & Napier. The only tenant, he noticed, who did not invest in a blinking light.

The shades were up. The front door stood open. He took a deep breath and went inside.

The transition from street noise to this pristine quiet reminded Dash of going underwater, when the sounds of the world vanished in a tranquil, lonely silence. He expected a modest abode like that of the National Association of Women Lawyers, but the firm of Meyers, Powers & Napier was a much flashier affair. Black and gold wallpaper with repeating diamond shapes surrounded the room. Side tables of black marble with white ivory inlays held vases that followed the same procession of color: wide black bases with narrow white tips. Lamps with flat, two-dimensional shades threw light at perpendicular angles, creating dramatic shadows against the walls. Two empty gold loveseats to Dash's right and left were for waiting clients. At the head of the waiting area was a rectangular bronze desk held up by a pair of narrow Greek columns on each corner.

A hallway behind the desk had four closed doors, two

on either side. Offices, Dash assumed. One of the doors at the farthest end opened and out stepped a woman dressed in a white suit—a woman's suit, Dash noted—holding a thick notebook. She turned and saw him.

"Oh hello," she called. "I didn't realize anyone was out there."

She hurried towards the waiting room. The white jacket with black trim was loosely draped on her narrow shoulders, her white shirt with gold tie was equally shapeless as was the long, white skirt. The suit gave her the appearance of long legs and hardly any torso.

She smiled as she took her place behind the bronze desk. "Do you have an appointment?" Her brown hair was cut short and rounded in curls. A subtle red blush had been added to her cheeks, a not-so-subtle red paint to her lips.

"I don't," he said, "but I do have an urgent matter to discuss with Miss Prudence Meyers."

"I see."

"I hate to be a bother and show up unannounced like this but . . ."

The secretary waved him off. "Not to worry. We're here to help. What kind of legal matter is this?"

Dash thought about the Müllers, Zora Mae, and the shadowy world they all seemed to inhabit, and took a chance.

"Criminal."

15

"Mr. Parker, how nice to meet you," Pru said, her voice a honeyed alto, her grip, like her voice, pleasant but firm.

The square office they stood in was done up in the same style as the waiting room, only instead of black and gold, it was blue and gold—*like the elusive female impersonator's dress on Sunday night,* thought Dash—from the rug on the floor to the walls to the vases.

"Thank you for seeing me on such short notice," he replied, sitting in one of two client chairs in front of the bronze desk.

"It's no trouble at all." She sat down behind her desk, a striking figure in a man's navy suit, trousers and all. Her black hair was cropped short, almost like a man's, yet her face was heavily made-up. Her lips were painted ruby, and her lavender eyes were surrounded by vibrant blue shadow and traced heavily in black ink, like the Egyptians the world was dying to imitate. Despite all the masculine dress, she came off as overwhelmingly feminine.

She folded her hands in front of her, getting down to business. "Tell me about this criminal legal matter."

Given all the subterfuge he used to find her, Dash gambled on telling the truth. "I'm being blackmailed, Ms. Meyers."

A curt nod. "That is most certainly criminal. Have you gone to the police?"

Dash shook his head. "I know you've heard this one before, but I can't."

"And why is that?"

Dash shifted in his seat. Even though she was dressed like a man—an illegal action if seen by the wrong cop—there was always a risk of admitting his nature out loud, especially in the daylight. He hoped she was as open-minded as her appearance.

"Because I am someone who's guilty of degenerate disorderly conduct, I believe the law says."

She blinked. "I see." She unfolded her hands and began to make notes on a pad of paper with an expensive looking ink pen. Without looking up, she asked, "Do you know who is blackmailing you?"

"Oh yes."

She looked up. "You do?"

"And unfortunately, I believe you do as well. Walter Müller."

She hesitated only slightly, but it was enough. She knew that name and that man very well. "Walter Müller," she repeated, the pace of her words slowing. Her eyes went back to her notes. "How did you find that name?"

"He gave it to me himself while he blackmailed me to my face."

More scribbles on the pad. "No notes or telephone calls or anonymous contacts?"

"It was very 'nonymous.' Apologies. Bad joke. Trying to find the humor in this has been trying."

"It's understandable. What were the terms of his blackmail?"

"He didn't ask for money, which is what I thought he'd do."

This surprised her. "Oh? Interesting. What did he ask for in return then?"

Dash swallowed. This would either go well or go very badly very quickly. "He asked me to find you."

She stopped writing. Her head remained down, her eyes on the paper. "I'm sorry?"

"To find you. And a female impersonator." Dash started speaking hastily. "Before you panic, he doesn't know I'm here and I won't tell him I've found you. But, Miss Meyers, he is most keen on the subject and if I don't give him some kind of answer, he will turn me and my friends over to the police for degeneracy and serving illegal liquor."

She frowned, looking up again. "You broke the Volstead laws?"

"I own a speak."

A curious intelligence peeked out of her lavender eyes. "No," she breathed. "It can't be. The bruise. Of course. You're the speak owner Walter punched. What's it called again? The speak, I mean. It had something to do with suits."

"Pinstripes. You remember what happened that night?"

"A bit hard to forget. Walter made quite an entrance. I thought the entire club would come to your defense."

"They would have, too."

"I don't condone violence, but thank goodness that little boy in the green suit incapacitated him. I'd hate to think what Walter would've done otherwise."

"As I've recently learned," Dash said, "he'll do most anything."

She put down her pen and folded her hands in front of her again. "This is a most distressing situation."

"Indeed. What makes it all the worse is Karl dying and I—"

"Excuse me. What did you say?" Her face showed confusion mixed with panic.

She doesn't know.

Dash took another deep breath. "Karl. He's been killed."

Incomprehension still crowded around her frown lines. "Killed?"

"Murdered."

Dash then sketched out for her what details he knew and added in Karl's time in Harlem, including the telephone call he made.

"Next thing I know, Walter is back at my club— drunk, I might add—telling me it's my fault Karl is dead and to atone for my sins, as it were, I'm to find a man who dresses in drag. Along the way, I discovered your name."

He shook his head in disbelief.

"It's all like a bad dream." He focused on Pru, who seemed to be half-listening to him. "If I may ask, how did you know Karl, Miss Meyers?"

She raised a hand. "Excuse me. I need a moment to absorb this information."

She focused on breathing in and breathing out. Her complexion somewhat paled.

"You're telling me Karl Müller has been murdered?"

Dash nodded.

"Do you know who killed him?"

"I do not."

"It wasn't Walter?"

"Believe me, the thought has crossed my mind, but I can't say for certain of his guilt or innocence, Miss Meyers."

"Please, call me Pru. I think it's appropriate, given the circumstances." She paused. "Karl is dead." No longer a question, but a statement.

Dash asked again, "How did you know him?"

"Through a friend of a friend."

"Which friend? The man who dresses in drag?"

She ignored the question. "And Walter wanted you to find a female impersonator? Did he give a name for her?"

"He did not, but I think her name is Miss Avery."

"How did you come across that name?"

"Karl. He said it was Miss Avery's idea to come to my club that night."

"What else did he tell you?"

Dash adjusted his posture in the chair. "His brother works for the Committee of Fourteen handling their finances. Karl said he is . . .was . . . Walter's assistant, but I suspect he was lying about that. I also learned he was handing out rent party cards for Harlem's 'Baroness of Business,' a very determined and dangerous woman named Zora Mae. I'm supposed to meet her tonight. Have you met her?"

She replied carefully, "I know *of* her and have seen her once or twice from across a crowded room. But if you're asking if we're friends or acquaintances, the answer is no."

Her answers were so meticulously worded, Dash could feel she was tiptoeing around the truth. Not lying, per se, but not being completely honest.

"I see," he replied. "It seems Karl spent some time in Harlem outside of the watchful gaze of his brother, who apparently is uncomfortable around such non-white company. Before Karl disappeared from his hiding place—"

"Where was that?"

Dash paused. He didn't see the harm in telling her. "The Oyster House. It was there he mentioned you, that you were an attorney, and that you had a plan that failed. He was later overheard on the telephone trying desperately to reach someone. I found out yesterday he'd left several messages for Tyler Smith—as did you, I might add. Messages which Tyler Smith never collected. After unsuccessfully reaching for Mr. Smith, *poof!* Karl is gone."

Dash exhaled slowly. All of his cards were on the table. Now he would see if his gamble on the truth paid out.

"That's helpful, thank you."

Pru composed herself, a drawbridge going up to seal off the emotions that threatened to escape. She was all business now.

"How did you find me?"

"I visited the Bar Association, who referred me to the National Association of Women Lawyers."

"I'm surprised they did that, considering what they think of us. You're quite resourceful, Mr. Parker."

She freed her hands from each other and began to adjust items on her desk. The notepad. The pens. The stack of files.

"You wouldn't happen to be a detective, would you?"

Dash shook his head. "Not in the slightest."

"You certainly act like one. Back to Walter. Does he think this female impersonator had something to do with Karl's death?" The fingers of one hand began to absent-mindedly drum the surface of the desk.

Dash shook his head again. "I don't believe so. It's what he *says,* but he's after something else." He leaned forward in his chair. "What is Walter looking for? He mentioned how this female impersonator would never leave Karl behind because Karl had something she needed."

"That's rather vague."

Dash was unable to keep the urgency out of his voice. "Pru, please."

She leaned forward on her desk, her expression shrewd. "If you think he's lying about the reason to find her, what makes you believe him about the rest?"

Dash ran a nervous hand through his misbehaving brown hair. "I don't know. If he is lying about that, then he's after revenge."

"Revenge?"

"According to Walter, this female impersonator corrupted his brother, and she was the last person to see him alive."

"Second to last," she said. "I believe you are the man who has that honor."

"True enough." He sat back in his chair. "Miss Meyers, why were you in my club that night? Karl said it was for a special event. Not a celebration, he was quick to add, but something else."

She just stared blandly at him.

"Alright. The telephone call he was trying to make that night. Do you know why he was trying to reach Tyler Smith? Karl was most insistent about it. Panicked, really."

No response.

Dash blew out an exasperated breath. "Pru, I could use some help here. What about your plan?"

"Are you asking because it could lead you to this female impersonator?"

"Yes."

"What will you do if you find her? Turn her over to Walter? Turn me over as well? What is the goal you're working towards?"

It was a good question. His response came out

awkward. "If I can find you both, find out what it is Walter is really after, maybe we could work together to stop him."

Pru processed his response behind opaque eyes. After a moment, she said, "Mr. Parker—Dash—unfortunately, I am unable to help you. Your situation comes into great conflict with an existing case of mine."

"An existing *case*?"

"And client-attorney privilege means I cannot reveal my client nor the case itself. My advice to you is to go to a trusted member of the police."

Dash smirked. "There isn't one."

"Or find a different attorney. I can refer you, if you like."

"But Pru—"

She was adamant. "I'm sorry. I . . . really, truly am."

Dash was at a loss. He had been so sure she'd help him, that they'd band together against Walter Müller with the law as their weapon. Now she was shutting the door on his hopes and all because of a case? What case? And what did it have to do with Walter or Karl? He looked into her lavender eyes and saw steely resolve. She would not budge, he knew that.

He stood up, taking a shaky breath. "Thank you for your time, Miss Meyers."

He took out a card with the address of Hartford & Sons printed on the front.

"This is where you can reach me if you change your mind."

Her eyes flicked down to the card, then back up again. "Good luck, Mr. Parker."

He forced a smile. "Same to you."

Dash returned to Hartford & Sons, defeated and in need of a drink. He'd sneak a beer out of the secret stash. Joe would give him hell for it, but he didn't care. What a disappointing day this had been.

While he was fumbling in his pants pockets for the tailor shop keys, he slowly became aware of the leisurely tapping of a cane behind him. He didn't make too much of it—lots of people walked with canes in the city. The sound, however, stopped abruptly behind him.

Dash turned to see an air-tight man dressed better than most who visited his shop during the week. The downward-looking gent wore a matching boater jacket and slacks, the print a luminous shade of blue with wide, tan stripes. The shoes were a sharp brown leather like teak on a boat. Atop his head was a summer straw hat with a wide navy band around the middle. The tapping was courtesy of a bamboo cane curved around the man's wrist.

Money.

"There you are," the man said, his voice a pleasing bari-tone. "And here I thought you were closed." The man looked up and gave Dash a full view of his lovely face: warm, chocolate eyes, thick, pink lips, and a carefully culti-vated jaw line. "You are the tailor, unless I am mistaken."

The good looks of the man startled Dash. He hoped the surprise—and the attraction—didn't show. He managed to say, "You are not mistaken." Keys finally in hand, he said, "I'm sorry, sir, did we have an appointment?"

The man shook his head. "Not officially. I was in the neighborhood and thought I'd stop by. I have a dinner party coming up, and I'm in desperate need of a new jacket. Are you Mr. Hartford?"

Dash inserted the key into the front door's lock. "Mr.

Hartford is no longer here, I'm afraid. I'm his replacement, Dash Parker."

"Nice to meet you, sir. My condolences for Mr. Hartford." The man pointed to the spot where Walter had struck Dash. "A nasty bruise you have there."

Dash reflexively reached up and rubbed his sore spot. "A bit of trouble a few nights ago."

"The city seems to invite it." The corners of his mouth seemed to twitch with amusement. Dash thought those lips were downright kissable.

Don't be distracted by beauty. Keep your wits, Dash. He's far too charming to be what he seems.

The man nodded towards the shop. "Shall we go in?"

Dash turned the key and opened the door. "After you, sir."

The man with the kissable mouth stepped inside and took in the surroundings while Dash opened one of the windows. He hoped the stuffiness would soon dissipate.

"You're not the father or the son?" asked the man, referring to the sign out front.

"No, sir," Dash replied, hanging up his own jacket on the coatrack in the back corner.

"The Holy Ghost then?"

Dash smiled. "I've been called a lot of things in my short little life, but 'holy' has never been one of them." He rolled up his sleeves. "Now, how can I help you today? You mentioned a new jacket?"

If he didn't ask about, or suggest, pinstripes, then he was not in the know. And if he wasn't in the know, then he was either an innocent walking in here or something else. Dash heard of undercover federal agents carefully entrapping speak owners and their patrons. He wondered if this man could be one of them.

"Yes," the man replied, "I have a dinner party coming up. A white jacket type of affair. And unfortunately, my current one doesn't seem to fit anymore." He patted his midsection. "Too much rich food these days."

He's not one of us, Dash surmised. *But could he be the Feds?*

He appraised the man's frame. When he moved, Dash could see a thickness around the middle, but it wasn't overbearing nor unattractive. His height helped. That alone could've meant *cop,* but there was also a sense of wealth about him. Dash's own privileged childhood taught him their calling cards—or as they'd say in the gin joints with illegal poker games, their tells. The way they carried themselves, the style and fit of their clothing, the clear pronunciation of their words. The wealthy had a distinct air.

"I take it the old coat is too tight when buttoned?" Dash asked.

The man nodded.

"Let's see what we can do about that. Take off your jacket, please."

The man gave him a sideways look, but then did as instructed. Dash took the boater jacket, folded it neatly, and draped it over his desk chair.

"Where should I stand?" the man asked.

Dash pointed to the center of the room. The man complied, his back to the front windows. Dash grabbed the tape measure from the side of the floor length mirror and came up behind him. "Hold your arms out," he said.

When the man did, Dash wrapped the tape measure around the upper part of the man's chest. Subtle cologne with a citrus fragrance tickled Dash's nose. He thought he knew the brand. The elegant lavender, rosemary, and jasmine was balanced by a light musk. It made him want to get closer to the long neck, which led upwards to small ears that dared to be nibbled.

He's dangerous, Dash old boy. Resist temptation!

Dash announced, "Forty inches around the chest."

"Comes from rowing."

Dash dropped the tape measure and then focused on the man's arms. The muscle definition was apparent as he laid the tape from shoulder to wrist. Could these muscles have come from military training? "Which university?"

"Princeton. I still do it, you know. A man has to have exercise to keep from becoming a complete blob."

"I don't see any threat of that with you. Sleeve is thirty-four. Would you need pants as well?"

That little smirk again. "Very well. If the jacket doesn't fit, why should the pants?"

Most certainly not *in the know. Who are you, sir? Why are you here?*

Dash took the tape measure again and wrapped it around the man's midsection. "Thirty-four and a half."

The man sighed. "I remember when I was thirty. The waist, not the age. I guess there's no coming back to that, is there?"

"You look fit and healthy to me, sir."

"Thank you, Mr. Parker."

"Please, call me Dash."

"Alright."

Dash dropped to his knees. "Now your inseam. Do you mind?" He held up the tape for the man to hold.

Instead, the man replied, "Not at all."

He made no move to take the higher end of the tape from Dash and place it on the inside of his thigh. Many of Dash's customers did this because they weren't necessarily comfortable with the proximity between Dash's hand and their delicates. This man was apparently comfortable with the thought. Was he an invert as well? Everything about this man was just slightly askew, a millimeter off-balance.

Who are *you?*

Dash kept his face blank and continued with his work. He placed one end of the tape near the man's ankle and the other high on the upper inside thigh. "Thirty-two. You're a tall man, mister."

"I've been told once or twice like a beanstalk."

Still on his knees, he asked, "And what will be the name on the account, sir?"

There was a slight pause. Then the pleasing, sensual voice said, "Surname is Fife."

16

Dash froze.

He misheard. He must have misheard. This cannot be the notorious gangster who sent Lowell Henley to approach him.

"First name?" Dash managed to ask.

"Nicholas. Although some in the newspaper business call me 'Slick Nick.'"

Dash lowered the tape and looked up at the man, who no longer seemed handsome nor playful. There was a darkness to his eyes, a menace to his lips. Fife's face hadn't exactly changed expression, per se, but like Adam taking a bite of the apple, Dash felt the innocence fall away from his eyes and saw the world take on a new tint. Down on his knees, his throat within grabbing distance of this killer's hands, he felt beyond vulnerable. He felt naked.

Fife said, "I would've been here sooner, but a man of my position is rather busy."

Dash's throat was suddenly dry, his mouth mealy with fear. He concentrated on keeping the shakes from his voice as he lowered the tape measure. "I can understand that."

"You sent away one of my associates. Was the contract not agreeable to you?" The voice was maddeningly calm, flat seas in contrast to Dash's roiling ocean.

"I don't like to sign contracts without further investigation."

Fife nodded. "I see you're a savvy businessman. I'm a savvy businessman too. And savvy businessmen don't like to negotiate with an associate."

"I just wanted to try the merchandise first."

"You're a bar owner, you need to know what will be behind your bar. A bar that could be protected from . . . let's say . . . legal nuisances."

"Your associate did mention that."

"Yet you seemed unimpressed."

Dash gave what he hoped was a calm shrug. "I pay the police now to ignore my club. What additional protection do I need?"

Fife considered his response for a moment. "It amazes me how naive some men can be. I didn't think you were one of them, considering your nighttime activities. But let me educate you on how this world works.

"A man like myself provides the needed goods to make the businesses of men like yourself run. Without my goods, no one would attend your lovely little club. Well . . . maybe to engage in some degenerate fucking. That would make you nothing more than a madam, a den mother to whores. You strike me as the kind of man who's a little too well-bred for that." He paused.

Dash held his breath.

Fife continued. "As in any industry, there are competitors. Others who provide the same goods—inferior goods, I must add—and they act aggressively to compete. You understand economics, don't you?"

Dash nodded, never taking his eyes off the gangster's face. His knees began to stiffen, but Dash refused to adjust his position.

If I had to, could I make a run for it?

Probably not. He wasn't poised for flight.

But the windows are open. People can see in. Surely, he wouldn't kill me in broad daylight.

Yet how many stories had he read where gangsters had done exactly that? Too many to mention.

Fife's pleasing voice said, "I see you are a quiet student. I hope that means you're listening." He smiled, then just as quick as it formed, the smile uncurled itself and settled back into a flat line. "Economics, to be uncouth about it, is a form of war. Everyone is trying to be on the positive side of scarcity. That's what war really is, by the way. It's not fighting injustice or defeating an evil enemy, like a warlord Kaiser. It is, simply put, the acquisition of limited resources. Land. Gold. People—*especially* people. All are elements to be used in the creation of more wealth and more power for those in charge. The goal is to be the leader everyone fears so no one will come after you and take what you've killed to get."

The gangster began to adjust the cuffs of his sleeves.

"The Romans were quite effective in this regard. The slightest infraction, however minor, was met with brute force. It was said that a Roman could walk down any street without fear of harassment because of the unspoken, but always executed, threat of the Empire."

The cuffs now fixed, Fife smoothed out his sleeves, running his hand from shoulder to wrist and back again.

"My competitors have never tried to come after me. Nor have they ever tried to steal a club that's under my control. A free agent, like yourself, is vulnerable to their attack. You see, while you're paying that sack of lard of a policeman to protect yourself and your employees from jail, you've left yourself wide open for someone to waltz in and take your club by force. *And they. Will. Do that."*

Dash flinched at the sudden surge in intensity.

He knows about us bribing Cullen McElroy, just like he knew about the delivery truck we use. How long has he been watching us?

Sleeve inspection complete, Fife then adjusted his collar. "I am a fair and reasonable man, Mr. Parker. I do business; I don't do anarchy. Some of the others in this city?" He shrugged. "They have bullets and liquor and no idea what to do with either. You can be under their control; in which case you will find yourself in the middle of endless turf wars. You've read the papers. You've seen the damage they cause on a regular basis. God forbid an innocent bystander be hurt by that. You. Your customers. Your doorman. The Irish bartender who loves you so thoroughly."

Dash's face turned red.

The gangster smiled. "Oh yes, my associate has been following you for quite some time. You really should get better shades in your window. But then, I don't think my associate would've enjoyed the view half as much."

Dash tried to speak. "Mr. Fife—"

Fife raised his hand to cut him off. "I don't care what you do with your cock. Or what the Irishman does with his, for that matter. We all have our appetites to satisfy. Unfortunately, my competitors are not so understanding. They'll want to own your club, but they'll have disdain for the clientele to which you cater. Which begs the question, how much will they protect you from the police? From the Feds? From their own rivals? They may even sell you out to the highest bidder. Law enforcement, tabloids, or both."

Dash replied, "I can re-read your contract again, if you'd like. I still want to see the goods you would be providing my business." He refused to be *completely* intimidated, dammit, even if it was foolish to hold onto any crumbs of pride.

The gangster paused for so long, Dash thought he had crossed the line. Again.

And this time, I won't survive it.

Fife's expression changed to one of admiration. "I can respect that. It will be arranged. Just remember this. Whomever you make the deal with, always consider if that agreement will keep you on your knees"—he lowered his hand, causing Dash to flinch. The hand grasped Dash's own and pulled him up from the floor—"or let you stand. I let people be on their feet."

Dash now stood face-to-face with this man, practically toe-to-toe. That smirk again. That damnable smirk.

Then, without warning, the gangster cupped Dash's face with both hands and gave him a long, gentle, wet kiss. The lips were surprisingly tender and deft, inspiring Dash's own mouth to naturally respond.

When Fife pulled back, he whispered, "I know you've wanted to do that for quite some time now."

He winked before turning away to collect his coat, hat, and cane. Once he was put back together, he strolled to the shop door and opened it, letting in the hellfire of the August heat.

Full voiced, he said, "I'll be in touch."

Joe roared, "He just came to the shop?! In broad daylight! The nerve of that man!"

It was close to sunset and they were standing out front

of the Cherry Lane Playhouse, watching folks line up for the box office for tonight's show, the second night of previews. They smoked cigarettes off to the side near their apartment entrance. The sky was a brilliant pink overhead.

Dash took another nervous drag and said, "That's generally how these men operate."

Joe gave him a pointed look. "I can't believe you didn't tell me about him sooner." He meant Lowell Henley.

"I'm sorry, Joe. I didn't want to worry you and Finn and Atty until there was something to worry about." Dash looked down at his feet. "I suppose now there is."

Joe reluctantly nodded, his form of accepting Dash's apology.

A "normal" couple, radiating energy, came up to them. "Is this the line for the box office?" the man asked. His cheeks were cherub red, as were hers.

Dash shook his head and pointed to their right. "It's over there."

The woman lightly bumped her elbow to his arm, her manner good-natured. "I told you so."

"Yeah, yeah, yeah." The man tipped his hat to Dash and Joe. "Thank you, gentlemen."

"Happy to oblige," Joe replied.

The couple left them to get in the correct line.

Joe snubbed out his cigarette in the teacup they used as an ashtray, placed it on the ground, then seized Dash by the shoulders. "I'm sorry, lad. I should've been there."

Dash looked into Joe's emerald eyes. "What do you mean?"

"Ya could've been hurt. Or worse."

Don't remind me.

The moment Nicholas Fife left the shop, Dash practically fainted into his desk chair. All of the tension which had built up like steam in a boiler burst through. The rush of relief at having still been alive was quickly followed by the mounting dread of what would happen next.

Fife is always watching. Is he watching us now?

Dash looked up and down the street, saying to Joe, "How could you have known he'd pay us a visit? I had advance warning, what with Lowell offering me the contract and all, and even I didn't anticipate this."

Joe released Dash's shoulders and sighed. "We'll have to do it, won't we? Sign the agreement?"

Dash's eyes stopped patrolling the street and settled back on Joe's face. The freckled forehead was wrinkled with worry, and the corners of his eyes held lines of regret. An old feeling rose up in Dash's chest and he quickly swallowed it down.

Shaking his head, he replied to Joe's question, "I don't see how we have a choice."

They didn't have many choices these days, what with men like Fife, Müller—hell, even McElroy—in their lives.

Did you really believe freedom was possible?

Another couple, this one older, their hair completely gray with faces lined like crumpled paper bags, walked up to them.

"Excuse me, sirs," the older gent said. "Is this the line for the box office?"

Joe turned his head to the side and blew out a line of cigarette smoke.

Dash pointed to their right. "The box office line is over there."

Joe muttered, "Where the bloody box office is."

The old man registered Joe's sarcasm with a slight pause and a flash of the eyes.

The woman on his arm, Dash supposed his wife, said, "I told you, Harold."

The man cleared his throat and a forced smile. "Thank you very much."

The couple moved off.

Joe said to Dash, "We can make it work, lassie. With Fife. If his booze is as good as he claims, it might not be so bad."

"I'm supposed to try it sometime."

"When?"

Dash shrugged. "Whenever is most convenient for Fife, I imagine."

Another couple, this one in their thirties, came up to them. Before the man could speak, Dash pointed to his right. "Box office line is over there."

"See?" the woman said, as they moved away. "I told you it wasn't possible the line was that short."

Dash didn't hear the man's reply. He said to Joe, "As if we don't have enough to do with this Walter mess, I've now got to find a suit for Mr. Fife."

Joe shook his head. "He was just using that as an excuse to get into your shop."

"Somehow I doubt that."

The sidewalk was increasingly busy with those going to dinner or to a show. A derelict man was stumbling among them, bumping into a man in a brown suit and offering a pantomimed apology. The man in the brown suit glared at him, using a handkerchief to wipe off any street grime that may have transferred from the derelict's dirty rags to his jacket and shirt.

As the derelict got closer, Dash could see scraggly whiskers hiding his face. Dirty gray hair in need of a trim cascaded over his ears and down to his shoulders. The suit he wore was covered in patches on the knees and elbows, the fabric a different color. Surprisingly, the man didn't smell, though Dash had expected him to.

The derelict stopped right in front of them.

Joe gave the man a wary look. "No spare change and no spare booze, partner."

The derelict replied in a familiar voice, "Well I never! Is that what you call Catholic charity, you brute? May the goddesses never see such selfishness."

Dash squinted his eyes. "Finn?"

The derelict reached up and pulled off the long, gray hair. It was a wig. Underneath was the dark-haired Finn, his grin unmistakable behind the fake whiskers.

"I told you it would be a marvelous disguise."

Finn tossed the wig to Joe, who jerked away as if Finn had tossed him a tarantula. The wig floated to the ground.

"Finney!" Joe bellowed. "Why ya playing the fool?"

A hand went to his breast. "*I* didn't play the fool, but I daresay our Mr. Müller did."

Dash said, "He didn't recognize you?"

Finn crossed his arms, clearly pleased with himself. "He never gave me a second look."

Dash smiled. It was about time they had some good news. "Where did he go?"

Yet another couple came up to them.

Before Dash could give his usual response, Joe barked, "This is not the bloody box office line. Yer late. The line is already halfway down the street and it's back that way." He gestured to their right.

The couple flinched at the harsh brogue and moved along, casting furtive glances over their shoulders.

"I see your usual graciousness extends to strangers as well," Finn said.

He began to take off his disguise one layer at a time. First went the whiskers.

"These blasted things are just itching my face. Honestly, the things I do for you people."

"Finney," Joe said, "tell us what happened."

Once the whiskers were off, Finn examined them. "He's an odd one, that Walter. First, his darling mother walked him all the way to the front door."

Dash asked, "Of the apartment?"

The coat was next. Finn slid it off his shoulders and folded it over his forearm. "Of the *building*. She stood there and waved him goodbye. She watched him leave, almost like she was making sure he left. I didn't dare move from my spot until after she went back inside."

"Well played, Finn."

Finn grinned as he picked up the wig from the ground. "I'm going to pretend I don't hear a note of surprise in your voice. It would be *shameful* if the two of you doubted my abilities."

He shook out the wig and added it to the garments draped over his forearm.

"I was half a block behind him the whole time. Needless to say, he did *not* go to the Committee of Fourteen."

A man in his twenties came up to Finn. "Excuse me, are you an actor in this playhouse?"

Finn gave him a most thorough once over. "Hello, stranger. Why do you ask?"

The man pointed to Finn's disguise. "You're coming from another performance, aren't you?"

Finn was amused. "In a manner of speaking."

The man leaned in and lowered his voice. "Can you help a gentleman out with a ticket? All the preview performances are sold out and I'm dying to see this show before the ticket prices go up."

Joe intervened. "Look, lad, we're having a conversation here."

The man held up his hands. "I apologize. I didn't mean to offend." He tipped the brim of his fedora. "Have a good night, sirs." He turned and walked towards the box office line.

Finn whirled around to Joe. "How *dare* you interrupt what was an obvious flirtation. Goddess knows, I need a distraction as my poor, sweet Valentino is still laid up after his surgeries."

Dash asked, "Any news on that front?"

Finn sadly shook his head. "Still waiting and seeing."

Joe's fiery brow wrinkled again. "Who cares about that Valentino bloke. Finney, where did Walter go?"

Finn rolled his eyes. "All over. I must say, I am just exhausted after today." He reached into his front trouser pocket and pulled out a scrap of paper, unfolding it. "I wrote down all the places he visited. Maybe you can tell me what they mean, because darlings, I have no earthly nor heavenly idea *what* that man was doing."

He squinted as he read from the paper.

"First, he went to a café on 86th and Madison for breakfast. Then down to some of the Times Square cinemas and caught a couple of motion pictures. *The Big Parade* and *Ben Hur,* if anyone's interested. Then he went to the German motion picture theatre back up on 86th. Last stop was the bank. Then he went home."

Dash couldn't conceal his puzzlement.

Finn returned the piece of paper to his pocket. "I trust you're as confused as I."

Dash said, "He's acting like a man of leisure."

Joe added, "A man without a care in the world."

"Do you think he knew he was being followed?"

Finn shook his head with disgust. "Again, with the doubt! Boys, he never once looked back nor over his shoulder. Didn't stop in front of shop windows to catch someone in a reflection. I crisscrossed the street several times, so I was never directly behind him or across from him at any time. Trust me, there's no way he spotted me."

Dash laid a hand on his friend's shoulder. "Good work, Finn. I apologize."

"I'll accept that apology over a drink and a sailor."

A foursome of women walked up to them. Without missing a beat, Finn pointed to their right. "Box office line is that way, dearies," he said before they could ask.

As the foursome moved away, Joe said, "What does this mean, lads?"

Dash replied, "I'm not sure, but I think it's telling he lied about being employed by the Committee. Oh! Remember, Joe? Walter wanted information by Thursday, and I asked if we needed to bring it to the office? He was quick to say to bring it to his apartment." Dash smiled in triumph. "That's because he doesn't work at the Committee at all."

"Well, lassie, hold up. What if he took off a few days to let the bruising heal?"

"Yes," Finn said, "he really took a beating that night, much deserved. Perhaps he didn't want his colleagues to know he'd been in a fight. I imagine anti-vicers look down on brawling."

Dash nodded. "You're right."

Joe added, "And don't forget, the Committee spies on entertainment places regularly. Maybe that's what this lad was doing."

"But Karl said he worked in the finance department, not in the field."

Finn said, "Maybe Karl was lying."

"It's possible." Dash looked up at the purpling sky. Night was coming. "Let's see if he goes to work tomorrow. If not, then he's lying to all of us as well as his mother."

Joe grunted. "Makes ya wonder why."

Finn held up a pointer finger. "Excuse me, but let's go back a bit. Did you say we owe him information by this Thursday? As in *tomorrow*? We don't have anything to tell him!"

Dash replied, "We might, gents. We just might."

He filled them in on his conversation with Prudence Meyers.

"A legal case?" Joe said.

"Criminal by the sounds of it. If Pru is building a case against Walter, then we might see some interesting behavior in his daily activities."

"How do ya know Pru's building a case against him?"

"Educated guess. I can't see this woman working for the likes of him, but I absolutely can see her working against him."

"Never underestimate the power of money," Finn warned. "Most people's principles go out the door when a bunch of sugar is poured out on their desks."

"He's right, lassie," Joe said. "It's a buy-and-sell world now. As proved by this Fife fella."

Finn cupped a hand behind his ear. "Say who again?"

Joe shook his head. "I'll tell ya later."

Finn placed a hand against his chest. "Oh, I do *not* like the sound of that."

17

At midnight on the dot, the cab dropped Dash off in front of Flo's building. She stood there in an emerald-green dress with sparkling fringe. A yellow sunflower had been clipped to the side of her hair.

"Miss Russell," Dash said as he walked up. "You look ravishing."

Flo rolled her eyes. "Come on. Let's get this over with."

They walked to 135th and Seventh in silence, earning a few curious glances. A white downtowner and a black woman wasn't an entirely unusual sight, but could, in some neighborhoods, get one or both of them physically assaulted. Luckily for them, this part of Harlem saw its fair share of downtowners.

The Harlem streets were teaming with people, all done up in dresses and hats and suits and ties. Laughter ricocheted off the sides of the brick buildings. Windows on the upper floors were wide open, and the sensuous sounds of jazz and blues floated down to the pavement, following them as they walked. The moaning vocals, the piercing cornets, the low boom of the bass blended in with the purr of motor cars and the brass of their horns. The marquee of the Cotton Club flashed its bright neon, making it almost as bright as day. To Dash, it felt like being in the center of a Christmas tree, all that glitter and tinsel and lighting surrounding them.

The foot traffic flowed as fast as the Hudson, an aggressive current of black citizens and a few white downtowners quickly moving across the blocks. Flo and Dash headed east at a clip.

While the Hot Cha was a new club to Dash, he knew of several in this neighborhood, thanks to some of his band members. There was Small's Paradise, which featured café au lait girls and dancing waiters. Across the street was the Yeah Man!, a downstairs bar that always answered the question "Is there anything going on tonight?" ("Yeah, man!"). Nearby was the Log Cabin, a small, intimate space perfect for romance or its facsimile; Tillies, which his drummer Calvin claimed had some of the best fried chicken in Harlem; and the Theatrical Grill, which gave you Broadway performances without the inconvenience of having to go to Broadway. Dash had to admit that while the Village was a hopping spot, it couldn't compare to the red-hot sizzle of Harlem.

Once Dash and Flo hit their cross street, they left the river of excitable, loud-talking young people.

Soon they descended the steps on the corner of 134th and Seventh towards the basement. The door of the Hot Cha had no sign, no marquee, no indication of what lay behind these walls. Flo rang the buzzer and they waited for the eye slot to open. It did with a bang. Brown eyes—and nothing else—stared back at them.

Flo said the code words: "I'm here to walk Clarence's dog."

"Step to the side," said the voice, male and deep.

She did as instructed.

The eyes narrowed. "He with you?" the voice asked.

Flo replied, "Don't mind him, he just the dog walker."

The secret code for white downtowners.

The eye slot slammed closed. Then there was the sound of a series of locks being undone. The door opened slightly, and Dash and Flo stepped into the darkened corridor.

The doorman was a tall black man, fittingly dressed in a tuxedo, all long arms and long legs. Dark hair cropped close to his skull shimmered with some kind of oil. His hands and feet were incredibly large, almost a caricature, like when a child draws a full-grown man. There was a wooden stool behind him and what might've been a jug of liquor resting behind it.

The man closed and relocked the door, not saying a word. Then again, he wasn't paid to socialize, just to keep watch and make sure no men in blue barged in here.

Regardless of his silent state, Flo thanked him and walked down the darkened hallway. Dash followed. The music was muffled at first, but slowly intensified the closer they got to the entryway. They turned a corner and stepped through the archway into another world.

Men—gorgeous black men—were everywhere. On the dance floor, sitting at the round tables, or serving drinks. All dressed to impress. Tuxedos and pinstripe suits, checkered and houndstooth jackets, bow ties and long ties, shoes as shiny as freshly polished motorcars. Women were dotted about like daisies in a field. Most were dressed in white, shimmering in silk chiffon and sleeveless cotton blouses or dresses. Above them all—besides the cigarette smoke—was the sweet voice of Jimmie Daniels and the rhythmic pounding of Garland Wilson on his upright piano. Dash had heard of them through the grapevine but had never seen them perform. A chill went up his spine as his ears were tickled by the music. Jimmie and Garland were *that* good.

A thin man in black pants and a white jacket appeared in front of them. "How many, sugars?" he asked, his voice high and smooth.

"Just two," replied Flo.

"You together?"

"No, just acquaintances."

"Two fine dinners like you?" The maître d' looked at Flo, then Dash. "What's the holdup?"

Dash smiled. "Different tastes."

The man nodded, understanding the situation. "I'll seat you two at the bar. With luck, someone will strike your fancy. Let's see." He pointed at Dash. "A buddy ghee for you." He then pointed at Flo. "And a barbecutie for you?"

Flo nodded.

The man smiled, ivory glittering between his lips. "Right this way."

They followed him as they meandered around the haphazard seating arrangement, tables and chairs seemingly plopped down at random. Glasses clinked as waiters whizzed by with cocktails spilling over the brim. Laughter, light and breezy like a chandelier tinkling, filled the air. The bar hugged one of the far walls and was about three-fourths full with a mix of suits and dresses, their backs to the action. Dash was the only white person here.

True to his word, the maître d' sat them next to a stunning man in a slick black tuxedo and a lovely woman dressed in purple with white sashes. Painted lashes fluttered Flo's way. Flo smiled politely but didn't exude too much warmth. The man in the black tux sent an interested look to Dash, who replied with a smile.

Flo slapped his shoulder. "We're not here to make friends tonight, Mr. Parker."

"No reason not to be polite."

"Uh huh. Keep it in check. I need all the blood to be going to your brain, not elsewhere."

She got the attention of the bartender, a short and stout man in a checked brown suit jacket with a flat cap on his square head. He came her way. A slow, smoldering smile followed.

Flo murmured to Dash, "Pretend you're not with me."

Dash nodded. She was going to use her feminine wiles to find out where Zora Mae was in this sea of men and women. Dash backed away, standing closer to the man in the tux giving him eyes, and pretended to watch the band while eavesdropping on Flo's conversation.

The bartender said, "Now *how* can I make you happy this evening, baby?"

"You can get me a Gin Rickey and don't be stingy with the gin. I'm not asking for sugar water."

He laughed at that. "A woman who knows what she wants and ain't gonna settle for less. Coming right up."

He set about making her drink, stealing glances back at her whenever he could.

Poor man, Dash thought. *He's going to waste his hype.*

When the bartender returned with her cocktail, he said, "It's a tragedy when a beautiful woman is all by herself."

She held up her glass. "Nothing a good drink can't cure." She tasted it and smiled. "Good to know you can follow directions."

The bartender leaned in close. "I follow directions *very* well."

Dash suppressed a smile.

"Uh huh," Flo said, making her voice low and husky. "That so?"

The bartender started drawing tiny circles on the bar with his fingertip. "Oh yeah. You tell me what to do and I'll do *exactly* what you say."

"Exactly what I say, huh?"

"And I won't stop until you tell me to."

She licked the gin and stray crumbs of sugar lining the glass from her lips. "I need you—"

"Woo! Music to my ears!"

"—to get me the Baroness."

It took a few seconds for her request to register, then for disappointment to show. "Say again?"

She took another healthy sip of her drink. "Do I really need to ask you twice?"

His finger stopped swirling on the hardwood of the bar, and he stood up straight. "I get drinks, not people."

She slowly wagged a pointer finger at him. "You said you follow directions. You said you'd do exactly what I say."

"I did but—"

"But nothing. I gave you my instructions. Unless you want to disappoint me." She gave a theatrical sigh. "A shame, really. I don't entertain men who let me down."

One of the men at the other end of the bar called for him. The bartender kept his eyes on Flo. "Who should I tell the Baroness is wanting her?"

"A friend of an employee of hers."

"Who's the friend?"

Flo snapped her fingers, getting Dash's attention.

He turned and said, "Dash Parker. Tell her I have, sadly, some bad news about Karl Müller."

Flo jerked her head towards the bartender. "Give him the card."

She meant the blue card Karl had.

Dash reached into his inside jacket pocket and handed it to the bartender.

The bartender flashed a look at him. "I see she got you trained like a dog." He returned his eyes to Flo, anger slowly widening the pupils. "This dog doesn't do tricks without a treat."

Oh my, Dash thought. *Normal men get so angry when they are denied female attention.*

Flo slapped a quarter on the bar with a hard *thwack!* "You'll get another one if you give us the answer we want." She didn't blink as she stared at the bartender's face.

The bartender smirked, then slid the quarter into his palm, glaring once more at Flo. He went down the bar, whispered to one of the waiters collecting drinks, and then set off to get his next order, only paying half attention to his new customer, as he kept glancing back at her.

The man in the tux sitting next to Dash said, "The Baroness sure knows how to throw a party."

Dash turned and regarded the man with an interested gaze. "Does she now?"

The man nodded. "Best time I ever had. Got to see some things I never thought I'd see." He turned and set his warm, brown eyes on Dash. His voice became a little softer. "Got to *do* some things I never thought I'd do, too."

Dash felt a tingle at the base of his neck. "And did you like it?"

The man laughed. "Oh yes! Yes, sir, I did. Whenever she throws a party, I make sure I'm there. Have you ever been to one?"

Dash shook his head.

"Well, if you want to go to her next one with somebody—"

A female voice called out, interrupting them, "Whatchu want with Miss Mae?"

Both Dash and Flo turned their heads. The woman in the purple and white dress glared at them from her barstool.

Is this Zora Mae's moll? Dash thought. *The crazy one?*

Realization dawned on Flo too. Trying to keep it casual, she shrugged, making her voice nonchalant. "A conversation."

"Uh huh. We both know that's bushwa." The look hardened. "Zora belongs to me. *I'm* her Sheba, got it? So, whatever you say, it better be quick. And then you and your ofay pet here better get gone."

Dash tried to intervene. "Miss, you have nothing to worry about. Our interest in Miss Mae is strictly professional."

Those jealous eyes bored into Dash's. "It better be, mister. It. Better. Be."

The bartender came back, decidedly less flirtatious this time around. He had the sulky look of a child being asked to do chores. "The Baroness would like you to join her table."

Flo asked, "Where is she seated?"

He pointed across the room to the far-left corner.

"Thank you, sir." She reached into her purse and slapped another coin onto the bar, only this time it was a nickel.

The bartender picked it up with disgust. "I thought I was gonna get another quarter."

"You shouldn't have pouted. I don't reward pouty boys."

The bartender cursed under his breath.

Flo stood up from her barstool, giving one quick glance

at Zora's moll, and then said, "Alright, downtowner, you on your own."

"Pardon me?"

"This conversation has nothing to do with me, and the less I know about it, the better." She pointed a finger at him. "And remember what I said, now. Whatever trouble you bring upon yourself, it does *not* come back to El and me. Understand?"

"I do."

"Good." Another glance back at Miss Purple and White. "Be careful with Crazy Eyes over there."

And with that, she left the bar.

As Dash turned to go to Zora, the man in the tux reached out and grabbed his hand. "You think about my offer now."

The bartender cut in. "Tully, find some other white meat to chew on. He apparently is Miss Mae's boy now." His eyes slid over to Dash's. "And God help him."

Dash forced a smile at the man in the tux and left to go meet the Baroness.

18

She appeared to Dash in flashes in between the dancers on the floor. The white cloche hat on top of her head. The glow of her pearl earrings. The high black fur of her collar. The sparkle of her diamond necklace laying against bare skin. And finally, the intricate pattern of the white dress.

Then there was the woman herself. A caramel dream with eyes so warm and inviting, they practically whispered an invitation. A small, upturned nose leading to a richly painted mouth. Skin smooth as the silk draping over it. Her frame was thin but formidable. She wasn't just beautiful; she was powerful.

Zora's fingers tapped the tabletop idly to the music, keeping time with the piano player as her eyes kept watch of the dance floor. A faint smile appeared from time to time, as if she was delighted by something—or someone—she saw. She sat alone with a martini. Dash got the sense she didn't entertain company unless she requested it and she could also dismiss it as fast as she got it.

When she noticed Dash standing to the side of her table, she gestured to an open chair. She waited until the song ended, then gave a rousing round of applause. The twosome announced they were taking a break. The dancers left the floor and the noise diminished by half.

"That Jimmie," she said. "Voice like a sweet angel. I never get tired of hearing him."

"He is a fine singer, Baroness. Or do you prefer Miss Mae?"

Zora turned to Dash and measured him up, taking in every inch of his frame. "A downtowner at my table," she finally said. "And a bruised and battered one as well. Will wonders never cease? Miss Mae will do. What's your name again? I'm afraid I've forgotten it already."

"Dash Parker. I'm here about—"

"Karl Müller, yes, Mr. Johnson said. Bad news, if I remember correctly."

She held up the blue card Dash had given the bartender, then slid it over to him. Dash left it on the table for the time being.

"You should know, Mr. Parker, I have many folks handing out my cards."

"Yet bad news about Mr. Müller granted me permission to sit at your table."

Her thin brows arched over intelligent eyes. "You're very astute." She took a sip of her martini. "The name is familiar. I can't quite picture the figure who goes along with it."

"Young German kid, about my height." Dash reached into his pocket and pulled out the photograph Walter had forgotten to take with him when he left Pinstripes. He handed it to Zora.

She studied the picture. "Ah, yes. I remember him now. Such an innocent. Such purity. I'm sure whoever seduces him will find him as tender as veal." She glanced up at

Dash. "My, my, you're quite taken with him. Have you bed him yet?"

Dash felt his cheeks burn. "We didn't have that kind of relationship." Something told him to hold back the news about Karl's murder. "He came to me for help but then he went missing Sunday night. The last time I knew where he was, he was at the Oyster House."

"Ah. Guilt. Another delicious emotion. Almost as aching and wonderful as lust."

"Before he left the Oyster House, he made a telephone call. He couldn't reach someone and then disappeared. I'm wondering if he was trying to reach you."

Zora seemed amused with his question. "And you came all the way up here to Harlem to find out. Not many white men would've braved such a meeting."

"Why be afraid of a Baroness?"

She laughed low in her throat. The tip of her finger began to trace the circle of her martini glass.

"I'm a single woman from a poor family, and yet, I'm one of the most powerful women in Harlem. Do you know how I did that?"

Dash shook his head.

"I learned long ago that human nature always, *always* wins out. Doesn't matter how well you're raised or how devout you are. When the sun goes down and the rooms get dark, we're all just animals."

Her finger stopped tracing the glass. She licked the gin off the tip and then swept her arm across their view of the dance floor.

"Look at 'em. They love the music. They love the liquor. They desire the company more. Dancing is, after all, just the prelude to other things. An overture to the main act.

Pansy clubs. Bulldagger joints. We all go because we can't get it anywhere else."

"You own clubs?" Dash asked.

"I own clubs. I own houses and apartments that host special kinds of salons—some with stories and acting; others that specialize in pleasure. And people pay for the privilege. That's what boys like Karl were helping me with handing out those cards. Karl tempted you with it, didn't he? Despite his innocent nature, he was quite the temptress. Or perhaps he was the temptress *because* of his innocent nature. An interesting thought to ponder, don't you think?"

She grinned flirtatiously.

"I'm not only in the business of animalistic tendencies, Mr. Parker, lest you think I'm completely debaucherous. Like I said before, I learned about human nature. It's true, we all give in to desire. We also have a want—no, a *need*— to be forgiven. To be made pure. To start anew."

"Salvation," Dash said. "How do you sell that? You own churches?"

Zora laughed. "Not quite, though I do have a preacher or two in my pocket. I have shares in certain facilities, which specialize in rehabilitation. From booze. From sex. From inversion."

Dash looked at her with horror. "You're an invert yourself! How can you—"

"Because it's damn good sugar." Her eyes were no longer warm and seductive, but cold, black coals. "Listen, my pretty, there's only one thing that matters in this life, and that's money. Not because of the things it can buy, but because of the *freedom* it can get you. Money *is* freedom. Make no mistake about that."

"Money is the root of all evil," Dash replied.

"Quoting Timothy, are we? And it's *for the love* of money. Money itself is neither good nor bad."

Zora leaned forward, her manner intense.

"I'm a single black woman, Mr. Parker. You think if I didn't have piles of sugar, I'd be free to walk around and do what I want? Say what I want? *Have* whoever I want?" She shook her head. "I'd be married to some man who may, or may not, hit me across the mouth if I say something smart. Popping out babies and scrubbing floorboards. No allowance 'cause my man don't want me outta the house. Let's not forget that south of Harlem, I'd be somebody's maid. Trapped in a life of *yes, missus* and *no, missus* and *I'll get right to it, missus.* Well, no sir. I refuse to be caged and I *refuse* to be tamed."

She leaned back in her chair, pausing to pull out a cigarette from her bag and light it, one of those long ones that required a special holder. The activity of preparing her smoke as well as the nicotine itself dissipated the tension that was mounting at her table.

Once she finished the inaugural puff, she said, "I grant you, some of what I do may be distasteful. It's a messy means to a most gorgeous end."

"How Machiavellian," Dash replied.

Zora gestured towards him with her smoldering cigarette, her manner once again flirtatious. "An educated one. You certainly fit right in here, Mr. Parker. Would you like me to find a gentleman who can match you wit for wit? Oh, I forgot."

She then picked up the photograph of Karl and placed it against her breast.

"You already have one. Can I keep this? I know it may be hard for you to part with it, but in case I stumble upon him and need to remind myself what he looks like."

Dash shrugged. "You can keep it. It won't do you much good. The boy is dead. Someone killed him Sunday night. Strangled him in Central Park."

Zora held his gaze for a few seconds. "I see. That's the bad news. I thought you were simply chasing after him. Well. I would say thank you for the information, but I suspect you're here for other reasons."

"I'm talking with people he might have run to that night."

Her manner was dismissive. "What makes you think he would run to me?"

"He was very keen on getting out. Changing his name, starting a new life. He was fleeing from something, or someone. You're a powerful woman, as you've said. If anyone could get him out of a bad situation, it would be you."

Her voice came out flat. "I don't take in strays."

"He mentioned that. How did Karl Müller come to work for you, anyway? If you don't mind my saying so, it seems like such an incongruous match."

Zora took a deep, long drag of her cigarette. "He attended one of my pleasure parties. One of my mixed-race ones. He stood out like a sore thumb, poor boy. What he saw widened his eyes." She chuckled. "Men and women everywhere, mostly unclothed, watching and exploring. I believe when he saw one of my boys take a lover on the dining room table, he rushed outside. Curious, I followed him.

"He was smoking a cigarette and shaking, though it wasn't cold out. I said to him, 'Did you like what you saw?' He took his time answering, because we both knew the answer was *Yes*. Then I said, 'Do you want to join in the festivities?' He shook his head. 'Shame, you might enjoy it.' He replied, 'I know other boys who would enjoy it more thoroughly than I.' By the next week, he was advertising for me."

"Who bought him to the party?"

"I have no idea and I never asked him."

"Was he a good employee?"

"He was effective. My patronship went up. He was clever too. I didn't have to explain my color system more than once."

"Color system?"

"Rent parties are in black folks' homes, Mr. Parker. Not everyone is as accommodating of downtowners as I am." She tapped the blue card advertising her upcoming party. "See this? Blue means whites are welcome. Red means blacks only. Green means whites only. Savvy?"

"You seem to think of everything."

She smiled. "I do indeed."

"And Karl didn't come here Sunday night?"

She shook her head. "And even if he had, I wouldn't have taken him in. My lady wouldn't appreciate it."

Zora turned and looked back at Miss Purple and White, who was still sitting at the bar. She was watching them intently. Had she been there staring at them the entire time? Her angry glare at Dash immediately changed to a kittenish smile towards Zora. The change in expression was so drastic, so quick, that Dash felt again the fluttering of anxiety.

Zora said, "She's quite protective of me."

"Some would say jealous."

"That too. I bet you right now she's wondering how she can stick a knife in your back without anyone noticing."

Dash took a deep breath. He doubted Zora spoke in exaggerations. "What's the name of my would-be attacker?"

"Why would you want to know that?"

"Seems polite, under the circumstances."

Zora broke her gaze from Miss Purple and White and laughed.

"My, my, you are funny, Mr. Parker." Another drag of her cigarette. "Sonya," she replied in a cloud of smoke. "Sonya Sanders. Lovely alliteration, don't you think?"

Dash nodded, glancing back at Zora's moll. The kittenish smile was gone and replaced by another hateful scowl.

"I can see why if Karl was running from trouble, he wouldn't be safe with you."

"Indeed not. Although what trouble would he be running from? An innocent like that couldn't have been involved in *too* much."

"Whatever it was, it required a lawyer. He was friends with—or working with, I can't quite tell—a white bull named Prudence Meyers."

"A woman lawyer? Now that just makes her more delicious."

Dash leaned forward. "You know her?"

Zora shook her head. "I don't know her, but I have seen her once or twice here. Luscious cream in a suit. I wouldn't mind adding her to my coffee. She'd often come in with Karl and two other men. The club usually attracts a more male audience, which I find tiresome, but I do love Jimmie's voice. When she walked in, I took immediate notice."

"Did you speak with her at all?"

"A lady never kisses and tells."

Zora was enjoying toying with him. Dash couldn't decipher whether she was lying or simply stringing him along.

Sensing his frustration, she said, "Oh my, someone remains impatient. You want answers so badly, don't you,

Mr. Parker? Perhaps if you grieved for the German boy you wanted but couldn't have, you might find some peace."

He ignored her comment. "Karl mentioned that Prudence Meyers's plan didn't work. Do you have any idea what that was about? Did you ever overhear something about a plan in their conversations?"

Zora clicked her tongue against her teeth. *Tisk, tisk, tisk.* "Eavesdropping is very unbecoming in people of our stature, Mr. Parker. I can say they seemed to speak with great earnestness, almost as if she was trying to convince the little boy to do something."

"Karl?"

"No, the other one."

Dash said the only other name he could think of. "Tyler Smith?"

"That's the one."

So Tyler *had* lied to Dash and Joe after all about not knowing Pru and Karl's other friends. "When was this?"

Zora looked up to the ceiling in thought. "I want to say . . . last Saturday? To be honest, all my days and nights blur together."

Dash was barely able to contain his excitement. "Did you ever see a female impersonator with them? Tall, dark hair. Prefers dresses with fringe and sparkle. Possibly going by the name Miss Avery."

Zora's grin was wicked. "Mr. Parker, you just described nearly every queen in the city. But no. I never saw one with them."

Damn. Still, Dash had established connections between Karl Müller, Tyler Smith, and Prudence Meyers. Were Karl and Tyler working with Pru on her case? Or were they her clients?

"No matter," Dash said. "I intend to ask Tyler Smith later what's really going on."

Zora watched him carefully. "Come again?"

"Mr. Smith. I met him yesterday morning. He claimed he didn't know Pru or any other of Karl's friends, but according to you, he knows them quite well. A few of them at any rate." Dash clapped his hands together. "The little grifter. I can't believe he thought he'd get away with that lie. Isn't it amazing what people think they can get away with?"

Zora's gaze was filled with dark amusement. "Hmm," she purred.

Dash's triumph was short-lived. Something was off. "What is it?"

"Nothing," she replied.

An awkward smile. "It must be something. You seem amused."

Her brows arched. "Among your obvious intelligence and skills, you didn't tell me you were also a spiritualist. I find that particular talent to be so *very* interesting."

"A spiritualist? What do you mean?"

"You *do* know what a spiritualist is, don't you? Someone who communes with the spirit world."

"Yes, I know what they are, but why would you suggest I am one?"

Zora puffed a perfect oval of smoke into the air. "Because, my dear, Tyler Smith is dead and has been since Monday night."

19

Dash stared at her, slow in comprehending.

"Dead?"

Zora relished giving this news. "As the proverbial doornail."

Dash shook his head, trying to comprehend this new bit of news. Dead? "When was this again? When he died, I mean."

"His body was found Monday night, wrapped in a sheet in the alleyway behind the Shelton Hotel. Apparently, the poor man was bludgeoned to death by an ashtray, placed in a laundry cart, and wheeled out back."

The shards of glass and crumbs of ash on the rug I stepped on . . . the red wine stain in the corner . . .

Dash asked, "How do you know this?"

Zora smiled. "I have my sources."

"Wait a moment. Just wait a moment." Dash shook his head, trying to clear his thoughts. "You said Monday night? Are you sure? Because just yesterday morning, Tuesday, I was talking with Tyler Smith in his own hotel room."

"Like I said, you must be a spiritualist."

"This can't be," Dash said, more to himself than to Zora. His eyes stared down at the table, as if the answer could be found on the cheap wooden surface. "He was there. He had pointed a gun at us, and then poured us cocktails. He *spoke* to us. Unless . . ."

He looked up at Zora.

"What does Tyler Smith look like?"

"I thought you met him?"

"I thought so as well, but I may have met an imposter."

"A lot of those running around the city. Tyler Smith is—or was, I should say—on the short side, a little round. Balding, though he wore a ghastly toupee. Vain little man, but very charming. Of course, money does buy a certain level of charm."

Dash stared at the enigmatic woman. "That's not the man I met at all." He then described his "Tyler Smith."

Halfway through his description, Zora nodded. "Ah, you met a friend of Mr. Smith. The other man who came in with Pru, Karl, and Tyler."

"Who?"

She held up a pointer finger and wagged it slowly, chastising Dash's boyish impatience. "How much is it worth to you?"

"I'll pay it."

"So eager, so willing, *so* impatient." She raised her martini glass to her lips and leveled her gaze at Dash. "Be careful what you ask for, downtowner."

A warning.

A sudden, chilling thought occurred to Dash. He had been to the Shelton, asking for Tyler Smith. A dead man. A murder victim. Thank God he and Joe hadn't given their real names. Still, they had appearances worth remembering, especially Dash's face. Why hadn't the front deskman held them there and called the police? Here were two rough-looking men asking after a corpse. And then later, Dash pretended to be said dead man to get those uncollected messages. How had they escaped disaster? Perhaps the front desk staff didn't know. Wouldn't be the first time word-of-mouth didn't reach everyone in an organization. In any event, Dash couldn't risk going back to the hotel again. He and Joe got lucky once with two hotel employees who weren't kept in the know. Odds would not be in their favor a second time.

"Mr. Parker," Zora said, coaxing him back to the present.

He roused himself. "Apologies. Yes, I understand the implications, Miss Mae, but I'm also in a bit of a quandary."

"I should say so. Two dead men in your orbit. You're a dangerous man to know. Tell me, do all of your acquaintances meet a sudden end?"

She took another sip of her martini, swishing the gin around her teeth.

Dash replied, "I could ask you the same question, since we *both* knew them. Makes me wonder if perhaps you were involved."

She laughed as she set the glass back down again. "Why would I strangle that German boy? Or bludgeon the vain Mr. Smith? They were nothing to me."

An idea appeared. "Maybe they threatened your operation. That's why Pru was here. Not to have a drink or listen to music or talk with Karl and Tyler and whomever in private. Maybe it was to meet with you."

The more Dash spoke his thoughts aloud, the more he liked this theory.

"Yes," he said, "Pru was putting together a case against you. I imagine you wouldn't stand for that."

Zora's voice turned cold. "I'd be very careful what you say, ofay. Because I would do anything to keep what I've got. *No one* will take it away, Mr. Parker. *Never.*"

He forced a smile. "Just thinking out loud."

"Perhaps you shouldn't."

Her face was stony.

Dash nodded. "Apologies. Sometimes my mind moves faster than my sense."

He bandied about for a more neutral subject of conversation.

"Let's go back to Tyler's friend. The one I seem to have met yesterday instead of the real Mr. Smith. This man is very important to me."

"Why?"

"Because he is hiding something."

"Aren't we all?"

Zora then watched him for a long, unsettling moment.

"I have money," he said, cautiously.

She laughed. "I don't want your money. I want a favor." Her tongue caressed the last word.

Walk away, said the voice in the back of Dash's mind. He knew he should obey the warning, tell this woman no deal, that he'd find another way to get this information. Yet the blazing blue eyes of Walter Müller burned in his memory. The threats to his safety and to the safety of Joe, Finn, and Atty.

"What is the favor?" he asked.

Zora smiled again. "I'll let you know when I need it granted."

She reached into her bag and pulled out an expensive looking piece of stationery with the letter Z monogrammed at the top. An ink pen followed. She slowly unscrewed the cap and then wrote out an address. Once she was finished, she picked up the paper and gently blew over it to dry the ink. When it was, she folded it and handed it to Dash.

Dash took the paper. "Thank you, Miss Mae."

She kept her grip. Her voice, like her fingers, were iron and steel.

"Remember our agreement. When I call in my favor, you will not refuse."

They held eyes for a moment, then she released the paper. Dash read the elegant cursive. *Paul Avery.* Miss Avery. An address was listed, an apartment on Christopher Street, close to Dash's apartment and club.

He looked up at Zora.

She anticipated his remark. "I told you I didn't know a *Miss* Avery, but I do know about a Mister."

"Is Paul Avery a female impersonator?"

"Does he dress in drag? I don't know."

"Do you think he killed Tyler?"

"Why would he do such a thing?"

"I don't know. He was impersonating a dead man in that dead man's apartment. I may not be a professional detective but even I think that's significant. Don't you agree?"

Zora was no longer interested in pursuing possibilities with him. She asked, her voice now bored, "Where can I reach you to reclaim my favor?"

"The Cherry Lane Playhouse. I live above it."

"Bohemia! Decadence disguised as art. I do love it so."

The band started up again. Zora turned away from him and watched the singer, a placid smile on her face. She hadn't said so, but Dash had been dismissed.

He stood up from the table, folding the piece of paper and placing it in his inside jacket pocket.

"Don't forget my rent party card," Zora said, keeping

her eyes on the band. "I think you should come and see what the 'Baroness of Business' is all about."

Dash reached down and slid the blue card into his pocket. Some survival instinct told him he was being watched and he looked up. Sonya Sanders, Zora's moll, was glaring at him again, but this time, her face smoldered with pure hate.

She thinks Zora gave me a telephone number.

He wanted to cross the room, sit down at the bar, and correct her. Yet he didn't believe she'd listen to reason. Reason was beyond her. She was all emotion, all Id. All crazy.

Suppressing a shiver, Dash left the club with the name of a possible murderer in his pocket—and a possible murderess watching him leave.

Thursday morning found Dash watching the light slowly illuminate the cramped bedroom. He hadn't been able to sleep at all. Two men, former lovers, murdered at almost the exact same time. Perhaps even the same night.

Who could've killed them? Walter?

It wasn't outside the range of possibility, given his rage at the queer sex. Dash could easily picture Walter pushing his way into Tyler's apartment and seeing Karl there. Enraged, he strikes Tyler on the head with the ashtray, chases his brother into another room, and strangles him to death.

But why move the bodies to two different places? An alleyway for one, Central Park for another seemed such an odd choice for a murderer to make. Not to mention the Park was a trek from the Shelton. Even in the dead of night, Walter would've been seen by someone.

Maybe they were killed in separate places?

That seemed more likely.

But if Walter had killed Tyler Smith, then why send Dash and Joe to visit him? That part didn't add up. Unless Walter had struck him down in not only a moral rage but a drunken one. Monday night, when Tyler's body was found, he was a slurring and cursing mess in front of Hartford & Sons before he blackmailed Dash and his friends. Perhaps he killed Tyler Smith and quite simply didn't remember it. An ashtray as a weapon seemed to Dash to be a spontaneous choice, something selected during an alcohol-induced argument.

Dash could figure Walter for Tyler. But what about Karl? If Walter was responsible for his brother's death, why the obsession with Miss Avery? Walter had said it was Karl who had something Miss Avery needed, but what if he lied? What if it was the other way around, that Miss Avery had something that Karl or, closer to the truth, *Walter* needed?

And what, if at all, did the murders of Tyler Smith and Karl Müller have to do with Prudence Meyers and her case?

Dash sighed. Zora Mae inspired more questions instead of providing more answers. And tonight, he had to go back to Walter's apartment and give that horrible man information he frankly didn't have.

Joe was still snoring on the cot, having lost the coin toss and having drunk too much whiskey to fight over the bed.

How unfortunate, Dash thought. When Joe was conscious again, he'd tell him about Paul Avery and what happened to the real Tyler Smith.

Frustrated, he got himself ready for the day, dressing in a three-button dark navy pinstripe suit with white shirt and turquoise tie. Starving, he briskly walked to West Fourth and opened the door to the Greenwich Village Inn, immediately regretting it.

The bloated globe of Cullen McElroy stood at the bar, waiting for Emmett to pay him his "donation."

Dash cursed under his breath. Monday was his bribery day; Thursday was Emmett's. Usually McElroy stopped by earlier, but he was apparently running late today.

The odious man turned and smiled, his teeth a nauseating quilt of gray and yellow. "Ah, Mr. Parker. Fancy seeing you here."

Other than Emmett and McElroy, the only other witnesses to police corruption were the three Ex-Pat Wall Street traders. They sat in the back corners, trying to blend in with the shadows.

Dash took a deep breath. "Mr. McElroy—excuse me —*Officer* McElroy."

McElroy chuckled. "You're learning. That's good, Mr. Parker."

He flashed a look towards Emmett, who had his back turned and was counting out money from the cash register. Even from the back, he looked pouty and sullen. Not that Dash could blame him.

"Perhaps you can teach grandpa here how to show the proper respect."

Emmett replied, "I was taught respect was earned."

He turned around and re-counted the bills on the wood bar.

McElroy's eyes shifted from Dash to Emmett. "I haven't shut you down, have I? For your politically radical clientele. I think that's earning not just respect but gratitude."

He held out his fat hand.

Emmett left the bills on the bar.

The two stared at one another, both not willing to budge. A queasiness sickened Dash's stomach. While Emmett's insubordination was admirable, it could lead to violence or arrest or both. Whether they liked it or not, the police had the upper hand.

McElroy considered his response and opted for the easy way out. He smirked as he slid the money from the bar into his meaty hand. He pointed a stubby finger at the white-haired man.

"One of these days, grandpa, I'm gonna lose my temper. And I won't be responsible for my actions."

Emmett's snowy brow remained fixed in a frown. "I've lived through worse than you."

Another chuckle. "So you say, grandpa, so you say." He glanced at Dash. "See you next week, Mr. Parker." He nodded to The Ex-Pats sitting in the back corners. "Good afternoon, mutes."

All eyes were on the officer until he strolled out of the Inn.

"Jesus," hissed Emmett.

Dash looked at him. "You can't antagonize him like that, Emmett. He could really hurt you. At the very least, he can put you out of business."

Emmett waved him off, irritated. "I can't stand having to suck up to him. Who does he think he is?"

"The law, unfortunately."

"About time we changed that. The usual?"

Dash nodded as he pulled out a barstool and settled himself at the bar.

While Emmett set about making his sandwich, he said, "Emmett? You read the news every day, right?"

A raspy voice from behind Dash replied, "Multiple times a day."

A higher tenor voice added, "Multiple papers a day."

A granite bass voice finished the triad chord with, "Got a memory like a steel trap about every story too."

Dash turned around to see The Ex-Pats staring at him. "They speak," he said.

Emmett asked, "Why do you ask?"

Dash swung back around to face the bar. "Do you remember a few days ago, let's say Monday or Tuesday, reading a story about a body found behind the Shelton Hotel?"

Dash wanted to make sure Zora Mae wasn't playing with him about Tyler Smith. And Emmett's memory of news stories, as the bass voice attested, was usually faultless.

Emmett squinted as he thought. Then he nodded. "Yep. One of the tenants. Big scandal they tried to bury on page twenty. Nobody wants to check into a hotel to be murdered."

How could the concierge have not known about the story? If one's business was in the news for something awful like murder, wouldn't everyone you work with be a-buzz?

"It does ruin one's plans," Dash said. "When did the story hit the papers?"

"First story hit the papers Tuesday, the morning editions, though the body hadn't been identified. He was found by the trash cans in the back alley Monday night. No papers or anything like that on him. The papers didn't list his name until the Wednesday evening editions."

Emmett poured coffee into a mug and passed it over to Dash.

"That's why the concierge didn't know," Dash muttered to himself.

The name wasn't announced until the day after he and Joe visited the Shelton.

He took a sip of coffee and asked Emmett, "How did they find out who he was?"

"They took a photograph of his corpse and sent it around to the buildings in the area, the hotel included. The night staff identified him. Apparently, he was a night owl, and the day staff never saw him before."

"Did they say anything else about him?"

"Yeah. The fella was a high roller. Paid in cash for his room. Kept to himself largely, which hinders the police finding suspects—or at least finding innocent people to blame. Why do you ask?"

Dash shook his head. "Too long of a story. When I have more time, I'll tell it to you." Another sip of coffee. "Did the papers mention anything about what he did?"

Emmett shrugged. "All they said was bachelor, rich with family money, though they're estranged, and a New York native. Front desk said he spent nearly every night out, usually came back half-seas over. He was harmless and he was rich, so they looked the other way."

"Anything else?"

"Yeah. One strange bit: He was leaving the Shelton for good. Gave his notice. He'd be moving out the end of this month. The staff said they were sad to see him go."

Dash perked up at that. One of the many messages Tyler Smith hadn't picked up was a travel agency confirming his tickets across the Atlantic. Two tickets. Dash once again wondered who was going with Tyler.

He asked, "What was the reason for leaving?"

"Didn't say. Decision was sudden though, according to the staff." Emmett leaned on the bar, his weathered eyes flashing with cunning. "I bet he was running away, but somebody didn't want him to leave."

"You should work for the NYPD, Emmett."

The old man smiled. "I can't. I actually have a conscience."

After he finished eating, Dash left the Inn to open Hartford & Sons for the day. Standing there waiting for him was Prudence Meyers. She had donned a brown suit, her jacket open to expose a vest and white shirt with a high collar, topped with a bow tie. The gold link of a chained pocket watch scooped from the lower part of the vest to an interior pocket. A dark brown bowler perched on her head.

She smiled as he approached. "Mr. Parker."

"Miss Meyers. What brings you here? A suit, perhaps?"

She shook her head. "Can we talk?"

20

Inside the shop, the air was thick and musty, yet still degrees cooler than being on the street. Dash left the CLOSED sign in the windowsill to keep the two of them from being interrupted. He took off his jacket and laid it across the writing desk. Next was his usual routine of opening the windows. Pru took off her hat and did a short walkabout, taking in all the decorations and accoutrements of the tailor shop.

"This is cozy," she said once she finished her visual inspection. "One would never know a most exquisite speak is in the back."

"I wouldn't call our place exquisite."

"Come, come now. Don't be so modest. Your band is entirely unique for the Village."

Dash was suddenly wary. "What brings you down here, Miss Meyers? I pictured you as more of an uptown girl."

Pru went to inspect the hats on top of the wardrobe. "I'm an all-town girl, if I do say so myself." She selected a fedora and examined it. "I'm here to first apologize. Normally I don't turn away clients, but extenuating circumstances being what they are . . ."

"And what *are* those circumstances?"—Dash held up a hand—"I know, privileged. Alright, let me fill in some of the blanks and you tell me if they're the right answers. You've been seen around town with Karl Müller, Tyler Smith, and a man named Paul Avery, who may or may not go as Miss Avery when the sun goes down."

She went perfectly still. "Where did you get those names?"

"I've been keeping myself busy, Miss Meyers."

"I see. And we were seen by whom?"

"A woman named Zora Mae. Up in Harlem. The 'Baroness of Business'? I said yesterday I was going to see her, and the conversation proved to be quite interesting. It seems the four of you would go up to the Hot Cha and have earnest conversations. Miss Mae noticed you in particular were trying to get this Tyler Smith to do something for you. I don't know what, and she didn't say. Now Tyler Smith has been murdered, assailant unknown . . ."

Dash paused to see if, unlike with Karl, Pru had heard *that* bit of news.

She nodded once, sadness dulling her normally vibrant self. "Yes, a great tragedy."

Dash nodded as well. "And this Paul Avery fellow was impersonating him as of this past Tuesday morning."

She turned around, her brow furrowed. "Excuse me. Impersonating?"

"As in, he introduced himself to me as Tyler Smith. *In Tyler Smith's hotel room.* Tried to pretend he didn't know you, Karl, or Zora Mae, which—let's save the denials, shall we?—we both know are lies. So. Here's Mr., or perhaps Miss, Avery, pretending to be a murdered man, aiming a gun at me and my bartender."

"He had a gun?" This alarmed her.

"Oh yes. No idea how to use it, which made it all the more terrifying." Dash placed his hands on the writing desk and leaned forward. "When I came to visit you, did you know Tyler Smith was dead?"

She looked down at the floor. "Yes," she said, her voice small.

"Did Paul Avery kill Tyler Smith, Miss Meyers?"

She looked at him, her lavender eyes clear. "No, and it's Pru, remember?"

"Then why would he be in Tyler's apartment?"

"I don't know!" The surge in volume surprised them both. Her eyes cast downward to the fedora in her hands. "I honestly don't know about any of that. It's news to me." She looked up, her voice decisive. "But Paul Avery did not murder Tyler Smith."

"How can you be so sure?"

"Because we are working towards the same goal."

"Which is what?"

They both replied in unison, "That's privileged."

"Right," Dash said. He let go of the desk, straightened his posture, and crossed his arms over his chest. "Pru. Help me. Please. I'm in the same boat as you."

"Not quite. You don't know what sea you're in whereas I am the captain." She returned the fedora to its perch on top of the wardrobe. "Of a sinking ship, apparently."

Ships. "Who was planning to travel with Tyler to Paris?"

"How do you know about Tyler's travel plans?"

He reminded her about the uncollected messages at the Shelton's front desk. "Was Paul Avery going with him?"

The corners of her lips twitched slightly. "Not hardly."

"Who is this Paul Avery? Is he another attorney?"

"Absolutely not."

"A detective? A client?"

She walked towards Dash, her hands pressed together as if she were praying, the fingertips lightly touching her mouth. She chose her next words carefully.

"I can't tell you what we are trying to do. Too much is at stake, and too many people are already in danger. I know I have no reason to ask this, especially given your circumstance, but this is the second thing I wanted to tell you: please leave us alone. We are so close to accomplishing something important, something vital for people's freedom. We just need more time. I know it's frustrating to wait, but I promise you; it will be worth it in the end."

Time. Waiting. Suddenly Finn's words came flooding back to Dash. *He was always checking his wristwatch and the door—back and forth, back and forth—like watching Helen Wills on the court.*

Dash kept his eyes on Pru's face. "Who was Karl waiting for?"

The question caught her off guard. A wrinkled line creased her forehead. "What do you mean?"

"My waiter saw him checking his wristwatch and checking the door, as if he were waiting for somebody. Seemed nervous, too. Who was it?" He didn't wait for an answer. "It was Tyler, wasn't it?"

A quick blink of the eye gave Pru away.

"What was he bringing to you?"

Pru tried to evade his question. "What makes you think that?"

"Karl's demeanor. He wasn't anxious being in a queer club. I saw him in the Oyster House, and he looked right at home. Sure, some things made him blush, but there was a sense of childlike wonder seeing men and women being themselves. And if he was handing out rent party cards for the Baroness, then he certainly attended his fair share of 'degenerate' spaces. No, something else had to make him nervous—afraid, really—and that could be the safety of the man he loved."

Dash arched an eyebrow.

"How am I doing so far?"

Pru's lavender eyes flashed. "A strong volley. Any guesses on what he was allegedly bringing us?"

Dash shrugged. "Evidence. For your case, though what kind of evidence for what kind of case, I don't know yet." He tapped his chin. "Walter said Karl had something this Miss Avery wanted. This makes me think there was a trade somewhere, or there was supposed to be, but it got interrupted. Either way, it's something Walter desperately wants back."

"I thought you said it was Tyler who had the evidence?"

"It's possible the trade was from Tyler to Karl."

"Then why Karl's anxiety? Why the fear?"

Good questions.

"I don't know," Dash said. "Perhaps because Tyler wasn't there at my club, and he was worried Walter had done something."

"He very well could have," Pru replied. "From what I can tell, both Karl and Tyler were killed around the same time."

Dash nodded, having come to the same conclusion himself.

"Pru," Dash said, "Walter is out for blood. I have to give him a report tonight, and I have nothing of real value to give him. Sooner or later, he will make me tell him what I know. Whether I want to or not. And I . . ."

He glanced around the shop, trying to ignore the swells of panic rising in his chest.

". . . I don't want you or anyone else hurt."

She reached into her jacket and pulled out a pistol in a brilliant blue finish.

Dash raised his hands. "What is that?"

Pru admired the pistol in her hand. "A Remington Model 51 .32 caliber. It's an automatic. First manufactured in 1918 but overshadowed by the Colts and Russian models. I never preferred them much. Remington is my man."

"And what do you intend to do with that?"

"Defend myself against Walter Müller, of course. Don't worry about me or Mr. Avery. We can handle the likes of him."

She returned the blue pistol to her inside jacket, where Dash caught the flash of a holster.

"Do what you need to do, Mr. Parker. I'm not afraid." She headed for the tailor shop's front door. "If anything, Walter Müller should be far more afraid of me."

"Do you have it, Pru?"

Dash stopped her at the door with his question.

"The evidence? Was Tyler Smith successful?"

She gave him a long look, then said, "Goodbye, Mr. Parker."

At closing time, Dash returned to the apartment. Joe had roused himself and wanted to know where they stood with this "bloody Müller Problem." His brow darkened during Dash's recount of Zora Mae, the murder of Tyler Smith, and the visit of Pru.

"Damn this Pru for not helpin' us. And damn that little

minx Paul Avery, too. Thought he could outsmart us by pretending to be somebody else."

"That Paul Avery very nearly did."

A voice from below shouted "Where the hell is Florence's dress? Anyone? Someone better answer me!"

Joe ran a hand through his tangled red hair. "Any idea why he'd pretend to be his dead friend?"

Dash shook his head. "None."

"Is he the impersonator Walter's been lookin' fer?"

"I think so."

Those emerald eyes stared into Dash's. "Do ya think he killed the lad?"

Dash remembered the gun in the man's hand. "It's possible. But then why be in Tyler's hotel room? It's one definite way to be caught."

Joe dropped his gaze. "Maybe that's why he killed him. Mr. Smith looked like he had a lotta sugar."

Dash followed Joe's train of thought. "Take on a new life. With a brand-new bank account. Finn told us how hard it is to get into the Shelton."

He paused.

From below, the beleaguered stage manager yelled, "This is why no one should touch the costume rack! Goddammit, we have two hours to curtain and *no* dress for Florence!"

Dash said, "Mr. Smith must not have had many close friends or relatives for Mr. Avery to pull off the deception."

"Aye, but there was at least one person who knew him well, lassie. Karl." Joe looked up at Dash. "Think we might turn over a man like that to a man like Walter Müller?"

I don't know. I'm not sure what Walter would do to him, given his hatred over his father's secret.

The voice from downstairs shouted, "Jack, where the hell is Florence? Did she take the damned thing home?"

Dash said, "First we need to know what his role is in all this. And then we need to make sure. I won't send another innocent into danger."

He found his gray homburg and perched it atop his head.

"What say you, Joe? Shall we pay Mr., or perhaps Miss, Avery a visit?"

Paul Avery lived in a three-story bright red brick building on the corner of Waverly and Christopher Street, almost around the corner from Hartford & Sons and Pinstripes. Dash and Joe walked up to the stoop and scanned the names written in the small metal box, finding Mr. Avery's name next to APARTMENT 2 A. No other name was listed.

"Wonder what he does for a living that he can live by himself," Joe said.

"It's not tending bar, that's for certain."

They rang the buzzer for apartment 2A, but there was no answer. They rang once more for good measure.

"He's not here," Joe said. "What now, lassie?"

Before Dash could respond, an old woman with a sack of groceries came walking up toward them.

Dash intercepted her, saying, "Excuse me, ma'am, we're looking for Mr. Paul Avery. Does he live here?"

Seeing her up close, Dash noticed rheumy eyes damaged by time.

"He does," she said, her voice trembling. "Though I haven't seen him today. Then again, I don't see most of anything these days. Can barely see you." She turned her gaze onto Joe. "Or you, though I can tell you're tall. Forgive my appearance, I'm just getting over a cold. Don't you find summer colds to be the most irksome things?"

Joe smiled. "You look marvelous, my dear."

She chuckled. "Your flattery is insincere but appreciated, nonetheless. May I tell him who was coming to call?"

Dash said the first name which came to mind. "Tyler Smith. Do you know when he'll return?"

"Mr. Smith! So good to see you again! I don't know if you remember me. I'm the landlady, Marjorie Norton. Spinster," she added with a wink. She extended her hand.

The news of Tyler's death had apparently not yet reached the Village.

Dash gently clasped her fingers, giving a warning look to Joe not to expose his deception. "Nice to see you again, Miss Norton."

"Please, call me Marjorie."

Joe said, "You own the building?"

Her chin lifted with pride. "I do. My husband left it to me after he died. There were no other men around in the family to take it from me, so it's all mine. I'm what they call a 'working girl' now and I'm having the time of my life. Isn't it wonderful that women are able to do so much more now than we did when I was a girl?" She pivoted back to Paul Avery. "Mr. Avery isn't in, dear, so you can drop off Mrs. Avery's keys."

Dash furrowed his brow. "I'm sorry, did you say *keys*?"

Joe couldn't help himself. "Did you say *Mr. and Mrs. Avery*?"

Marjorie's rheumy eyes slid from Dash to Joe and back again. Her eyebrow arched with amusement. "Why, yes! Mr. and Mrs. Paul Avery have been tenants for years. Then again, you'd know that, wouldn't you, Mr. Smith," she added with a wink.

Dash's words came out in a stutter. "W-w-why would I know all about that?"

Joe talked over him. "Have you seen this wife of his?"

Marjorie looked at Dash. "I can see you haven't told your friend everything. Discretion is a dwindling virtue in these modern days. Yes, I have, young lad. She's a gorgeous-looking woman. I'd see her sometimes while she goes out at night or sits on the fire escape smoking her ciggies, I believe the kids call them now."

"And you've spoken with her?"

"Oh yes, on several occasions. Very nice. She seems well suited to our Paul. I hardly ever hear them argue. As you know, Mr. Smith, my walls are quite thin. I hear all my tenants in the building, whether they know it or not."

A low laugh followed. Dash could only imagine what secrets she'd amassed over the years.

"Yes, they are quite lovely. They always say 'goodnight Marjorie!' when they go out for an evening together. Sometimes I see him propping her up when they come home after a night on the town." More chuckles. "Mrs. Avery sure knows how to have a good time."

Paul Avery had a wife—making him less likely to be Walter's female impersonator—but what about this keys business?

"Marjorie," Dash said, "tell me about Mrs. Avery's keys."

"She left them at your place, didn't she? Oh my, what was it, a few nights ago—"

Dash took a chance. "Sunday?"

"Yes, Sunday. Very late in the evening. She comes running up while I'm out getting some fresh air. The heat has been something fierce and I couldn't go to sleep, so I came out here to cool off. And here she comes up the walk, all breathless and shaken. I said, 'Careful you don't trip and break your ankle in those shoes, dear.' And that's when she said she needed me to let her in. She'd forgotten her keys at a friend's place."

Marjorie looked expectedly at Dash.

"Isn't that why you're here, young man? To return her keys? I assume the friend was you."

Sunday?

Dash's heart went pitty-pat. Another clue.

"I . . ." He shook his head, trying to clear his thoughts. "Why would you assume she was with me that night?"

Her grin was shrewd. "I told you I had thin walls, didn't I? I heard you talking with Mrs. Avery. She said your name quite clearly and you replied back. You both have spent a bit of time in the apartment while Paul was away." She lowered her voice to conspiratorial levels. "I won't breathe a word. You can count on my discretion."

"How do you mean?"

"Mrs. Avery has her life and Mr. Avery has his. Why, he's been hanging around that masculine woman for weeks now. I'm surprised Mrs. Avery hasn't mentioned her to you. Let me see, what is her name . . . ?"

Joe said, "Pru?"

"That's her! Striking woman, even if she flaunts natural convention wearing men's clothes."

Dash said, "Do you ever overhear what Mr. Avery and Pru talked to about?"

Marjorie lightly smacked his hand. "Now, now. If I promise *you* discretion, I must keep my word about *his*. Anyway, go on up there and return the keys."

She unlocked the door and let them in to the small,

cramped foyer. Wood floors, brick walls, wood stairs. The air was musty and smelled of mothballs and sour milk. A baby cried somewhere above them. Dash nodded to Marjorie and led the upwards with Joe at his heels. Marjorie stayed in the foyer.

"I thought you said this Paul fellow was our girl?" whispered Joe, as they climbed the creaking, groaning stairs. "What does this mean, lassie?"

"I honestly have no clue," Dash whispered back.

"Tyler and Mrs. Avery. Mr. Avery and Pru." Joe shook his head. "I can't make heads or tails of this."

They reached the second floor and made their way to apartment 2A. Conversations murmured behind neighboring doors, complemented by the rattle of pots and pans and the pungent aroma of sausages and onions. Apartment 2A was at the end of the hallway, towards the front of the building.

Joe's brow furrowed even deeper into the folds of his red skin. "What do we do if she answers?"

"First, we say hello and introduce ourselves."

Joe rolled his eyes as Dash knocked on the door.

Marjorie called up from below. "She's out! They both work and they usually don't come back until late. Just slide the keys under the door."

Dash and Joe looked at each other and shrugged. They waited a few seconds and then returned to the foyer where the landlady was waiting.

Dash tipped his hat. "Thank you, Marjorie. We appreciate it."

She smiled benevolently. "You are quite welcome. Tell her next time to tie her keys to a string and tie that string to her wrist."

"I will."

Dash and Joe waited until they were a block away, well out of earshot of Marjorie Norton.

Joe remarked, "The *hearing* that lady has!"

"I'd pay millions to know what she overheard from Paul and Pru. You know they talked about this case."

"If they were talking about a case at all."

"You believe Marjorie?"

"Hell, lassie, this decade, why shouldn't a masculine woman and a feminine man get together?"

"Why not, indeed."

They reached the next cross section of streets and were drowned in the sea of noise of the evening rush hour. The rattle of motors, the squeal of changing gears, the impatient blasts of horns. The clanging bell of trolleys and the shouts of cabbies as they zigzagged about.

Joe yelled, "What do we do now?"

Dash put his hands on his hips. "Damned if I know."

21

Despite Joe's objections, Dash returned alone to 86th Street to give his update, such as it was, to Walter Müller. Joe wanted to accompany Dash, to make sure he was safe against this "blackmailin' bloody bluenose," but Dash assured him he'd be jake.

"As long as he thinks he's getting closer to the female impersonator and to Pru," Dash said, "he'll keep us around."

Joe was skeptical. "I don't know about that, lassie. We're in over our head."

He wasn't wrong, but Dash couldn't afford to have a night without a bartender. They might need to buy their way out of this trouble, and if that was the case, they needed all the sugar they could get.

Dash soon found himself in an IRT car rattling east-bound, then northbound until 86th Street. The wind had picked up, a hot exhale blowing down the streets. He knew in his heart of hearts he couldn't turn in Paul Avery to Walter. At least not yet. Not until he had proof of something dastardly or murderous. And he couldn't in good conscience give up Prudence Meyers and her law firm. Yet he also couldn't give Walter nothing again.

Perhaps this meeting didn't have to be about them. Perhaps Walter needed to know Tyler Smith was dead. Dash was interested in the man's reaction. Would it be indifference? Surprise? Worry?

Dash found the nondescript building on 86th Street near Avenue A. He walked up the stoop, took a deep breath, and rang the buzzer. He had to buzz twice before he heard commotion above in the form of a door being opened and shut, followed by heavy, angry feet on the stairs.

Walter soon appeared on the landing dressed impeccably in a gray suit, which was in stark contrast to the purple bruising of his face, now turning blueish black. As if the man couldn't look more like a nightmare.

Dash put on his best smile. "Good evening, Mr. Müller."

Walter raised his hand. Dash winced, waiting for a blow. Instead, Walter was checking his wristwatch.

"You are late, Mr. Parker. "

"I apologize. The IRT is not the bastion of efficiency. I have something to report about your, uh, inquiry."

"Let's have it then."

Before Dash could respond, a voice called from the top of the stairwell. "Walter! Who is there?"

Mother.

Walter took a deep breath and ignored her. "Tell me, Mr. Parker, where you've found this pansy."

"Walter! Answer me!"

A door on the ground floor opened up, and a pugnacious, overweight man stuck his head out into the hall.

"What the hell do you think you're doing?" he said. "You can't conduct business in the hall!"

Walter turned and said to the neighbor, "Mind your own business."

"Hey, pal, you made it my business by yakking it up so that the whole fuckin' building can hear."

Mother's voice called again. "Walter?"

The neighbor pointed upstairs. "And tell that bitch to shut the hell up. Now go upstairs or I'm calling the cops."

Walter was about to reply when his mother called for him again.

The neighbor crossed his arms over his chest. "Now, pal. Do it *now*."

Walter blew out a frustrated sigh. He gestured roughly to Dash. "Come upstairs."

Dash hesitated, the threat of danger weighing his feet down like cement.

The neighbor in the ground floor apartment looked at Dash. "What are ya waiting for? Go the fuck upstairs!"

Dash nodded and stepped into the building. Walter closed the front door behind him with a slam, causing Dash to jump. Walter gave a withering glare to the neighbor, who ignored it completely, and proceeded up the stairs at a fast clip. Dash followed, his feet struggling to keep up.

At the top of the staircase stood Mother, looking fragile and pale in a lilac robe. Her hands shook as she tried to keep the robe closed against her chest. The signs of grief. It hadn't been more than three days since she learned of her youngest son's death.

Walter was obviously playing the caregiver. "Mother, go back inside," he said at the top of the staircase landing. His voice was surprisingly gentle.

Mother's eyes, glassy and big, looked at Dash instead. "Who are you?"

Dash replied, "I work with your son, remember? At the

Committee of Fourteen? A colleague of mine and I were here earlier this week."

"Oh," she said, "I remember now."

Walter took his mother by the shoulders and guided her back to their apartment. Dash followed, wondering if Mother registered the fact both he and Walter had bruised faces. Had she assumed they'd fought each other? Did Walter have a history of violence?

I sincerely hope not.

The apartment was cramped and unbearably hot. The front square-shaped room Dash walked into was decorated with severe German furniture made from heavy, dark wood. A Black Forest hunting cabinet hugged one wall; a high-backed sofa bracketed by end tables hugged the other. In the center was a round oak table with a square base. On top were a few books, their titles faded and unreadable in the dim light.

Mother said, "I'll go make some tea."

Walter replied, "There is no need. My colleague here will give a report and then be gone."

"Why is it so late? Why are people visiting you at all hours?"

Dash said, "It is an emergency, madame."

"What emergency could there possibly be?"

Walter answered that one. "A club, Mother. A club that must not be allowed to stay open for longer."

Mother rubbed the side of her head. "What could be going in that club? Oh Walter, you don't think it was like when Karl was—"

Whatever gentleness Walter showed quickly fell away. His voice was sharp, his words short. "Mother. That is none of this man's business."

She nodded. "It's just the similarities. The late night visit. The urgent news."

Dash looked upon her with interest. Was she talking about a night when Karl was arrested? Visit enough speaks, in particular their kind of speaks, and the odds of ending up in the paddy wagon rose exponentially higher.

Walter softened his tone. "Go back to sleep, Mother. I will handle this news."

Mother nodded again. "Perhaps I'll do more of my knitting." She shuffled her way down a narrow hallway to the right of the front room. At the far end was a half-opened door. Her bedroom, Dash supposed.

"Mr. Parker."

Dash turned and faced Walter, who was now sitting on the sofa. The end tables on either side held family photographs. The sight of an even younger Karl caused a moment of melancholy for Dash.

I tried to save him, I tried to . . .

Walter looked at him expectedly. "Well?"

"I'm having trouble finding the woman lawyer, but I have a few leads."

There was something odd about those family photographs. Dash looked past the image of Karl.

"And the pansy?"

There were just three figures in the frame: Karl, Walter, and Mother. Dash looked to another framed photograph of the family. The same three. And those frames which held single portraits only showcased either Karl or Walter, occasionally Mother. Where was the father?

"Still no sign of her," Dash replied. "It will be difficult to find her, given that she may have heard what happened to Karl and is hiding in plain sight. In men's clothes."

Dash raised a finger before Walter could voice his displeasure.

"One item of interest regarding Tyler Smith, Karl's friend at the Shelton."

"Yes, yes, the one you *claimed* you didn't find."

Looking back at the family photographs, Dash noticed the shape of the pictures didn't fit the frames. They were too small. The pictures had been cut. Dash could make out the clean edge where scissors excised a figure out of the family. The father. A chill set in to Dash's chest.

He cleared his throat. "There's a reason we couldn't find him. He's dead."

Walter blinked. "Dead?"

"Murdered. Bludgeoned to death with an ashtray." Dash gathered all his strength and bravery and gave what he hoped was an intimidating look. "Did you kill him, Walter?"

The man sat still for a moment, then laughed. It was a harsh, cruel sound.

"Why would I murder him?" Walter asked.

"Because your brother ran to him whenever your mother would kick him out for refusing to stop his way of life. Being the good dutiful brother, when you didn't find him at my club, you went to his usual rescue place. Perhaps this Tyler Smith wouldn't let you see him."

"And I what?" Walter said, his voice mocking. "Hit him over the head with an ashtray in a rage? Seems a bit trite, Mr. Parker."

"Not for someone who hates the queer sex as much as this household does." Dash pointed to the framed family photographs. "I see Father Müller's been effectively erased from the family. Will you do the same to Karl now that he's gone too?"

Walter took a few deep breaths, getting his anger under

control. "The next time we meet, you will give me their names and addresses. No excuses. Or there will be consequences you cannot fathom. Understood?"

This was no idle threat. This was a promise.

Dash replied, "Understood."

Walter gave Dash until next Tuesday, August 24. It wasn't much time—only five days—but it was more than what he'd given them previous. Back at the Greenwich Village Inn for dinner, much to his dismay, Dash discovered an argument was underway.

"This is America, and we should only support Americans," a male voice said among jeers of protest. "Why give money that's just gonna go to the Vatican in those collection plates? No offense to you Catholics, but where do you think your money goes? It ain't to your parish, that's for sure. And thank God Harding knew that, and Coolidge ain't futzing it up. You radicals would have us corrupted from the inside out."

A deep, female voice said, "Sir, this is a nation of immigrants."

"And look how well that's turnin' out for us. Violence in the streets. Neighborhoods being taken over. Jobs gettin' harder to find. I swear, I walk down these streets, in New York, one of the first cities of America, and I hear everything *but* English. Enough, is what I say. We did our part in the war, thank you very much, now Europe can keep their scum and deal with their own problems."

A cacophony of voices raised in protest followed while Dash searched for a seat in the crowd.

When the voices quieted down, the dissenter said,

"Hey! Nothing wrong with asking people in our country to behave like they should."

A male voice with a thick Irish brogue said, "And how, exactly, should they behave?"

"Speak English. Cut their hair. Have protestant names. And renounce their Pope."

"Ya bloody super patriot!"

Dash expected a brawl to break out. Instead, everyone just yelled, which was equally pointless. He continued his search for an open seat. His eyes spied the Wall Street Ex-Pats in the darkened corners. True to form, they didn't speak a word.

Do they ever go home? Dash wondered.

A man paid his tab and left the bar. Dash rushed over and claimed the seat as Emmett was pocketing the change the man left behind.

Emmett looked up when Dash sat down. "Can you believe this shit?"

"These are political times, Emmett."

"If he don't quit it, I'll have to toss him. He'll start a goddamn riot in here."

As if on cue, the Super Patriot raised his voice. "As much fun as it is to debate with you fine gentlemen and ladies, I best be going."

Encouragement followed.

"Get outta here, ya ignorant arse!"

"Why don't ya go and continue licking Coolidge's boots, ya mindless fuck!"

"Ya was an immigrant too once upon a time, you hypocrite!"

A man of about forty, grinning from ear to ear, dressed in a fine tuxedo and donning a black fedora passed by the bar.

Money, thought Dash. It was amazing how the surplus of dollars—or lack thereof—drove the majority of political opinion these days.

Emmett shook his head in disgust. "You need a drink? 'Cause I sure as hell do."

"Yes, *please.*"

Dash watched as Emmett set about making two Gin Rickeys. He poured them into teacups and passed one to Dash, keeping the other for himself. They both raised their cups in a toast and sipped.

The front door groaned open, causing both of them to turn warily towards it. A matronly woman in a shapeless pale pink dress and purple cloche cap tottered in, her shoes clunking against the floorboards. Her gait was unsteady and uncertain. Was she drunk?

She stumbled towards the bar.

"Evening, miss," Emmett called to her. "What can I get you?"

The woman replied, "A night of Rudy Valentino with a side of sailor."

Emmett seemed perplexed by the response.

Dash recognized it. And the voice. "Hello, Finn."

His friend removed the cloche hat and the gray wig. "Tah-dah!"

Emmett jumped, spilling some of his Rickey on his hand. "Jesus Christ!" His snowy brow jumped halfway up his forehead.

Dash said, "Emmett, meet my roommate, Finn Francis."

Emmett's mouth stayed gaped open, a reaction which caused Finn to laugh merrily. He tossed the gray wig onto the bar and looked down at himself.

"What do you think?"

The pink and purple worked wonders with the circles

of rouge on his cheeks, one of which sported the black dot of a mole, and the dark, blood-red paint on his lips. Thin black lines traced his eyes and green and gold brush strokes rose upwards from his eyelids to his eyebrows. The dress, while shapeless, was very modern, as was the matching bag that hung from his right shoulder.

Dash remembered the missing costume from this afternoon and pointed to it. "That wouldn't be Florence's dress, would it?"

"Who?"

Dash shook his head. "You want dinner?"

"Yes, please. I'm absolutely starved."

Dash held up two fingers. "Same order, Emmett?"

The older gentleman kept his eyes on Finn, nodding absentmindedly. "Coming right up." One more moment staring at Finn, then he turned towards the kitchen.

Finn pulled out a barstool and collapsed onto it. "Dear goddesses, this costume, though clever, is a total terror to wear." He reached down and undid the straps on the shoes. "My poor ankles are just about through."

"Where did he go this time?"

"Slight variations on the same theme." He began to take off his fake eyelashes one by one. "Just like yesterday, he saw *The Big Parade* at the Astor Theatre on Broadway at 45th, followed by an encore showing of *Ben Hur* on Broadway at 47th. I went inside with him this time. The galley fight and the chariot race were *most* thrilling, and the New Testament scenes were in color."

Finn looked over at Dash.

"I expect to be reimbursed for it."

He placed the eyelashes onto the bar and set about wiping his brow, which was beaded with sweat from the heat of the wig.

"A quick lunch at another café, then another movie at the German theatre, then the bank, and then home. As far as I can tell, the man does nothing for money."

"And he never went to the Committee of Fourteen?"

"Not unless it's hidden in Times Square."

"It's not," Emmett said, setting a Gin Rickey in a teacup down in front of Finn. "Their headquarters is on East 22nd."

Finn arched his brow. "There you go."

Emmett flicked another look to Finn and retreated back to the kitchen.

Dash tapped his chin. "Do we think Walter ever worked there? Or just claimed he did?"

"How in the world would we find that out? I doubt the Committee would tell us. Moralists like their secrets, I find. And before you ask, under no circumstances are we walking in there ourselves. They are the lions, dearie, and neither one of us is David."

"It's almost beside the point anyway. He's not presently working for the Committee, so now we have a different question to answer."

"Which is?"

Dash looked at Finn. "How is he making his money?"

───────

Dash left the Inn and returned to the Cherry Lane Playhouse to change for another night at Pinstripes. The box office was closed up, the doors shut, not a soul waiting outside. Another performance was in progress. As Dash walked towards the side door to get to his apartment, he heard his name called.

"Dash Parker?" The voice was monotone, completely void of humanity.

His heart stopped. He turned to see a nondescript man in a suit holding a gun. Instinctively his hands went up. In his peripheral vision, he noticed a car driving up to the curb. Black. Also nondescript.

The man asked, "Are you Dashiell Parker?"

"W-w-who wants to know?" Dash stammered.

The man waved the gun towards the black car. "Get in the car."

"I'm sorry?"

"I'm not asking again."

He heard a door open. The darkness inside the black Ford gave no indication of who waited inside.

Is this how it ends? he thought.

Who had sent them? Walter? Zora?

Fear momentarily froze Dash to the sidewalk until the man with the gun started walking towards him. Dash instinctively backed up, then turned around again to face the car. Hands trembling, knees buckling, he ducked his head and entered the backseat. There, in all his corpulent glory, sat Lowell Henley, Nicholas Fife's henchman.

"Hello, Mr. Parker," he wheezed. "I told ya I don't like high hats like you."

22

Dash couldn't follow where the speeding car was going. All he knew was that they took a right, then a left, another right, another left, the crooked streets of the Village blurring together in streaks of streetlights and lit windowpanes.

The gunman sat in the front seat with the driver, both of them nonchalantly facing forward as they drove through the city. They didn't seem to worry what Dash was doing in the backseat. And why should they? There were three of them and one of him. And Dash was pretty sure all of them had a weapon of some kind.

Dash kept his eyes on Lowell, who stared ahead with the same passive expression he had when he visited the Greenwich Village Inn a few days ago. Was he operating on Nicholas Fife's orders? Or his own?

Foolish boy, his father's voice said. *Always engaging in such foolishness.*

The silence inside the car was unbearable and he wanted to fill it. He tried to speak but his mouth was completely dry, his tongue too thick and heavy with fear. Besides, what would he say? If they were going to kill him, there was no reasoning with them. Killing was their job, just like pouring drinks was his. They might even take great pleasure in it.

Would they make it quick? Or would they make him suffer? And what would happen once he was released from this mortal coil? He never did much thinking about so-called spiritual matters. People said there was a heaven up there somewhere, but Dash didn't figure it. He couldn't see invisible souls rising up into the sky like lost balloons. Then again, maybe he should, for he was about to be released from the ground.

A bump jolted the car. He looked out the window and saw they were on a bridge. He looked back at the city. The shadowy buildings sprinkled with electric lights glowed in the night. So benign, so peaceful, so safe. They looked too far uptown for this to be the Brooklyn, which wouldn't have made any sense anyway. The Brooklyn Bridge didn't allow cars. One had to use the trolley to cross. Which meant this bridge was the Queensboro. They were taking him to Queens.

Born on the East Side, banished to Bohemia, only to die in Queens.

He felt giddy, like he did as a child when his best friends were coming over to play. That tingling, tickling feeling in his chest which begged to be scratched but couldn't be reached. He even had to suppress a laugh when the car jolted again as they landed in the borough.

I'm going to be buried in a borough.

Was this what being hysterical meant?

They made a few sharp curves and pulled up in front of a massive brick warehouse, which stood at least two, three stories up. Long rectangular windows overlooked the East River, the lighting behind the dirty glass muted, like

Lowell's eyes. There was very little light on the street in front where the car jerked to a stop.

Dash was told to get out. He thought about running for it. If they were going to shoot him, what difference did it make where and when? Yet fear—or was it hope?—kept him from bolting.

The driver stayed in the car while the still unnamed gunman and Lowell went with Dash. They made a three-man procession to one of the warehouse doors, the gunman in front, Dash in the middle, Lowell in the rear. Parked on either side of them were dozens of dark green trucks with QUEENS FURNITURE emblazoned in gold paint on the sides. Underneath were the italics *PIECES FIT FOR ROYALTY!* Dash felt another giggle bubble up.

One of the warehouse doors opened with a piercing shriek. The gunman stepped to the side and gestured for Dash to go in ahead of him. The giddiness now gave way to pure leaden dread. His body did not want to move, but he knew he had no choice. He swallowed bile. A deep breath followed, taking in the smell of grease, dirt, and slight decay from the River, then he stepped into the poorly lit warehouse.

The room was large. Impossibly large. Only a few lights overhead created the absurd effect of stage spotlights. Instead of singers and dancers, they illuminated large wooden crates stacked from the floor almost to the ceiling. Was all of this furniture? It couldn't be. It had to be, what? Liquor? If so, there was enough to drown all of Manhattan ten times over.

Dash heard a throat clearing. He faced forward and saw Nicholas Fife. The gangster stood at the very end of the warehouse floor, hands clasped in front, a smile on his face.

"Mr. Parker," he said in his maddeningly pleasing bari-
tone. "I'm so glad you could join us."

I had a choice?

The night was getting more and more absurd.
Kidnapped at gunpoint, yet here is a gangster who was
persistently polite. Dash half expected him to offer a drink.
Which he would've taken. He for damn sure would.

Fife gestured to the space around them. "What do you
think?" he asked, pride filling his frame.

Dash stood dumbfounded. When the gangster looked
him in the eyes, it was clear he wanted an answer. "It's . . .
it's impressive, sir."

"And it's just one of many. I would tell you where they
are but"—Fife grinned—"then I'd have to kill you." He beckoned with an outstretched hand. "Don't be so shy, Mr.
Parker. Come here."

Dash looked to Lowell and the gunman, who flanked
him on either side. They stood at attention, spines rigid, like
bell bottoms and soldiers. Dash forced himself forward, his
legs ever so slightly shaking. Fife waited patiently with that
damnable smile on his face. He was dressed in a black
tuxedo, the vest, shirt, and bow tie blindingly white against
the dark jacket and pants.

When Dash was standing directly in front of Fife, the
gangster opened his tuxedo coat wider.

"Do you see?" he asked, pointing to the tightness of the
shirt around his midsection. "My rowing hasn't kept my
middle from expanding." He let the jacket fall back to its
resting position. "We never did discuss when my new suit
would be ready."

"When would it need to be?"

Fife laughed. "See? That is the absolute correct answer.
When would it need to be? I love that."

He pulled Dash to his side and spun him around, his arm around Dash's shoulders, as if they were friends. Buddies. Chaps. The spice of his cologne once again filled the air. So pleasing, one would never think it was the aroma of violence and death.

His breath was hot against Dash's cheek as he leaned in and answered, "I'd like the suit next Friday, if possible. That's when I must look excellent for this white tie dinner. Dreadfully boring affair but one must entertain boring people sometimes."

He looked at Dash expectantly.

Dash nodded vigorously, causing another chuckle from the gangster.

Fife squeezed Dash's shoulder then patted his back. "Good! Now that *that's* settled, let's get to the real reason why you're here."

The gangster started walking.

Dash hesitated, then followed, staying a few steps behind. "The real reason why I'm here?" he repeated.

"You had concerns about the quality and—I'm assuming —safety of my product," Fife replied over his shoulder.

He led Dash to a side door, which opened with another piercing squeal. The gangster winced. "I apologize for that. The hinges need oil. Some even need new hinges. But I find I like knowing when doors are being opened and shut. It keeps me from being surprised by someone sneaking in . . . or out."

Together they walked through the doorway, Dash noticing that Lowell and the gunman stayed behind in the main room with the stacks of liquor.

They entered a narrow hallway with jaundiced lighting, the pale yellow sickly against the exposed brick walls. Unexplained puddles of water dotted the floor, and the smell of damp was ever present. Fife led Dash to the very end of the hallway where he made a sharp right.

There was another room much smaller than the one they had just left. Chemical smells assaulted Dash's nose, pungent, metallic, and acidic. Oppressive heat tugged at his clothes. The lighting, though still muted, was of better quality here. Dash saw shelves of glass beakers, containers, and strangely designed funnels; clear and colored liquids filled some, others remained empty.

It's a chemistry lab.

Fife turned around just as Dash had the realization. "This is where we manage and maintain quality control." He gestured to a spot behind him. "And this is who is in charge of it."

Dash stepped to the side to see around the gangster. A long wooden table held beakers, burners, and more of those elaborate glass funnels. Standing behind the table with rapt attention on a beaker filled with a mud-colored liquid was a short Italian man.

"Mr. Parker, may I present to you Angelo Avogadro."

The chemist had a long, oval face, which remained still, showing no reaction to the two visitors who had entered his lab. Without looking away from the subject of his intense scrutiny, the chemist said, "Yes, Mr. Fife?"

"Angelo, I'd like you to meet a guest of ours. He's expressed great interest in the quality and safety of our libations."

"Is that so?" Angelo's eyes were still fixed on the brown liquid.

Dash stepped forward. "What is it you're doing?"

"I am testing for methyl alcohol. It will make you very sick if you drink it."

Dash turned to Fife. "You've hired a chemist?"

The gangster was pleased with how quick Dash understood the situation. "I'm sure you've no doubt heard the stories of men and women having a drink that later on killed them. Some are rumor but others are quite true. This damnable law has people making their own liquor but without the necessary ingredients to do it properly. Not only does it taste like absolute horse piss, but it's made up of chemicals one should never drink: gasoline, grain alcohol, and rubbing alcohol being the most common. I've even seen a barber use the disinfectant he keeps his combs in."

Fife shook his head.

"What people will do for a drink. And what a wonderful opportunity for me. If I can provide them good tasting liquor that won't kill them—well, not right away; some will regardless be drinking themselves to death in short order—then I can make a substantial profit."

Dash gestured to Angelo and his workbench. "And he tests the liquor?"

Angelo responded this time. "Not only test it, but also renature it."

"What does that mean?"

Angelo set the beaker down, satisfied with what he saw. When he gave his attention to them Dash saw the full beauty of his face. Eyes heavy with mystery, cheeks smooth with youth and vitality, and thick hair dark and tangled with midnight possibility.

Angelo replied, "I restore it to its natural state. I take out all the additives that make the liquid poisonous and I can make it drinkable again."

Fife stepped in. "You see, Mr. Parker, the U.S. Government knows this Prohibition nonsense is the most laughable thing since Harding's crooked cabinet. Not that I mind such moral deviation, but I despise men who claim they're righteous when they're otherwise. The government knows Americans, particularly in cities, will keep on drinking despite what the housemaids who proposed Prohibition claim. And they also know enterprising citizens will scrounge around and find anything they can use. Industrial ethanol, for example, is just floating around out there, free for the taking. Now our morally upright government agents are seizing it and adding in chemicals that make it foul smelling, bad tasting, even nauseating. Unfortunately, they've gone a little too far in some cases, for they made a good bit of it even *more* poisonous. That particular process is called . . . what is it again, Angelo?"

"Denaturing, sir."

Dash was stunned. "You mean, our own government is purposefully trying to kill us?"

The gangster shrugged. "Not *completely* purposeful, but then, what's a couple of thousand dead drunks if it scares off the rest from drinking?"

"But that's . . . that's . . ."

"Deplorable? Yes, I know." He gave Dash a sideways look. "Compared to the boys in Washington, consorting with a man like me isn't so bad, now is it, Mr. Parker?"

Angelo asked, "Would you like to know how I do it, sir?"

Dash held up a hand. "I am not a man of science, so I'm afraid I won't be able to follow. Thank you though, Mr. Ava —" He stumbled on the last name.

"Avogadro."

Fife said, "Now I believe you mentioned to my man Lowell something about trying the gin? What was it? Ah, yes. 'If he has good gin, I'll sign right then and there.'"

Hearing Dash's own words parroted back to him by

such a dangerous man was oddly threatening. Dash cleared his throat. "I believe I said that."

"Good." Fife pointed to one of the beakers of clear liquid on a left-hand shelf. "Angelo, is this one renatured?"

Angelo looked to where his boss was pointing and nodded.

"Excellent." Fife picked it up and walked over to Dash. "Here you are. Take a sip. Or two. You look like you could use one."

The gangster placed the beaker in Dash's hand. Dash stared at it. Was this an elaborate ruse to kill him? Give him the federally poisoned gin rather than the renatured stuff? Or perhaps he would be drinking acid? Burning him from the outside out?

Fife seemed to read his mind and smirked. "Yes, I suppose it does feel like a game of Russian roulette. Does this chamber have the bullet or no?" He patted Dash's arm. "Only one way to find out. Bottoms up."

Oh well, if I have to go, might as well be death by gin.

Dash raised the beaker in a mock toast and then took a sip. He waited for some kind of horrible chemical reaction once it touched his lips, tongue, and throat. So far, nothing. In fact, it tasted pretty darn close to regular gin. It was almost *good*. Not like the real thing, but not like the lighter fluid he'd been serving at his own club.

He looked at Fife, who smiled at his reaction.

"Up to your standards, Mr. Parker?"

Dash nodded.

"And that's just our version. In the main room you've seen, I have what they call The Real McCoy. Booze made in the islands down south and boated up here. Of course, that costs more. Considerably more—as you can imagine it would—but it is delicious, is it not, Angelo?"

Angelo shrugged. "I do not prefer spirits so much."

"Oh that's right. He's more about the wine, which, lucky Catholic that he is, he can get the real stuff with the weekly sacrament. I might convert just for that."

Angelo smiled for the first time since Dash met him. It was a wonderful smile, complementing the beauty of his face. "Many people have, sir."

Fife said to Dash, "Would wine go well with your club? Or is it just beer and spirits?" He made an aside to Angelo. "He has a very specific club with a . . . what shall we call it? . . . very specific type of clientele. Though the music, I hear, is fantastic. Rivals that of Harlem. You might like it, Angelo."

The chemist tapped his temple. "Must keep the brain clear."

Fife smiled his magnanimous smile. "I do think you should have one night of sin every *once* in a while. It's unnatural to be so pure all the time. Well, then." He turned back to Dash and took the beaker from his hand, placing it on the shelf behind him. "I think you've seen enough. Shall I count you as one of my customers?"

Another pointed look.

Dash smiled.

Better the Devil you know.

"You can."

"Excellent!" Fife extended his hand. They shook. Fife said to the chemist, "You're a witness, Angelo. A gentlemen's agreement."

"Yes, sir."

The gangster reached into his inside pocket and withdrew a card. "Here is a number you can call at any time. If anyone gives you any trouble, any at all, you dial this number."

He handed it over to Dash.

If anyone gives you any trouble . . .

Walter flashed into Dash's head. One couldn't find a better definition of trouble than him. With this contract, not only was Walter threatening Dash and his friends, he was also threatening Nicholas Fife. And Fife knew how to deal with such threats, Dash had no doubt about that. Expediently and secretly.

But are you a murderer?

This question gave Dash pause. Fife would kill Walter, like Atty suggested days ago. And Dash had already said to Atty they weren't killers. He meant it. He believed it. Yet the stakes were getting higher and the dangers more precarious. Was it still murder if it was self-defense? And could he live with the knowledge of what he had done for the rest of his life?

Dash noticed Fife looking at him strangely.

"Are you all right, Mr. Parker?" the gangster asked.

Dash cleared his mind of these ruminations and said, "Right as rain."

Fife paused, keeping watch over his face. "Good," he eventually replied. "First shipment will be at your club in two weeks . . . *after* I get my suit, of course. And now, Mr. Parker, I must bid you goodnight. I have other customers to see. I look forward to wearing your work next weekend."

There was that damnable smirk again.

"What with the special care you took to get my . . . measurements . . . I'm sure it'll fit me like a glove."

23

Fife's driver dropped Dash off at the Cherry Lane Play-house. The lights were out, the doors locked, the box office boarded up. It looked like the abandoned warehouse it once was before becoming a theater. God knew what time it was.

Maybe I need a wristwatch like Walter. Or like Karl.

His trembling legs managed to get him up the flight of stairs to the apartment with minimal fuss. His hands were another story. They kept shaking, and it took several tries to get the keys into the locks. He finally was able to turn them and enter the safety of his home. Finn's room was empty, as per usual. Probably out with a fleet of sailors, trying to forget Valentino's fragile health. Joe was surprisingly still awake and lying in the main bed, not on the cot.

Once Dash closed the bedroom door, Joe looked up. "Lassie, what happened to you tonight? You have any idea how worried I was?"

The voice was the usual Irish brogue, but the eyes took on a different character. It wasn't anger. The emeralds didn't smolder the way they usually did when his Irish temper was set off. It also wasn't concern, at least not directly. Dash held Joe's gaze, trying to pinpoint the expression as well as the feeling rapidly flooding his chest.

"I'm sorry, Joe," he replied. "Something happened . . ."

Now the emeralds darkened with fear. "What—?"

Dash told him about being kidnapped and driven to Queens. Lowell's henchmen. The gun pointed at him in the dark. The warehouse far away from any sort of help. The gangster standing center stage. The narrative came pouring out of Dash's mouth, words tumbling over themselves in a rush of adrenaline. The fear of stepping into that car. The relief of stepping out of it again.

When he paused for a breath, Joe reached his arms out and pulled Dash onto the bed. He was enveloped in a tight embrace, his face pressing against Joe's broad, naked chest. He heard Joe's heartbeat, which was pounding beneath his ear. Listening to it brought tears to Dash's eyes.

He's afraid for me.

It was a long minute before they separated. When they did, Joe looked into Dash's face and said, "I'll kill him." So matter-of-fact.

The absurdity of the statement caused Dash to laugh. "I don't think you can."

"Oh, lassie, don't tell me what I can and can't do."

Dash nodded, sniffing back his tears. "You're right. You're a formidable man."

"Ya damn right I am!" His hands gripped Dash's shoulders. "I'm sorry, lad."

"For what?"

"For not being there once again."

Dash forced a smile. "How could you have known?"

Joe used his thumb to wipe away silent tears from Dash's face. Without consciously thinking, acting purely on impulse, Dash kissed him. A kiss so hungry, it was like Dash was a starving man having bread for the first time in years. He wanted to feel alive, to feel free, not caged in by men like Walter Müller and Nicholas Fife—or even by the dumb bribe-collecting copper Cullen McElroy.

Clothes were hastily unbuttoned and discarded. In a blur of movement, they were both completely naked. Joe laid Dash on his back. When their naked bodies touched, a shudder shook its way from Dash's tailbone all the way to the top of his neck. The normally stoic Irishman whispered, "Dear God, lassie."

After that, it was hot breath on skin. Hands guiding hands, legs rubbing legs. Joe seemed to be pushing Dash farther and farther into the mattress, the weight of Joe's coarse, hairy body threatening to smother him. Dash's fingers were entangled in Joe's fiery copper strands as the ruddy man's rough cheek rubbed against his neck with every thrust. Dash bit Joe's shoulder, tasting grit and salt, causing a moan in Joe's throat. Sweat covered their bodies as sensations began to overtake them. The cramped room, the shackles of secrecy, the claustrophobic world disappeared as everything was reduced to their core senses. Touch. Taste. Smell. Mouths opened as their breaths got shallower and quicker. An involuntary cry of surprise escaped Dash's lips as he trembled beneath Joe. A moment later, Joe cried out as well. They held onto each other, breathing heavily, before they fell into the deepest of sleeps.

***

"Damn my rotten luck!"

Dash jerked upright as Finn slammed his way into the bedroom again. He rubbed his throbbing head while Finn paced the floor, his hands a fury of gestures. What time was it? What *day* was it?

"What's wrong now?" Dash asked his friend, who was wearing a copper-red vertical-striped suit, the coat unbuttoned to show a disheveled vest and crooked tie. A tan hat with an auburn band around the middle threatened to topple from his head, the way he was whipping and whirling about.

"My Valentino," Finn said. "My poor, sweet, beautiful Valentino! What horrible news before the weekend!"

Friday. It was Friday. Dash's brain was slowly starting like a hand-cranked Chrysler.

"*Still* goin' on about that the actor bloke?" murmured Joe from beneath the bed covers.

It took Finn a few seconds to see Joe wasn't on the cot but in the bed with Dash. He stopped pacing. His painted eyes squinted at the two nude men. "Well I *never*. Look at the two of you!"

Dash tried to intervene. "Finn—"

"Pray tell, when did *this* happen?"

Dash looked at Joe lying on his back, the covers just below his waistline, his hairy, freckled chest exposed. Joe held his arms laid above his head, the hair in his arm pits sticking out like bushes, his ruddy face fat with sleep.

Dash turned to Finn. "I had a scare last night and we—"

Finn held up a hand. "Say no more."

Joe replied, "Ya ask'd, ya mug."

"It's what we call a *rhetorical question*, you stupid Mick." Though the words were confrontational, the grin on Finn's face was anything but. "I'm so happy for you two!"

Joe scoffed, "Happy fer what?"

Finn rolled his eyes. "If you have to ask—"

Dash interrupted before Finn told Joe how Dash really felt. "What happened with Valentino?"

The joy was immediately gone, and Finn's hands clutched at his chest. "I heard he fell ill again. Fevers, nausea, yelling out because of the pain in his back. The poor man had trouble breathing. The doctors are trying everything they can to fight the infection. They think sepsis or something."

"I'm sorry to hear that, Finn."

"Oh! My poor Valentino is once again knocking on death's door."

Joe muttered, "He isn't *your* Valentino."

Dash lightly jabbed an elbow into Joe's ribs to silence him. "I'm sure he'll be alright, Finn. Doctors have been known to work miracles."

The little man reluctantly agreed. "There's a vigil some of us are going to today. So many are just as distraught as I am."

Joe once again muttered, "Bunch of Rudy fools."

Dash pulled the covers over Joe's head to muffle any more asides that might set Finn off on another tangent. They needed another topic, and there was only one he could think of.

"Finn, I know you're upset right now, but did you follow Walter this morning?"

Finn blew his nose into a plaid handkerchief he pulled from his breast pocket. "Yes, dearest, I did; despite my *grief,* I went about my task as a *professional*."

Finn composed himself, folding the handkerchief and returning it to its usual resting place.

"We know how the last two days, he followed the same routine, yes? Well, this morning, I decided to do something different. It's always bothered me how his mother just *stood* there, making sure Walter left. As if she didn't want Walter to know what she was really doing while he was out."

Dash said, "What makes you think she has a secret?"

Finn rolled his eyes. "*Everyone* has a secret, dearie. Which is why this morning, I followed *her* instead of *him*."

Dash was still sleepy, so it took a moment for him to register. "You followed Walter's *mother*?"

Finn grinned, all traces of Valentino grief gone, for the man was entirely too pleased with himself. "Anyone want to guess where she went?"

A dramatic pause.

"A speak!" Finn was laughing now. "Momma Müller is a drunkard! She went to a speak under one of those vile little butcher shops. I followed her in and let me tell you, she put away those beers. There were so many dead soldiers piling up on the bar, it was like the trenches in the War."

Dash remembered Mother's shaky hands and pale skin. It wasn't grief he saw. It was a hangover!

Joe sat up now, tossing the covers from his head. "We finally got something on them!"

"And not only did she attend a speak, dear boys, she also stopped by a baker and purchased something in a paper bag. Methinks 'twas not bread."

Joe shook Dash's shoulder. "A chink in the armor, lassie. A chink in his bloody armor!"

"We've finally got, oh what's the term?"

Dash replied, "Leverage." Despite not wanting to get his hopes high, he was grinning along with the other two. "Perhaps our luck is finally changing."

Perhaps I don't need to tell Fife about Walter at all.

"And that's not all," Finn continued. "I kept my disguise —a respectable businessman—and went to the Committee of Fourteen."

"Finn!" Dash said. "I thought you said we shouldn't go to the Lion's Den?"

"As *ourselves,* dearie."

"Finney," Joe growled.

"Oh, all right, I was drunk with power—as it were. Do you two want to hear what I found out? Or do you want to sit and judge some more?"

Joe rolled his eyes while Dash said, "Apologies. Please continue."

"Thank you," Finn said. "Well, it turns out Walter Müller did indeed work at the Committee since 1924 in the finance department. One of the best record-keepers they had. However, he left earlier this summer under scandalous circumstances. Apparently, an anonymous tipster called the higher ups and alerted them that Walter's own brother was an active homosexualist and had been arrested in a pansy speak raid. Soon afterwards, Walter resigned."

Dash said, "How did you have time to find all this out this morning?"

"It's almost one o'clock, dear."

Dash leapt out of bed. "Hell! I overslept!"

"Good loving can do that for a man," Finn purred.

While Dash hastily dressed, Joe asked, "Where did you hear all this, Finney?"

"I befriended a secretary named Millie Madison. Lovely girl. Unfortunately for her employers, and fortunately for us, she hadn't learned the importance of discretion."

Dash was rapidly absorbing the information as he pulled on his trousers and white shirt. Mother Müller had intimated last night that Karl had been arrested in a raid. *The urgency, the late-night visits, it's just like when Karl . . .* And that raid costed Walter his career.

Joe said, "I wonder who called in the tip?"

Finn shrugged. "Maybe it was young Karl, trying to get back at his older brother. If my sibling made his money by prosecuting my kind, I'd do the same thing."

Dash shook his head as he put on a royal blue tie around his neck. "Karl wasn't spiteful. I can't see him doing that." A thought worked its way into his brain as he finished the knot. "But I think I know who might be . . ."

———

Dash swung by Paul Avery's building at Waverly and Christopher. The Averys didn't answer their buzzer, and Marjorie Norton swore she hadn't seen them that morning, though she did hear them last night.

Good, they haven't fled the city yet.

Since by now, it was almost 2:00, it seemed pointless to open the tailor shop, which was fine by Dash. He needed to find a suit for Nicholas Fife. The gangster had to have known that Dash was not skilled in this regard, yet he still demanded a new suit anyway.

Power, Dash thought. *It's all about power with him. He'll enjoy watching me run around the city trying to find a solution.*

Sadly, Dash's search that day was unsuccessful. Many of the other tailors he approached with his odd request of selling him a suit for alterations looked at him bewildered. Why, they wondered, would he want to essentially plagiarize his work? Didn't he have a reputation to protect?

By 5:00, he declared defeat.

He returned to Paul Avery's apartment on Waverly and Christopher. Still no answer to the buzzer. Dammit.

Dash stepped back and counted the windows to the

front right corner, the one he guessed to be the Avery's apartment based on its interior location when he and Joe "returned" Mrs. Avery's keys. The lights were out and the curtains drawn.

He positioned himself in the doorway of another building next door. He watched for two hours to see if his quarry would stumble home like Marjorie said they often did. So far, he saw nothing out of the ordinary on the sunset streets of Christopher. Couples walking briskly. Several dog walkers letting their mutts out for a folic. Men hailing cabs to head uptown.

As night descended upon the city, the walkers turned into staggerers, the cheap alcohol working fast and swaying men about. One man sang opera at the top of his lungs, his verve much greater than his talent. Surveillance, or "stake-outs," as the pulps called them, required the virtue Finn claimed Dash lacked, and his friend was right. Dash felt simultaneously bored and itchy with energy. It was when he paced the opposite sidewalk for a bit to stretch his legs that he noticed a narrow alleyway, not more than three feet wide at the opening, running beside Paul Avery's building.

A memory sparked.

Marjorie Norton, Miss Eavesdropper Extraordinaire, had said she'd spoken to Paul's wife while she was smoking cigarettes on the fire escape. He looked around to see if anyone was paying him any attention. Everyone was moving too fast to care. He slowly stepped into the alleyway. Night had painted deep shadows into every corner and crevice.

On the sides, the building had black iron fire escapes laddering up to the top floor. Dash flicked his lighter to provide some light in the dusky darkness and scanned the ground. Sure enough, on the gravel below were hundreds of cigarette butts. The city cleaning service, which gave cursory glances to the main streets themselves on a *good* day, flat-out ignored the alleyways. It was one of the (many) reasons summer smelled so awful.

Dash kneeled on the ground examining the butts, holding them up to his flame. More than a few were rimmed with red or pink lipstick. He closed the lighter and glanced upwards. The building was designed with four windows on this wall for each floor. The first window from the front of the building caught his eye. On the ledge of the fire escape was an ashtray.

"Gotcha," Dash muttered.

Hunkered down in between the metal trash cans, Dash ignored the flies buzzing around his head and the stench offending his nostrils. He itched for a cigarette but resisted the impulse. Instead, he settled in, knowing it could potentially be a long night. It reminded him of the hide-and-seek games he'd play with his older brother Max. Max and Dash, what a pair. Dash would find the most improbable hiding spaces: kitchen cabinets, bottom desk drawers, once even the dumbwaiter. He could barely contain the excitement tickling his chest, and it took everything he had not to pop out of his hiding space. The memories were trapped in amber, a warm glow always surrounding them. They were the last memories of his brother playing with him. Sometime later, Max decided he was too old to play such childish games. When they were both young men, Max still remained aloof. Perhaps he always knew Dash's secret and the disruption it would cause. Better to be distant than to endure substantial heartbreak. It was certainly a lesson Dash learned later.

An hour into his vigil, he heard the crunch of gravel underfoot. His senses heightened. This was unexpected. He anticipated the lights of the Avery apartment coming on once they entered in the usual way, and Dash would simply wait by the front door when they left. Now someone was coming down the alleyway. He willed his breathing still. More gravel crunching. Then a darkened figure entered Dash's line of sight. The features were hidden in shadow. A man, judging by the suit. Or could it be Pru?

The figure's gaze went right over Dash. It turned and leapt upwards and grasped the fire escape ladder. It climbed upwards to the second floor and then walked to the window of 2A. Dash heard, rather than saw, the figure slide the window upwards and step into the apartment.

Dash waited. What should he do now? Was this one of the Averys, as he suspected? A random burglar? Or someone else involved in the Müller melodrama?

He stayed put, tuning his ears and concentrating on what was happening nearby rather than the ambient noise of the city at night. Through the opened window of 2A, he thought he heard the clattering of shoes on the floorboards, doors and drawers being opened and shut, and the rustling of someone rushing about. Whomever was in there was moving fast.

The slide of the window again and shoes on the fire escape. There was a click and a loud *clang!* The fire escape ladder had been released and dropped to the ground. The figure muttered, "Damn!"

A pause.

Then the *tink tink tink* of someone climbing down.

Gravel crunched again, but instead of footsteps moving off, there was silence.

Have I been seen?

Dash held his breath again. The silence stretched for so long, Dash wondered if the figure was still even there. He fought the impulse to peek around the garbage cans.

A snick of a lighter. Cigarette smoke soon floated into Dash's line of vision. Ah, the person had paused for a smoke.

Now is our chance.

Dash abruptly stood up, startling the darkened figure, who said, "Shit!" Her cigarette fell out of her hand, the glowing orange end smoldering on the ground.

The figure was less than three feet away from him. A woman. Dash flicked his own lighter so he could get a better view. His quarry was dressed in a sleeveless dress that was olive in color, silk in nature. A matching stole decorated her right shoulder, and a butterfly beret was clipped to her short, black hair. She was stunning. She was also frightened.

"Didn't mean to startle you," Dash said. "But I'm afraid we need to talk, Mrs. Avery." He stepped closer. "Or should I say, Mr. Paul Avery?"

24

A sharp intake of breath. "I don't know what you're talking about," the woman replied, the voice pitched high.

Dash had exhausted all of his patience waiting for her. He closed his lighter, extinguishing the flame. "Yes, you do. We don't have time for this. Walter Müller is hot on your trail and it's only a matter of time before he finds you."

"The man's a brute but thick as a post. He won't find us."

"I wouldn't underestimate him, Paul."

"I prefer Paula, if it's all the same to you." A curious look. "How'd you figure out there was only one Avery, not two?"

"Marjorie's eyesight isn't that sharp. I figured you talked in two different voices. In the absent of a clear picture, her ears filled in the rest."

"Hmm, clever."

Paula then rummaged around in her bag. Dash panicked, wondering if she was reaching for the gun she had at the Shelton. Instead, she came up with a brass tin, extracting a cigarette from it, and a brass lighter. She hastily lit another cigarette, a line of smoke escaping her lips as she sighed.

"Well," she said. "What happens now?"

"I was hoping you'd tell me. What's going on, Paula? Pru's being all cagey, and you've been impossible to get a hold of. What are the two of you afraid of?"

"The same thing you're afraid of. Walter-fucking-Müller."

"Why? What is the case you and Pru are working on?"

"How do you know it's about a case?"

"Come on, Paula, give me some credit! I know you, Tyler Smith, Karl Müller, and Prudence Meyers all met at the Hot Cha. You talked earnestly, according to my source."

"Where did you hear that bunk?"

"Zora Mae. The Baroness of Business herself. She's the one who gave me your address."

Paula eyed Dash uneasily. "Did she now?"

"The Baroness was very observant. She said that Pru, a lawyer, let's not forget, convinced Tyler to do something the night before Walter showed up at my club and made his mark on my face. Next thing we know, Karl's dead and so is Tyler."

"A series of unfortunate events. Just like what happened to your face." She gestured towards him with her cigarette. "Did you know Walter Müller before he did that to you?"

"No."

"See? You randomly got caught up in his orbit but there's no previous connection. Karl just happened to be Walter's brother. Tyler just happened to be a former lover. Tyler just happened to be friends with Pru and I. They had nothing to do with what we were working on. End of story."

"I don't believe you."

A bark of laughter. "Well, dearie, then I don't know

what else to tell you."

"You can tell me why you and Pru and Karl were waiting for Tyler that night in my club. You were the one in the blue and gold dress, were you not?"

Paula considered denying it but thought better of it. "It's a stunning little number, isn't it? Certainly caught *your* eye."

She thought while she inhaled another puff.

Her smoke-filled reply was, "We were going to wish Tyler bon voyage. He was moving to Paris."

That matched what Emmett had read in the news reports of Tyler's murder. But it didn't match what Dash already confirmed with Pru.

He said as much to Paula, who said, "Jesus, what *don't* you know?"

"The story with Walter. That's the piece I'm missing."

They stared at one another for a moment.

Paula took another drag of her cigarette. "You won't stop until you find out, will you?"

Dash shook his head.

An exasperated, smoke-filled sigh. "Alright. A few months ago, Karl confessed something to Tyler and Tyler came to me. At first, I thought he was joking. Then I thought he was drunk. But he managed to convince me."

"Convinced you of what?"

Paula paused to squash out the finished cigarette and light a new one. As she went through the ritual again, she said, cigarette bobbing in her mouth, "Do you know how Walter makes his money?"

"I know it's not from the Committee of Fourteen."

A smirk. The *snick* of the lighter and the inhale of smoke. "You have been busy. Good, we can go straight to the good stuff. Walter is a professional blackmailer."

Dash stared at her. "You mean, Walter was extorting money from other people?"

"He blackmailed you. Why wouldn't he do the same for others?"

"But who?"

She gestured with the lit cigarette in hand. "Us, dearie. Pansies. Bulldaggers. And everyone in between."

Dash paused. The pieces started to fit together. Karl saw what was going on, and Dash could only imagine the pain it caused. Even though Walter rejected Karl's true self, there's still something unnecessarily cruel about one's own brother persecuting men and women like him.

Cruelty is in our nature more than kindness, I'm afraid, Karl had said that night at the Oyster House.

"No wonder he wanted to leave," Dash said, then rubbed his forehead. "Poor Karl."

"Poor Karl? Poor *Karl?*" Paula's voice turned mean and vicious. "How do you think Walter found the people to blackmail in the first place?! He'd have Karl go to an underground club, get to know a few targets. Rich targets. Then Walter would have the club raided and everyone arrested. After the raid, he'd send a letter, demanding money or else."

Dash watched Paula. "Is that the truth?"

She relished ruining Dash's memory of Karl. "Oh yes. Everyone thought Karl was such an innocent. So kind-hearted, so naive. Ha! The boy was a spider, just like his bluenose brother. Worming his way into Tyler's life like he did. It was clear as day he just wanted Tyler's money and influence. You saw that wristwatch Karl just *had* to show off? A gift from Tyler, the fool, who had it engraved with that, that *spider's* initials." She shook her head. "The fool. In love with a traitor."

Dash tired of Paula's character assassination of Karl. He

said, "And this is the case Pru is working on? Walter's blackmail?"

"It's quite extensive. His list of victims I would daresay is over a mile long."

Dash leveled his gaze at Paula. "Were you one of them?"

She scoffed.

"What about Tyler?"

"That's a ridiculous question."

"Did you kill Karl?" Dash demanded again. "You obviously loathed the kid. He took away your best friend, he betrayed your kind. Seems like a perfect motive to me."

A satisfied smirk. "It's a good theory, except I was with Prudence Meyers all evening. After we left your club because of Walter's sudden appearance. You can ask her, if you like."

"Oh, I will." Dash looked off to the side. He didn't like this development, and Paula knew it. "Did you call the Committee of Fourteen and report that their finance maestro had a homosexual brother?"

"Why on earth would I do that?"

Dash just looked at Paula.

She smirked. "Sure, I did it. Why not? The man had it coming."

"Was that before or after Tyler came to you with Walter's blackmail scheme?"

Paula didn't answer.

Dash answered for him. "It was before, wasn't it?"

"How do you figure?"

"Because Walter's blackmail scheme was his new way of income. You effectively ruined his career. New York's a small town at its core, so word would have gotten around about his brother." Dash paused. "In effect, one could say it was *you* who caused the blackmails. Without your little stunt—which, let's both be honest, was to get back at *Karl,* not Walter, who would certainly punish his brother—Walter never would've come up with such an idea."

"That's the most absurd thing I've ever heard. Blaming *me*? For what the goddamn *Müllers* did? Ha! That's rich as all get out." Paula adjusted her handbag over her shoulder. "Now. You have wasted enough of my time, and I am quite late to an engagement."

She started to turn away.

Dash asked, "How did you lose your keys?"

She stopped. "My what?"

"Your keys," Dash said. "Marjorie said the night Karl died, you didn't have your keys and she had to let you in."

Paula replied with gnashed teeth, "Why that little busybody—"

"Where are they, Paula?"

"Oh, for goodness sakes. I lost my keys running out of *your* club when Walter Müller came barging in."

Dash watched her face. "Is that the truth?"

"Why are you looking at *me*? I'm not the dangerous one." Her voice turned shrewd. "You want to know who's dangerous? I'd look to the Baroness. Miss Zora Mae? Don't you find it strange she knew us so well? Even to the point of my address?"

The question was so obvious, Dash was startled by it. "Yes. At the time, it didn't seem odd but . . ."

He didn't finish the thought, which was *I was so desperate to get out from under Walter I took it at face value.*

Paula seemed to read Dash's mind and smirked once again. "She knew us because we spoke with her. You see, *she* was a victim too. Or rather her little moll, Sonya Sanders. She was arrested in one of Walter's little raids.

Imagine what a woman like Zora Mae would do once she found out the little boy who was handing out her rent party cards got her girlfriend locked behind bars."

Dash returned to Pinstripes, pulse racing. Zora Mae was more than just a passing observer of the Müller drama. She was a key player. He thought back to how she had toyed with him, teased him, and ultimately extracted a promise from him. Expertly done. He never considered she was involved.

When there was a break in the crowd, Dash told Joe and Finn about the Müller's blackmail scheme.

Finn gasped. "That is despicable. Utterly vile."

"Aye," Joe said, "we knew Walter was bad. But Karl?" He looked at Dash. "I'm sorry, lassie. I know ya took a likin' to him."

Dash shook his head. "I'm not so sure he was a willing accomplice. Look at us. We're doing Walter's bidding, to a point, and *we're* not in cahoots with him. I got the sense Paula was trying too hard to make Karl the villain. I think in actuality Karl was forced into it."

"Explains why he wanted to leave," muttered Finn.

"Exactly. *And* why he wanted a new name. He wanted to get out of that hell, to start over, to get clean of it, to begin anew. Only . . ." Dash sighed, surprised at the sudden pain that pierced his chest. ". . . only he never got the chance."

Joe rubbed Dash's shoulder. "Ya alright, lassie?"

"I'll be fine."

Finn asked, "What do you think it was that Tyler stole from Walter?"

"Not sure, but my money is on evidence of some kind."

Joe said, "Can it be used in court if it's stolen?"

Finn rolled his eyes again. "You haven't seen a trial in a while. Nobody's asking where the evidence comes from, especially if it confirms the popular verdict."

Joe smacked the bar. "Well, how is he gettin' the bloody money? You've been following Walter for days and all he's been doin' is *spending* money, not collecting it. Goin' to shows, the cinema, and the like."

Finn shrugged. "Maybe his victims mail the money?"

Dash shook his head. "Too easy for a mail carrier to swipe." He scratched his head while he thought. "Finn, he always went to the bank afterwards?"

"Everyday."

Dash smiled. "Ah ha! I know how he's doing it. Or, I should say, where he's doing it."

"How?!"

"He's meeting his blackmail victims. In the darkness of the cinema and the theater—maybe in the WC—but that's where the transactions are taking place. It's why he's seeing the same films every day."

Dash looked at Joe.

"He's not spending money there; he's *collecting* it there." He then looked at Finn. "And then he goes to the bank to deposit his earnings."

Joe shook his head and poured them all drinks. "Slimy bastard. What do we do now, lads?"

Dash rubbed his face and said, "I think we need to return to Harlem and have another chat with Zora Mae. Let's not forget, gents, Karl was closest to her in location than any of our other suspects."

Joe set the three glasses in front of them. "How did she even know he was there?"

"He called somebody from Leslie's office. Maybe it was

her."

Finn piped up. "Karl said she didn't take in strays. He said it right in *our* water closet. Why would he change his mind?"

"Desperate?" Even to Dash's own ears, it sounded weak and circumstantial. "I'll concede the point." He thought some more. "What if the person he was trying to reach would've gone to Zora? And he went there to intercept them somehow?"

Joe scratched behind his ears. "Who would tha' have been?"

Dash shrugged. "Any one of them. We know Pru, Tyler, and Paula went to the Hot Cha."

Joe looked over at Dash. "Ya think Zora would admit anything to ya?"

"Worth a shot. Her heaven and hell party is this coming Sunday night, and we do have Karl's entry card."

"I'm going with ya."

"No, you're not," Finn said. "If anyone is going to that party, it is *moi*."

"She's not some society lady, Finney. She's a mobster, sure as I'm sittin' here."

"Once again, I have to prove myself to you. I am not some frilly little yearling who doesn't know the ways of the world, *O'Shaughnessy*."

"Enough!" Dash said. He looked at Joe. "I understand your concern, but we'll be fine. Zora is not going to 'off us' at a party. Besides, I've already promised him the night off."

"Exactly, you brute," Finn replied.

Joe ran a frustrated hand through his thick, tangled hair. "I can't win this argument, so I'm not gonna try. Just be careful, the both of ya's."

Finn raised his glass. "Yes sir, missus sir, yes sir."

25

Sunday, August 22, couldn't come fast enough. Before Dash left Pinstripes that Friday night, he enlisted the aid of Atty in trying to find a suit for Fife. He handed his doorman Fife's measurements and said, "Don't steal it, Atty. We're already breaking enough laws as it is."

Saturday just crawled by. The only event of note was Saturday afternoon when Atty stopped by Hartford & Sons to tell Dash he had found a suit to alter for Nicholas Fife.

"It's a beauty," Atty said. "The finest materials. I never seen a sharper suit. And the best part is, it didn't cost too much sugar."

"How did you manage that?"

"Man the suit was made for died suddenly."

"A lot of that going around."

"One man's bad fortune is another man's blessing. I'm working on it tonight."

Dash smiled. "Thank you, Atty."

"Anytime, Boss. You, uh, still having problems with that Walter fella?"

Dash sighed. "Unfortunately, yes."

Atty reached into his pocket and pulled out his Smith & Wesson, inadvertently aiming the barrel straight at Dash's stomach. "Youse want to borrow my gun?"

Dash put his hand up to lightly push way the barrel away from him. "That won't be necessary."

"You sure? It's a nice piece. The sights are a little off, so I just aim to the far right."

"That . . . explains a lot, Atty. Thank you, but I'll do just fine on my own."

"Whatever you say, Boss."

Eventually Sunday night descended upon them, and Dash found himself dressed to the nines with Finn in a cab heading uptown to the address on Karl's blue card, to the corner of 150th Street and St. Nicholas. To Sugar Hill.

When they exited their cab, Finn whistled at the sight. "We are definitely not in the Village anymore."

Dash, equally impressed by the sight before them, replied, "You got that right, Finn."

Even though Dash knew what kind of grandeur they'd find up here, it still shocked him. Many whites, especially in Dash's former circles, assumed the black part of Harlem was nothing but dirty speakeasies and overcrowded slums. But many didn't know about Sugar Hill. Sugar Hill was where Harlem's rich and famous lived, where castle-like mansions and stately townhouses and rowhouses lined the streets like in New York's gilded age, when the Vanderbilts and the Rockefellers lived on Fifth Avenue before they retreated from the city. El told him once that Duke Ellington and Cab Calloway lived up this way, and Dash wondered—or rather, hoped—they might see them at Zora Mae's party. Harlem Royalty, indeed.

The mansion, which took their breath away, was a wood and stone wonder done up in the Queen Anne style. The first story was awash in gray stone and granite, the second story covered in crimson red–painted shingles matching the roof, the attic done up in white. The left-hand side of the house was box-y, utilizing a typical A-frame at the top. But the right-hand side was rounded, climbing upwards towards a gumdrop turret. Windows were everywhere, all opened— those that weren't stained glass, that is—and music and laughter spilled out onto the street below. Inside the window frames were the shadows of patrons, some standing, others dancing, all radiating joy. The porch below was decorated with electric lights on a string, like those at Coney Island. Potted plants with large, elephant-like leaves stood on either side of the door, as big and elaborate as the headdresses on Broadway dancers.

Dash and Finn were the only whites in line and, just as Zora Mae had warned, they got more than a few wary glances their way.

"Isn't this just grand," Finn purred, oblivious to the stares. "I'm going to have a hard time picking just *one* man tonight."

"Finn, stay focused. We're not here to have a good time."

"You know, if you stay this serious, you're going to die a young death."

We all very well may if I can't figure a way out of this mess.

They got to the porch stairs and walked up to the stoop. Above the front door was a long, rectangular piece of stained glass. Underneath it stood a tall man in a black tuxedo and white gloves. He gave them a baleful look. "Gentlemen?"

They placed Karl's blue cards onto the blinding white of his outstretched palm.

The doorman looked down and saw the color of the card that, as Zora Mae claimed, was the all-clear for whites to enter.

The doorman looked up and said, "Welcome to Dante's Inferno. Upstairs is Heaven, where angels and their singing will great you. The ground floor is Purgatory, where you may pause to consider the state of your soul. And the basement is Hell, where sinners are greeted with open arms. Enjoy."

As they walked into the foyer, Finn muttered, "I love the drama of this party! So theatrical."

Dash looked at Finn. "We shall we start?"

"Can we just stop and marvel at this *hall*? Dear goddess, no *wonder* they call this place Sugar Hill. Look at how much sugar is on display!"

Dash, having grown up in wealth, looked around to see the hall through Finn's eyes. Mahogany wood archways carved into intricate patterns led to rooms to their left and right. Glass panels embedded in the opened doors portrayed Victorian men and women in a variety of poses, stories that must've meant something to the owners. A silver chandelier with six bulbs encased in crystal hung above their heads, as did the carved wood ceiling. This was Old Money through and through.

It reminded Dash so much of his former family home, he felt slightly ill. "It's grand, alright," he managed to say.

"It's more than grand! It's capital!"

Dash was puzzled. "Capital?"

"A British sailor I entertained last night said it often. I think I'm going to adopt it from now on."

Recovered, Dash asked again, "Where shall we start? Or do you want to stand and stare some more?"

"No reason to be a bearcat." Finn considered their

options. "Let's go up to Heaven and begin our descent down. Just like Dante."

Dash nodded. "The lady hath spoken."

They found a wooden staircase and ascended to a landing filled with angels in white sheets and robes, their wings sewn to their backs and sparkling behind them. The walls were also covered in white sheets, and miniature Roman-Greco columns lined the floor in even lines. Heaven was apparently the Parthenon.

Dash and Finn were directed to a doorway to their left, where they were greeted by Gabriel, a massive black man wearing a royal blue robe that flowed around his muscular frame. Unlike the other angels, his wings were golden, fanning out to the sides and arching above his head. Heavy eyeliner made Gabriel's eyes appear even more striking and a slight dusting of makeup emphasized the sharp angle of his cheeks and jawline.

"Gentlemen," he said, his voice booming with granite, "welcome to Heaven. The Good Lord has been expecting you."

He opened the door and the free form, bent notes of jazz washed over them. The room they entered was essentially a ballroom with a vaulted ceiling high above their heads and chairs pushed against the walls, leaving the floor in the center wide open. People filled the space, doing dances Dash had never seen before. Complicated moves that had shoulders rolling, hips rocking, hands up in the air with fingers waving, legs bowing out and coming back in. Twirls, turns, kicks, and slides. One couple even performed a flip.

Makes my club look absolutely tame.

Like in Pinstripes, some of the men danced with other men. Same went for the women. No one seemed surprised or offended by what they saw, which meant this party was a safe place. A few whites stood at the perimeter, clearly intimated by the sheer physicality of the other dancers.

A six-piece band played at the other end of the room, its members dressed in white. All the instruments—drums, bass, piano, cornet—were painted white. A singer, a beautiful black woman with short hair and smooth curves, wailed about lost love in a voice that was so spirited, it sounded as if she were celebrating rather than mourning.

Finn said his ear, "What are we looking for, Bossman?"

"I'm not sure yet."

They traced the edge of the room, careful not to step on the feet of the spectators watching the floor flushers. The singer finished her lyric and turned the song over to the cornet player, who blew with abandon. The dancers suddenly parted, as if on cue, and a trio of women dancers donned in white silk and fringe took to the floor. One of them was Flo Russell, El's friend who had introduced Dash to Zora Mae. She was in the lead position, and Dash could see why. Her movements were so agile, so natural, it didn't look like a planned dance at all. Rather it was a story, an extension of the singer's melody, conveying heartbreak, anger, sadness, and triumph through movement. It was exhilarating to watch.

Halfway through the dance break, Dash saw Flo looking at him. Though the smile stayed on her face, her eyes darkened. She was not pleased to see Dash.

The singer came back in with the vocals, and the whole floor swarmed with people again, Dash losing sight of Flo in the throng.

When the song was finished, the dancers took a break and Flo came straight over to Dash.

"What are you doing here?" she said without preamble.

Her abruptness took Finn by surprise.

Dash too. He said, "Zora Mae invited us." Which was *mostly* true.

"Uh huh. You can't stay away from trouble, can you? I told you nothing better find El or me."

Panic filled Dash's chest. "What happened, Miss Russell?"

"What happened is now I gotta work this party on account of introducing you to Miss Mae. That goddamned bartender gave me up and somehow, she tracked me down. I had to give up my spot tonight at Connie's to an understudy who is just itchin' to take my spot. Every night I'm not there, she's weaseling her way into the director's good graces. Now, downtowner, I didn't dance my soles off to be replaced by some young thing with two left feet and two pennies for sense."

"I apologize, Miss Russell, I—"

"Don't apologize, just *leave.*"

Finn spoke up. "But we just got here, dearie, and I don't know about you, but I am just in love with the whole aura of this place. Classic decadence in classic décor. I mean, what more could a girl ask for? It's all so capital!"

Flo stared at Finn, not sure how to react.

Dash replied, "We will, as soon as we find Miss Mae."

Flo jammed her pointer finger into Dash's chest. "I mean it, downtowner, do *not* cause any more trouble. Or you're gonna find my dancing shoe in a place shoes don't belong."

She turned on her heel and stormed off.

Finn said, "My, my, making friends wherever you go."

Dash shook his head and turned towards Finn. "I don't see Miss Mae up here. Let's see if we have better luck in Purgatory."

Finn snorted. "Now that's a sentence you don't hear often."

When the first doorman had mentioned "pausing" in Purgatory, he wasn't lying. The room must've been a salon, but it was hard to tell, given that all the furniture had been removed. On the floor were piles upon piles of pillows, all upholstered with plum and burgundy fabric. On top of the pillows, stretched out in a hazy bliss, were men and women, still in their glad rags, eyes blank, slight smiles on their faces. Lying beside them were long bamboo pipes.

Opium.

Finn made a move to go further inside the room. Dash put a hand up, stopping him. Finn gave him a puzzled look, and Dash shook his head, saying softly, "We need to keep our wits about us tonight."

Finn, for once, agreed. "Shall we go to Hell then?"

Dash smiled. "I thought Walter Müller already sent us there."

"Good one, Bossman."

They found a steep staircase heading down to the basement. The lighting here was much darker. The lightbulbs had been painted red, casting a crimson tint over everything and everyone. Unlike on the other two floors, in here there were shadows. A face or two was visible, but the darkness cloaked their actions. Given the urgent whispers and the sudden gasps, Dash had an idea of what the shadows were hiding. The chalky brick walls and the dusty floors led to a bar at the other end of the room, where two men were mixing and pouring drinks.

Finn said, "You can deprive me of men, but you will not deprive me of a drink."

He strolled over to the bar, leaning forward to whisper into the bartender's ear.

Dash stood where he was and looked around. He expected the Hell portion of the party to be the loudest yet. The gnashing of teeth, as the Bible had promised. Instead, Hell was quiet, seductive. Like the Devil himself.

Like Nicholas Fife.

And Walter Müller.

A husky voice began to sing over a piano. In the corner next to the bar was a shiny, black upright piano. And behind it sat El Train in her black tuxedo. He shouldn't have been surprised to see her. If Flo was here for introducing him to Zora, then why wouldn't Zora also get Flo's best friend to accompany her? A woman as powerful as Zora Mae would want to have a woman as famous as El Train at her grand party.

El sang the intro, slow and smoldering:

I just saw a maniac
Wild, and tearing his hair
Jumpin' like a jumpin' jack
Child, you should've been there

Laughed so loud I thought I'd cave in
When I heard that silly, daffy dilly ravin'

El noticed Dash standing there for the first time. She gave him a flat look, arched an amused brow, and continued to sing, turning a fox trot number into a minor key simmer.

Five foot two, eyes of blue
But oh, what those five feet could do
Has anybody seen my girl?

Turned up nose, turned down hose

Flapper, yes sir! one of those
Has anybody seen my girl?

A female voice said behind Dash, "Hello, there."

Dash turned around. The Baroness of Business Zora Mae had appeared from the shadows. He took in the sight of her. Bobbed hair shiny and black. Lips the color of crushed cherries. Lashes long and thick. She wore a dazzling scarlet red dress that, even in the crimson dimness of the room, still managed to sparkle and shine.

She recognized him. "Mr. . . . Parker, is it?"

He turned on his most charming smile. The practiced flashing of teeth he once used daily when he lived among the upper crust. Where manners—or the appearance of manners—was more important than the morality they supposedly upheld.

"Miss Zora Mae, so lovely to see you again."

He took her hand and gently brushed his lips against her knuckles. Honeysuckle perfume, light and airy, tickled his nose.

El sang:

Now if you run into a five foot two covered in fur
Diamond rings and all those things, bet your life it isn't her
But could she love, could she woo?
Could she, could she, could she coo?
Has anybody seen my girl?

"You certainly know how to treat a lady," she said.

"Are ladies treated any other way?"

An eyebrow arched. "You'd be surprised how ladies are treated most of the time. Tell me, Mr. Parker, how are you enjoying my little soirée?"

Dash looked around, taking in the surroundings. "The most elaborate soirée I've ever seen."

Zora swelled with pride. "Yes," she said, "this one is a special occasion. Definitely one of my most literate parties. I was re-reading a copy of the *Inferno* I stole from a library back in my youth —a whites-only library—when the idea just came to me."

"It is ingenious."

"Come now. I know you may not have much experience with the opposite sex, but unlike men, a lady doesn't need to be *constantly* flattered. We're not quite as desperate for the validation. Just a sprinkle of compliments will do."

Dash acknowledged the admonishment with a slight nod. "I must say, though, I'm a little surprised by Hell. It's not quite what I thought it'd be."

"It never is. Now that we have the pleasantries out of the way, tell me why you are here. Oh. I remember now. Your friend. The little German boy who got himself strangled. Did you find any of his enemies?"

> *Love made him a lunatic*
> *Gee! he hollered and cried*
> *Like a monkey on a stick*
> *He was fit to be tied*

"A few, actually," Dash replied. "In fact, I may be looking at one."

It took her a moment to understand what he was intimating. Her voice dropped to a low growl. "Are you threatening me?"

"I would never. I can't say the same for Walter Müller and his blackmail of you. Or rather, of Sonya."

When we asked him for his wife's description
He just answered all of us with this conniption
Five foot two...

As if saying her name conjured her, Sonya Sanders appeared in the back of the room. It was too dark to read her expression, for which Dash was grateful. If he saw what he expected to see, he would be frightened out of his wits.

Zora noticed her and gave a little wave, then she gestured to a far-off corner. "Let's talk."

They sat in an alcove on a red velvet love seat just off to the side of the bar. The seat was designed for snuggling, though that was the last thing Dash or Zora had in mind.

"I take it you know about the Müllers little setup?" Zora said.

"I can quote chapter and verse. Tell me about Sonya."

She considered her response. "She was arrested. Simple as that. At the Au Lait. A case of bad timing."

"And you received a letter?"

"I did. Bring the money to the House Beautiful—the Lafayette Theatre—on 132nd and Seventh, sit in the back row to the left, and leave the money in an envelope underneath. Then get up and leave before the show finishes."

His hunch was confirmed. "Miss Mae, did your blackmail letter state who it was the sender?"

She shook her head.

"And when did you learn the Müllers' identity? Before or after Karl started working for you?"

"After, of course. Do you honestly think I'd have let him anywhere near me or my girl if I knew what he'd done?"

They both looked out from the booth. Sonya still stood against the back wall, her eyes watchful, her face full of anger, her hands in fists at her sides.

Keeping an eye on her, Dash said, "Miss Mae, did you kill Karl?"

A mirthful laugh. "I credit you for bravery, Mr. Parker. Not many men would be as forward to me as you are now."

Dash nodded towards Sonya. "Did she?"

"I don't watch her every second of every day."

They turned away from Sonya and looked into each other's eyes.

Zora said, "We have the motive, I admit. No one threatens my people and gets away with it. The fact that Karl was being used by Walter to raid black clubs, well, sometimes retribution is the only answer."

Dash swallowed a lump of fear in his throat. "Did you kill him?" he asked again.

"We have the means as well. I never like getting my hands dirty, but my girl? She derives a distinct satisfaction from the physicality of violence." She held up a pointer finger. "But—and this is important, Mr. Parker—where is the opportunity?"

She sat back against the booth, a self-satisfied smirk on her face. "We didn't even know that traitorous little worm was up here until you came to visit me at the Hot Cha."

"Someone at the Oyster House could've told you."

"Who?"

Dash shrugged. "Any of them. In the audience, at the bar, behind the bar. I'm sure you have operatives all over Harlem. Maybe one of them recognized him and told you."

"You're reaching, Mr. Parker."

"Perhaps I am. And even if you did kill him, you'd never tell me, would you?"

Her eyes glittered. "Do you remember when I gave you the address of Mr. Paul Avery? And when I gave it to you, I said it was in exchange for a favor?"

He regarded her warily. "What is the favor?"

"Don't look so glum. I suspect we'll both get enjoyment out of it." She paused. "I want you to kill Walter Müller."

Dash's eyes widened. "You want me to . . . ?"

"Kill Walter Müller, yes, that is correct."

He shook his head. "I am not a killer, Miss Mae."

"Nor am I, yet you're convinced I could be one."

"Miss Mae—"

Her voice turned hard. "You would do well to listen to what I say. I don't ask for favors. I demand them. You will do it. If you don't, I will make your life so miserable, you will wish you were dead."

She slid out of the booth.

"Good evening, Mr. Parker." She glanced at Sonya, whose face was still dark with rage. "Be careful as you leave. I'd hate for anything bad to happen to you."

The Baroness then slinked off into the darkness.

Dash's lower back and armpits were damp, his breath short. He needed to find Finn and get them both out of here.

26

Dash left the booth as El finished her song. She caught his eye and motioned him over to her piano.

When he got there, she said, "What are you doing talking to Zora?"

"I found out what Karl Müller was running from."

Her reaction to the blackmail scheme was one of resigned disgust. "I tell you," she said, "these bluenoses are the reason we got so much crime and bullshit." She lightly smacked his arm. "Now what were you *thinking* threatening her like that?"

"I didn't threaten her!"

"You most certainly did when you accused her of murder. And not only that, you accused her moll, too! Didn't you hear anything I said to you? This is not the world you're used to, downtowner. This is a world of shadows and shivs, and you're skipping through it like Little Red-goddamn-Riding Hood!"

He felt his cheeks burn with a blush.

She's not wrong. And now you're on the hook for killing a man.

"I just asked a question." He didn't like how meek his voice sounded.

"Sometimes asking a question does more than just state curiosity, Dash."

"It doesn't matter anyway. She didn't know Karl was even in Harlem." He sighed. "Karl left to go somewhere and wherever he went—and whomever he saw—that's the answer to who killed him."

"Why do you care who killed him? You got what you need to get Walter off your back. Blackmail, a drunken mother, *and* a drag-wearing dead father? Seems to me your problem is solved."

Dash shook his head, glancing down at his shoes. "It would take too long to explain."

And he still didn't know how Tyler Smith's murder fit into all this.

When he brought his gaze up, he saw two figures in the foreground. He squinted, his vision clearing. "Is that . . .?"

El turned to look behind her. "Oh yeah. That's Les."

There he was, Leslie Charles, plain as day, wearing a gray pinstriped suit with fedora in hand.

Dash said, "But he's talking with Zora Mae?"

The enigmatic woman and the sapphire-eyed man were in a deep, intense conversation.

"Of course he is! How'd you think I got this gig here?"

"Does he know her?"

"They go way back. Grew up in the same neighborhood, I believe. How'd you think I knew so much about her?"

Dash watched as the two of them bent their heads together, their faces partially hidden by the dim light of the room. A possibility entered Dash's thoughts. If Zora found out about Karl—and she most certainly would have if Pru told her what was going on—then Leslie Charles would've heard about it as well. And if Leslie put two and two together that Sunday night . . .

Wait a moment. Didn't Horace say he had something to say to me?

The night El took him to meet Flo Russell. Tuesday. Horace mentioned it was about the woman he was going to meet. Zora Mae. El was in a hurry to make the introductions to her friend Flo Russell in between sets, and, given all that had transpired, Dash never went back to the Oyster House.

"Maybe," Dash breathed.

El turned and looked at him. "What?"

"Maybe Karl wasn't the only one who made a phone call that night." He brought his eyes up to El's.

She immediately began shaking her head from side to side. "No, Dash. I'm telling you right now, drop this. Nothing good is going to come from it."

"El, Karl was a victim of Walter's too! Why should his death go unpunished?"

"That's too simple a view of life."

"Sometimes life *is* simple, El!" Dash looked around. "Where's Finn?"

He found his friend at the bar chatting up a beautiful, tall black man in a tuxedo.

"We've got to go. Thank you, El. I promise I'll be careful."

"Dash!"

But he didn't wait to hear the rest of her response. He quickly walked up to Finn.

"Excuse me," he said to the tall black man and turned to Finn. "We've got to leave."

Finn was incensed. "Ex*cuse* me, but I was having the most *lovely* conversation with . . . ?"

The black man replied, "Chester." His voice was deep, full of granite.

"Chester! And I would appreciate it if you let us be for a few moments."

Dash smiled for the sake of Chester. "Normally I would but we have an emergency to deal with. Chester? Pleasure meeting you. Love that tuxedo. Very nice fit."

Chester looked down at himself. "Thank you, sir."

Dash grabbed Finn's arm and pulled him away. His friend muttered indignities until they were outside.

Once they left the mansion, Finn said, "What the *hell* has gotten into you?"

"I'll explain on the way."

"On the way *where*?"

———

The line outside the Oyster House was as long as ever. Dash and Finn bypassed it and walked right up to Horace, who was welcoming a black couple to the club. When Horace saw them, his face lit up.

"Mr. Parker! So glad to see you." His eyes then narrowed. "What's wrong? You look like a man who's being chased."

"I feel like it sometimes, Horace."

Finn cleared his throat.

"Oh, excuse me, where are my manners? Horace, this is Finn Francis. He's a partner of my club."

Finn extended his hand like a royal debutante. "Charmed."

Horace didn't know how to respond, as he was

expecting a regular handshake. He glanced over at Dash, who nodded slightly, then he gently grasped the end of Finn's fingers.

"Charmed, Mr. Francis. Or should I say, miss?"

"Whichever you prefer," Finn replied, then he dropped his voice into a lower register. "I can be whatever you want me to be."

This time, Dash cleared *his* throat. "Finn, another time. Horace. You were going to tell me something when I was here a few days ago—when El and I were going off to meet someone to introduce us to Zora Mae. Do you remember what that was?"

The black giant looked up at the sky, as if the answer were written in the stars pinpricking the charcoal canvas above them. "Oh! I do remember."

His eyes came back down to Dash's. They were cloudy with concern.

"I don't know what it means. I'm not sure I *want* to know what it means."

Dash's lips curved into a compassionate smile. "I know the feeling, Horace. I've been feeling that way for a whole week now."

"Yeah, and I don't like it. Not one bit." He licked his lips. "Normally I don't stick my nose into other people's business. Everyone's got a price to pay to make it in this city, even Harlem. Perhaps *especially* Harlem, so I don't begrudge how the sausage is made, if you catch my drift."

"I do."

"But this might be a bit too rotten."

Dash's pulse was climbing. He bit back the urge to rush the gentle giant along. Finn, for his part, amazingly kept quiet.

Horace sighed, took another deep breath, and said, "It

was closing time Monday night, right after you left. When you said something bad happened to that little German kid. You remember?"

"I remember."

"You were mighty upset. Anyway, I was having a sip at the bar, you know how I do after a shift. I went outside for a smoke in the back alley, and, all of a sudden, I'm hearing Les speak. At first, I thought he was talking to me, because I remember saying, 'what was that, Les?' And he didn't answer me. I peered over to his office window. His back was turned, talking on his telephone."

"Just like Karl on Sunday night. The night he disappeared."

Horace nodded vigorously. "Exactly! I thought I was having a, what do they call it? Déjà something."

"Déjà vu," Finn replied. "The feeling that you've already been someplace, or done something, before."

"That's it!" Horace said. "Yes, exactly that. I didn't mean to overhear, Mr. Parker. You gotta trust me on that."

Dash nodded. "I do, Horace."

"I don't want to be seen as no gossip. That don't get you anywhere in life."

"Except maybe in the newspapers," muttered Finn.

Dash discreetly, and lightly, stepped one shoe onto Finn's toes.

The pressure caused Finn to say, "I apologize, Horace, you were saying?"

"Right. I still had my ciggy to finish, so I kept still. And Les said, 'Hey Miss Mae, how does it lay?'"

Horace looked at Dash.

"I remember the name because El mentioned she was going to take you to someone who was going to introduce you to her."

His gaze went to a place just above Dash's shoulder. It was like the past conversation was a moving picture at the cinema and the screen was just behind Dash.

"He say, 'uh huh, uh huh, right. You remember that white kraut? That's the one. Well, it's been taken care of. That's right. Just thought you should know.'"

Horace's eyes returned to Dash's.

"When I found out that the little boy you were trying to help was found dead, well, you can see why I don't want to know what I know."

Dash gave a sympathetic smile. "Thank you for telling me, Horace. I appreciate that."

"Do you know what it means?" The gentle giant's face was pained.

Dash's smile turned sad. "I think I do."

Horace's face fell sad as well. "Yeah. I think I do, too."

The rattle and hum of Harlem street traffic swirled around them while Dash processed this new piece of information.

He looked up to the giant. "Is Leslie due back to the club tonight?"

"Yes, sir. He had to run an errand."

An errand that involved Zora Mae. "I see. And does Leslie come in the front way or the back?"

Horace was puzzled. "Why do you want to know?"

Leslie Charles whistled as he strolled down the alleyway.

For the second time that week, Dash was crouched down behind metal trash cans, breathing in the aroma of rotting garbage and his own sweat, his teeth grainy from the dust of the city. As soon as he heard Leslie, Dash stood up and, once again, caused a startling effect.

"Jesus fucking Christ!" yelled Leslie.

"Good evening, Mr. Charles."

Leslie grabbed his chest as if he were having a heart attack. "What the hell are you doing hidin' out in my alleyway?!"

Dash forced a smile. "We need to have a little talk."

The club owner took several deep breaths. Even in the dark, Dash could see Leslie's sapphire eyes widen in anger.

"Talk about what, ofay? We've got *nothing* to talk about." He began shaking his head and walking towards the back door to his club. "El may put up with your bushwa, but not me, brother, not me."

Dash stepped forward, which prompted Leslie to say, "Get away from me. You in Harlem now. I can kick your ass if I want to."

Dash held up his hands in a peaceful surrender. "I just want to talk about you and Zora Mae and a little phone call you placed last week."

"What phone call?"

"I like how you didn't bother to deny knowing Zora. It makes my job so much easier."

Leslie put his hands on his hips. "*What* on earth are you talking about? Did you take some dope?"

"Leslie, when I dropped off Karl Müller last week, did you recognize him? Or rather, recognize his name?"

"You talking about that little sauerkraut? Why the hell would I care about him?"

"Because his brother blackmailed Zora's moll. And I do believe we both know how Miss Mae would feel about that."

Dash took another step forward.

Leslie tensed. "Get away from me."

Dash ignored the warning. He was getting closer to the truth, he knew it. "Did you call Zora to tell her Karl was in your club?"

"Why would I do that?"

"You're friends, are you not? I heard since childhood."

Leslie licked his lips and cleared his throat. "So?"

"*So,* here's this little ofay dumped on you against your will and he just so happens to be connected to a hateful, immoral blackmailer, who just so happens to have black-mailed your childhood friend's lover. The Müllers threatened Zora's freedom and possibly her livelihood. I have a good sense of what lengths she'd go to protect herself."

"Oh really?" Leslie crossed his arms over his chest. "What lengths, ofay? *Please* enlighten me."

"Tonight, she told me to kill Walter Müller."

That stopped Leslie.

Dash continued. "Did she tell you to kill Karl Müller?"

No response.

"Did she, Les?"

Those sapphire eyes went cloudy as the club owner calculated his risk. His eyes cleared. "She did, but"—he held up a pointer finger—"and listen to me closely now, I am *not* a killer. You got me? I didn't give two shits about him. I didn't even *want* him in my club. I don't like you ofays. You cause trouble. The only reason I allow them in my club is because of their sugar. And baby, I will take *all* their sugar. It's the least y'all can do for all the pain and suffering you cause."

Dash stepped back. "If you didn't kill him, did you see him leave?"

"Nope."

"Do you know why he left?"

"How much is it worth to ya?"

"Les, goddammit, just *tell* me!"

"Hey, boy, you on *my* property now, and you don't have the right to speak to me in that way."

Dash held up an apologetic hand. "You're right. I was out of line."

Leslie stared at him, his sapphire eyes shining bright in the dark. "He overheard me," he murmured.

"I'm sorry?"

Leslie took a deep breath and said through clenched teeth. "He overheard me talking to Zora. I told her I had him and what would she like me to do with him. Then she told me."

"And Karl understood what was going on from just hearing your side of the conversation?"

"He got the gist he wasn't safe."

"And so he ran."

In Dash's mind, he could see the kid panic, try to reach somebody on Leslie's telephone after the club owner left, and then take off. But where would he have gone?

"How come you called Zora the night after he left and said 'it's been taken care of'?"

"How do you know that?" Leslie answered his own question. "Goddamn Horace."

"Leave him out of this. He's only trying to help."

"Get me in the jailhouse, that's how helpful he is."

"Answer the question, please."

An exasperated sigh. "Because *you* told me someone strangled that little fuck! Jesus Christ, you honestly thought I'd dirty my hands by wrapping them around his neck? And then drag his body to the Park? Please. You must be on dope."

Dash felt his cheeks burn with embarrassment. "Why'd you call Zora a second time?"

"'Cause it gets me off the hook! She asks you to do something, it's not a request, ofay, it's a demand. And she wants results."

"Why were you at her Heaven and Hell party tonight?"

Suspicion glared at Dash. "How'd you know I was there?"

"Because I was, too. Karl invited me before he died."

"I see," Leslie said. "Not that it's any of your business, but she wanted El to play her party, and I was there to make sure El played her party. You know, you and her got a lot in common. You both disrespect men on a regular basis."

His lips widened into a shrewd smile.

"At her party, she asked you to kill Walter, didn't she?"

Dash remained silent, but it was still an admission.

Leslie smirked. "Ha! Now you gotta do what she asks, and baby, I don't think you're going to get as lucky as me." A low chuckled rumbled in his chest. "No, sir. You are fucked, Mr. Parker. You're about to get your lily-white upper-class hands dirty like the rest of us."

He pulled open the back door.

"By the way, keep your ass outta my club."

He went inside, slamming the door behind him.

27

The following morning, Monday, August 23, a full week since the nightmare started, Finn burst into the bedroom with tears streaking down his face.

"My Valentino!" he wailed. "He's gone!"

Dash sat straight up in bed. He rubbed the sleep from his eyes. "Gone where?" he said mid-yawn.

Joe replied softly from the sheets next to him, "He died, lassie."

That snapped Dash into focus. He took in the tear-stained face of his friend. "I'm so sorry, Finn. What happened?"

Finn recounted how the actor succumbed to his infection. All the modern medicine in New York couldn't save him. There would be a public viewing tomorrow.

Dash's friend was inconsolable. He kept repeating over and over again, "My Valentino!"

Joe looked over at Dash. "What do we do?"

"We stay here, and we comfort our friend."

"Lassie. It's Monday."

Damn it to hell. It was NYPD Donation Day. The last person Dash wanted to deal with right now was Cullen McElroy.

He groaned and slid out of bed, leaving behind a crying Finn and a consoling Joe.

Shaved and dressed in his Banff blue pinstripe suit, he returned to Hartford & Sons, where McElroy was already waiting.

He snapped his watch shut. "On time this week, Mr. Parker. Very good."

Dash counted out the bribe and handed it more brusquely than he should have to McElroy. "Here you go, sir."

McElroy's eyes flashed. "No need to have *that* attitude. After all, I'm doing *you* a service."

Some service. It hadn't protected him from mobsters or blackmailers.

Dash swallowed down the anger and bitterness. "Apologies. I'm having a rough morning."

McElroy grunted. "So's everybody. They're all crying over this actor guy Rudolph." He scoffed. "I don't get it. So he was in a couple of pictures. What does he have that I don't got?"

A waist.

Dash kept his commentary to himself.

"Something might interest you," McElroy said. "Someone was offering me some sugar to tell on you."

"I'm sorry?"

"A blond kraut. Wanted to know where you lived and such."

Walter.

"And did you tell him?" Dash asked.

McElroy's eyes sparkled. "Not yet. I was wondering how much it was worth for me *not* to tell him."

"How did he find you?"

"Must've asked around for the flatfoot working this neighborhood, so he knows where you work. I'd be careful with him, if I were you."

"Why do you say that?"

McElroy glanced off into the distance. "I checked him out. I figured with a name like his he was up in German-town, so I spoke with a few coppers in that precinct, and whattaya know? He had a brother who was murdered last week."

Karl.

"He did?"

"Yessir. Strangled in the Park. Robbed, too. Nothing left on him except his identification card. Messy business. Found him Tuesday morning, but he'd been dead for a while. Looked as if someone was trying to hide him under the bushes and such. A walker found him and reported it."

"I see."

McElroy turned his head back towards Dash. "Ya didn't have nothin' to do with it, did you?"

Dash gave an awkward laugh. "Me? Why would I be involved in anything like that?"

McElroy shrugged. "Seems odd the brother of a murder victim is asking about you, that's all."

Another rotten smile.

"Should I tell him to bugger off? Or give him your address?"

Goddamn men like you. The leeches of New York.

Dash reached into his pockets once again and handed over a few more dollars. "You're a credit to the uniform, McElroy."

Desperate and sleep deprived, Dash returned to the law firm Meyers, Powers & Napier. When he had spoken with her twice before, he didn't know all the facts. Now he knew the story, or nearly all of it, and it was time to get confirmation. Confirmation and help.

It was time to stop being polite.

The secretary—this time wearing blue and gold, like the dress Paula wore in his club the night this fiasco began—smiled upon his entrance. That smile quickly frowned when he walked straight past her, saying over his shoulder, "Is Prudence Meyers in?"

"Sir," called out the secretary. "Wait one moment, sir!"

Dash found the last door on the left, turned the knob, and pushed it open. Pru looked up, surprise framing her lavender eyes. She wore a tan suit with faint pinstripes, her white shirt faintly ruffled at the collar. The sleeve had been pulled up from her wrist to avoid the ink stains as she made notes on a stack of papers.

A gray-haired man in the client's chair, dressed all in navy, swiveled his head around to face the interruption.

"Excuse me, sir, we're in a meeting," he said, his voice full of gravel and authority.

"Mr. Parker," Pru said, "this is most inappropriate."

"It's Dash, and we need to talk now."

The secretary caught up with him. "I'm so sorry, Pru, he just *barged* in here—"

"This is most outrageous," the gray-haired man said. He swiveled his creaky head back towards Pru. "What kind of business are you running here?"

She held up a placating hand. "I apologize for this

outburst, Mr. Williams. Frannie, can you show Mr. Parker out, please?"

Dash crossed his arms across his chest to prevent Frannie from attempting to grab his arm and pull him out. "I'm not leaving, Pru, until we talk."

Her lavender eyes burned with anger. "I am speaking with a client, Mr. Parker."

"Either we can speak in private or we can speak in front of him. He's a client; it's privileged, correct?" Dash then sat in the other client chair next to Mr. Williams. He held out a hand. "I'm Dash Parker. Nice to meet you, Mr. Williams."

The man stiffened, his disapproval sounding like a cough caught in the base of his throat. "This is most absurd. Perhaps I should find another lawyer."

Somehow Pru managed to calm him down. Even more testament to her negotiating skills, she got him to wait until after this conversation was completed. When she closed the door, shutting out the sight of Frannie patting Mr. Williams's hand, she let out a hissed sigh.

"Alright, Mr. Parker, you have exactly one minute to state why you're here before I call the police."

She turned and resumed her place behind her desk.

Dash sat forward in the chair. "I know it all. Paula getting Walter fired. The Müller's ensuing blackmail scheme. The clubs they raided and some of the people they targeted, one of whom is Zora Mae. Or rather, her moll. I know Tyler Smith was to get some evidence for you. I know that Walter Müller will do anything to get it back. What I don't know, Pru, is whether Tyler gave that to you or if it's still missing."

They both sat silent.

The room seemed to tick, though Dash saw no evidence of a clock.

Finally, she said, "What is it that you want?"

"I'm not here to blackmail you! I'm here because I need your help. Walter is a very dangerous man, and he is threatening me. If you're really trying to help people like us—people like me—then stop letting it be an esoteric legal argument and make it real."

They locked eyes.

Another length of silence stretched to its breaking point.

Her nod was slightly imperceptible. "I will do what I can, though I fail to see how this information will help you."

She paused, her hands coming up, her fingers forming a point against her chin while she gathered her words.

"A case like this, a blackmail case, depends upon evidence and the scope of the extortion. Because the letters were sent in the mail, it's considered a federal offense. But even then, the FBI wouldn't take much of an interest unless either the blackmailer was a person they despised anyway or the blackmail victims were high enough in society that their money and status would force the authorities into action."

"While their money and status would keep their names out of the courts and the papers."

"Correct. Karl had mentioned such people to us when he was detailing what he and his brother were doing. We needed that confirmation to know if we even have a shot of ending Walter's extortion."

Dash sat back in his chair. "What kinds of people?"

"Nephews of Astors. Cousins of Vanderbilts. Sons and daughters of those in Tammany Hall."

Dash whistled.

"Exactly. When the FBI sees those names, they'll have no choice but to act."

"Especially when some enterprising young Fed sees a chance to make a name for himself."

"That too."

"Do you think it was intentional on Walter's part?"

Pru shook her head. "I think it was a happy accident. Most of his victims couldn't very well pay the blackmail, but these gentlemen and ladies could. They could afford to pay indefinitely."

"It's why he could survive being asked to leave the Committee of Fourteen." Dash looked at her. "What kind of evidence would Tyler be stealing?"

The moment he asked the question, he had the answer.

"A ledger."

Surprise lit Pru's face. "How did you know?"

"Karl told me Walter worked in their finance department and kept meticulous records. I guessed a habit like that is a hard one to break."

He leaned forward again. Now for the important question.

"Do you have it, Pru?"

Her guard came back up. "That's really none of your concern."

"Let me tell you why I want to know. It's not to tell Walter Müller."

"It's not?"

"*Somebody* killed Tyler Smith and Karl Müller, Pru. And the answer hinges on if the ledger was found and by whom."

"Not necessarily. Walter could have done it."

"Then he'd have the ledger."

"Not unless he'd hidden it."

Dash shook his head. "Tyler would've never let Walter into his room."

"He could've forced his way in."

"There's a tightly run lobby downstairs, plus an elevator man. Even if Walter got past those two, Tyler still wouldn't have opened the door. And the door was not broken open. I know because I saw it a day later. Whoever killed Tyler was someone he knew and trusted."

He watched her face carefully. Her eyes lost their sparkle. Her jaw went slack. The skin on her face paled to an ashen white.

"You have it, don't you?" Dash said, his voice soft.

She nodded.

"Who gave it to you?"

She shook her head. "He couldn't have. He was with me that night, hiding out in my apartment."

"The whole night?"

She paused. Her voice dropped in volume, so soft it was almost a whisper. "Not before we met at the club, no. But we didn't have it until days after Tyler was killed."

"Timelines are easy to fudge, Pru."

"No, I refuse to accept it."

"Why is that?"

"Because it makes no *sense!* What's the motive?"

An idea materialized, so clear and so simple, Dash couldn't believe he hadn't thought of it before.

"Pru, when did Tyler break things off with Karl?"

Whatever she was expecting Dash to say next, it wasn't this. "Excuse me?"

"The breakup. When did it happen?"

An uncomfortable laugh. "That's absurd. Tyler didn't break things off with Karl. He wouldn't have. They were going to Paris together at the end of the month. Where on earth did you hear such a preposterous idea?"

"From two men. The first was Karl—"

"What? That can't be!"

"—and the second was the man pretending to be Tyler." Dash gazed hard at Pru once more. "I think we found our motive. Tell me, Pru, who gave you the ledger?"

Tuesday at mid-morning, Dash and Joe first went to Paul Avery's apartment. Not surprisingly, he wasn't there. Dash managed to charm Marjorie Norton into giving him Paul's employer.

Scorsoni Construction was located uptown on 77th Street and Madison. After paying the cabbie, they walked towards the building's entryway with purpose.

Dash glanced at Joe, who was at his side. "Are you ready?"

"Aye, lassie. You?"

"Ready doesn't begin to describe it."

The building housing the construction company was surprisingly nondescript, a boxy square rising four stories into the sky. It dwarfed the buildings next to it, allowing for SCORSONI CONSTRUCTION to be painted on its sides. Underneath was the epigraph: NO JOB TOO BIG, NO PROBLEM TOO SMALL. DRIVEN BY THE AMERICAN SPIRIT.

Inside, they spoke to the doorman, saying they had a 10:00 appointment with Paul Avery. The doorman called up. The secretary had no record of such an appointment. Dash pressed that there must be a mix-up and successfully implored the doorman to ask the secretary to patch him through to Paul. They must've reached him, for the doorman asked for their names. Dash was pretty sure their names would get the man to at least come down.

Mr. Avery had serious stones. He invited them up.

The office was on the third floor. The setup reminded Dash of newsrooms, where multiple desks were arranged in the open air, sitting two at a time. It was mostly women who sat there, typing on large typewriters or chatting on phones.

One woman was in an argument and, in a thick Brooklyn accent, said, "Listen, wise guy, I don't care what you *think* was in the agreement. I'm looking at the contract as we speak and we did *not* promise a twenty percent bonus if you deliver on time . . . Why would we reward you for simply doing your job . . . ? Do I sound like I'm joking?"

Three closed doors sat at the far end of the room. One of them opened and out stepped Paul Avery, dressed in a light blue suit.

"Gentlemen," he said, his voice purposefully low in pitch.

Knowing his secret, Dash found the voice to be strained, an unconvincing disguise for a man who preferred Chantilly lace and face paint.

Paul gestured for Dash and Joe to join him in his office. As Dash passed the argumentative Brooklyn girl, she said into the receiver, "Ya talk to ya mother with that mouth . . . ? Just 'cause you *can't read* doesn't mean my company is gonna shell out some dollars . . . Oh yeah? I got some words for you too!"

And then she slammed the receiver down, ending the call. The Brooklyn girl leaned over to her desk mate, a woman whose eyes never left the fast-moving typewriter. "Can you believe that jerk? What a cad!"

They stepped into Paul's office, which was moderately big. A large mahogany wood desk covered with stacked papers sat on one end. On the opposite side, two chairs for guests. Two filing cabinets hugged the wall to Dash's right.

To Dash's left, a coatrack where Paul hung his matching blue fedora.

Paul closed the door and return to his place behind the desk. He folded his hands in front of him and said, "To what do I owe the pleasure?"

Dash didn't beat around the bush. "You can tell us why you killed Tyler Smith."

28

The silence that followed was profound.

All three men stared at one another. Dash didn't move nor blink. Neither did Joe.

Paul broke first. "What do you want?" His voice was drenched in fear.

Joe replied, "We want answers, *Paula*."

Paul flinched at the voice of his female namesake. "Please," he said, "not so loud."

Dash leaned forward in his chair. "I'll keep quiet as long as you tell me the truth. The moment you lie to me, I tell the police everything I know. Do we have an understanding?"

Paul took a deep breath. "Don't make me do this."

Joe said, his voice gruff, "It's happenin', lad, so just accept it."

Dash tapped the arms of his chair. "I know the plan for that night. Pru told it to me. The Müllers went out for dinner. Karl gave Tyler a key to their apartment. Tyler broke in and found the ledger."

Paul flicked him a look. "Of course, you know about the ledger. You want it back. To give it to *him*."

He looked off to the side, his expression darkening.

Joe scoffed, "We're not workin' for that bloody bluenose. We're victims of him, for chrissakes!"

Dash continued. "Tyler was to bring the ledger to my club."

Paul nodded. "We figured it was safe because it was still relatively new. Walter would've never heard of it. Except Dumb Dora Karl led him straight to it."

Dash nodded. "When the Müllers returned home, Walter noticed something was amiss. No offense, but Tyler was an amateur thief. Despite his best efforts, he wouldn't have been able to leave everything the exact same way it was. Walter put two and two together and when Karl left with whatever excuse he gave—get some air, meet a friend, go to church for Sunday evening prayer—Walter followed his brother downtown. Walter asked me to find a female impersonator in Pinstripes, so he must've seen you two together at some point."

Paul replied, "Perhaps when we met up in front of your club."

"Did you have the ledger with you then?"

"I didn't! I never met up with Tyler that night!"

"Then how come Pru has it now?"

"We knew something went wrong with Walter's appearance at your club. We were hoping Tyler saw Walter and ran. When we didn't hear from him, I went back to the Shelton the next day, and didn't find him there. I went back the day after that and he *still* wasn't answering, so I . . . snuck into his apartment."

He took a moment to compose himself.

"The apartment was empty. And I thought, while I'm here, let's see if the blasted ledger is, too. I was in the middle of searching for it, actually, when you two showed up. I swear, I was not there Sunday night. Only that Tuesday morning."

Dash watched his face, which was still half-turned away from them. "That's not all of it."

"Why are you *doing* this? I tell you, that is exactly what happened."

"I'm afraid it's not. You *did* go to the Shelton Sunday night."

"That's a lie. Who said that?"

Dash looked over to Joe. "Should we show him?"

Joe shrugged. "I suppose we have to."

Dash reached into his pocket and brought out a piece of paper. He handed it to Paul, who regarded it with suspicion, then with trembling fingers, opened it. Dash watched his eyes as Paul read the forged note he had spent all of last night writing and rewriting. Dash tried his best to copy Walter's handwriting from the piece of paper on which he'd written his address the night he first blackmailed them. Walter claimed earlier he had taught Karl how to write. Dash hoped their writing styles would be similar.

Paul's face whitened as he read the words:

Dearest Pru,

I am writing this in haste as I don't know how much time I have before I must leave. I witnessed something terrible tonight. Unspeakable. I went to Tyler's apartment before we met at the club, and I found him dead!!! Struck in the head. And Paula was in the apartment. She must have killed him for reasons we all know. I ran out of there, and now I don't know what to do or where to turn. I couldn't say anything at the club for fear of my life. I hope one day I can return to you, but now I must go into hiding.

Sincerely, Karl

Paul looked up at him. "You wouldn't. Betray your own kind?"

Dash kept his face stony. "When my own kind is a killer, yes. I have no qualms about doing that."

"Why would I kill him? I loved him."

Joe replied, "Precisely why, lad. Ya loved him too much to let him go."

Dash went on. "Tyler must've told you about his escape to Paris. With Karl."

"Leaving ya. For good."

"Forever."

"I'm sure ya didn't mean to kill him, lad. Sure it was an accident."

"You couldn't persuade him to stay. It was too much."

"Ya picked up the ashtray and hit him."

"All right!" Paul shouted.

Dash could hear a silence on the other side of the door. His coworkers had heard the shout and were no doubt murmuring *What is going on in there?*

Paul didn't seem to notice or care. His face was withdrawn, his mouth trembling. "I didn't mean to. I just wanted him here. He had to stay here. As long as he's here, I could convince him one day that I was—"

He stopped and took a deep breath.

"I loved him. So. Much. I didn't understand why he couldn't love me back in the same way."

He sniffed back more tears.

"It was before we went to your club. I was to meet him there to make sure he got back from the Müllers' safe and sound. Instead of handing over the ledger, I found him *packing*. I wanted to know where he was going. That's when he told me about Paris, about him and Karl going *together*. I couldn't believe what I was hearing. Him and Karl? In Paris? As a couple? I begged him. *Begged* him."

Paul dropped his head and lowered his voice.

"He wouldn't listen. He said he loved that, that *boy.* Loved him! Can you imagine? After all we'd been through together. After all the times I . . ." He swallowed hard. "The next thing I knew, the ashtray was in my hand."

There it was. The confession. In front of two witnesses. Dash looked to Joe, whose face was locked in a grimace.

After a moment, Dash said, "And then you moved the body to the alleyway using the room service cart. That's how you truly lost your keys. Not in leaving my club but while moving him."

Paul was silently weeping now. "I didn't mean to. I just wanted him—I just wanted him to stay. Why didn't he? Why didn't he want to stay? With me?"

The unspoken answer hung above the room like a cigarette cloud.

"After that, I didn't have time to get the ledger. I ran to the club and pretended everything was fine. When Walter showed up and started fighting you, I hid in the bathroom with Karl."

"That's where you told him Tyler no longer wanted to see him." Dash turned to Joe. "That's why he was so upset and panicked."

Paul snorted. "Please. He didn't deserve Tyler's love. Given what he'd done with his despicable brother—"

Joe interrupted, "He was helping ya put his own flesh and blood in jail. That should count for something."

"Not enough! It wasn't enough. He hadn't earned redemption in my eyes."

Dash said, "So you decided to break his heart."

"No," Paul replied. "That was just a happy accident. I

didn't want him going to the Shelton and starting trouble by asking about a dead man."

"Why not? Seems to me, you could've easily framed him for murder." As soon as Dash said the words, he understood. "The ledger. You didn't get it the first time, being too distracted by Tyler's packing. You needed to search his room once more."

Paul nodded. "I couldn't have them looking for a tenant. Not yet, at any rate. If they found his body, they'd seal off the room. I got called away Monday to a job site and couldn't break away. I was a nervous wreck, hoping they wouldn't find him. That Tuesday, I told them I was ill and ran to his apartment." He scoffed lightly. "Imagine my surprise when the two of you walked in on me."

"Hence the pistol."

"It was Tyler's. I was telling the truth about not knowing how to use the blasted thing."

Joe said, "We thank ya's for not accidentally shooting us."

Dave flashed a warning glance to his friend and said to Paul, "And Karl?"

Paul sniffed again. "What about Karl?"

"I want to know what happened to Karl."

The mere mention of the kid's name irritated the man. "I don't know a damn thing about what happened to Karl. I didn't even know he was dead until *you* told me!"

"Stop lying, Paul." Dash's voice was hard now, anger building up inside him. "What happened? Did Karl not listen to you and go to Tyler's? He was trying to reach some-body that night. I think it was his lover. Did he not buy your lie about Tyler breaking things off?"

"This is preposterous! I was not at the Shelton on Sunday night. Ask Pru."

"She went to sleep, didn't she?" Dash was gathering fury, his face flush, his cheeks hot. "You could've snuck out of her apartment, gone to the Shelton, found Karl, and did what you've always wanted to do."

"No!"

"You strangled that kid and threw him away like the garbage you believed he was."

Paul was bewildered. "I did no such thing!"

"Liar!"

"Lassie," Joe murmured.

Paul's mouth gaped open. "You're insane. You know that? I, I admit, I accidentally hit Tyler, but I didn't go on a, a murderous *rampage*. I am not a violent man, I swear. I just lost my temper that one time . . . that one time I wish I could . . ." The tears came back. ". . . wish I could change. Oh God, Tyler, I'm so sorry."

Paul began to quietly weep.

Dash's surge of anger began to subside, replaced with a growing confusion. He was so sure Paul Avery killed them both. But this pathetic man mewling grief in front of him had seemed so . . . what was the word? . . . *sincere* in his denials of killing Karl. Could Dash be wrong?

There was a knock at the door. One of the secretaries opened it and poked her head in. "Mr. Avery? Is everything alright?"

Paul averted his face so she wouldn't see the pink cheeks and the trail marks of his tears. "Yes, Gladys."

She looked doubtfully from Paul to Dash and Joe. "All right," she said slowly. "There's a package for you. You need to sign for it."

"Thanks, Gladys." He wiped his face with a handkerchief and stood up. "Would you gentlemen excuse me?"

Dash replied, "We're not quite finished here, Mr. Avery."

Gladys leapt to her boss's defense. "Excuse *me*, gentlemen, but you can wait one moment while he gets some air and gets his package. I don't know what could be so important."

Joe said, "It's very important, miss—"

She cut him off with a single raised finger. "Not now, gentlemen. You can wait." Her voice softened. "Right this way, Mr. Avery."

She gave them a withering, warning look as Paul left the office.

As soon as he cleared the threshold, she said, "You two don't mind, I need to find a file. Last I saw it, it was in here somewhere."

Gladys walked into the office and closed the door behind her, effectively trapping Dash and Joe inside. She sat down behind Paul's desk and began opening the drawers, keeping one eye on them as she searched. Dash mentally tipped his hat to her. She was clever. And fiercely loyal. He hoped Paul paid her well.

Joe murmured to Dash, "Will he try to run?"

Gladys paused, staring at them. Joe forced a smile and stared back. The seconds stretched into what felt like half a minute before Gladys broke away her gaze and concentrated on the bottom drawer of Paul's desk.

Dash murmured back, "Most assuredly."

"What do we do?"

Gladys said, "What are you two muttering about?"

She shut the bottom drawer with a slam, her head coming up. She folded her hands and leaned forward on the desk. Her expression said she expected an answer.

Fiercely loyal, indeed.

Joe replied, "With all due respect, ma'am, it's none of your business."

"I see. If it has anything to do with Mr. Avery, then it *is* my business. Why are you here? And why have you made that dear man so upset?"

Dash said, "It was unintentional, ma'am."

She sniffed. "Don't seem to matter if it was intended or not, the effect is just the same. He's about to leave on the trip of a lifetime, and you two barge in here—"

Dash held up a finger. "Excuse me, what did you say? About the trip?"

Gladys stiffened. "Not that it's any of *your* business, but Mr. Avery was leaving for Paris. He's always wanted to go, and now he gets that chance. And you two are just ruining—"

"Joe." Dash looked at his friend, who nodded. "Thank you, Gladys, but I believe we'll be going."

He and Joe both stood up. The movement startled Gladys, who said, "What are you two doing?"

Joe said, "Apologies, ma'am."

He jerked open the office door and the two of them ran through the office at a fast clip with Gladys yelling from behind. The women at the desks gave them concerned looks as they excused their way out. The elevator was going to take too long, so they took the stairs, two at a time, until they hit the lobby. No sign of Paul Avery.

"Hell!" Dash said.

He went to the doorman.

"Excuse me, sir. There was a gentleman in a light blue suit who came down here. Do you know where he went?"

"Certainly. He signed for this package, then said he had an emergency and took off. He gave me the package to hold."

"Which way did he go?"

"Lemme see. He took a left out of here and not too long ago, too. You might be able to catch him. Say, is it the same emergency as his?"

Dash didn't give a response. He and Joe took off in pursuit, bursting through the lobby doors and out into the open air. Once on the street, Dash searched the blocks ahead. In the late morning foot traffic, Dash saw flashes of Paul's blue suit a block and a half uptown.

"There!"

Running up Madison, the two men dodged oncoming pedestrians, some of whom raised their voices and yelled, "Slow down, ya maniacs!" The intersections weren't timed for their benefit, but they ran into traffic anyway. Dash hoped the oncoming taxis and delivery trucks would stop. Miraculously, they did, though they honked their horns and shouted out curses.

They were soon only a block behind Paul, who gave a nervous look behind him. They were gaining ground, the distance between them shortening.

We're going to catch him. By God, we're going to catch him.

Their good luck ended right there, for a thick crowd of people suddenly loomed into view. Thousands—maybe even tens of thousands—clogged the streets and the sidewalks.

"What the hell is that?" Joe called.

Paul's blue suit disappeared into the throng.

Dash said, "Oh no, no, *no!*"

They followed him into the mass of people, most of them women and young girls crying. Many were saying, "Oh Rudy! My dear sweet Rudy!"

The Valentino viewing.

The papers had publicized that Rudolph Valentino's body would be lying in state at Campbell's Funeral Parlor on Madison and 81st. Only the crowd was so massive, Dash and Joe hadn't yet reached 81st; they were only at 79th. It looked like half the city had shown up to get a glimpse at the famous actor.

Dash and Joe tried to push their way through, stepping around and, in some cases, shoving aside the grievers. Every once and a while, Dash caught sight of Paul's blue coattails ahead of them.

A young woman yelled in Dash's ear, "I need to see him! I need to see him one last time!"

Dash gripped his throbbing ear and looked over the crowd. Where the hell was Paul? There was shouting ahead, then a scream. Suddenly, the crowd surged forward, knocking Dash off balance. He almost fell but regained his footing. What was happening?

A stampede.

By the time Dash registered it, he was caught in the current of people. Police horses stood off to the side. The mounted officers blew their whistles to no avail. Bodies jammed against Dash's back and front. He was pushed into the small body of a young girl, whose height was perfectly aligned to Dash's stomach. He felt the wind leave his diaphragm. The pain was sharp, and he couldn't breathe. Another woman shoved his right shoulder, turning him left. Another shove to his left, turning him right. Something caught his legs and before he could stop it, he went down.

Feet pounded the pavement by his head. He placed his palms on the sidewalk, trying to push himself up, but hard wooden soles stepped on his fingers. He cried out in pain and surprise. He brought his hands underneath his chest to protect them from being broken. He turned his body slightly and looked behind him. Above him was a sea of skirts and dresses. Below him, the mass that had entangled his legs turned out to be a woman who had also fallen.

He shouted, "Stop! Stop! You'll hurt her!"

A shoe kicked his head. The world slid out of focus. Colors and shapes blurred together. He thought he heard his name being called, but it was hard to tell over the cries of others. He felt hands hook themselves underneath his arms. The sea of legs and shoes changed to that of hats and hair. He turned. Joe was speaking to him, but he couldn't rightly understand him. Nausea overtook him and the world began to spin. The last thing he remembered seeing was Joe yelling to the crowd around them.

29

Dash's eyes fluttered open. At first, he didn't recognize the room. Then he saw it was his bedroom and he was lying on the bed. Joe was sitting in the corner, staring at him with concerned eyes. Finn was in the other chair, blowing smoke rings out the opened window overlooking Commerce Street.

At that moment, a truck blared a horn, and the sound was murder on Dash's head. He sat up and said, "Close that window, will ya, Finn?"

"Look who's returned to the land of the living," Finn said as he shut the window.

"Jury is still out on the living part."

Dash felt coldness on his head and realized an ice pack had been placed there. He reached up and removed it. He said to Joe, "Don't tell me the other side of my face is now black and blue."

Joe shook his head. "Just a nasty bump on your head."

Finn said, "It was utter chaos out there! I heard it was tens of thousands of people who showed up to see my Valentino."

Joe rolled his eyes. "Finney, they all tried to kill us."

Finn placed a hand over his own chest. "*Such* is the power of the world's greatest lover."

Joe shook his head and said to Dash, "How ya feelin', lassie?"

Dash took a deep breath. "I've had better days. What happened after I went down?"

"I picked ya up and carried ya off the street. Wasn't easy with all them Valentino nuts weeping and shrieking. Never heard such noises in all my life. Once I got us to the cross street, I whistled for a cab. Miracle of miracles, we got one before the coppers started shutting everything down."

"You carried me?"

Finn replied, "Over his shoulder and everything. I saw him coming into the apartment. *Such* strength. If he wasn't with you, I'd have found a way to faint so he could pick *me* up."

"Finn," Dash warned. A question popped into his throbbing head. "Why weren't you at the viewing?"

"I tried, dearie, honest I did, but the crowds were too much. I heard rumor they would have another viewing tomorrow."

"I see." Dash looked to Joe. "Did we lose Paul?"

"Aye. Disappeared without a trace. Called the construction place. He never came back. Went to his apartment while you were sleeping. Marjorie hasn't seen him neither."

"Damn." Dash sat back against the headboard. "What time is it?"

Finn replied, "It's a little past one." He turned to Joe. "And *I* am just about starved. What say you to lunch? I could just about murder some deviled eggs and jam."

Joe snorted. "I could just about murder you. Dash here

is laid up in bed—all because of you and half the city's obsession with this *Val-en-tin-o* bloke—and you're talking 'bout eggs."

The two men started arguing. Finn wanted to go to the Crystal because of the champagne. Joe wanted to know how Finney could afford champagne, since he knew good and well what he was paid.

Dash couldn't take it. "Boys! Please continue this conversation elsewhere."

His whole body felt sore. God knew how many times he was kicked and where. His knuckles ached, his head throbbed, and his ribs were probably bruised. On top of that, his legs felt stiff, and his stomach still smarted from when he ran into that little girl, her head making a perfect fist. He felt like a prizefighter. Only he hadn't won.

Joe said, "C'mon, Finney. Let's let the man be." He looked at Dash, "Get some rest, now. I'll be back to check on ya."

"Thank you, Joe."

Dash drifted in and out of consciousness. His dreams were feverish, often nightmares, and he'd awake startled to find himself alone. Sometimes the dreams would blur into reality, the images staying in the room until he went back to sleep.

As the sun began to set, Dash rolled over to see a figure standing by the dresser, his back towards Dash. "Joe? Joe, I need some water."

The figure set off to the washroom, but before he could return, Dash fell back into another dream.

A sudden crash of thunder caused Dash to sit up straight in bed. Joe was sitting in the chair by the window, watching the storm batter against the glass.

"There he is. Ya have a nice rest?"

"I believe so. My head certainly hurts less than it did." Dash looked around the room. "Did you bring me some water?"

"Water? When did ya ask for that?"

"A while ago. At least, I thought I did."

Joe stood up. "I think you were still dreaming. You haven't said a word since I've been here."

He left the bedroom and went to the washroom.

Dash eased himself out of the bed and limped towards the window. The glass was streaked with rain. Lightning flashed in the distance. On the street below, people scurried underneath black and gray umbrellas, dodging puddles on the sidewalks and in the streets. He heard a creak behind him and turned to see Joe with a glass of water.

Dash said, "You're an angel among men."

"And you're a silly goose. I'm opening Pinstripes now, though I doubt anyone will be out in this weather. You stay here and keep resting."

Dash made a salute. "Aye aye, captain."

Joe rolled his eyes and left the apartment. Dash saw his figure below, joining the throngs of people sloshing through the storm. He sipped the water, grateful the nausea had long since passed.

Another crash of thunder. What a horrible night to be out. It was then Dash realized it was Tuesday night and he owed Walter a name. He groaned. If he missed another deadline, Walter would for certain turn them in. Pinstripes would be raided, and he, Joe, Finn, and Atty would go to jail. He couldn't let that happen. Not after all they'd been through.

Dash finished the water and dressed slowly and carefully. He didn't want to risk pulling a Boone and passing out. Outside in the downpour, he waited a good ten minutes before he could find a cab. Drenched to the bone, he dripped in the backseat as the cab made its way up to Sauerkraut Boulevard.

Out front of Walter's building, Dash rang the buzzer, hoping he wasn't too late. He heard someone coming down the stairs, but instead of Walter, it was Mother. She wore a severe black dress with sleeves, the skirt stopping well past the knee. Her long, white pearls were draped low across her neck.

She looked at him with confusion. "Who are you?"

"Good evening, ma'am, I'm a friend of Walter's. I'm supposed to meet him here."

She regarded him with suspicion. "Walter doesn't invite people over."

"Yes, ma'am, but it's important. Another update on the project from last week."

"So many urgent meetings. He is not here at the moment. He stepped out."

"I see. May I come in? It's really coming down out here."

She pursed her lips, but surprisingly, she acquiesced. He followed her upstairs to their apartment. He hung up his raincoat to drip in the short hall and walked into the parlor.

Mother gestured to a room off to the left of the parlor. "Would you like some tea to warm up?"

"That would be lovely."

She nodded once and set off to the kitchen. When she was gone, Dash realized what a golden opportunity he had been given. He looked around to see if Mother was anywhere in sight. She wasn't. Making an educated guess, he went down the other hall and found the bedrooms. There were only two, which meant the brothers had shared a room. Mother's was easy to identify. It was the master bedroom at the end of the hall. The brothers slept to the right of it.

Dash stepped inside and turned on the lamp. Two small beds were positioned on opposite sides of the room, each having their own nightstand. Two knitting needles and a pile of dark navy yarn laid on the bed to Dash's right. Mother's knitting projecting, the one she mentioned the last time Dash was here. A small writing desk was in front of the one window in the space. Dash could picture Walter sitting there, writing his evil blackmail letters. Anger once again filled his frame.

What a horrible, horrible man. Such evil hiding behind such pious morality.

And if that didn't perfectly define these Prohibition days, Dash didn't know what would.

The floorboards creaked behind him. Dash turned to see Mother in the doorway holding a cup and saucer. "I see you found his room."

"Yes. I hope you don't mind. I get wanderlust if I'm stationary for too long."

He took the cup and saucer from her hands. A quick sip. It was only hot water. Mother had apparently forgotten to put in the tea bag.

He smiled, murmuring compliments about the tea. He looked around the bedroom, seeing the paintings of the German countryside on each wall in heavy wooden frames. He nodded towards them, saying they were lovely.

Mother didn't seem to hear what he said. Instead, she said, "That forgetful boy. He left his timepiece here."

Dash was startled at the non sequitur. "Pardon me?"

"The timepiece. Walter just got it last week, and he sometimes forgets to wear it. You wrap it around your wrist. Look."

She pointed to the nightstand on the right side of the room. Dash assumed this was Walter's side. There on the nightstand was a wristwatch.

Dash slowly looked from the nightstand to Mother and back again. "You say Walter got this last week?"

"Why, yes."

Dash went over to the nightstand and picked it up. He wasn't well versed in these new inventions, but he could've sworn it was the same one Karl had on his wrist. But both Walter and McElroy had said the boy's pockets were picked clean. Why take all the contents out of his pockets but leave his watch? And if Walter was brandishing this since last week, after Karl was found dead in Central Park, then . . .

Dash slowly turned the timepiece over. There, on the back of the face, were the letters "к м." Karl Müller's initials. This was the wristwatch Tyler Smith had engraved.

Dash looked back at Mother. "Mrs. Müller, the Sunday before last, did Karl come home?"

Karl was contemplating a new life. He overhead Leslie Charles promising to turn him over to someone else. He had to run. He must've come home to pack.

Mother belatedly answered his question. "Karl?" She thought to herself. "I believe so."

Dash's pulse started to climb. "He came back here to this apartment the Sunday before last? You're absolutely certain?"

She nodded as she stepped forward, the motion causing her to lose a bit of her balance. She steadied herself with a hand on the bedroom doorframe. It was apparent she was not sober. Dash wondered if she ever was.

She said, "He was packing when I found him. Told me he was leaving and said goodbye."

Dash set the wristwatch back onto the nightstand. "You spoke with him? That night?"

She entered the room and sat on the bed next to the pile of knitting. Her eyes were glassy and wet. They gazed off into the distance. "He said he couldn't live this way anymore. His heart was broken and there was nothing left for him here. I told him he had his family, but that did not console him. I told him he was being silly for behaving such in a way over a girl. The city is full of them. He'd forget her in time."

She wrapped her arms around herself in a tight hug.

"Then he said it wasn't a girl. He said a man's name. And he cried. My son *cried* like a weakling. He said he missed his lover."

Her mouth shook.

"Lover. He used the word *lover* to describe a man. I was so—so—disgusted."

Her hands reached for the pile of knitting. She placed it in her lap, where she began to pull at the thick woolen threads.

Realization hit Dash just as another crash of thunder pounded outside. "Mrs. Müller, what did you do?"

Her voice took on a dreamlike quality, as if she weren't talking to anyone other than herself. "I told him he couldn't be such a thing. It would jeopardize Walter at the Committee. He would bring shame to our family."

Her voice changed. It became sharp and mean.

"He said he didn't care. What he wanted was *sin*.

Perversion. Just like his father. My son would not live a life like that. He would *not!* I wouldn't allow it."

A flash of lightning, a boom of thunder.

Her hands continued to pick at the woolen threads in her lap, wrapping them around her fingers. Dash visualized them wrapped around Karl's neck. Mother holding them there until the boy was subdued. Had she meant to kill him? Or was it an accident?

The time lapse. McElroy had said it, but it didn't register with Dash at the time. Karl's body was found Tuesday morning. Yet Monday night, Walter was at Dash's tailor shop, drunk, claiming he'd caused Karl to be dead.

"Mrs. Müller."

"Walter came home and helped me take Karl to the Park. Karl loved the Park. He could spend hours upon hours there, never getting bored."

Dash watched her in horror. A mother who killed her own son.

No wonder she gets blotto every day. She can't face what she's done.

She shook herself out of her alcohol-infused trance. "If you'll excuse me," she said, untangling the threads from her fingers. "I'm not feeling very well. I need to lie down."

She stood up, the knitting pile falling to the floor. She turned and slowly shuffled her way out of the room and down the hall to the master bedroom. The door closed behind her.

Dash felt the apartment start to spin. He would've broken down and cried over the horror right then had he not seen familiar stationary on the writing desk.

He set the cup and saucer down on the nightstand next to Karl's wristwatch. He walked over to the desk, his head pounding like the rain outside. Illuminated by the strobe of lightning was the letter Z. For Zora Mae. And underneath it was Paul Avery's address. The same note she had given Dash last week at the Hot Cha. How on earth had Walter gotten this?

The figure in Dash's room. He had thought it was a dream. What if it was Walter?

Walter had run out of patience. He must've followed Dash from somewhere or found out where he lived from that backstabbing rat McElroy. Then he broke into Dash's apartment, searching the place while Dash was out cold. Walter would've found the addresses of Paul Avery and Prudence Meyers stored in his dresser.

"Oh no," he said aloud.

Dash turned and ran out of the apartment and down the stairs. Outside in the rain, he ran until he found an available cab. Paul's address came out in a rush.

"And step on it!" he told the cabbie.

The rain slowed traffic to a crawl and it took almost an hour to get back down to the Village to Christopher and Waverly. Dash tossed money at the driver and ran to the building. He pressed the buzzer to Paul's apartment. No answer. He pressed again.

He then pressed Marjorie Norton's. No answer either. He was about to press all of the tenant buttons until someone let him in when he saw the front door was slightly ajar. He wrenched it open and raced up the stairs. At the top, he knocked on Paul's closed door. No response. He knocked again. Something told him to try the doorknob. He turned it, finding it unlocked, and the door swung open.

He entered the apartment, saying, "Paul! Paul, are you—"

He stopped. At first, there was incomprehension. Confusion about the scene before him. Then slowly, like floodwater creeping up his ankles to his shoulders, dread filled every inch of Dash's tall, trim frame.

For that's when he saw the dead body lying in the center of the floor.

30

Dash had only been face-to-face with death a handful of times, usually those of family members. And it occurred to him, as he stared at the lifeless corpse of poor, innocent Marjorie Norton, that a room has an odd quiet when it hosts death, as if all the sound is taken away along with the person's soul. The air in this musty, cramped space was certainly still, almost reverent. The electric current, normally humming in the tableside lamps, quieted itself for the first time. Even the shadows seemed to retreat far into the dusty, webbed corners. Death demands such respect. More so than God. God can be praised and cursed in the same breath with the cocky certainty He will forgive the blasphemous words escaping your lips. Death did not forgive. Nor did it forget.

A pool of blood surrounded Marjorie, who lay on her stomach. Her head was a pulpy mess of bone and hair. The smell of copper mixed with the pungent smell of gunpowder. Whatever had happened here, it hadn't occurred that long ago.

She must've heard Walter barging in. She went upstairs

to investigate. Maybe he even forced her to open the door. And then he . . .

Dash turned away from the body, bile rising in his throat. He thought he was going to vomit, but thankfully he didn't. He waited for the spasms in his throat and stomach to stop. Then he turned his attention to the rest of the apartment. The front room was a mess. Furniture toppled over, books and papers scattered across the floor. There had been an immense struggle.

A horrible thought occurred to Dash. Walter could still be in the apartment. Dash wished he had taken Atty's gun when offered. Now here he was, standing next to a dead body, and her killer was armed while he had nothing with which to defend himself.

He backed away and closed the door. Poor Marjorie. Her only sin was curiosity. Damn that evil Walter.

As Dash walked down the hallway, he thought about where Walter would go next. If Paul didn't have what he was looking for, then he'd go to Pru.

"Oh no," Dash moaned.

He ran down the stairs and out into the rain. It took another ten minutes to find an empty cab in this weather. Time was ticking, and Walter was cleaning up all the loose ends from his brother's betrayal.

"Please, please," Dash kept repeating to himself in the back of the cab.

The cab driver glanced back at him with uneasiness, but Dash barely registered the movement. He kept thinking, *please let me be ahead of Walter Müller for once.*

The cab roared up to Tammany Hall. Dash paid the driver and ran through the downpour to the offices of Meyers, Powers & Napier. The flashing neon of the

Olympic and the Central Hotel felt mocking and absurd given the tragedies of the night.

At the law firm, the door hung open, nearly ripped off its hinges. The wrath of Walter Müller. Dash waited a moment outside. If he saw another mangled body, he didn't think he'd be able to withstand it.

He took a deep breath. His only hope was that Pru wasn't here; that Walter had just found the ledger in Pru's safe. And he had no doubt that's where it was.

If any one of us could open it, it would be him.

Dash wouldn't have been surprised if the German used dynamite. Walter was beyond stealth at this point. He was a blunt battering ram, leaving destruction and debris in his wake.

Dash stepped through the law firm's doorway. The storm continued to rage outside but inside the office, the noise level dropped by half. Dash kept the door open in the hopes a good citizen would come along and report a break-in.

The front room was dark. The air was still. Only loud, ragged breaths could be heard. Dash looked around, trying to find their source.

Pru? Where are you, Pru?

It took half a minute for him to realize the breaths were his own.

"Thank the Lord," Dash muttered to himself.

"The Lord is not here."

Dash froze in place. At the end of the hallway that stretched behind the secretarial desk stood the shadowy figure of Walter Müller. He had been searching Pru's office. A gun was aimed at Dash's chest.

Dash's hands rose up slowly. "Mr. Müller. Fancy meeting you here."

Walter raised his other hand. The missing ledger was in it.

"I found my ledger. So strange seeing one's work like this. Filed and documented."

"Where is Pru?"

"I've spent the last few days wondering how I got here." The shadowy figure started toward Dash, inching its way down the hall. "I've had a lot of time for self-reflection, as they say."

Walter entered the front room. He gestured with his gun for Dash to move to the side. Dash did as instructed, carefully sidestepping, never taking his eyes off the German. Something inside Dash told him to keep Walter talking. Talking was time.

And I may not have much of it left.

Dash focused on keeping his voice steady and strong despite the fear flowing throughout his body. "I know everything, Walter."

The two men had circled until Dash was on the other side of the room with the secretary's desk behind him and Walter ahead of him, blocking the front door.

Walter smirked. Lightning flashed behind him. "Do you, Mr. Parker? I told you not to go snooping into my business."

"Your *business* was quite clever. Using your brother to find pansy and bulldagger speaks so you can have them raided and the occupants blackmailed. Quite inventive."

Dash looked around for a weapon. He could grab the desk lamp and hit Walter over the head with it. Yet he doubted he could move faster than Walter's bullet.

Walter's voice was slick with derision. "Those so-called men and women would pay anything to keep their secrets hid."

Another low growl of distant thunder and the tabloid flashbulb of lightning. Could Dash duck behind the secretary's desk before the bullets would fly? Would the desk even *stop* the bullets?

"A creative solution for being fired from the Committee," Dash said. "I bet that anonymous phone call was a surprise."

"My brother's indiscretion costed me my job. And so, I would punish him."

Now it was Dash's turn to feel disgust. "You used your brother in the most horrible manner possible."

"I disciplined him."

"You tortured him!"

"Sin is *not* to be rewarded, Mr. Parker. Our God is a vengeful God, and sometimes he uses one of us to carry out his judgment. That is what I was doing. Administering judgment. To my brother. To those despicable, disgusting sodomites."

"Really? I thought you profiteering."

"Enough!"

"But something unexpected happened. Something that threw a wrench into your 'judgment.' Karl fell in love."

"He did *not* love him!" Walter's face was red with anger. Veins protruded from the sides of his neck. "You people are incapable of love! What you do is *not* love! It is perversion! It is sickness! It is disgusting!"

Dash waited for him to finish his tirade. When Walter finally quieted, he said, "What you didn't count on was Karl asking Tyler—*the man he loved*—for help. Tyler went to Paul, who got Pru involved. They would document your blackmail, collect evidence, and have you put away."

Walter smirked again. "They thought they could stop me. How foolish were they?"

"They must've been some threat to you. Otherwise, why have me track them down?"

"Which you did beautifully. And now, I have my ledger." He shook it once in his hand. "No more evidence. And soon, no more witnesses."

Dash stared down the barrel of the gun in Walter's hand, the icy fingers of fear working their way down his spine.

Death does not forgive. Death does not forget.

The charcoal metal flashed brightly with the lightning outside. One of the flashes illuminated the figure of Prudence Meyers crouched just outside the doorway. In the next lightning flash, Dash saw her blue steel pistol clutched in her steady hand.

Walter cocked the hammer of his own gun, the motion making a sick-inducing *click*. "Mr. Parker," he said, his voice calm and serene.

Dash hoped Walter hadn't seen the surprise he felt on his face. He needed to stall until Pru made her next move— whatever that would be.

"What about your brother?" Dash said. "We both know what your mother did."

Walter fake pouted. "*Tsk tsk tsk.* Do you think I'm that stupid? Do you think I'm that sentimental?"

"You were blotto the night you had to move his body from your apartment to Central Park. Ever since, your mother's been drinking herself to death. I think you both realize the horror of what she has done."

Walter shook his head from side to side. "No, Mr. Parker. That will not work."

"Oh?"

Pru slowly raised up, using her other hand to shield the Remington from the rain.

"You don't feel any remorse over what you did to your brother? You don't feel any shame over a mother murdering her own son?"

Pru was now inching towards the entrance. How could Walter not sense her? He must've been too focused on Dash.

Keep his attention.

"Carrying your brother's lifeless corpse must've filled you with such rage. That's how you and Mother did it, am I right? Carrying him as if he were a passed-out drunk."

Walter just grinned his sick grin.

"But if you didn't love your brother, why you were drunk the next night? Stumbling around West Fourth, shouting how I killed him."

"I was drunk because my one source of income was now dead. And it was because of men like *you,* who filled his head with nonsensical things. Of how he could live as he wanted. In sin."

Dash shook his head. "No. You actually *cared* for your brother."

Walter adjusted his shoulders. The heavy gun must've been difficult to keep steady, to keep still. "Let me show you how sentimental we Müllers are. You know about my father, yes? How he dressed as a woman in the underground cabarets of Berlin?"

Dash nodded. "It was his nature, Walter."

"Ha! Nature? Nature would never allow that! No, it is sin; it is the Devil, Mr. Parker. And it must be banished, snuffed out, destroyed. My mother knew that. It was why she called the Nazis, told them about the club, told them about *him.*"

Dash's eyes widened.

Walter laughed. "So you see, we do not cry over dead perverts such as yourself."

"It doesn't explain why she's drunk every day and every night, Walter. Perhaps the thought of losing two men in her family—a son and a husband—was more than she could bear."

"I will show you how much we can bear," Walter snarled. "First, I will aim this pistol at your foot and shoot it. I will do the same to your elbows and to your hands."

Pru had just crossed the threshold and was a mere few feet away from Walter.

Dash said, "That's a lot of bullets, Walter."

The German patted his pockets. "Don't worry. I have enough. I will keep you alive as I shatter every joint in your body, Mr. Parker, even if you are begging for death. For as long as possible, I will make you suffer."

The dreadful mix of fear and anticipation was almost more than Dash could bear. He swallowed, his tongue thick, his throat dry.

Hurry, Pru, hurry!

He said, "Did they teach you that in Germany?"

Walter hummed a trill of a laugh. "We Germans are an incredible people filled with incredible strength. And it takes a lot of strength to pull the trigger."

Pru by that point was directly behind Walter. She brought the blue steel Remington up in one smooth motion and placed the barrel against his temple.

"You got that right, mister," she said.

Then she fired.

EPILOGUE

Round white headlights barreled towards Dash. A cab cutting through Jones Street. He stayed on the south side of Jones Street until the cabbie roared past.

It was Friday evening, August 27, and Dash was determined to return the bounce to his step. He breathed in deep, taking in the sounds of the city at night. He wanted these sights and sounds to replace the ones currently living behind his eyes.

In the last few days, he'd barely gotten any sleep. The events of the previous Tuesday night kept playing in a loop. He saw Mother's dreamy expression as she described the killing of her son and the moving of his body as *taking him to the Park.*

Then the dead body of Marjorie Norton and the bullet passing through the temple of Walter Müller. He didn't think the images would recede anytime soon.

Shortly after Pru had fired her lethal shot, she picked up the ledger from Walter's lifeless hand and grabbed Dash's live but trembling one and led him down the hallway.

"There's a backdoor which leads to an alley," she said.

"How did you know to come here?"

"He broke into my apartment. I figured he'd come here next, if he hadn't been already."

Dash tried to look back at Walter's corpse, but Pru's forward momentum prevented him from doing so. "What do we do about him? About Walter?"

They took a sharp turn at the end of the hallway.

"Listen to me," she said, her voice firm. "We don't have much time. Someone's going to report the shots. The cops will be here soon."

"We can't just leave him there!"

Another sharp turn. A triple-locked door. Pru set about undoing the bolts. "You were never here. Neither was I."

She wrenched open the door. "Go home!"

He didn't understand but by that point in the evening, after all he had seen and heard, his mind had begun to shut down. He simply nodded, went out the backway, ran down the alleyway, and grabbed the first cab he could find. He returned to the Cherry Lane Playhouse, where he couldn't speak for hours. Not even to Joe or Finn.

Dash awoke the next morning to newshawks reporting a sensational breaking-and-entering at the law firm of Meyers, Powers & Napier. An unidentified man was found shot dead on the premises, and the firm's safe was found hanging open, its contents emptied. Police surmised the unidentified man had a partner who got greedy and decided to keep the safe's treasures for himself.

The newshawks went on to describe the novelty of an all-female law firm, with a quote from Prudence Meyers saying, "We women are just as strong and just as tough as our male colleagues. Possibly more so, because we have so much more to prove." Dash hoped the publicity would send defendants in droves to their doors.

He later learned from the afternoon paper editions of a sad suicide in the new Germantown. After Dash had left Mother Müller—whose real name was Helga—to go racing to Paul Avery's apartment, she had taken a bunch of sleeping pills with several glasses of bootlegged vodka. She died before the sun rose the next morning.

Too much death, Dash thought. *Far too much death.*

He pretended to go about his schedule as normal. Breakfast and lunch at the Greenwich Village Inn, where Emmett watched him with concern. "You're as silent as The Ex-Pats," he said Thursday morning, nodding to the traumatized former Wall Street traders.

Dash only shrugged. "I think we've all seen some things we wished we hadn't."

Soon the globe of Cullen McElroy walked into the Inn, leaning against the bar as Emmett paid his weekly bribe.

"Thank you kindly," the rotund officer said, pocketing Emmett's hard-earned money.

Dash was so exhausted, he couldn't muster the energy to be disgusted by the man. He kept his eyes downcast.

McElroy noticed. "Mr. Parker, are you well? You don't seem your usual smart self."

"Late night," he managed to say.

McElroy chuckled. "You young ones. Never a dull minute."

You speak the truth.

"Whatever happened to the blond kraut fella?"

Dash's eyes flashed up. He almost said "Walter?" but managed to stop himself. "I couldn't say."

McElroy grinned. "You paid me to keep quiet about you."

"But you gave him my address anyway, didn't you?"

McElroy shrugged. "He paid me more. Did he find ya?"

"In a manner of speaking."

"What did he want?"

"The name of an honest cop."

McElroy stared at him for a long moment. Then he laughed and shook his finger at Dash. "You young ones. You've got sass for days." He looked at Dash once more, then nodded at Emmett. "I best be goin'. Thank you both for your contributions!"

Emmett glared after him, muttering under his breath.

"Easy, Emmett," Dash said. "Last thing we need is him causing trouble."

Thursday night, Dash met with El at a Harlem speak after her set at the Oyster House. She said, "Les is still upset with you. Not sure when he's going to let up." She gave him a pointed look. "Not the smartest move accusing him of murder."

"The clues were pointing towards him."

"Uh huh. Clues have a way of pointing in the wrong direction sometimes. What ended up happening anyway? Did you find out who did it?"

Dash recounted for her the last few days.

When he finished, El could only say, "Good Lord, Dash. You've been one cursed downtowner."

"That about sums it up," Dash replied. "At least I fulfilled Zora's favor, even if I didn't pull the trigger."

Just like what happened to Leslie.

El nodded. "Be thankful for that. You're not a killer, Dash."

"I'm not so sure of that. My actions caused the deaths of several people, El. How am I going to live with that?"

"Don't make me slap some sense into your fool head," El warned. "People will do what they're going to do. Karl? He could've stayed put, could've done what you told him, and he'd be alive. Yeah, he overheard Les, but Les wouldn't have done anything. He talks a big game but he's no killer, same as you. He made a choice. A bad one. Then you were forced to make choices, some bad—like Zora Mae—and some good, like helping your friends. That's all life is, making choices and hoping for the best. There's no sense in reliving it because it doesn't change anything. Are you listening to me?"

Dash nodded. He knew what she was saying was right, but he couldn't shake the regret pressing down on him like the August heat.

Friday morning, Paul Avery was apprehended at the shipyards trying to board a boat to Europe. It turned out Pru had turned him in to the authorities. Under her advice, Paul confessed to the murder of Tyler Smith, claiming temporary insanity, for a reduced sentence.

Now here it was, Friday night, and Dash wanted the swagger of his youth to return.

My youth. Ha! Twenty-six and already a Father Time.

He shrugged the thought aside and strolled up Jones Street, whistling a popular tune, trying to get into the mood. He decided to go inside Hartford & Sons to pick up a hat to replace his that was lost in the rainstorm of Tuesday.

Look sharp, feel sharp.

It wasn't yet opening time for Pinstripes, so Atty wasn't at his usual post. Dash unlocked the shop doors and went inside, turning on a lamp and opening the wardrobe. He pulled out a few options. Satisfied with a gray-blue one, he went to his desk to notate the inventory "loss." Just as he sat down at his desk, there was a creak from the back of his shop. He froze. He turned his head to see Nicholas Fife exit the curtained-off changing area and walk towards him.

"I hope you don't mind my letting myself in," he said,

"but I'm in need of my suit. And I must say, it looks *exquisite*."

Yes, Atty did a fine job.

"Good evening, Mr. Fife," Dash stammered.

Fife went to the opened wardrobe and ran his fingers through the silk ties on display. "You've had a very interesting week."

"I have?"

He picked up one of the silk ties. "Oh yes. My men had a helluva time keeping up with you. Uptown, then downtown, then uptown again. You were very, *very* busy."

Panic flooded Dash's chest. How much did Fife's men see? "Mr. Fife—"

The gangster held up a hand, silencing Dash. He turned around, the silk tie now between both of his hands.

"Running around, asking people questions. To them, it looked like you were playing detective. And I said, that couldn't be true. You are a speak owner. Why, if you are a detective, then knowing the location of my warehouse and the work of my chemist would make you a . . . well . . . *threat* to me."

The gangster began wrapping the tie around his fists.

Dash slowly stood up. "Mr. Fife, there's something you need to understand. We were forced by a man named Walter Müller—"

"You know what strikes me odd about it all? The disguise. A tailor shop owner with a degenerate speak in the back. I have to say, that is *quite* elaborate. Over-the-top."

Fife was walking towards Dash now, blocking his path to the front door.

A trickle of sweat slowly slid down Dash's back. "This Walter Müller blackmailed us, Mr. Fife. His brother was murdered, and he wanted us to find out who did it."

"And did you?"

"I, I . . . I suppose I did."

The gangster gasped in mock surprise. "Lookee there. My men were right. You *are* a detective. Are you private? With the cops? Or with the Feds?"

"Neither! I told you, we were forced into it."

By now, Fife was face-to-face with Dash, so close their noses almost touched.

"No man is ever forced to do anything. We all have free will, do we not? And we all make choices. And choices, Mr. Parker, have consequences."

He then slid the silk tie around the back of Dash's neck.

Dash swallowed. My God, was Fife going to . . . strangle him? Despite the awful realization, fear and disbelief—heavy, like lead—kept him rooted to the spot.

Fife took the two sides of the tie and began to make a knot at the center of Dash's chest, like a father does for his son wearing a suit for the first time.

"You haven't answered me. Who. Do. You. Work. For?" The gangster began slowly sliding the knot up to Dash's neck. "Private? The coppers? Or the Feds?"

The knot was now snug against Dash's Adam's apple.

"Mr. Fife, I work for none of them."

The knot began pressing harder against Dash's throat as Fife continued to slide it upwards.

"Now, now, don't be modest," Fife said, his pleasant baritone maddeningly calm. "A man of your accomplishments must be recognized."

The tie was beginning to cut off Dash's oxygen supply. He felt his cheeks begin to flush. He tried to answer but couldn't. His chest was on fire from the lack of oxygen, and he could feel himself start to fade. His pulse was pounding against his temples, so hard he struggled to understand Fife's words.

"Can you hear me, Mr. Parker?"

Dash couldn't speak but he could shake his head, albeit barely. The gangster watched him struggle some more before releasing him. Dash grabbed at the tie's knot and pulled it away from his neck. He took several grateful gasps of air, bending at the waist. He coughed, his throat scratchy and raw. He heard the creak of the floorboards and looked up.

Fife had returned to the changing area and walked out with his suit on the hanger. He went to the shop's front door and opened it. "Thank you for my suit, Mr. Parker. I truly believe you are a man I could have much use for."

He looked over his shoulder.

"And remember, I'm always watching."

Dash stared as the air-tight man straightened his jacket and walked slowly down West Fourth. Once Fife was out of sight, Dash rubbed a hand along his neck.

This is what I signed up for, he thought. *No one runs a speak and remains completely free.*

And all he wanted, like all men and women in the world, was to be free. More than ever, he needed to be around his kind, to be around friends, to be around *life.* And Providence smiled upon him, for walking up to the tailor shop were Atty, Joe, and Finn.

"He lives!" Finn shouted as they entered.

Joe grinned, saying, "Do my eyes deceive me?"

Atty clapped Dash on the shoulder. "Welcome back, boss! Good to see youse!"

Dash forced a smile as he stood, pleased his legs weren't shaking too much. "You slay me, Atty. You act as if I've been gone for months."

"Feels like it, boss. Say, did that fella who I got the suit for, did he like it?"

Dash looked over Atty's shoulder to the outside street. All he saw was shadows and people strolling along the sidewalk. Yet he knew Fife was out there, watching, waiting, like a wolf on the hunt.

"Yes," he replied, "yes he did."

Atty began walking towards the changing room. "Good. That means we're gonna get much better booze."

"And speaking of booze," Finn said, following him, "I am in *desperate* need of some."

Joe shook his head as he trailed after them. "Easy, lass. Don't start so hard first thing in the evening. Ya gotta save your strength for later."

He gave a casual wink to Dash.

Dash felt himself blush.

Atty pushed the right spot of the changing room mirror and led the way into Pinstripes.

Finn said, following after him, "Is that so?" He looked over his shoulder at Joe. "Tell me more, Mr. Night Life."

"Ya know what your problem is, Finney? Ya think you're too clever by half."

"You know what your problem is?" Finn called from behind the wall.

"No, but I'm sure you'll tell me," Joe bellowed into the secret doorway. He glanced back at Dash. "You coming?"

Dash smiled and stepped towards him. He brushed past Joe who whispered to him, "Welcome back, me lad. Or is it me lass?"

Dash whispered back, "Whichever you want." He crossed the threshold of the club's secret entrance.

Joe leaned back and laughed as he followed Dash into

the club. "Whichever I want, he says! Praise be to the Mother Mary! The power I shall have!"

Finn was seated at the bar next to Atty, rolling his eyes. "Dear goddess, why are you making him *more* insufferable?"

"Insufferable?" Joe scoffed. "Use yer head, lassie, I'm the barman filling your orders." He ducked underneath the bar, coming up with glasses and bottles. "What will everyone have?"

Dash stopped at the head of the bar and looked at his friends. His heart was filled with gratitude that they were all still together after the most horrid week and a half of their lives. They were safe and sound.

For now, at least.

He said, "I know exactly what I want. I will have good jazz . . ."

"Hear hear," said Atty.

". . . good men . . ."

"Hear *hear*," said Finn.

". . . and not least of all, some good gin."

Joe, Finn, and Atty all replied in unison, "Yessir, missus sir, yessir!"

THE 2ND HIDDEN GOTHAM NOVEL

Read on for an excerpt from
The Blind Tiger
to be released December 2021

EXCERPT FROM THE BLIND TIGER

The royal-blue Stutz Vertical Eight Sedan bounced across the intersection, rattling Dash Parker's trim six-foot frame against the ceiling. He rubbed the top of his head, simultaneously patting down his misbehaving brown hair. He hadn't had the time to bathe, shave, and change, something he'd normally do before the nighttime festivities. After all, it was 1926, and the city was popping like a champagne cork at an Astor wedding. One simply didn't *wear* one's day suit after the sun went down. But a man waving a gun would change the plans of even the most stubborn and stylish man.

"He can just ask to see me, you know," Dash said. "No need for the entourage and the private chauffeur."

The corpulent shape beside him rasped, "Where is the fun in that?"

In the darkness of the backseat, Dash saw the giant bald man smile.

He would be amused. This is the part of the job he enjoys.

He certainly enjoyed the first time Nicholas Fife sent for Dash. A faceless man lunging out of the shadows in front of Dash's building. The car sliding up behind him, the door opening seemingly by itself. The polite, but firm, request to get inside. When Dash did, shaking as he went, he saw Lowell Henley, Fife's lead torpedo in the backseat with that same closed-mouth grin, that same raspy breath.

Now here they were again, sitting in a five-passenger luxury car outfitted in a pale blue interior with teak-outlined windows while a nameless driver sped through the grid of Manhattan. The streetlights whipped by, their balls of yellow blurring and stretching into comet streaks.

If only Fife would come around once every hundred years.

"I'm not a toy he can toss around for his amusement," Dash said.

Lowell turned his head, his eyes glassy and black. "You'll be whatever he wants you to be." He faced the front again. "He'll like that suit though. You'll have to make another for him."

Dash looked down at the Banff blue pinstriped fabric that set his hazel eyes aflame. The crisp white shirt underneath allowed the bright red tie to flare like a firework. The topper, the gray felt homburg, he held between his hands. He mentally accepted the compliment, but he longed for his usual tuxedo. At least then it would *feel* like he was going to a party instead of to . . . wherever he was actually going. Which, he was certain, wasn't to his death.

Reasonably certain. One never knew with Fife.

He said, "You know I don't make suits, Lowell."

It was the honest-to-God truth. Though Dash owned Hartford & Sons Tailor, he was not gifted with needle and thread. Quite the opposite. But that wasn't why the Greenwich Village men visited the shop on West Fourth between Barrow and Jones—just to the west of Washington Square

Park, to the east of Seventh Avenue, and in the heart of Manhattan's Bohemia. It was the secret club called Pinstripes hidden behind the changing room mirror that brought them in droves.

Lowell kept his face forward. "You took his measurements."

"That's the one part of the job I *can* do. An associate does the rest."

He meant his club's doorman, Atticus Delucci. One wouldn't think the short, balding Italian with muscles thick as a boxer's would be so adept with needle and thread. And yet, every night, he would sit in the front window of the shop doing the alterations, giving the illusion Hartford & Sons was a legitimate business. It also kept Atty from being bored senseless and provided them with extra sugar to bribe the neighborhood cops. A necessary evil.

Like Nicholas Fife.

Lowell said, "I'm told you took great care with his measurements. In fact, he said his suit was fitted down to the very last millimeter. In all the right places."

The driver of the car flashed a look at Dash over his shoulder and smirked.

Dash could read his mind.

Well, Dash had been called worse. He preferred what the driver was thinking to what the nanny lawmakers called him and other men and women like him: "degenerates." It wasn't just a derogatory word; it was a legal term. He supposed they should feel flattered the nannies felt so threatened they made a special law just for them. Now in addition to being arrested for buying and selling alcohol, Dash and his kind could be charged with "degeneracy" and sent either to prison or to a mental institution. It all depended on the wealth of your family.

Dash's family had wealth, but these days they wouldn't intercede. That only happened once when Dash was younger, and they promised never to do so again. Especially when, just before his twentieth birthday, Dash defied his father's orders to stop his secret foolishness.

Ah, but isn't all love foolish?

"Turn here," Lowell said to the driver.

The Stutz careened around a corner, tossing Dash against Lowell, then shuddered with a large bounce as the car began climbing upward. Dash looked out the window and saw they were on the Queensboro Bridge.

Just as he suspected.

He was being driven to one of Fife's several Queens warehouses, where there were crates stacked upon crates of re-distilled liquor to be sold to the thousands of illegal speaks and clubs throughout the city. Even Pinstripes received some.

Dash adjusted his tie. "Did Fife find out something about her?"

It had to be the reason he was summoned: Fife had discovered a crucial clue about the girl who died. Dash didn't much care for the idea of he and Fife being linked in more ways than just liquor—especially when that link was death—but he put still managed to put on a brave face.

Lowell took a raspy breath. "He didn't say, and I don't ask."

"I'm sure he appreciates your discretion."

Lowell didn't take the bait on that one, so Dash sat back and looked out the side window. The lights of Manhattan had been replaced by the inky void of the East River. During the day, it was noisy and crowded with ships, boats, yachts, sea planes, and anything else mankind invented to get from point A to point B. At night, the river was empty, its earlier activity replaced with a sudden darkness and a profound silence.

How many secrets does this river hold?

And then, a terrifying thought: *Will I be one of them one day?*

Given what he and Fife shared, it wasn't outside the realm of possibility.

How certain are you that you're not being driven to your death?

Cold sweat flashed across his palms. His stomach began boiling with tension. Fife's world thrived on secrecy, as did Dash's. Yet Dash's four a.m. decision one night had blown that secrecy sky high with big, bold newspaper headlines and column after column of newshawks ruminating, insinuating, and, in some cases, flat out lying. Given who she was, though, how could they have possibly avoided the press frenzy? It was inevitable!

He wanted the body at the bottom of the Hudson.

Dash swallowed a large lump of fear. His reluctance to let her family suffer indefinitely over her disappearance had angered Fife. Dash had argued it didn't matter. A disappearance or a death would've inspired the same breathless prose so favored by newspapermen. Fife eventually had agreed with him. Or seemed to. Had the mercurial man changed his mind?

The car landed on the other side of the bridge with a thud, jolting Dash out of his head and back into his body. The driver careened around sharp curves, throwing him against the door of the Stutz. It felt like they were driving in circles with all of the right-hand turns, but soon they pulled up to an average-looking riverfront warehouse.

Lowell exited the luxury car, assuming Dash would follow. Stepping outside, Dash's nose was overtaken by the smell of pungent salt and sour decay. The East River in all her glory. He looked up at the warehouse expecting to see the familiar sign of Fife's cover business saying QUEENS FURNITURE, *FURNITURE FIT FOR ROYALTY!*

Or at least it had.

Now it said *DANZIGER PAPER.*

Dash looked to the fleet of delivery trucks surrounding them with the new moniker and a new tag line to go along with it: *THE CLASSIEST OF SALUTATIONS WITH THE BEST OF REGARDS.* Even the trucks themselves had been repainted, a pale blue with the new text in a rosy pink.

Dash pointed to the fleet. "New business?" His voice was only slightly shaking.

"New business," Lowell echoed.

Dash arched an eyebrow, trying to be nonchalant. "Gotta stay up on the latest trends."

The driver said with a proud smile, "Danziger's the name of a girl I go with. She's thrilled."

"I bet."

"Sal," Lowell said, "keep your trap shut."

Sal, properly chastened, replied "Yes, sir."

"Stay here. You," Lowell pointed at Dash, "come with me."

Dash nodded. "Right."

He looked to Sal. The driver's face was blank. No worry. No pity. Not even excitement. He gave no indication whatsoever as to what was in store for Dash.

"Mr. Parker!"

Dash looked up to see Lowell halfway to the warehouse. The large man beckoned with his hand.

Never let them see you sweat, his older brother Maximillian used to say. *Even if you're scared out of your wits, never let the other man see it.*

One of the few pieces of familial advice Dash still recited to himself. He took a deep breath and hurried after Lowell, who bypassed the warehouse's main two doors and instead went to a side entrance.

They entered a narrow hallway with jaundiced lighting. The smoky smell of exhaust, the tarry bitterness of oil, and the earthy dampness of mold was overwhelming and oppressive. Exposed pipes ran above their heads, the joints emitting little droplets of water that fell to the uneven concrete floor below, their splashes tinkling in the puddles polka-dotting the narrow hallway. Dash avoided them but Lowell walked straight through, not caring what the water— or whatever it was—did to his shoes.

At the end of the hallway, Lowell turned and knocked on a closed door. A muffled voice responded on the other side. Lowell nodded to himself once, then turned the knob and entered.

Dash hesitated for a moment, thinking, *should I run? Give myself a fighting chance?*

A Dumb Dora idea. He was in the middle of nowhere. Where could he go for safety? And no matter how fast he ran, Lowell's bullets were undoubtedly faster.

The bald head peeked out from the room he just entered. "You coming?"

Dash saw in his eyes the torpedo was hoping Dash would be resistant, be difficult, so he could engage in his well-practiced violence.

You're not getting that satisfaction tonight, you big lug.

Dash forced a smile. "On my way."

AFTERWORD

This fictional work stands on the shoulders of many researchers, whose work helped to inspire (and correct) many of the characters, scenes, and plot twists of *The Double Vice*. Specifically, George Chauncey's *Gay New York: Gender, Urban Culture, and the Making of the Gay World 1890-1940;* James F. Wilson's *Bulldaggers, Pansies, and Chocolate Babies: Performance, Race, and Sexuality in the Harlem Renaissance;* Frederick Lewis Allen's *Only Yesterday; An Informal History of the 1920s;* Deborah Blum's *The Poisoner's Handbook;* and Joshua Zeitz's *Flapper.*

To help with capturing the queer slang of the times, Mae West's three plays: *Sex, The Drag,* and *The Pleasure Man* proved to be quite fascinating (and entertaining!). Cab Calloway's *Hepster's Dictionary* helped guide the dialogue of those in Harlem's cabaret world.

The archives of *The New York Times* and *The New Yorker* provided context for what was happening elsewhere in the city beyond my characters' plight.

The character of El Train is an inspired mashup of

Gladys Bentley, who also performed in men's tuxedoes (sometimes backed by a chorus of drag queens), and Lucille Bogan, who was famous for songs such as "B.D. Women" and (the absolutely NSFW) "Shave Me Dry." They kicked at the walls of convention in the 20s and defied what women were supposed to look like and sing about, particularly as women of color. Their influence on music and performance should not be overlooked any longer.

Certain fictional places were also inspired by their real-life counterparts, such as The Oyster House being a fictional version of The Clam House (where Gladys Bentley often performed). The mansion of Zora Mae's Heaven and Hell party is a mashup of the Bailey House on 10 St. Nicholas Place and the house of 14 and 16 St. Nicholas Place. Dash's own Pinstripes was inspired by an inter-racial club reportedly in the East Village during the same time period.

Other settings, such as The Shelton Hotel, the Hot Cha, and the Greenwich Village Inn, were real, but finding descriptions of their interiors—beyond publicly filed floor plans, that is—proved to be difficult. So, like all good fiction authors, I made them up. Same with Dash's tailor shop Hartford & Sons, which is based on a 1920s photograph of a Greenwich Village storefront.

Street names have a way of changing in New York City. For instance, the Cherry Lane Playhouse is now on Cherry Lane, but back in the 20s, it was called Commerce Street. Unfortunately, the New York Public Library didn't have a street map from 1926, so I did my best to maintain accuracy with what was available.

I want to thank all those whose works and archives have helped with the development of this book. Any errors or misinterpretations are mine and mine alone.

ABOUT THE AUTHOR

Chris Holcombe is an author of LGBTQ+ historical crime fiction. *The Double Vice* is the first novel in his *Hidden Gotham* series, which showcases New York's lively but criminally under-represented queer world of the 1920s. He is also an award-winning songwriter, winning "Best Folk Song" at the 2009 Hollywood Music in Media Awards, as well as an accomplished brand strategist in marketing and advertising. He lives with his husband in New York, where he is hard at work on the next *Hidden Gotham* novel *The Blind Tiger*.

For more information, visit www.chrisholcombe.com and follow Chris on:

 facebook.com/thechrisholcombeauthor

 twitter.com/thechrisholcom1

 instagram.com/thechrisholcombe

Made in the USA
Middletown, DE
24 January 2022